Death Is Contagious

By

James. E. Moore

*Especially to my friends
Bill + Ellen*

*James E. Moore
10/13/02*

ISBN: 1-4033-1282-6

This book is printed on acid free paper.

1stBooks - rev. 05/08/02

Dedicated to all my hunting buddies, jointly and severally, who have shared with me the experiences of fighting mosquitoes in duck blinds, briars in search of fowl and saddle sores tracking the big game of the west.

CHAPTER ONE

The riders were no longer visible. The advance party, following the winding trail down the mountain, was obscured from Paige's view. The woman had first observed the hunters on their home-bound trip about fifteen minutes earlier, as they snail-paced their way along the rock-scarred ridge. She silently pled for speed from the horses that seemed to move in slow motion.

On her right, Hand Mountain extended northerly, casting its shadowy, ghostly profile across the plains. Configured like an arm severed below the elbow the weathered range portrayed a macabre rendition of a human right hand. Along its southern tip extended five ridge lines, or fingers. The hunters, winding along the near slope of the middle ridge, cut the distance to the lodge.

Why were the hunters moving so slowly? Paige's anguish intensified with every passing moment. If their arrival was delayed, it may be too late, she thought.

Even with binoculars, Paige had been unable to distinguish specific individuals among the hunters. The distance had been too great. Lashley would probably be in the lead cluster following Frenchie's guide, she reasoned. That team should be the first to arrive at the lodge, the base camp for the hunting party. Lashley arriving first was not just her silent request, Paige considered it more of a desperate prayer. Heather was missing. She had been gone for more than four hours.

Extensive search efforts, initiated by those who had remained behind at the lodge, proved fruitless. Heather had not been found. Paige, now fearing the worst, urgently needed the assistance of two particular men in the inbound parties. Among all of its members, only those men held her confidence. If the lost woman was to be located, Lashley and Frenchie would find her.

"Be careful," Crisco, the barrel-chested cook, had shouted when Heather Baldwin announced to Paige her determination to jog along the trails leading from the lodge. "This mountain ain't called 'The Death Hand' for no good reason. The Hand will close into a fist and hard strike a stranger with little warning."

Several guests scurried into the porch area to eavesdrop on the verbal exchange as the cook expanded upon his warning.

"The Hand ain't too kind to even us who've lived here a lifetime. Don't get out of sight of the lodge," continued Crisco, gesturing toward the weathered mountain that served as a back drop for the remote hunting camp. Its fingered ridges, broken and scarred, like the rough hand of an old saw mill worker, callused by usage and age, dominated the landscape.

"The mountain acquired its name from earlier pioneers traveling the Oregon Trail. Legend says the mountain had grown from the missing, right arm of Venus de Milo," added the cook.

"I just need to get some exercise," Heather told Paige. "I've not exercised since we left home."

"Besides, these mountains are gorgeous," Heather continued. "This is my first time to the west, and I want to see them in their splendor. I didn't join on this hunting trip with the intentions of being cooped up in a rustic lodge for a week."

The woman's decision to jog had occurred late that morning. Heather, after finishing an early light lunch, accepted the cook's warning to stay clear of the ridges and departed. Two hours elapsed before Paige expressed concern about her long absence. An unstructured, halfhearted search had followed, consisting primarily of yelling Heather's name out the front and back doors of the lodge.

At Paige's insistence, the base camp members launched a greater effort. Major Jerry Greer, an air force officer, with an abrasive autocratic approach, assumed command. He divided the lodge's guests into groups. Captain Tyrone Mitchell, a muscular black man in his early thirties was assigned to coordinate the second command, consisting mainly of the female guests.

Prior to departure, the major assigned one pistol to each group with the instruction that, upon locating the missing woman, the party should fire two, well spaced shots. Should the circumstances require emergency assistance, an alarm of three shots was planned.

Any visitors repeating a trip to The Hand knew and understood the mountain's deadly power. Lashley spoke to Paige often that this magnetism was the primary reason why many hunters selected the rustic Cottonwood Guest Lodge. He claimed it was an outdoorsman's challenge to face the danger the mountain offered, an opportunity to successfully surmount each appendage. In the process, each hoped to bag a trophy animal from secluded crevasses. Hunters knew that however challenging one of the mountain's fingers might be, another ridge always appeared, even more revealing, equally as demanding, and just as prone, in turn, to conquer the intruder. As such, the search for Heather Baldwin had been undertaken with vigor.

* * * * *

Knowing more clearly the winding contours of the trail leading westerly up the steep canyon behind the lodge, Greer opted for this route. Ray Horne, the assistant cook, volunteered to join the major. The cook was youthful and strongly built, slightly hampered by a crippled leg. Cottonwoods and yellow-leaved aspen bounded the trail as it rose sharply, twisting and hair spinning up the canyon like a carelessly discarded rope.

A swift, forty-five minute climb produced no discovery and left the major completely exhausted. Even hobbling from his handicap, the youthful cook made the climb with minimal effort. Greer was impressed by the man's tenacity.

The wind changed abruptly in an uncomfortable, gusty, down-trail direction, making the men's attempt to break the tree line difficult. Upon reaching a gentle sloping point just beyond the timber break, Greer called a break.

The lodge, far below, had been obscured by vegetation for the final fifteen minutes of the ascent. During the upward climb, an occasional dim sight of the lodge served as the men's fixed point of reference.

The building quickly disappeared, as the trail switched back.

As the men rested, the Cottonwood Lodge lay spread below and appeared as if it were an aerial photograph.

The sun light reflected on the fish pond, shimmering with the wind in silver white, erratic designs. The lodge had a high-pitched roof over the primary structure, set in a cluster of supporting buildings. It was the setting and not the architecture that counted. The wooden lodge, accentuated by the rusty red barn, corral, and assorted support buildings, contrasted with a towering white structure serving as the cold storage unit. The layout was a miniature arrangement for a model train display.

From what the major understood, the Cottonwood Guest Lodge had been constructed by Frenchie Hebert's grandfather over a hundred years prior as a two roomed log cabin. Over the ensuing years, modifications had been added to the original structure, first by Frenchie's father who attached a kitchen along the western side and glassed porches along the southern and eastern sides. The youngest Herbert, now in his early fifties, added the bunk house and a closed walkway connected to the base structure. These additions were adapted to service the demands of hunters and dudes desiring to experience a western-style survival, with only the bare necessities of modern living.

The Cottonwood Lodge nestled, pinched between two ridges named the Thumb and Trigger Finger. Once, the lodge had been crested by an umbrella of cottonwood trees, but a blight had long since destroyed the closest trees. Large, round stumps remained as silent testimony of the trees' former magnificent size and as memorial sentinels guarding the surroundings.

Major Greer considered the alternatives. At this juncture, the trail had reached a steep slope extending upward from the timber line toward the Knuckle of the Thumb. As the contours shortened, mountain grass sprinkled with broken roots and occasional pinion pines dominated the landscape. The journey upward to the first crest was more strenuous as the horse trail became less defined across this rocky terrain.

Upward, toward the ridge line, the landscape appeared to be in synch with nature. No disharmony was visible. Everything appeared in place among the scattered sage and dwarf juniper. It was not reasonable that Heather Baldwin would have passed upward beyond this point had she selected this canyon trail for her jogging route. Whatever spectacular view she might have sought, it would have ended where the men now rested. Up slope, the view deteriorated in to monotonously rough, broken ground. Little could be accomplished by proceeding farther along the trail, so the men began back tracking.

Retracing their steps on the descent, they asserted more attention to any signs that might indicate an individual had deviated from the trail. But it was difficult. There were too many places to search. A trip and fall from the steep trail afforded many obscure depositories for an injured body. It would be pure luck if the men spotted the woman lying in a recess among the trees.

Early afternoon shadows were blanketing the lodge when the two returned down the canyon, devoid of news.　In their absence, Captain Tyrone Mitchell reported to Greer that he, together with his team, had searched easterly along the rutted road - the sole artery back to the asphalt road and ultimately to civilization. Unable to locate any signs of Heather, the captain had quickly altered his team's course and had swept southeasterly around the tip of Trigger Finger.

Pearl Gavin and her boyfriend, Joel Guarimo, had volunteered to remain at the lodge on the off chance that Heather might return, undetected by the search parties.　Pearl, a heavy-set woman with a strikingly beautiful face, appeared relieved to be excused from the physical tasks required to endure the rigorous, exhaustive walking search.　But Joel Guarimo, a strong man with an athletic physique, had not been so easily excused by the major.　Finally, Guarimo was able to persuade Greer that if Heather returned, he could signal with the firearm, as Pearl was not familiar with weapons.　The wait for those remaining at the lodge was in vain.

Crisco, the camp cook, along with several women guests, vainly searched the barn and all of the out buildings. Empty handed, Crisco's team had shifted northeasterly around the end of the Thumb. Their efforts as reported produced nothing useful.

After what each party considered a reasonable search, they retired to the lodge to compare notes, and pondering a new alternate strategy for the next effort. However, there was more discussion, suggestions and confusion than action. Even the major, with all of his command abilities, was unable to reform the search efforts.

* * * * *

Paige now stood alone. As bearer of bad news, she leaned against the gate post, nervously awaiting the return of the hunters into the lodge compound. Darkness was near. The sun had dropped behind the mountain and shed an uncomfortable expectation of darkness over the lodge. Its retreat dampened the afternoon heat. The woman shivered, both from the cold and fear. Already the mountain's shadow began to race easterly across the broken plain.

11

A lead horse broke the horizon, freed from the low wash that continued to embrace the remaining hunters. The lodge's two resident dogs loped beside the inbound hunter. The rider was close enough for her to recognize Perrie Hebert, the head guide and owner of the Cottonwood Guest Lodge. Frenchie, as he was commonly known, operated as the point horseman for the inbound hunters. Stooped shoulders crowned by a large head, topped with grey hair that balanced a weathered cowboy hat clearly distinguished the guide even at this distance. Paige's prayers had been answered. Lashley, she knew, was hunting with this party.

Moments later, Howard Lashley rode into view. The woman was disturbed to observe Lashley rein his horse, move off the trail and lean sideways in his saddle. He appeared to be observing something on the ground. She watched the dogs sniff the area indifferently. Frenchie reined his horse beside Lashley's halted mount.

Hurry, she thought, almost emotionally destitute. Don't be distracted now, Lashley. She needed him.

Paige's anxiety about the missing woman approached a deeply rooted fear. Heather appeared to Paige as a rather affirmative female. Slim, with the confidence of an athlete, Heather was extremely attractive. The least directed to vanity among the women in the party, Paige felt Heather was the most compatible of the females. She liked the missing woman. Although she had only recently made her acquaintance, Paige considered Heather a friend.

"The hunters are in!" Paige yelled over her shoulder toward the main lodge building.

At the lodge, the front door flew open to accommodate the exit of the two military officers. They broke into a double-paced trot to join Paige at the gate.

Three hundred yards out, Paige observed Leo Rich spur his jaded mount, urging his horse forward into a galloping Caesar's triumphant entrance. It was vanity she thought which drove the man to impress the welcoming committee at the base camp.

"Whoopee!" Rich bellowed like a stray calf as he passed Paige. "I took a real trophy today. It'll be listed in BOONE & CROCKET. A fuckin' three hundred and fifty yard shot at a running target. Broke its goddamn neck in two shots."

Her skin crawled in rebellion at this performance. Rich was a car dealer and a livid bragger. If Paige could categorize the man, she would label him as crude, insolent, and dominating at his best. He was the epitome of a male chauvinist, vulgar when performing at his worst.

Beryl Carter and Lewis Fulcher passed the gate turning their lathered horses toward the corral. Beryl, a tough, stocky but friendly man, commented as he dismounted, "I got a good buck, Paige. Nothing compared to Leo's, but it beats anything I've racked before."

Further down the trail, two mules labored under the load of the day's kills. The youngest outfitter, Cinch Wilkinson, lead the trailing animals' final measured step to unloading and fresh oats. Paige saw Frenchie hold back, riding the last tortuous yards parallel with Lashley. The men were talking.

* * * * *

"Cinch told me about that buck. It's your trophy," the head guide told his riding partner. "He watched the kill from up along that ridge. When the buck jumped, Rich didn't see it until it made its first stop. When it broke again, he shot twice. Missed both times, Cinch reported to me. Deer was less than two hundred and fifty yards out from him."

Shrugging his shoulders, Lashley spurred his horse and the two men rode down the trail. Short on speaking, Lashley preferred to communicate with body language.

This year's trip was his second hunt at the Cottonwood, but his third visit to the lodge. During the previous summer, Lashley had spent two weeks on horseback traversing Hand Mountain and its five finger-like ridges. He felt more at home in the rugged mountains than in urban surroundings.

"Four hundred and seventy—five yards down slope from you where you shot. Open sights," Frenchie continued.   "That was some shot the way Cinch figured it."

"Five twenty-five," Lashley responded.   This correction was not intended as a brag. It was more of a confirmation of a fact. "Crosswinds. Maybe ten knots. Couple inches off target."

"You didn't claim the buck as you had a right to do. That Rich is as full of conceit as a kitchen cat. I figure you've got something you spotted last summer that will beat this one," Frenchie said. "Rich has got to suspect that deer's not his kill."

Lashley shrugged again and advanced forward to pass through the gate where Paige and the lodge guests gathered. He noted Paige stood in a rigid, stoic stance. The look on Paige's face caused him to rein in his horse. Frenchie drew up beside him. Their horses, jaded by long hours under heavy loads, shifted restlessly, pawing the ground with their iron shoed hoofs.

"Heather's missing, Lashley," she spoke, fighting involuntary tears. "Almost five hours now. We searched everywhere. No luck. I'm desperate. She

16

said she was going for a short jog. Wanted to get a good view of the mountains. Crisco warned her to keep in sight of the lodge. But I guess she didn't listen."

"Searched? Where?" Lashley asked the woman. During the year she had been his close friend, he had seldom witnessed such emotion from her. This current temperamental display was an exception to her usually stable countenance. Their relationship had matured, augmented by her ability to handle stress. No bitching, whining woman would have ever received his invitation to participate as a companion on a hunting trip. If Paige was driven to the verge of tears, Lashley had little doubt that something was seriously amiss.

"Major Greer took the young cook, Horne, up the canyon behind the lodge," the woman explained through short, strained breaths. "They couldn't find Heather in that direction. They said there were too many places to search off the trail, what with all the trees up there."

She paused as if waiting for some acknowledgment or comprehension, choking on her own tension. Lashley nodded in union with her concern.

.   "One group covered the barn and the other buildings. I went down the road, that way." She pointed.

"There?" Lashley asked as he swept his hand to the south, off the point of Trigger Finger.

"Just a little way down to the spring, but there was too much area to cover on foot. We yelled, honked horns. Nothing," she replied.

Lashley pivoted in the saddle and again faced the head guide, who had remained silent during Paige's explanation.

"What say?" the hunter asked. Several of the women, newly arriving at the gate, breathlessly watched the process.

Frenchie pondered for a brief moment. "How would you handle it, Lashley?" he asked.

Lashley stared into the deep weathered face of the guide. After some reflection, he said decisively, "Frenchie, take the black bitch."

He pointed to one of the dogs the lodge used to flush deer from rough terrain. "And Rich. Work up the trail behind the lodge. No more than half mile. Let the dog do the work. If the woman is off the trail anywhere, the bitch will find her. I'll work from here toward the new house. I'll take Wilkinson and the cur."

Lashley's selection of Cinch Wilkinson was not mere happenstance. Of all the regular employees at the Cottonwood, Lashley had been most impressed by the wiry, narrow-hipped youngster. Extremely agile and well poised, with quick hands, he had the facial features characteristic of his Native American ancestors, dark brown. His hunting outfit reflected the abuse of too many barbed wire fence crossings, briar entanglements, and strong detergents. Lashley reasoned that the cowboy was a choice pick in a pinch.

"Got it covered," the top guide responded, already giving instruction for Leo Rich to remount and follow. As the bitch dog trailed, Frenchie explained to his riding companion the need for haste.

"Carter, you and Fulcher remount. Search around that antelope spring down there." Lashley pointed to a place southeasterly of the barn where the horses found water. "See if you can find Miss Baldwin. She's missing."

"Wilkinson, come with me," Lashley instructed the cowboy. "Call the cur. Major, you take care of the mules and game. Hold the other incoming hunters in check here at the corral. Don't follow. Let them wait for our call."

Lashley and Cinch rode diagonally, crossing the front of the barn, up an inclined trail to a gate. The young cowboy, dismounted and opened the gap, allowing both horses to pass.

The mongrel dog located his personal passage through the fence. Lashley knew the dog's experiences. Drawn from years at the lodge, the animal was preconditioned to expect, at the end of a successful hunt, a nice rest with a few tidbits as the fresh kills were skinned and dressed. Now there was to be no rest. The canine was needed for an important mission.

Lashley rode several hundred yards inside the fence and stood full height in the stirrups, stretching for better surveillance. The wind at this lower altitude was subsiding, signaling an official end to playtime. Preparing for the darkness, nature altered its direction.

The circumstances forced Lashley to place his mind parallel to that of a novice desiring a scenic track. Where would the woman jog from the lodge? He was weary, and he had little time to ponder. More than six hours in the saddle, enduring windy canyon updrafts blowing grit into his face, had left him fatigued and sunburned. He wanted to rest with a bottle of Jack Daniels at his elbow, but those comforts could wait. Heather Baldwin must be found.

Lashley gauged his position. At the butt of the Thumb lay a triangular plateau, its left side adjoining the Arm. The south base extended a half mile due easterly from the tip of the Thumb. Bordering the third side was a jagged cliff line, varying in heights from twenty-five to 100 feet. At the apex of the triangle was an abandoned, two-story structure. This plateau was occasionally used as a landing strip by inbound hunters with small aircraft. Its flat area accommodated only craft equipped with STOL—Short-Take-Off-and-Landing capabilities.

Mentally, Lashley had immediately rejected the steep canyon trail behind the lodge as a route that a jogger would select. Dispatching Frenchie Hebert and Leo Rich to search for the woman upward through the canyon had been a mere precaution. That trail afforded a difficult and strenuous route, an arduous tour for a flatlander. Many of the views along the canyon trail were obscured by trees, which, even in early fall, still retained sufficient foliage to conceal the scenery.

Alternatively, this plateau, especially from the cliff's edge, presented a panoramic scene easterly across the rolling plains toward a distant mountain range. Along the tip of the Thumb, the plateau's easily accessible location designated this site as Lashley's choice for a jogger, seeking a spectacular vision within easy distance. He was convinced he would locate Heather nearby.

Cliff lines are magnets for a tenderfoot. Their edges spell the most obvious danger for the curious. An awkward step on loose rocks along the ledge, or merely poor judgment as to the proximity of the edge, could signify death or serious injury. Discovering a crumpled woman at the bottom of the cliff would be a disastrous end to this hunting trip. Lashley feared that such a find was a reasonable possibility.

From the start, Lashley had been opposed to allowing women to join the hunting party, but he had been overwhelmingly outvoted. Lashley contended that women would destroy the best hunt. He knew that when the men were hunting, they would think of screwing. And when they were screwing, they would think of hunting. Either way, the two activities just don't mix.

"You," he pointed to Cinch, the young guide. "Check the new house. I'll take the cur and cover the cliff line."

Describing the abandoned structure as the "new house" was somewhat of a misnomer. Constructed for Frenchie's in-laws during the brief duration of his marriage, the two-story, irregular building had been unoccupied for over twenty years. The building lay half a mile away at the northern most point of the plateau. Just by chance, curiosity might have led

Heather there to observe the old, western-style homestead.

"Come dog," Lashley commanded as the riders parted. The cur, as if fully understanding his mission, moved easterly ahead of the horse.

Lagging his tongue, the dog moved outward to skirt the rim line. He acted as if he knew when the job was done there would be scraps. In less than five minutes, the dog sniffed the ground.

Lingering behind, Lashley watched the mongrel dog, until, at the cliff's edge, it stopped. By the animal's erect and stationary stance, Lashley knew the search had ended. He galloped to the point, reined in beside the dog, hastily dismounted, and approached the inert figure.

Reality was worse than he had imagined. Conditions might have been better if the woman was lying at the bottom of a ravine. Lashley knelt down and curiously examined the woman. He paused, lingering over the prone figure for several minutes. Returning to his mount, he reached for the rifle in his saddle scabbard, extracted it, and discharged three distinctly spaced shots.

CHAPTER TWO

The four men crouched cowboy style, spooning their supper from tin plates.   Under the back door stoop, cords of carefully stacked firewood secured both sides of the overhang, a barrier against the evening's dying winds.   Their coffee cups steamed, protesting the dropping temperature.   A stream at the edge of the stoop provided a natural melodic background.

Absorbed in their own thoughts, the men ate in silence.   Pale, yellow light emitted from a kerosene lantern in the kitchen.

The local electric cooperative had determined that serving the isolated Cottonwood Lodge, was not economically feasible.   Because the lodge was located over sixteen miles from a paved road and the closest transmission line, the lodge was short on the basics of modern living. Frenchie was forced to use ingenuous and basic methods.   Minimal electrical needs were captured by a wind turbine which generated a blower system on the fuel oil furnace serving the bunkhouse.

26

Such rudimentary facilities contributed to the mystique of the lodge and attracted a heartier clientele.

From inside the lodge, conversational voices drifted out to the men under the stoop. The tone of the party was subdued compared to the festivities of the previous evening meal, their first night of a scheduled six-day booking. Jovial exchanges, boasting, and heavy betting had served as a side dish for last night's supper. Tonight, the mood was modified. Heather Baldwin's disaster had a subduing effect upon the hunting party.

By Cottonwood standards, the hunting party was above average in size, and thus taxed the building's accommodations. Eight men and two women had been designated by Leo Rich, the party's leader, as the hunters.

Rifle-toting females were a rarity at the lodge. When Patricia Stanford and Myrtle Wallace were identified as hunters, Lashley knew Frenchie had been especially surprised, since this was a Leo Rich team. Rich relegated women to mere bed companions, never saddle partners.

Nine non-hunting guests were paired with the ten hunters. A staff of two cooks and six guides, including the owner, rounded out the population of the lodge. That was more than the permanent residents of many Wyoming towns.

Under the stoop, one of the men shifted, nervously extracting a circular container from his hip pocket. He pinched a bit between his forefinger and thumb and placed it between his cheek and gum.

Somewhere in the distance, a coyote challenged the moon to expose its mystical reflection. His challenge was ignored. The first half of the night was going to be dark, until a quarter moon rose somewhere after midnight. To the apparent disappointment of the baying animal, only the stars responded, twinkling vividly in their display, as was their exclusive right in the high altitudes of the Rockies. Jupiter was especially radiant that night, as its yellow tint shone even more brilliantly among its other flickering peers.

Frenchie began acting uncomfortable. The silence under the stoop was unnerving. He sucked his lower lip between his teeth, adding seriousness to his appearance. His eye ticked nervously.

"The moon will still be up in the late morning. Deer should move long after daylight. Tomorrow should be good hunting for the timber line buck," he blurted, obviously delaying as long as possible the inevitable conversation about Heather Baldwin.

"Not so sure," the youthful Cinch Wilkinson replied. "Looks like a southeast wind tomorrow. Never kill nothin' on an east wind on the Hand."

Draining the final drops from his cup, Howard Lashley encircled his arms around his bent knees. He studied the three men. "By now, some of the women must have figured out what happened to Heather," Lashley commented, focusing the conversation to the real issue. "At least those who assisted in cleaning her up know. Everybody else reasons she fell."

Frenchie sighed. "How do you figure that?"

"You don't get abrasions on your body with your clothes on. Heather's clothes weren't torn. But her body was pretty messed up though. Plenty of cuts and bruises," Lashley answered softly.

"Was it that obvious?" Hank Stringfield, the older of the cowboy guides, asked. String, as he was commonly called, was a weather—beaten man, tall, with hips and shoulders disproportionately broad. His wiry grin revealed rotting teeth, a by-product of excessive dips of snuff. The cautious type, he favored both belt and suspenders.

"Yea, it was that obvious. It's bad enough we've got to report it to the authorities," Lashley stated. "She needs medical attention."

"Can't get out on the east road till after morning light," Frenchie replied. "This afternoon there was a washout down in the valley. Did you see it?"

"Yea," Lashley said. "Came in a tad after noon."

Rainstorms at this time of the year were unusual but the temperature had not been cold enough to produce snow. A southerly moving front had passed through the valley. Shortly after midday, pregnant clouds had birthed a downpour of surprising strength.

From the knuckle of Middle Finger, Lashley had watched the discharging water cascading in its search for the most expedient route to the North Platte River.

Plunging with a knife's edge, the water had cut a ribbon path through the washes in the lower country, slicing the rutted road that serviced the lodge. Until repairs could be completed, ingress by that route was out of the question.

"How about the other road, the north one? You know, the one up to the Diamondhead Ranch. Could we use that one?" Cinch Wilkinson asked.

Lashley considered this alternative. He had traveled that rutted road once. He found it to be a difficult route. Bending sharply, the ruts eventually turned easterly toward Sleeping Camel Rock. Miles farther it joined with Route 220. South from that intersection, the hard surface road led to Rawlins.

Using that trail would take much longer, maybe four to five hours. It was possibly as distant as twenty-five miles of rough ruts before a vehicle would reach the asphalt road.

During World War II, when the region had been used as a bombing range, the Army Air Corp had installed a sizable culvert across the upper gulch on Diamondhead road. Whenever a washout occurred

31

along the lower stream bed, Lashley knew Frenchie alternately used the northern route as an emergency exit. The longer route was used just long enough for ranch hands to affix a plow to a pickup truck and grade around the erosion. Never a major project, the grading was more of a time-consuming inconvenience. Accustomed to constant battles with the elements, westerners accepted such occurrences as a way of life.

"I wouldn't try that north road at night. Not until it's checked," Frenchie responded. "You'd be like a jack rabbit caught in short grass. It's an easy site for an ambush. We don't know if those who attacked Miss Baldwin have that road covered. Better we wait for daylight and go out the direct route. They can't very easily set up an ambush there. Not without us seeing them. No, we must use our usual route. It's our only chance."

"How do you suggest we handle it?" the young guide asked. "The whole thing's loonier than a sheep herder in early fall. After spending all summer with a bunch of sheep, he's crazier than a goose under a chokecherry bush."

"Meet it head on," Lashley said. "Call the men together. We'll tell them what we know."

Frenchie let the suggestion digest for a moment. "Man, I don't want to face that. As far as I'm concerned, that's like using a corn cob in the privy. It may get the job done, but it ain't comfortable."

"You can't hide daylight from a rooster, Frenchie," String said, as he spit out across the stream.

His employer responded, "I feel like the last man on 'crack the whip' at school recess. I'm fixin' to be flung out on my own. I'll be as helpless as a cow in a mud bog."

"Frenchie," String added, "we're behind you."

"Yea, but that's somewhere on the far side of the Tetons. That's how far you are behind me," Frenchie responded.

"You know better than that," Lashley stated with his usual confidence.

"What about the women? Who carries the tale to them?" Frenchie asked, knowing but still dreading the answer.

"You must tell the men," Lashley stated. "Let each of the men handle it with their companion as they deem best."

"Okay. Now is as bad a time as ever. I'm as crowded against the fence as I'll get," the head guide said. "String, you get the women grouped in the dining area and keep them there. Cinch, you brief Crisco and the rest of the crew. Let's curry the burs out of our tail, and get it behind us."

Assembling the men around the billiard table proved more difficult than anticipated. Frenchie's request that the men peel off to plan tomorrow's hunting arrangements met stiff resistance.

Elliott Thornton, the most portly and least profane member of the hunting party, clung to his beer as though it were a life ring on a stormy sea. From the bar stool, he bellowed, "I shall comply with all edicts and regulations communicated to me through regular channels. Until officially summoned, I will remain on this pedestal as my sanatorium of refuge."

His bed partner Katherine, a red-head in her early fifties, smiled sweetly at Elliott's comments.

Demurring, Beryl Carter shook his head. "Not now. Dunsey and I are retiring early, if you know what I mean. I'll be back in an hour or so for my instructions." He flicked a wink to his girlfriend, Dunsey Martin, who moved closer and planted a kiss on his cheek.

"You don't need me or Mitchell," Major Greer responded. "We aren't hunting. You need Wallace and Stanford from our detail." By military habit, he referred to individuals, of either gender, by their last names.

Lashley intervened, "Major, let's get the men together as Frenchie requested." He paused and took a slow deep breath forcing calmness. "Respond please!"

From across the room, Paige St. John's expression evidenced her suspicion that something was amiss. Lashley responded with an affirmative gesture. He crossed over and whispered in a low tone, "Help String keep the women in the dining area. This is very serious. Hope it won't take long."

The kerosene lamp's low candle light produced a pale, yellow backdrop for the gathering. Crouching

35

below a window sill, Lashley surveyed the ten men who formed a semicircle before him.

Leo Rich, owner of a prosperous car dealership on Florida's Gulf Coast, was their leader. The originator of the trip, Rich invited and recruited from his local friends, hunters for each year's trip. To his knowledge, this was Rich's sixth visit at the Cottonwood. For the last four years, he had assumed the leadership role, vetoing and selecting participants. Heather Baldwin accompanied Rich as his latest girlfriend. The crude man had a biting sense of sick humor.

Lashley accepted that Frenchie tolerated the car dealer in his own way, as a fly in a coffee cup - extract what you desire and disregard the unpleasant residue. Rich paid premium prices to select the choice days of the hunting season. Money talked even in the remote reaches of the Cottonwood Lodge. Rich had enough money to be called "Mister." But the man was still as obstinate as a cow with a sore throat.

Beryl Carter, an asphalt contractor, was returning for his third trip. He was a big man, heavy set. His bull-shaped neck and sun-weathered face were topped with a closely cropped hairstyle. The husky Texas native, in spite of pugilistic proportions, possessed a reserved temperament which Lashley admired. Designated as the financial officer for the hunters, Carter organized, through Frenchie, the booking deposits and any other special financial arrangements. The bookings were a tad difficult since the Cottonwood had no phone. On prearranged dates Frenchie would drive to Alcova, the closest service station, and contact the contractor to plan the arrangements for the season's hunt.

It was during one of the phone calls that Carter had made Frenchie aware that women would accompany all hunters during this year's hunt.

Women on a hunting camp were not a novelty at the Cottonwood. This trip was an extraordinary exception, Lashley recognized. Rich, on all of his previous hunts, had brought a bed-warming companion, but none of the other hunters in his party had copied his tradition.

37

Lashley, having made previous trips to the Cottonwood, was knowledgeable of Frenchie's business. During the summer, when the Cottonwood operated as a dude ranch, women were occasional guests. If there was anything a cowboy dreaded it would be a fancy acting woman. Many of the female guests acted like sick calves, moaning about the rustic accommodations. The men guests rarely complained. The guides especially dreaded a hunting party heavily loaded with females.

Frenchie, as he told Lashley, was at first reluctant to comply with Rich's decision to include nine women. He had ultimately acquiesced by increasing his fees, and all of the repeaters recognized this as an indirect means of showing disapproval. Horses and women are a poor mix, Frenchie believed. He knew that friction, usually petty jealousies, always developed when mixed groups shared such close quarters for a week-long hunt. But it was the men's money and their hunt. They could spend their dollars however they choose.

It was always shocking for the women to discover the lodge had no electricity. On this particular trip the bitching had started early, but soon subsided. These females adapted more quickly to the primitive conditions.

Members of the hunting party varied over the years, but the true veteran for duration was, as Lashley understood, Elliott Thornton, a hard drinking, real estate broker. For ten years, he had attended the hunt religiously, like a part-time Presbyterian at Easter sunrise services. He was devoid of qualifications as a hunter, but he compensated with experience as a drinker. Frenchie claimed he could not recall Thornton ever discharging his rifle during any visit to the Cottonwood. The guide nurtured a deep—seeded suspicion that Thornton's rifle always had an empty chamber and clip. The hunt was the man's freedom to drink, fully liberated from the nagging tongue of a spiteful spouse.

For insurance agent, Robert Stevenson Farrow, this was his sixth hunt. He was small in size, the opposite of Rich. A highly efficient, details man, Farrow was the humorous asset which bonded the various elements of the hunting party into a homogeneous team.

Two members of the party were most puzzling for Lashley. Air Force Major Jerry Greer and Army Captain Tyrone Mitchell, both clearly athletic, were not designated hunters. When the hunting parties departed that morning, the men had remained at base camp. Their female companions, Patricia Stanford and Myrtle Wallace, had mounted horses with experienced ease. During the day, the women had demonstrated outdoor skills, superior to many of the males. Stanford, the older, was a plain but attractive woman.

Captain Mitchell and Myrtle Wallace were the first blacks to register at the Cottonwood under Rich's leadership as Lashley had been informed. Blacks had hunted with other parties at the lodge before, but this was an absolute first for Rich's usual redneck outfit.

Myrtle Wallace proved her skills when earlier in the day she bagged a four-point buck. She took it with one shot at three hundred yards. It was not just a lucky shot, as one of the guides reported. The kill was evidence of hours spent on a firing range. She appeared to be tough female and not one easily short tied to a snubbing post.

The next individual seated to the guide's left was a person of unknown quality for Lashley. Joel Guarimo was a first-timer and a last minute recruit for the Rich party. On this first day of the hunt, claiming a queasy stomach, Guarimo, had remained at base. High altitudes sometimes had such effects on flatlanders. Thus, the request to beg off from a grueling six hour saddle ride was not unusual. Frequently guests required time for their personal systems to adjust to the extreme change in elevation.

If Guarimo did not assume more participation with the group, Lashley reasoned that Rich would not extend a return invitation. The man was aloof, humorless, and a constant complainer. He suspected that the closest Joel had ever been to a cow was a rare tenderloin on a silver platter. He reasoned the man was a certified stall-fed tenderfoot.

He knew almost nothing about Joel Guarimo, the electrical supplies salesman. Rich had given a few details. He had been selected by accident. Pearl Gavin's brother, Mitchell, a Cottonwood veteran from two previous hunts, had taken ill suddenly. He persuaded Rich to include Pearl and Joel by vouching for their compatibility. Rich acquiesced.

Thyus Harder and Lewis Fulcher, on Lashley's far left were both second-timers. Eager, though inexperienced as hunters, both Harder and Fulcher had the qualities of good team members. Fulcher was as quiet as a down pillow. It was surprising that he elected to attend with no bed companion. Harder, by contrast, was more outgoing and had brought Grace Hancock, a slightly plump but cute partner.

As the tenth member of the hunting team, Howard Lashley positioned himself selectively on the guide's right. This placement afforded him an unobstructed view of the balance of the party.

"What's the latest word on Heather?" Beryl Carter directed the question to the guide.

"That's why I asked y'all here to join us, so we could discuss it," Frenchie nervously began. "Miss Gavin and Paige St. John have been attending to her. We placed her in the back room of the main lodge building. Miss Gavin had volunteered to continue as a nurse. Mr. Guarimo will need to bunk with Rich tonight."

A sudden chuckle came from R.S. Farrow. "That'll be a shocking experience for Leo. I bet he hasn't spent the night in a room with a male since he was ten years old at youth camp."

"Fuck you, R.S.," Rich yelled quickly over the heehawing of the group.

"Joel can stay with me," Fulcher volunteered. "They won't have to remove Heather's personal belongings to make room for him. It would be more convenient for all."

"About Miss Baldwin," Frenchie interrupted as he silenced the chuckling men by slowly raising his left hand. "We need to discuss the incident." He struggled in a diplomatic way to convey the touchy revelation. "She…uh, she…uh…"

A plaintive voice came through the silence. "What are you saying?"

"She's been assaulted," Lashley interjected.

"What the hell is this, Frenchie," Rich demanded.

43

The guide took a deep breath before the words finally came. "There ain't no easier way to say it. While the hunting party was out, Miss Baldwin was attacked and sexually violated. It happened somewhere on the rim, just off the little landing strip."

There was another anxious pause as the gravity of the disclosure took effect. The room swelled with several audible gasps and curses.

"You're saying she's been raped? Who did such a terrible thing?" Elliott Thornton questioned, impulsively sobered by the disclosure.

"Raped?" several voices echoed.

Additional voices challenged, "It can't be."

"Not Heather?" Lewis Fulcher responded in a tone of painful precision.

"Yeah," Rich inquired, with a voice sufficiently raised to include the females in the dining room. "Which of you, sons of bitches, fucked my girl? I'll kill the mother fucker with my bare hands!" Rich pointed his long, bony finger at the two military officers.

Lashley noticed two women startled by the outburst moved to stand in the dark shadows of the doorway.

"Don't point at me when you say that." Major Greer snarled in rage. He moved toward the car dealer. Fifteen years his senior, Lashley judged Rich would have been no match for the physically well-conditioned officer. Everyone in the room recognized the mismatch.

R.S. Farrow, typically the mediator, stepped between the men. "Calm down," he yelled, trying to be calm himself. "Hear Frenchie out. We might have some answers then."

"It appears to have been someone outside the lodge. A party who has no association with this hunting group," Frenchie stated. "Too bad the bronc was not raised on this spread. If so, we could fix him."

"Whom then?" Thornton, fully sobered now, inquired.

"We aren't for sure," Frenchie answered, flinching as soon as he had responded as though his ambiguous answer was an error.

"What do you mean you don't know who? Then it's a God damn cover up," Rich responded again, raising his voice. His eyes glared viciously at the head guide.

"You're protecting that shit-eating cook, Crisco," the dealer continued. "He's already served time for rape. There was a cowboy who worked here for several years, Jimmy Hunger. He gave me the scoop on Crisco, our erstwhile cook. I'll castrate the bastard for messing with my pussy!"

Major Greer moved again, this time to block Rich's movement toward the kitchen. "That's a lie! Crisco was in sight the whole time. Until Heather was noticed as missing, Crisco was serving food or cleaning up. After that, everybody at base camp was searching with some other person. When we couldn't find her, we returned to the lodge and reviewed everyone's whereabouts. Everyone's time was adequately accounted for." His anger voiced his conviction.

"Then someone else at lodge did it," Rich pounded his fist.

The major's rage became more acute with every passing second. He forced a pause. "Hey," the officer directed his wrath to Rich, "what about you? I think you slipped off the hunt, rode back, and assaulted her. Did she get tired of your abuse and finally refuse your advances?"

Rich swung his fist at the officer, who artfully dodged and delivered a retaliatory blow to Rich's midsection. Quickly, both men were restrained while Rich groaned obscenities at Greer.

"You blue suited son-of-a-bitch. I'll cut your nuts out for that," the car dealer croaked through pain clinched teeth.

Five men had remained behind. Lashley had confirmed that Greer had talked extensively to Crisco. Joel Guarimo had wandered aimlessly about the building and spent some time talking to Horne about the set up at the lodge. The electric supply salesman had gone outside around the barn and the vehicles. Paige had confirmed she had occasionally observed him during his ramblings.

Lashley was almost certain that none of the men were absent for sufficient time to have attacked Heather. It all pointed to outsiders, unless several of the guests were jointly lying. Maybe he had missed something. Could Leo Rich be right? Had someone at the lodge been a part of the attack? It was too difficult for him to fathom, though he tried.

Captain Mitchell, from what he had heard, was an Afghan veteran. Mitchell had just transferred to Tyndall Air Force Base in the panhandle of Florida. As an Army inter-service exchange officer, he now observed the Air Force's operation with the F-16 jet fighters.

Mitchell's companion was Myrtle Wallace, a civil servant. Light-skinned, the color of heavy cream, she was tall and thin. Her dark straight hair accentuated the striking features of her face. The commanding general of Tyndall had secured an invitation, through Leo Rich, for a western hunt for herself and Patricia Stanford.

Contrasting with the close knit Rich hunting party, these four military connected individuals were true outsiders. The group ate and separately conversed as a foursome, and maintained minimum social intercourse with the balance of the guests.

Frenchie shifted uneasily. Always nervous in front of an audience, he obviously was not accomplishing what he was attempting. His explanation was falling short, its meaning lost. He needed assistance.

"Help me, Lashley. I'm not doing well. I'm as clumsy as a new born colt doing this kind of stuff," Frenchie implored.

Lashley surveyed the men, making deliberate eye contact with each individual. His eyes swept the group like a broom chasing cobwebs. The process took longer than a minute, and the intervening silence was eerie. It might have been his ability to arouse fear with his piercing eyes or merely the commanding sharp tone of his voice. Whatever the method, he demanded undivided attention.

Lashley spoke, "I'll explain the circumstance using the facts that I know, with minimum speculation. I'll request no interruptions or comments. When I've concluded, we will discuss our alternatives. Agreed?"

Upon obtaining acquiescence, he proceeded.

"When Heather left this lodge, she exited the gate just below the fish dam. That's the same trail that our horses departed on this morning. When returning this afternoon, a few several hundred yards out, I noticed small rubber soled tracks. Because the footprints were over the hoof marks of our outward bound horses, I concluded they had to have been placed there after nine o'clock.

"Just above the spring where the antelopes water, the prints turned easterly down into the small draw. It was evidently a single track. None came back. When I later found Miss Baldwin, I realized that her shoes were of a matching configuration and size to the tracks I had earlier noticed on the trail. I thus conclude she made the first limits of her jog down by the antelope spring."

He paused and slightly lowered his head as though speaking for such length was exhausting.

"How she arrived from the water hole to the rim of the cliff where I located her is to some extent speculation, but there is some factual basis for my next assumption," Lashley continued. "After midday, there was a spectacular storm off the north rim of the Arm. Lightning, rain, and rainbows. Maybe she desired a box seat for this display. Your search parties obliterated any track she made crossing the plateau. But the cur picked up her trail inside the fence line along the flat. She must have jogged out to the edge of the cliff, following along the rim about halfway toward what Frenchie classifies as the new house. It was at this point where she was first attacked."

Lashley again paused, surveying the impact of his information.

"First attacked?" someone murmured under low breath. "Then was she attacked again?"

Slumping in the doorway, Myrtle Wallace and Patricia Stanford had become a permanent part of Lashley's audience.

Lashley continued, ignoring the question. "Someone had been standing on an outcrop just below the cliff line. He had been there for a long period of time. At least eighteen cigarette butts had been discarded by this sentinel. Most likely, he is from an urban area. Any person raised in this dry, open country always crushes his butt. Too much chance for a wild fire. Our assailant was careless with his smoking. He was no local."

Lashley stopped, waiting for reaction. Then, after a long silence, he again commenced. His audience shifted uncomfortably.

"At the point where this guy was ultimately flushed from his hiding place by Heather, there were signs of a struggle," Lashley elaborated. "He must have overpowered her and drug her down the foot trail that leads to the base of the cliff. While the balance of you transported Heather back to the lodge, I back-tracked her assailant's course to a stand of chokecherry bushes about 300 yards east of the base of the cliff. A vehicle had been parked in that thick undergrowth. Signs indicated that there were at least three occupants. It was at that location where she was raped.

"Afterwards, she was administered some type of medication or drug that rendered her unconscious. There's a single puncture wound in the bend of her left arm, a needle mark. She was then physically carried back to the rim's edge and discarded.

"That's where I ultimately located her. In addition to the medication, I'd say she was suffering from exposure. She lay in the cold for several hours. No purpose is served by describing the details of her condition when she was finally discovered, but it is sufficient to say that it was not pleasant."

Lashley paused. Even as he out lined the scenario, the explanation sounded unbelievable, incomprehensible, even to him.

"That leaves us some immediate assignments," Lashley continued. "First we need medical attention for Heather. Since the Cottonwood is so remote and surrounded by mountains, cell phones don't work here. We might use the lodge's radio but even that has limited range. Since we can't get help to come in, we will have to go outside to contact the authorities."

"Hell no," yelled Rich, no longer able to restrain his emotions. "We're not going to get the police involved in this. We'll have every newspaper in the country on our asses. It's all I need for my wife to be notified. That's not going to happen. Period!"

Farrow interjected, "Leo, Heather must get medical attention. Treated, you know, for diseases and things."

"I'm not against that, R.S. That's not what I'm saying. I wouldn't touch her myself till she gets a clean bill of health. Take her to some local doctor for testing but not to the police. The police are definitely out. O-U-T. OUT." Rich demanded.

"You crude S.O.B.," Major Greer interjected. "You're more concerned for yourself than you are for the woman. That's heartless!"

"I'll take no lip from a desk jockey who lets his cunt do his manly hunting for him. You came on this trip on my invite, and I'm now uninviting you. Pack your wheel-caps and leave some tire tracks on the road," Rich ordered emphatically.

"Leo, cut it out," Farrow pleaded. "The major is just as concerned about what's happened as we all are. We have to do what's proper even if that means involving the police. We all have the same possible exposure."

"Damn it R.S. I can't get caught again. My wife will clean me for everything but my hood ornament. It can't happen," Rich responded.

"What happened to Heather is serious," Farrow pleaded. "It's got to be reported. It's like trying to keep secret a gold strike. It gets out no matter how tight you screw on the lid."

"Serious my ass," Rich said. "Somebody's plowed in her pee patch. It's not the first time that a dent's been put on her maidenhead and it won't be the last. Her wheels were spinning when I found her, and they'll continue to churn when I'm in the shop. I will not risk any chance of exposure."

"Rape isn't the same as having sex," Carter quickly interjected. "Even you have to acknowledge that, Leo."

"We aren't talking about some sixteen year old virgin," Rich insisted vigorously. "Heather has been around the dirt track plenty of times. She's got a body right out of Part's Pups and she's advertised it in the most appropriate show rooms. I'll put some hard cash on her, maybe twenty-five thousand. That will restore the damage to its original condition.

"That's gross," Fulcher interrupted. "Don't even speak of such a despicable solution."

"This is my hunt and my pussy. I'll drive both courses the way I choose. There will be no yellow flags waved at me on this track."

Frenchie elected to let the argument go its course. He bent down to Lashley. "Rich's pissing in a stove pipe, and it can only come out one way."

"I agree," Lashley responded. "The coon hounds are gaining, and there's no tree in sight."

"But there must be some area of compromise," R.S. Farrow interjected, "that can accomplish both purposes. Let's hear some ideas from Lashley."

"Access is impossible. We can't get out from the lodge until morning," Lashley said. "Today there was a washout on the road. Frenchie can quickly repair the water damage after first light. One of the guides can take Miss Baldwin to a doctor in Rawlins. The Major can accompany the group. There will need to be two women volunteers to assist the guide. The balance of the party can continue their hunt without interruption."

Lashley intended to split the antagonists. This would allow sufficient time for healing.

"One of our guides, George Poulen, you know him as Chainsaw," Lashley continued, "is familiar with the locals in Rawlins. He lives there. Heather is a guest at this lodge. My name can be recorded as finding her. No one else needs to be mentioned. I'll front any investigation that follows. Now let's turn in early. Tomorrow will be a rough day."

The offer was more than a suggestion. He delivered it as an irrevocable command. Quickly disbursing, most of the men drifted away whispering to each other about the day's event. The women emerged, pairing with their companions, anxious for details of the conference. It was now time for rumors and speculation to be sowed, reaped and then served like instant grits Lashley thought.

Rich remained behind. "It's bull shit, Lashley. And you know it. You may con the balance of this crew with your used car story, but you'll not draft me into it. As long as I'm kept out of any publicity you can run the showroom."

Rich secured a confident step toward Lashley and sneered, "The first hint my name's attached to the paint, and you'll have skid marks on your back."

As Rich pivoted and stalked off, Captain Mitchell moved closer.

"When the sun rises, there's going to be a man hunt. You're going to neutralize the perpetrators unless I miss my guess," Mitchell said as he squatted beside Lashley. "I have the feeling you have withheld vital information from the rest of us. Whatever your motives or personal reasons, I'll accept them."

Indifferently, Lashley shrugged his shoulders and Mitchell continued. "Tomorrow, I'd like to accompany you on your mission."

"What mission, Captain?" Lashley asked the large, burly, black man.

"I want to be a part of that operation."

Lashley was silent, evaluating the squatting man. He adopted the wise owl look and posed the question as a visiting professor lecturing on unfamiliar subject matter.

"Can you use a gun?"

"I was raised in South Alabama, Wilcox County. Hunted all my life. Even though I do desk work now, early in my military career I went through both ranger and paratrooper training. I was engaged in ground action in Afghan."

"Sounds qualified," Lashley said. "But could you stalk a man?"

"Yes, I believe I could, under these circumstances," Mitchell responded.

"Then you may join me, but take fair warning. Tomorrow will be a tough day. A killing day."

CHAPTER THREE

Nothing was in focus. The noise was irritating, unidentifiable. Flickering in the distance was a tiny flame, possibly a candle. The image was not discernible, yet. The man felt numb. His body, like a cork on a fishing line, bobbed and jerked. He floated, but could not break free of the weight dragging below him. Confined, he needed urgently to flee and run. He wanted to escape, but the thought passed. There would be no escape, and he knew it.

Had the candle caused the explosion which was consuming his very existence? Flames were everywhere, and the volume of burning material was increasing. The pressure of the heat made his head throb. The noise increased in volume. It was a sound he knew, but its identity was remotely beyond his comprehension.

Howard Lashley felt a force tightening around his neck, tighter and tighter. His throat constructed, cutting off his breath. Strangulation! He gasped, no longer able to catch his breath. Then from a distance, he heard a faint voice, slowly becoming louder and clearer.

"Wake up, Howard!" Paige St. John said emphatically as she shook her bed partner. "It's that dream again. Wake up."

Bolting upright in bed, still gasping, Lashley jolted awake as sweat covered his body even in the chill of the room. In the fireplace, glowing coals remained from the fire last stroked hours ago.

The young woman looked puzzled and queried. "It came back, didn't it? The dream."

"Yes," he conceded. "It's been a long time since the last one."

"Maybe three months?" she insisted.

"I guess about that long," he responded at once.

Utilizing the corner of the blanket, she mopped the sweat from his brow. "I'd hoped the dreams were gone this time, Howard."

Paige was the only person of his acquaintance who called him by his first name. He introduced himself as

Lashley and corrected any deviation of that name. But he never corrected Paige.

Characteristically, he shrugged his shoulders. The small, closed room revived a sense of days he had spent in the Five Pines Hospital. For the past three years, it had been difficult for him to be in a closed room. At home when he slept, even in the cold or damp weather, he insisted that some window be open. Only then would he reach a minimum comfort level. Encouraged by Paige, he was at last conquering his phobia or so he thought.

"What happened to Heather must have triggered it, Howard. I know last night you were so concerned about her," she said.

Last evening, after the men had conferred, the couple had retreated to the sanctuary of these sleeping quarters. Small, by the rest of the lodge's standards, the room was considered the least desirable by most guests. Lashley coveted it for the isolation. The open fireplace provided the sole source of heat, and by morning, dying embers would struggle to combat the invading cold. For Lashley, that was the charm of the room.

Barely twelve feet long by fourteen feet wide, the room's furnishings were sparse. It consisted of a bed and small end table bound by two wooden chairs. High on the wall over the iron bedsted, was a glass window covering one half of the wall. The window gave the room the openness that Lashley desired. Lengthwise, parallel over the bed, was a deep shelf that serviced as a type of linen storage. Extra blankets, quilts, and towels were neatly stacked on the shelf. Wooden pegs, strategically placed along the remaining walls, served as storage for the guest's gear and as gun racks.

"Let's go, Paige," Lashley had requested when the men's strategy conference had concluded. He picked up a fifth of Jack Daniels, Black, and a pitcher of cold water, requesting Paige to bring two glasses. Thus prepared, they retreated to their secluded room.

As she mixed the drinks, mild for her, three fingers for him, Lashley stroked the fire with a long metal poker. Quickly, the flames had warmed the room. He moved the wooden straight-back chairs to face the fireplace and motioned for her to sit. Three stiff swallows were sufficient to relax him, warming his interior as the fire warmed his outer body.

Depositing his glass on the floor, he reached for his rifle. As he cleaned the Remington 30.06, he explained to her, in summary form, his briefing of the men.

When he finished, she said, "I helped them treat Heather's wounds. They were awful. I just feel that something was terribly amiss, but I don't know the extent of it. What happens now?"

He told her. Later, when they had sought the comfort of bed, he felt the tension in his body. They did not make love. His action was not a rejection directed toward her personally. There were secrets retained, best left untold. And so they had slept as they had for the past year, spooned together until, in early morning, she awakened him from those jerking motions she had come to associate with his devastating dreams.

Lashley checked his watch. It was barely 4:00 a.m. From the kitchen, sounds filtered out as Crisco and his helper, Ray Horne, made preparations for the morning meal. Unable to return to a sleeping mode, he swung off the bed, pitched some wood into the fireplace, and punched the embers. He crouched in front of the fire and extended his palms as a welcome to the heat.

"It's been more than three years now," he said thinking out loud. "Three years of living in twilight, not a whole person."

Paige, propped on her elbow, watched his profile in the dim light.

He continued with a weakened and almost defeated voice. "Awakening in a hospital with no remembrance of who I was or any trace of my history is like being born an adult, with an adult knowledge, but absent childhood."

He rocked backwards on his hands, creating a moving silhouette along the opposite wall.

"It's all right," Paige reassured. "It doesn't matter to me. I love you, with or without a family history."

He recognized she sensed his frustrations. He had spoken of them, not often, but frequently enough for her to be aware of the thwarted desires eating at his soul. In their early acquaintance, he had maintained stoic silence for days at a time. But now, especially in these last four months, he had become more open with his concerns. He talked with caution. In bits and pieces, his story slowly unveiled.

"What if I'm married or have children? How does that compete with your feelings?" he stated abruptly.

Her brow wrinkled with concern as a small tear streaked down her cheek, barely visible in the firelight. Her sadness touched him as it always did when he talked of his frustrations. The dreams always produced this despair. Just when would it end?

"We've been through this so many times," she spoke softly. "There are ways to work it out if we just stand together. I'm ready for a firm commitment from you. No more of this ambiguous stuff, but you know I'm not pushing you. I'm ready when you are. But even a proposal of marriage has a time limit. You have my offer, unconditional. I don't want to push, but you need to make up your mind." She quickly wiped her tear.

"It wouldn't work well for you," Lashley leaned forward, and she caught his smile in the fire light. "If we tied the knot it would end your invitation on these outings. Married women are not allowed on hunts. At least if they are married to one of the hunters."

He ducked the pillow she threw, leaned over and kissed her gently on the forehead. He ran his hand through the nape of her gown and cupped her breast. It was a tender, loving motion he had conveyed many times before. His emotions stirred once again, as with all of the other times he touched her.

Especially at this time, he needed emotional support. Heather's rape had adversely affected him. Outwardly, he attempted to show no discernible change. But he and Paige had lived together long enough that he knew she could detect his internal personality deviation. She squeezed his hand tighter to her breast, warming to the touch.

"Please tell me your troubles," she requested. "Please, please tell me the extent of this danger."

But his answer was silence.

"Go back to sleep," he finally said. "Frenchie will need help to get the blade on the truck. After the road's repaired, you are going into Rawlins with Chainsaw."

He made a stop at the community restroom on the enclosed walkway connecting the main building with the bunk house. At this early hour, the facilities were unoccupied. With military precision, he performed a quick cleanup and shave. With the exception of the room at the far end, which was occupied by Leo Rich, none of the bunkhouse rooms had toilet accommodations. Everyone used the gender-separated facilities on the walkway.

After splashing cold water on his face, Lashley checked his features in the mirror. Early thirties, he assumed. His face was darkened, sunburned by the hours he spent running along the beach training for marathons. Physical activity was an obsession for him, as he felt no necessity to engage in financial endeavors. In some convoluted manner, he received a substantial monthly check from an undisclosed trust. It more than satisfied his humble desires. His hair was dark and curly, but premature gray stubble spotted his chin. He always maintained a neat appearance, even on hunting trips.

"No dividends for the wild and woolly hunter," he mumbled.

Crossing the darkened dining hall, he entered the kitchen simultaneously with Frenchie Hebert and Chainsaw Poulen. He poured a cup of cowboy coffee, strong and thick. It activated the desired effect. Haunting dreams hastily retreated into memories to be forcibly locked away for the day. The bitter taste of the cowboy brew jolted him back into the presence of reality.

The kitchen's size accommodated a table spacious enough to serve the guides. The active wooden cooking stove guaranteed warmth. In the early morning chill, the kitchen was the social center of the lodge.

"Has String exposed his bearded face?" Frenchie asked the cook crew, as he prepared for his first caffeine injection of the day.

Ray Horne, the younger assistant cook, hobbled about the kitchen with efficiency, collecting and scrubbing the dishes.

In the kitchen, the wood stove furnished the hot water. The tin coffee kettle, scarred by years of abusive use, stood ready to instantly scald any cowboy's unsuspecting innards. Ingeniously, the Cottonwood had provided adequate indoor water for plumbing and cooking. Upstream, the cowboy had constructed a sunken cistern. It collected water from an adjacent creek. Through pipes, gravity fed, the water flowed with sufficient pressure to fulfill the needs of the lodge as efficiently as a municipal utility system. Water heaters, fueled by kerosene, furnished the guests with minimum hot water for the showers and taps.

"Not yet, Frenchie," Crisco responded. Crisco was a medium build, barrel-chested man with a grunt face tanned by years of excessive exposure to the harsh climates of the mountains.

"He's enjoying the last flicks of his wet dreams," Frenchie said and turned to Lashley. "String sleeps in the room over the barn 'cause he claims our snoring and farting disturbs him. But I think it's his strange love life that distances him from our lofty quarters."

The men laughed at their boss' comments. Even a small crew required one man to serve as the butt of ranch hand jokes. By default, the honor was bestowed upon Hank Stringfield, the oldest of the crew.

"Go get String up, Cinch," Frenchie instructed the youngest guide, Cinch Wilkinson, who just entered the room wiping matter from his eyes. "And close the trap on the cooler while you're down that way."

He watched the cowboy reluctantly slip into his jacket and depart into the cold morning air.

Crisco handed Lashley a tin platter filled with a pair of egg yokes staring upward, fenced in with thin strips of fried ham and topped with a biscuit.

Balancing the platter and cup, Lashley located a table that received adequate light filtering through the kitchen door. He swung his leg over a chair and sat down. Shortly he was joined by Frenchie and Chainsaw.

"Lashley, I've got to thank you for the way you handled the situation last night." Frenchie said. "I'm not sure I could have made it without your help. Cottonwood's had hunters coming in for more than seventy years under my grandpop, my dad and now me. Nothing like this has ever happened. Thanks again."

Lashley shrugged his shoulders in acknowledgment.

"It's hard to fathom. The whole thing is unreal. Just unbelievable." Frenchie continued. "It's one thing to talk about violence, but it's something else when you become a part of it. My crew starts talking about the next rodeo for six months before the event. One day and it's over, broken bones and all. That's a kind of violence I can understand. But violence against people, I just can't comprehend. It's like finding a camel in the Klondike. You can't explain it."

"Making chin music about it won't help," Chainsaw interjected. "A man that straddles a wire fence is going to come away with a sore crotch. We can't stop just to breathe our pony any longer. It's time to apply some leather to the rump, and go after the people who did this."

"That's exactly what I had in mind. Come daylight, I'm going to start trailing," Lashley answered.

"What support do you need?" Frenchie asked.

"Two mounts and the cur dog. That captain, the quiet one, Mitchell, has volunteered to trail with me. Appears to be the man to assist. Has good qualifications, on paper, at least." Lashley responded.

"It's really my responsibility. I should be doing it," the guide said, as he sopped the yokes with his biscuit.

"You stay with the guests. They are entitled to the hunt they paid for," Lashley said.

"Frenchie could spare String for today's hunt," Chainsaw suggested through hurried bites. "Let String take the women into Rawlins. I could be free to back you up on the tracking. It could be dangerous out there. You don't know what to expect or the numbers you're up against. There's a lot of unknowns. Could be as dangerous as platting a mule's tail. Could get kicked when you least expect it."

Lashley considered the offer. George Poulen, a native of Wyoming, was a top notch ranch hand. He had met Poulen during his past summer's trip to the Cottonwood. A short stop into an Alcova bar disclosed few locals who would talk to a stranger, but Poulen did. A friendship nurtured during the consumption of a six pack of beer. Lashley hired Chainsaw, as he was nicknamed, to teach him the finer points of the rugged west. Working out of the Cottonwood, they covered Hand Mountain together, spending grueling days in the saddle. Chainsaw was a knowledgeable teacher and Lashley was an apt pupil. The two became friends. At Lashley's suggestion, Frenchie hired Chainsaw to guide exclusively for the Rich party.

"No, Chainsaw," Lashley said. "You're the only man I can trust to minimize the impact with the local authorities. You are known in Rawlins. No one else is. We don't need a full-blown investigation of the lodge's occupants. We need the local sheriff to direct his attention to locating Heather's assailants."

"I assure you I can handle that," Chainsaw suggested between bites.

"How do you plan your tracking?" Frenchie asked.

"I'll work high enough along the east slope of the Arm to stay out of rifle range. It's best to keep that broad gulch visible. You know, the one that parallels the road as it passes north. Keep a distance but close enough where I can glass it. Chainsaw and I worked that gulch last summer. I know it well enough."

He paused to sip his coffee and continued, "There isn't adequate foliage in the bottom to hide a vehicle, except in a few isolated places. At the south boundary of the Diamondhead Ranch, along the fence line, where the road turns east and crosses the draw at the government culvert, I'll change tactics. I'll come off the Arm and flank the road south along the lower flats. If I haven't found a vehicle in seven or eight miles, we'll consider they've vacated the area. However, if I locate them, I'll tree them and send the Captain back for help. Cut your hunt short today. Be back at base by 2:00 p.m. sharp. If we've found anything, the captain should be back to the lodge with instructions by then. If he's not back as planned and neither of us has returned by dark, stay put. Wait till morning. I don't want anyone coming up on me in the dark."

"Okay," Frenchie said, as he swallowed the last of the biscuit. "But I think it's risky. We don't need any more casualties at the Cottonwood."

"Chainsaw," Lashley said, "it should still be daylight when you return from Rawlins. Send a deputy down the northern route. Check for tracks first. If that vehicle's tracks indicated he doubled back off the north road, skip it. Our game will have been flushed and long gone. But if the tracks haven't come out, let the deputy come on into the lodge around that road. Warn him to be careful."

"Got you covered," Chainsaw responded.

"Take my rented Bronco." Lashley extracted the key from his pocket, tendering it to Chainsaw. "It's probably the roomiest of the vehicles. Take the back seat out. Make a pallet on the floor. There are plenty of extra blankets and quilts in my room. Paige will help. Maybe Miss Baldwin's gained consciousness by now and can give some details of her attackers. It may give us a picture of what we can expect."

Cinch's hasty entrance into the dining room interrupted the men.

"Frenchie," Cinch croaked with emotion. "You better come. It's String. He's dead."

CHAPTER FOUR

In the gray morning darkness, the cold-storage building towered like a lighthouse in a storm. Fifteen feet tall, ten feet by ten feet for the inside dimension, it counterbalanced the lodge's rust painted outbuildings. Walls filled with eighteen inches of sawdust provided insulation for the cooler's contents.

The absence of electricity forced ranchers to harness nature's elements, converting them to friendly use. This particular structure substituted for refrigeration. It was an example of man's ability to ingeniously survive under harsh circumstances. In reality, the storage building was a colossal, modified ice chest.

Everyday at sundown, an employee would climb a ladder, opening a small trap door near the top. Elevated at such heights, the door was beyond reach of meandering varmints. The autumn nighttime temperature religiously plunged in this high altitude, and the cold entered the cooler through the gaping hole. When the small upper door was shut in the mornings, the cold air was thus trapped inside. Dressed game, hung inside, was protected just as well as if it was in a reefer at a meat market.

Cinch swung the heavy cooler door open, shining his flashlight inside. Deer carcasses from the previous day's hunt hung on racks. The young man's weak batteries furnished a dim light. The light hesitated, holding focused on the hanging carcasses. Then it swung swiftly to the right.

The appalling scene unfolded. Framed in the glow a man hung, a meat hook impaled in his back. In the standard position of a gun fighter, the man dangled with arms hung lightly to his side, knees bent, feet apart and shoulders crouched. His face, shrouded by shadows, was not distinguishable. But the worn, faded, leather vest was identifiable. Hank Stringfield dangled a foot off the floor.

"Jesus, String's deader than a broken bridle," Frenchie said, reacting to the scene.

The hanging cowboy had worked for the Cottonwood off and on for twenty years. Peculiar in some personal ways, Hank Stringfield, however, had been at least dependable during the hunting and dude season. During the rest of the year, when he was sober, he performed odd jobs around the lodge, tending to the horses and the few cattle Frenchie still retained.

Lashley had learned on his previous visits the connection the man held with the Cottonwood. String was especially adaptable with the remuda. Outfitting hunters required a substantial head of horses, usually double the highest number of guests scheduled for any given hunt. In recent years, the Cottonwood's herd had never dropped below an inventory of thirty mounts. Left on the range to graze during lax months, the horses would retreat to their wild habits.

String's job was preventative in nature. Every few days through out the off season, selective horses were saddled and ridden. Unruly stock was cut and sold. By the arrival of the first fall hunters, String's duty was to assure the riders were furnished a mount, gentle even for neophytes.

But now he was dead. Murdered. The man had been culled from the herd of mankind, as a horse designated for the glue factory.

"That's how I found him. The big door was opened. I was surprised String had been so careless. Then I found him. That's worse than a necktie party," Cinch said. "He climbed the golden stairs on a bent hook."

Lashley entered the room, gesturing toward Chainsaw. "Help me lower him."

Chainsaw stepped forward to assist. The men lowered String, as they gently placed the body lengthwise along the back wall.

"Bring the light closer," Lashley requested.

As Cinch complied, Lashley, with Chainsaw's assistance, moved the body for examination. In the middle of the body's chest, a bullet hole showed, marking a penetration of man's most vital organ - the heart. His shirt contained traces of powder burns, evidence that the killer had been at close range. If the projectile had not caused his death, the men shared little doubt the meat hook had succeeded.

"Cinch," Frenchie said extending the keys, "drive Lashley's Bronco closer to the lodge. We need to be on the move earlier than I expected. Leave the light here. We need to check some things."

No sooner had the young guide cleared the room than a muffled curse was heard, followed by an echoed yell. A pause succeeded. Then Cinch barked, "It's the dog! I fell over the damn dog!"

The three men joined the youngster who was still on his knees, his hand outstretched toward the bitch.

"She's dead, Frenchie. The bitch is dead," Cinch said.

Lashley leaned forward. The bitch dog lay on its side, as if sleeping and enjoying the warmth of a noon day sun. Never again would this animal relish such luxury. It had been shot once in the lower neck and again behind her front shoulder blade.

"I heard no shots last night. We're too close to the lodge to have missed hearing three shots being fired," Frenchie said.

Lashley responded, "My best guess is that someone used a weapon with a silencer. The dog must have surprised the killer. He then had to take her out. String must have realized something had happened. He came up to investigate and got bushwhacked." Lashley continued, "Cinch, go get the Bronco."

Under the dim light of the flashlight, the men watched Cinch disappear.

"A silencer at the Cottonwood? Can't be? We don't have any weapons like that," Frenchie stated. "We've got a madman loose out there somewhere."

"Frenchie," Lashley said, "call up the cur."

The head guide whistled and received no response. He whistled again. This time it was louder.

"Where's my other dog? That's funny," the top guide said. "He always responds."

"Could he have been scared off?" Chainsaw suggested.

"Maybe, but I don't think so," Frenchie responded in frustration. "He's tough. That cur's been known to tie in with a badger."

Lashley flashed the light around in the general area. The second dog lay a few feet away.

"Damn," Poulen said. "They got both dogs."

Sweeping the flashlight along the ground, Lashley found what he suspected, several twenty-five caliber cartridges.

"Well, we know the weapon he's using. That should narrow our search," Lashley said. "Don't find many twenty-five caliber weapons on a hunt."

To the right of the barn, a vehicle's light switched on, more effectively illuminating the surroundings. Cinch had reached the Bronco.

The light cast a ghostly shadow up the slope toward the lodge, 200 yards away. Sweeping the flashlight along the area, Lashley found what he suspected. To the left of the cooler, the gate to the corral hung open, the penned horses long since departed.

"The catch horses are gone! It'll take us hours to round up sufficient mounts for a hunt or for someone to track those thugs," Frenchie said. "What else can happen?"

"Frenchie, you'd better come over here," Cinch called from the Bronco.

"I think you're about to discover what else can go wrong, Frenchie. I'd say we're bare-ass naked in a nest of rattlers." Chainsaw responded, but his tone was far from playful.

Making their way across the front of the barn, the men found Cinch bending over the hood of the Bronco, peering at the engine.

Cinch commented on his discovery. "All of the spark plug cables are missing. It won't crank. Whoever did this is as dirty as a blue-tick hound."

"Damn. This can't be happening," the lodge's proprietor said in surprise.

"Cinch, you and Chainsaw look at the other vehicles," Lashley instructed them. "Hebert and I will take the flashlight and check the pickup in the barn."

After separate investigations, the men gathered at the Bronco. The verdict was unanimous. All vehicles were disabled, inoperative.

"It's going take hours to pirate parts to make repairs," Chainsaw commented. "That is, if we can find cables and some tools to put the parts together.

Don't look to me to do it. I'm not much good on electrical work."

Lashley recognized the horses posed an additional problem. Customarily the horses were left out to graze each evening. Two animals were always retained in the corral, and fed grain and hay. These pinned horses served as morning mounts to round up the necessary horses needed for that day's hunt. In the absence of the catch ponies, the guides would have to do the task on foot. It would be a difficult job. Scattered horses were like kids at recess, hard to regroup. The release of the catch horses and the disabled vehicles returned the lodge to man's original transportation mode - foot.

It was sixteen miles east to the nearest asphalt road. Traveling ten miles south, across extremely rough terrain, including a climb up a massive mesa wall, they might reach the closest ranch house. Either route would require a full day of strenuous hiking. Horses had to be caught, and quickly.

"What's the call, Lashley?" Frenchie asked.

"Best would be to use all available manpower to catch one horse. If we're lucky, that might not take long. Catch one and we can corral the balance we need. Once we have a couple under saddle, we'll send one rider south to the ranch on the mesa and another east to the highway. Let's see if we have the talent among us to get at least one vehicle operative. Then we can fall back to our original plan. Chainsaw takes the vehicle and the women out to Rawlins. He reports the incident. I'll go tracking."

"What about String?" Cinch asked.

"We'll leave him there in the cooler," Lashley answered. "At least until the police arrive on the scene. Chainsaw's going to have a tough time keeping a lid on this one. The Sheriff will now become involved whether we like it or not. There's a cold blooded killer loose. He's got to be run to ground. Drag the dogs to cover. Can't let the guests get more upset by seeing them lying in the open."

"Let's get back and face those hostile tenants," Frenchie said. "Standing here won't bring String back. Catching the horses might make the medicine taste better. Complaining won't help. Kicking don't get you nowhere, unless you're a pack mule."

Dousing the truck lights, the men started the climb upward to the lodge. They skirted left crossing the fish pond dam. To their backs, the morning sun fan-tailed on the horizon, painting the sky reddish amber. It was a red sky morning. The time had arrived for sailors to take warning.

The men crossed the foot bridge and entered the lodge through the side door. As if by automation, Crisco handed each a cup of caffeine, camouflaged as coffee. Ray Horne, the cook's assistant, began spooning Cinch Wilkinson a plate of vitals. At the foot of the stairs that lead to the crew's loft sat Fish Mackey and Fred Stumbough.

These last two rounded out Frenchie's team of guides. Both men had lanky, suntanned faces. Clad in faded blue jeans, denim shirts, with Lee jackets, their lean weathered faces made them appear aged beyond their years. Thin as men born to the saddle, they wasted no energy, moving with measured skills.

Fish was somewhat the wag of the crew. He forever hassled the cook, Crisco, who invariably responded with hostile reaction, occasionally making

Fish the target of a hard biscuit hurled more than in jest.

"Frenchie," the cowboy jeered. "This coffee won't be much help this morning. I've seen muddy creek water stronger than this. It's so weak the spoon won't float."

"How would you know, Fish?" the cook barked in retaliation. "You're so blind you wouldn't be able to tell a spike from an eight point at twenty yards."

"But it's my hearing that counts," Fish shot back. "Let them move an inch, and I can estimate their weight within ten pounds by the noise their balls make. The reason I can't guess your weight is because you've got no balls."

He leaned his head back and roared with good-natured laughter. Stumbough echoed the merriment. He was the only member of the crew currently married, but his conjugal visits were limited to three or four trips to Casper per year. Each visit was short in duration, usually for not more than a few days. He cherished, as had mountain men of generations past, the benefits of the infrequent visits to the cabin bed, while holding out for minimal tying responsibilities.

Observing the dead pan look on their employer's face, the men quickly let the joking pass.

Frenchie turned his backside to the wood-burning stove. A relic from the 1920s it had served the lodge faithfully, both for heat and cooking. It was a marvel that Crisco could cook anything on such an antique item.

Speaking in a low voice, intended as a briefing exclusively limited to his crew, Frenchie said, "String's dead. Somebody killed him and both dogs. Cinch found him hanging in the cooler. I want all of you to join me in the dining hall while I explain the details to our guests."

The men gasped and started popping questions, but the boss' haggard face squelched their inquiries. They dutifully followed him.

The lead guide entered the dining hall, which was now illuminated by strategically placed Coleman lanterns. It was the largest room in the lodge and was the guests' social center.

At the far end of the larger room, acting as a buffer to the glassed porch was a counter bar surrounded by four bar stools. The bar's counter top operated as a self-service lounge where the guests were free to accommodate their individual needs.

Off the stoop, a concrete box had been constructed in the stream, allowing for the free flow of cold mountain water. This contraption served as a natural beer cooler. During the past years, Elliott Thornton had kept the stoop door hinges warm with his numerous trips for the suds.

The early-morning guests crowded the dining room and were eating breakfast, chatting amicably, as if Heather's rape had been placed in some mental storage rack. Elliott assumed his normal position at the bar stool, taking in a morning eye opener.

The room's lighting reflected against walls of polished lodge-pole pine, surviving from the cabin's original construction. The various antelope and deer racks scattered along the walls cast grotesque dancing shadows. Vintage rifles and shotguns, mounted intermittently among the racks, gave the room a rustic touch. Four tables, accommodating six guests each, were supplemented by two four-seat tables.

By Lashley's hasty count, three guests were missing—two women, including the injured, Heather Baldwin, and Major Greer.

Tapping the table with a spoon, Frenchie asked, "Does anyone have an update on Miss Baldwin?"

Captain Tyrone Mitchell rose from his place at the table. "I've just checked. Her pulse and temperature seem normal, but she remains incoherent. My ex-wife was a nurse, so I have some limited medical experience. Either she's suffering from the lingering effects of the medication she was given, or there is some additional medical problem. I checked her head. It doesn't appear to have been subjected to any severe blows, so I'm not convinced it's a concussion. But I have no explanation of her disoriented condition. If anyone has any ideas, I'd welcome them. Otherwise, she appears to be resting well, with no outward signs of trauma, other than multiple bruises and abrasions."

Lashley continued to be impressed with this young officer's talents and resources. When and if the saddle's cinch loosened and the leather slipped, Mitchell would be a welcomed ally.

Frenchie stammered as he continued addressing the group, "There's some most unpleasant news that I must share. String, the outfitter mostly responsible for our horses, is dead. His death was not accidental, but we don't know the cause exactly. It has now become more important that the Sheriff becomes involved. We no longer have a choice. But there is a major problem facing us. Our horses have been scattered over the range and all of the vehicles have been disabled. Once the catch horses get loose from the corral, rounding them up is like trying to get cowboys to bathe on Monday instead of Saturday. It can be done, but it will take some persuasion."

During this moment of silence across the room, a woman sobbed modestly. Another voice muttered, "Oh my God."

The guide paused to study the effect of his announcement.

As expected, Leo Rich characteristically reacted first.

"Son of a bitch!" he shouted, rising to his feet and waving his arms in emphasis. "Frenchie, I don't know what's happening around here but you better tighten your lug nuts, 'cause I'm about to sue your seat covers off. How dare you involve me in something that attracts publicity where I can get in trouble with my wife. I'll drag you through every court in the land. I'll paper the walls of my shit house with judgments against you."

"Leo, back off!" R.S. Farrow retorted severely. "Frenchie isn't responsible for everything that happens in this place. There's got to be another explanation."

"The hell he ain't," the car dealer yelled again shaking his fist. "Who's the owner of this racetrack? It's Frenchie. That's who. I'm damn careful in covering my trail. Nobody, and I mean nobody, is going to fuel my wife's tank so she can drive me to a divorce in a classic car. I'd lose my dealership and all I've built 'cause Frenchie can't control a minor hunting party."

Beryl Carter stood and placed his hands on Rich's shoulder, shoving him to his seat. Leaning, he moved face to face with Rich.

"You shut up," Carter said in the harsh tone of an asphalt contractor. "I don't want to hear any more of your bawling. Others in this room have the same risk. Let's figure out the best way out of an underbid contract. Cut our losses. Either you help us solve the problem or you can stay out of the way. It's your choice, Leo. But any more outbursts from you and you can deal directly with me. Do I make myself clear?"

Rich spoke in a near whisper. "Beryl, you remember the last time? That bitch wife of mine almost got me castrated. She's got relatives in the Dixie mafia. Said she'd have them kill me if she again found peter tracks on my seat covers. They slashed my tires and broke the windows in my car, all because of that girl I was balling. I just can't go through that again. I don't need any more of that. Understand?"

"I understand," Carter responded. "We just got to stick together like a batch of bad asphalt. Let's see what we can do."

Rich weakly nodded affirmatively.

Carter then turned and addressed the party. "Let's excuse the women and any other bellyaches that might be squeamish. Let's get to the bottom line on this. A murder, if that's what you're saying, might not be everybody's batch of hot mix. But we're going to have to get organized and face it the best we can."

Murder. It was probably the first time Frenchie would even admit to the term. Murder it was and likely the only one at the Cottonwood. There had been mention of a hunter who had been accidentally shot by his hunting partner and had died. Another had suffered a heart attack. He later died of that condition. Death was not an unknown element to the Cottonwood. It was, however, Lashley understood, going to be difficult for Frenchie to come to grips with the term, "murder."

Dunsey Martin and Grace Hancock hastily excused themselves. Elliott picked up his beer, as he and his team mate, Katherine Pace, moved further along the porch out of the room. The restaurant owner, Lewis

Fulcher, joined them, picking up a cue stick and racking the billiard balls.

Myrtle Wallace said, "Stanford and I will stay. We're prepared to accept the details."

Paige waved to Lashley from the door frame. Satisfied with the silent instructions from his eyes, she remained in the room. Attendance had dwindled.

Carter said, "Let's start with the guide. String. What do we know about his death?"

Lashley uncharacteristically filled the void. "The best we can tell he was shot at close range. Whoever did it also killed the dogs, opened the corral, and let out the catch horses. Without those horses, it's going to be difficult to round up mounts to send for help. We're going to have to do a round up on foot because someone has also disabled all the vehicles."

Lashley paused to let the group savor his message. Then he continued. "Every available person will be required to assist in a foot drive roundup. The object will be to get a horse close enough for one of the guides to catch. When they're loose on the range, sometimes it isn't easy. Horses aren't willing to volunteer for a six-hour stint under a saddle on a regular hunting day. They'll figure it's going to be another hard day and they'll be squeamish. Once we catch one horse, the balance of the roundup will be just like it is every morning. Once we get the mounts, then riders will be dispatched in separate directions to get help."

Lashley hesitated momentarily, then continued, "While we're catching the horses, somebody's got to make an attempt to get one of the vehicles operative. Pirating parts from different vehicles and using a little ingenuity might work. We've got to give it a try. If we're successful, and it's only a slight chance to get motorized, we'll send a team to Rawlins for help. Using shovels instead of the blades, we can partially repair the washout damage sufficient enough to get a vehicle across the draw. It'll be rough, so Heather cannot be taken out on the first trip. We'll bring medical assistance to her."

"I might be some help," the young captain volunteered. "Repairing antique automobiles is one of my hobbies. I can't guarantee results, but I'll try.

These new vehicles are different, but the principles are the same."

"I'll help him," Carter said. "In the paving business, keeping your equipment rolling is a daily affair. In my younger days I jerry-rigged many a piece of equipment to keep it rolling. I'm willing to try."

"Do what you want to," Rich interjected, "but I'm going to arm myself. My .357 Magnum will keep that killer locked under the hood, and I want everybody to know that I am prepared to use it. If the killer's in this room, he better damn sure not cross me, 'cause I won't give him a second chance."

"Are you gonna bitch, or are you gonna help?" Carter rejoined him stoutly.

"It's that cook," Rich said softly, his eyes shifting nervously to the threshold of the kitchen. "He also served time for murder. It's bullshit about outsiders doing Heather in. Someone inside this building did it."

Speaking louder, he announced, "I'm going to give you guys two hours to get your motors in tune. If I'm not satisfied, then I'm going to take over this outfit."

"Leo," R.S. said as he affectionately placed his arm around Mitzi Rhodes. "You can't do that. Talk like that is not productive and it frightens the women."

"R.S., I organized this hunting party and selected the participants. I didn't come here for any floor plan in the show room. I paid. Frenchie contracted with me for exclusive rights to hunt at my pleasure during this week. The balance of you are here under my contract. I'll expel those who don't conform to my request. It'll happen so fast. Like hitting the lock button. Zap, and you're locked out."

"It's not a question of the hunt," Carter responded quickly. "We all agree that you have the veto on that. But we're talking about a bigger parking lot. Who dripped the grease on the asphalt? That's the issue. We've got to get some concrete curbs around our paving project to keep it from crumbling at the edges. Control. That's what we're talking about. How to set the edge. Frenchie's the owner here. In that respect he has the ultimate responsibility. He's like the captain of a ship. We've got to follow him."

"I'll listen," Rich angrily remarked to the contractor, "to whatever he proposes, but I'll make the final decision. Frenchie works for me by contract. I'm the key to the ignition. I'll crank it up or turn it off, if and when I'm ready. Two hours until I insert the key and move into the driver's seat for real."

Leo Rich rose and pushed back his chair with such force that it fell. Then he departed the room for the bunk house, swearing under his breath.

"R.S., you better calm him down," Carter interjected. He's been your friend longer than he has been mine. You played ball with him. I've only known him for fifteen years. In the lodge, he was in the south, when I was Master. He's always been a loudmouth bastard, but never to this extent."

Fulcher reentered the room in time to hear the last bit of Rich's tirade. "I always said you couldn't please Leo if you hung him with a new rope."

Thyus Harder, not to be outdone, interjected, "Leo can be a real no-good bastard most of the time, but other than that, he has few faults."

"You'll have to understand Leo," Beryl Carter apologetically offered the group. "Last year, his wife caught him dicking around. Her family is from Tampa. All of them are Italians. A tough bunch of Dagos who put a lot of emphasis on family values. A group of them shot out Leo's windows. That's true. But that's only half of the story. They took Leo and his girlfriend out in the woods, stripped them, and whipped them real bad. The girl disappeared shortly thereafter. Leo was told that was just a prelude to what he could expect the next time he started screwing around."

"I can confirm that," Farrow added. "For a while, Leo played it close to the vest. Then he started the careless skirt chasing all over again about six months ago. We've warned him, but he's bull headed."

"Leo's convinced right now that there's an odds-even chance that it's his wife's relatives out there. The attack on Heather appears to be a duplicate of the previous attack on his former girlfriend. His outburst has some basis, in fact," Carter concluded.

"Two hours is irresponsible. Nothing can be accomplished in such a short time," Frenchie inserted with enthusiasm.

"I'll work on him," Farrow said. "Give me a little time. We need to get moving to organize our relief effort. If things don't change in a hurry, the beneficiaries on some of those policies I've written for this group are going to have their lifestyles altered. There'll be some rich widows. How are we going to divide the labor?" R.S. asked as he helped Mitzi stand.

"Stumbough, behind String, is our best man with the horses," the head guide said. "Let's get as many as we can organized for a walking roundup. One team with Cinch will flank out on a straight line along the left side of the barn. The other group, with Fish, will go a half mile south down the trail. Then each will move, fan-shaped, forming a half moon. The idea is that maybe, just maybe, one or two heads are in that hollow where the antelope water. If so, if we walk cautiously, it will allow someone on foot to slip a halter on one. If we don't move too fast, one horse might be flushed up to the barn. Stumbough will be there. We won't catch one all day if they even get spooked. If one gets within eye distance, Stumbough can charm him in. Once they're flushed away from you, go back out the same way you came in. Too much pressure will drive them too fast, even for Stumbough."

"What if there are no horses in that hollow?" R.S. asked.

"Then we'll repeat the process covering other areas until we are ultimately successful. One horse is all we need to catch," Frenchie added.

A sand-lot, ball-game method of selection followed, dividing the guests into teams. "Ennie and Mennie over here, and you Moe, over there." If circumstances were different, it would have been a farce. But with the stench of death and rape invading their thoughts, Lashley reasoned, it was a serious selection for competition in a deadly game.

During the division, Fish Mackey approached his boss. "Our ham radio don't work. I can't raise nobody. It did the last time I checked it a couple of weeks ago, but not today. I'll keep checking it."

Leo Rich cornered Chainsaw as he stood beside Lashley. "Look here, Chainsaw," the car dealer offered, "I'll pay you twenty-five hundred bucks on the side if I don't get involved. Take the woman to the doctor. Don't report her assault to the authorities. Just let them know about the killing. That's all."

"What about Miss Baldwin's feelings. Shouldn't we consider whether she wants her attackers caught?" Chainsaw asked.

"Shit man, I'll make it up to her. I'll put a wad of money in her hand. That'll make it all right."

"I'm not sure if I can work that out," Chainsaw answered.

"You're blowing twenty-five hundred bucks?" Rich responded as he steamed off to the bunk house.

The early morning sun, balanced as a ball framed in the porch window, had cleared the mountain peeks east of the Pathfinder Reservoir. Lashley observed it was a little past eight. The morning chill gripped tightly to the ground, reluctant to surrender to the morning sun.

Motioning to his team, Cinch started for the front door. Before he could exit, the pane glass window, just to his right, shattered. It disintegrated. Slivers, tumbling and twisting, sought the refuge of the porch. Dunsey Martin, positioned closest to the window, screamed, brought her hands to her face and fell to her knees sobbing.

At the bar, Elliott gripped his latest beer as he was struck by splinters imbedding his back and fell to the floor.

"Oh, shit!" yelled Cinch, who seldom used profanity and never in the presence of women. "It was a shot," piped the young man. "Get down! Get on the floor!"

In the confusion, Lashley directed Dunsey from the porch into the dining hall. Initially, her injuries appeared to be more superficial than life threatening. Tweezers, rubbing alcohol and band aids should do the trick. The most difficult assignment would be to calm her down. He turned toward the other injured party.

Paige had guided Elliott to the billiard table, directing him to lean over. Three large splinters were embedded into his back. Lashley observed as the woman easily removed two of them. The last sliver, between the belt and ribs, resisted her first attempt. She jerked the glass. It yielded, revealing a three inch penetration. How medically serious could such a deep cut be considered Lashley wondered.

Cinch crouched, lifting his head just so that his eyes cleared the sill of the broken window. Lashley moved beside him.

"What happened, Cinch?" Lashley inquired of the young cowboy.

"A shot," piped the young man. "Someone shot the window out. I heard it just as I touched the door."

"Could you see where it came from?"

"No chance. It happened too quickly."

Frenchie joined the men at the door, receiving a brief report on the crisis. "Could it have come from the barn?" he asked.

"Don't think so, Frenchie," Cinch replied. "Sounded farther off than that. Maybe three hundred, three hundred fifty yards out. I thought it was somewhere off to the left." He gestured toward the north of the barn.

His employer straightened, gazed intently through the broken window in the direction Cinch had indicated. "That could be any of a hundred places out there," Frenchie responded. "What do we do now?"

"Cinch's going to stay here and watch," Lashley said emphatically. "You and I are going to call the roll. Account for everybody and their whereabouts when the shot came."

As they moved, a second shot cracked. This time the projectile struck the building with a thud just under the broken window.

CHAPTER FIVE

"It's been more than an hour," Frenchie Hebert said as he sipped his coffee. He leaned forward in his chair, squinting between cracks in the hastily boarded window space. "What's happening?"

"He's waiting us out," Howard Lashley responded, crouching against the wall peering out toward the barn.

"Why? What's the logic of that?" Chainsaw Poulen asked.

Lashley shrugged his shoulders in an uncertain response.

Pandemonium within the lodge had prevailed, following the second shot. Leo Rich, returning from the bunk house in his most obscene style, had pitched a fit, calling Frenchie every epithet known to the English language. Concerted efforts by both R.S. Farrow and Beryl Carter finally calmed him down. Under protest, Rich extended his deadline to twenty-four hours. He then proceeded to direct his attention to trying to convince any one of the women to retire to his secluded bunk house room and enroll in a course of carnal knowledge. During Leo Rich's tirade, Joel Guarimo, tall and slender-limbed, inclined to early stockiness in the midriff, joined with Grace Hancock and Mitzi Rhodes in a lengthy praying session. Dunsey Martin, in a hysterical fashion, repulsed numerous offers by Captain Mitchell to administrate to her wounds. It took a concerted effort by Paige St. John and Tyrone Mitchell to successfully comfort the woman.

Order in the dining room was restored when Lashley began delegating assignments. Keep them busy, he thought. People who are active are not as likely to be concerned about personal problems. Idle hands are the devil's tools, or something along that line, so he remembered from some childhood colloquialisms.

A rather tedious task of removing the glass splinters from the porch was assigned to two women and three men.

A couple of guides removed some of the shelving from the pantry and nailed the boards over the gaping window space. As they worked, each labored carefully to remain unexposed targets for the sniper. The back end of the south porch was designated as the infirmary. There, Elliott and Dunsey were moved for further attention. Katherine Pace became her boyfriend's Nightingale. She brought Elliott a beer and nursed one of her own.

Armed with his 30-30 Winchester, Cinch, the young cowboy, had been assigned to maintain guard at the front door. With binoculars, through a peep whole, he scoped the lower property, barn and outbuildings for movement. In the hour since the second shot was fired, there had been little to report. Cinch informed Lashley he was fairly certain the second shot had come from the barn from the upstairs window on the left side. He thought he had seen the muzzle flash. Once, he detected movement behind that window, but it was so quick, so fleeting, that he was unable to discern anything more definite.

From an occasional glint, Lashley had the impression that someone was likewise scoping the lodge. Smoke trailed from the stove pipe. Someone was stoking the fire in String's loft.

The sun cast a shadow on the upside of the barn. Like Cinch, his observation was further obscured by the position of the sun, now a quarter up from the horizon. Within another few hours, the advantage would shift. The sniper would be facing the sun, provided the lodge held out that long.

The sniper or snipers, Lashley was convinced, were apparently holding up in String's room, located in the upper northern portion of the barn. Years before, String, a loner, had converted a portion of the upper barn loft for his personal shelter. It was a large room, simply furnished. Access to the room was from two directions. One entrance was from the outside stairs. The position of the barn made this entrance invisible from the lodge. Occasionally during heavy winter snows, String could drop down from a trap door to the barn's interior and administer to the needs of the horses and cows that were wintered inside.

Poorly constructed, String's room had previously been drafty and cold, but the older guide always preferred its isolation to the bunk room above the kitchen. Over the years, in order to minimize the room's discomforts, he stuffed newspapers in the walls and feed sacks as wall paper to further insulate the cracks. His efforts had eliminated most of the draft problems but not all of them. The loft was a less desirable accommodation as far as the other lodge hands were concerned. A rusty potbelly stove provided the sole warmth of the room. String, Lashley reasoned, was not even buried, and the killer had the gall to occupy the dead man's home.

As the lodge's occupants settled into their defensive routine, Frenchie, Chainsaw, and Lashley sat together on the porch to confer and evaluate the situation. Captain Tyrone Mitchell, a chair in tow, joined the group.

"You want to know how I feel? I'll tell you," Chainsaw said after the black officer sat down. "It's like having the wagons circled, but there are too many gaps between each tongue and the next axle. The Indians are pouring in like sand through a crack. There's no way to stop them."

"Think the shooter is gone?" Frenchie offered, knowing the answer before it rebounded into his court.

"No. It's now a game of nerves. Two shots close together, one breaking the window, and the other impacting the wall. That's deliberate planning," Chainsaw responded, as he shifted for a better vantage point.

"Why is somebody sniping at the Cottonwood?" Frenchie asked. "It's crazy."

"You tell us," Lashley demanded. "Considering all the people in this lodge, Frenchie, you are the most likely target. It'll take someone who knows the territory and how the lodge operates. It would be tough for a flatlander to target this lodge without some inside knowledge."

"Anyone got it in for you, Frenchie?" Mitchell asked. "Say, like rival outfitters, a mad hunter or something?"

"I don't think so," Frenchie said. "Over the years I've pissed some people off maybe. Don't think it would be a hunter though. If they're dissatisfied, they just don't come back. The disgruntled hunters simply engage another guide. If they're that mad, I'd refund their money before they left anyway. I've done that a time or two in my career, but that was years ago. Nothing recent."

"How about some locals?" Chainsaw asked.

"You know how it is what with the Cottonwood located in a couple of square miles surrounded by government ranges," Frenchie said. "A few years ago, one of the cattle lease holders under a government contract accused some of my hands of being responsible for a few missing cattle. Some of his hands showed up, liquored to the hilt, and spoiling for a fight. Nothing ever came of it. Best I can remember the herd had drifted into a blind canyon. Later, they found the steers that were missing."

"Anything else?" Chainsaw pressed with no animosity in his voice.

"Once or twice on the Diamondhead Ranch, north of the Hand, there were complaints of cutting fences. But that's always been settled."

"Any other possibilities?" Lashley questioned for an answer with the calm persistence of a trial lawyer.

"The type of guiding I do wouldn't conflict with any locals. I don't do any pressure advertising or contracting out-of-state hunters who have applied for licenses as a means of getting them to come to the Cottonwood. All clients get here by word of mouth, or they are repeat hunters. I don't see that as a problem."

"Possibility it could be something else?"

The head guide thought a minute before he responded.

"During the summer there'd be an occasional sheep missing from herders up on the high meadows. We do slip up there every now and then. Kind of need a variety in our diet. The owners don't like it much, but usually it's minor stuff. The only thing we ever get is a stray or lamb that's been hurt or something and never would have lived anyway."

"Anything else?" Lashley pressed.

"Nothing I can think of," Frenchie answered.

"What about your present crew?" Lashley interjected.

"Not that I can imagine. String got drunk occasionally when he went to Alcova. He's had several fights, but nothing serious. As far as the other employees, Fish and Stumbough, I don't know too much about their background. Like Chainsaw, here, Fish just works during hunting and dude season, not all year 'round. The cooks, now, Crisco and Ray Horne, his assistant, they're different. I know them pretty good. No problems I know of."

"Tell us about Cinch," Lashley requested, pressing for details about the young cowboy.

"Came to work here at age sixteen or so," Hebert recalled. "He ran away from some trouble down in Laramie. Nothing real serious, but the girl's family didn't see it that way. He's tough and as smart as a cowhand can be. He could use a cactus for a pillow. Quick. Kin to a rattlesnake on his mother's side. Prefers the open sights of a Winchester repeating rifle, old style. With it, at a hundred and fifty yards, he's good enough to drive the cork into a bottle without breaking the neck. Shot for shot, he's equal with me."

"What about Horne?" Mitchell asked.

"He's Crisco's nephew," Frenchie responded. "Been here about five years. He was real good with horses. He rode them so fast that he only hit the ground in high places. Two winters back, his horse got squeamish, gave an unexpected buck that broke the saddle girth. The fall busted Horne's leg pretty bad. We set it for him. Maybe we didn't do the best job, and now he walks with a limp. Can't ride so well anymore. So, he became Crisco's assistant."

"What about Crisco?" Lashley inquired.

"Well, when he was younger, maybe seventeen, he was accused of raping a girl. He has denied it to this day. Later, I heard she'd changed her story, but Crisco had already served five years. I'm not sure he isn't a eunuch or somethin'. After that prison term, I've never known him to associate with women. He keeps to himself. Seldom leaves the Cottonwood. He may not look like it, but he's not towing an empty wagon. In many ways, he's real smart."

"Rich said he killed someone," Lashley said. "Any truth to that?"

"Yeah. In prison, he killed a man in self defense. Some lock up problems. As I understand it, the warden was glad he took that man out. Made Crisco a trustee cook and gave him time off for good behavior for killing that man. That's where he learned his cooking skills."

"What about someone within the hunting party?" Chainsaw asked. "Any leads there, Lashley?"

"I don't know that much about them. They're not in my social circle. Mostly, my contacts with them are minimal meetings to plan the hunts and limited accidental meetings."

As the men conversed, Lashley observed the barn through the cracks in the boarded window. From his view, they were pinned down. Trapped like rats in a cage.

"How are the injured?" Frenchie asked, directing the question to the silent officer, catching him off guard.

"O.K., I think," the captain answered. "Dunsey's face is patched up and she's resting. I don't see much chance of scarring. She was lucky. All of her splinters, though bloody, were minor. Elliott, I'm not sure about. The lower puncture was pretty deep. He's at least satisfied right now with a beer. We need to keep a close eye on him."

"That's good information," Lashley interjected.

"What's our plan of action now that we've scrapped our horse drive and automobile repair class?" the officer inquired.

"Move closer if you want to," Frenchie said as he motioned to a closer location as though it was a welcome mat for the conference.

"Can we rush them?" the captain asked, as he moved.

"Risky," Lashley responded. "Clint's pretty certain the last shot came from String's room up in the barn. But we can't be sure he's still there. The stairs aren't visible from this angle. Besides, if he's part of the gang that assaulted Heather, there are at least three of them, possibly four. I identified at least three separate tracks down there among the chokecherries. There's been insufficient movement to target their location. Or, more importantly, count noses."

"Who do we have that can carry out such a military operation?" Frenchie interjected.

"That's a squad action," Lashley answered. "It takes some deployment and flanking movement. Possibly we could give sufficient covering fire with all the weapons we have here at the lodge, but we could expect casualties. Civilians aren't going to be committed to those risks."

"I'll take that risk," the captain volunteered. "Maybe I could slip out and flank the barn. Come up behind them. You could give me some covering fire from here."

"No," Lashley answered as though his decision was a command. "I think not. It's what they're waiting for. Flush us out, one at a time, like jumping a covey of quail. Pick us off as singles. It's too much of a long shot. Let's play their waiting game for a while. Time is on our side. If we don't show up for the plane back home by our scheduled arrival time, someone is going to start looking. They'll back track up here. That's five days from now, but we don't need any more of our group dead."

Frenchie almost laughed. "You don't believe you can keep this many people confined in this lodge for five days. This ain't Caesar's Palace where there's entertainment, gambling, and diversions. In that length of time, they'll be killing each other. There'll be more danger inside the lodge than from the outside."

"I agree with Frenchie. We can't wait that long," Mitchell said.

Lashley shrugged, sipped his coffee, and leaned sideways, flexing his back. "Give those at the barn a little more time. Let them show their hand first. In the meantime, let's gather all the information that is available. Then we can develop a workable plan. Let's get a relief guard for Cinch, and put the food bag on."

The group departed leaving Lashley crouched near the broken window, watching, thinking, and analyzing the bare scraps of data within his knowledge. What logical conclusions he could generate did not fit any pattern. Like the window, his data was shattered into pieces that must be reassembled.

Grace Hancock cleared her throat to attract Lashley's attention. He turned and stared at the woman.

"Mr. Lashley, I need your help," Grace Hancock said softly as she handed the lean man a plate covered with burgers and flat fries. "Paige fixed this for you, the way you like it. She said it was okay for me to talk to you. She's not jealous or anything."

He noted the woman's full figure. Her sharp distinctive features were disguised behind designer glasses. When speaking, she habitually glared over the upper rims. It was a cute gesture that accentuated her usual, natural humor.

Lashley silently accepted the tendered plate, nodding absently for her to sit down. With a practiced motion, she removed her glasses, wiping her eyes with the back of her hand. Absorbed in his thoughts, Lashley had been unaware of her emotional stress. Her reaction disturbed him.

"You've got to help me. You're my last chance," Grace sobbed softly. "I'm desperate." She stared down awkwardly at Lashley in his crouched position.

A frightened, uncontrollable woman was all that was needed to add to the confusion. Everyone handles the pressure of danger differently. One thing that could not happen was to lose control of just one individual. One person running loose, unhinged, would be a catastrophe. Grace's request had to be addressed, and quickly.

"Why me?" Lashley protested. He lifted his shoulders and extended his palms upward.

"Because you are a decent and kind man," she blushingly whispered.

His eyebrows raised in an inquisitive expression. His shoulder shifted again, asking why but disclaiming the allegation.

"I saw what you did for Heather when you found her. I was on the stairs, out by the barn, using field glasses. When you got off your horse, you covered her with your coat. You delayed before giving those three signal shots. You took the time to redress her. Put her clothes back on so all the men wouldn't see her nudity. At the time, I really didn't know what you were doing, but when I was helping Pearl Gavin clean Heather up after she was brought to the lodge, I figured out what you had done. That was kind and decent. I mean, dressing her like that."

Lashley shrugged, suggesting it was no big deal and remained silent. Now comes the clincher, he thought. She wants me to get her out of this mess. Save her alone above all the others. Be her hero, no less. How would he be able to succumb to her wish when he had no idea how to protect Paige, who by his selection had become an involuntary draftee in this range war?

Grace was no longer crying, but for confidence she nervously played with a ring on her finger. She looked down at her lap apparently fascinated by her hand movements. "I'm having a problem with Leo Rich," she continued, struggling with each word. "He's coming on to me real hard. What with suggesting, no, that's not right. He's really demanding that I have sex with him. Not meaning to be crude, but I've told him I don't do windows and I don't do blow jobs. But he won't listen."

"Talk to Harder. He's your companion on this trip. Why can't he solve your dilemma?" queried the man.

"I can't get any help from Thyus," she pleaded and looked across to Lashley with a sigh. "Leo and he

125

have some huge real estate deal going on. Thyus has a big commission pending. Leo threatened that if Thyus can't convince me to give into his sexual demands, he'd take the deal to another real estate agent. So, Thyus is pressuring me to do it."

Lashley clicked his tongue. Another blind canyon.

She paused to regroup her thoughts. "Maybe what I do with Thyus is wrong in some people's eyes, and maybe deep down I know it's wrong. But I'm divorced and have a two year old daughter. I have a hard time making it. My job in the courthouse doesn't pay much, so Thyus helps me financially. I couldn't make it without his assistance. He'll never leave his wife, and I understand that, even if sometimes I have difficulty accepting it. At home the men that are my age are either drunks or abusers. I take what pleasure and security I can get within bounds, but I'll not lower myself to sleep with someone I don't care for. And to me, sex with Leo Rich is the lowest thing I could do. If he forces me to do it, I'm going to hurt him real bad."

Grace's dilemma was worse than Lashley had imagined. Killers stalked them on the outside, while within the lodge violence was embodied by a pair of panties. Rich was the fester of a boil, a magnitude beyond his conception. History demonstrated the obvious. Battles cannot be fought on two fronts simultaneously. These internal distractions were disturbing Lashley's concentration. Absent concentration, Lashley could find no solutions, and death was the only alternative.

"I'll speak to Rich and Harder for you," he said with little enthusiasm.

"Oh, thank you, Mr. Lashley," she sighed contentedly, leaned forward and kissed him on the cheek and departed.

The report of a gun shot distracted Lashley. Chainsaw was beside him in an instant, straining for a look. Starting at six minutes after eleven, during the serving of a course of venison burgers, the lodge received its next calling cards. At intervals of one minute, three shots were fired, targeting the same location. Each bullet impacted the porch wall under the broken window. It was as if a bull's-eye had been painted on the porch's exterior wall and someone was engaged in target practice. Then the firing abruptly ceased. Five minutes passed. Nothing.

"He is firing from the same location," Lashley said to Frenchie, who had also joined him after the third shot. "Lower left corner of that window. Keeps the muzzle close to the window sill. Doesn't extend the barrel out, so I can't identify the weapon. Also, there's no forewarning of when he's going to shoot. That's very clever. He's erratic with his firing. At this point, I can't discern any intentions other than harassment. Chainsaw, get Thyus Harder. Ask him to join me for a few minutes. Frenchie, check with Fish to see what he has observed."

Harder just settled beside Lashley when the sniper's weapon barked again. The spacing was now measured at a little over five minute intervals. How many shots in the latest pattern? Nine, he thought. He was losing count in all of the confusion. It was definitely a new pattern. What did it mean?

Something was happening, but what? Lashley was not sure.

"I'm recruiting Grace for a special assignment. I want all of her things brought out on the porch. She is going to work under my supervision. I can't discus why I need her or her job description except to say it is important to our safety."

Harder exhaled deeply. Lashley believed the man had initially objected to Rich's intimidations. Rich's request had probably been repulsive to him. Lashley suspected that Harder cared for Grace. But he also knew that the timber deal Rich held over the real estate agent's head was powerful leverage. Carter had discussed some of the details with Lashley. If the deal fell apart, Harder would suffer financially. He was hurting and in tight economic distress. Several bank notes were coming due that Harder could not meet without refinancing. Rich was the key to that situation. This one transaction would satisfy Harder's outstanding obligations and leave a substantial reserve balance. Any surplus would be needed for medical expense if his wife's health continued to deteriorate.

Rich played the key role in Harder's future plans. Under this pressure, Harder, Lashley suspected, had finally forced him to consent to Rich's demand for sexual favors from Grace.

"Why did you select Grace?" he inquired of Lashley who recognized the move as weak attempt to resist Grace's assignment.

"Pearl Gavin is full-time with Heather," Lashley responded. "Paige and Mitzi Rhodes are rotating to give her some relief. Katherine Pace, to the extent she can, is nursing Elliott. Dunsey Martin is injured. The two women with the officers, Stanford and Wallace, will have other duties. That leaves Grace, doesn't it?"

"What right do you have to direct people?" the real estate agent angrily questioned.

"I don't have any right," Lashley responded. "I'm just doing it. If you want to discuss it, go down to the barn. Maybe our friends down there can explain it with more clarity. In the meantime, I don't have time to argue the details. That's my decision, and it's not debatable. Cross me once, and whatever fear you have of Rich will be nothing in comparison."

At four minutes and seventeen seconds, another shot resounded. A pattern was developing, but why? People did not act randomly, even killers. At times, the victim is selected by chance. But it requires forethought for the killer to get out on the street, to accomplish anything. The pattern of shots indicated forethought. Something was coming down. Lashley did not know what.

Thyus Harder was visibly shaken. Whether it was due to his proximity to the front line where shots were fired or due to a pending show down with Rich about Grace, it really did not matter. Lashley was uncertain about Harder. He had other problems to resolve. The subject of Grace Hancock had drawn out too long.

"Now there are three things I want you to do, and they need to be done now," Lashley instructed the real estate broker. "First, send Grace back to me here at this door. Second, you tell Leo Rich about our discussion. While you're doing that, if you need any help, recruit Beryl and R.S. You tell that son of a bitch Rich he better stay out of my way, or he'll be hiking a path to the barn alone. Lastly, get a guide to help you move Grace's gear out here. Set her up in that corner. She can use the couch for her working area and she can sleep there. Now move."

Grace approached Lashley with a question, "Thyus said you wanted to see me?"

"I want you to be my recorder," he told the woman. "Keep tabs of the time of each shot. Where it originates, if that can be determined. Record any unusual events. I need a log of what is happening. Can you do that for me?"

Grace smiled. "Yes, I'll be glad to do it."

Lashley turned back to the boarded window. Because he had been subject to continuous distraction, it was a moment before he realized the deviation in the pattern of shots. It was such a minor movement that he almost missed it. He was not sure it was a movement or that his eyes had tricked him.

At four minutes and five seconds, the shots continued. But it was the shadow on the bunk house roof that he almost missed. Fish Mackey, the jester guide, relieving youthful Cinch Wilkinson, was to Lashley's left, stationed near the front door. Fish was

132

unable to detect the movement. It was beyond his line of vision. The enemy's soft probe had begun.

"Get over there," he hissed at the woman, shoving her toward the couch at the end of the room. "Fish, hold tight. I'll send Cinch to join you."

"Chainsaw," Lashley yelled over his shoulder as he picked up his rifle, moving out on the walkway heading toward the bunkhouse. There were footsteps overhead. Someone on the roof was moving in the direction of the main lodge building.

Chainsaw and Frenchie joined him. The purpose of the closely spaced shots was now apparent. The shots were intended to confuse the occupants of the lodge, to direct their attention to the barn and away from a flanking movement. It was a cover to allow a man to reach the bunkhouse and climb upon the roof. Studying the intent of the pattern was distraction enough to catch the spectators watching the game on the wrong end of the playing field.

"How'd he get there?" Lashley asked the head guide who joined him on the walkway.

Frenchie offered, "I'd say he crawled up that ditch on the far side of the service road we use to get to the back side of the lodge. There's a culvert. He must have crawled through. Could have brought a ladder from the barn to get on the roof."

Mitchell slid in beside the two men. When he had regained his breath, he pressed, "What are they doing?"

"I'm not sure," Lashley answered. "Send Cinch to cover the front door with Fish," he instructed Frenchie, who quickly moved away.

Following the sound of the footsteps on the roof, Chainsaw and Lashley entered the dining hall. Captain Mitchell followed them with a pained facial expression.

Lashley pointed to Mitchell, "Get everyone on the floor, keep them in place. Nobody is to move until this is over."

The captain nodded and motioned for compliance. Most of the guests obeyed. Those who demurred, he pushed to the floor.

"He's over your room," Chainsaw said as they entered Lashley's quarters, pointing toward the ceiling as the perpetrator moved along the roof.

In the fireplace embers from the dying fire smoldered. Small tongues of flames licked the back fire bricks. Lashley tossed a log among the coals. Sparks drafted up the flue.

The steps overhead stopped near the chimney. Silence was followed by an indiscernible noise, a scraping sound. Then smoke, back-stroked from the chimney, filled the room.

Lashley considered the scene for a moment. "He's clogged the chimney," he announced.

"He's cutting off our heat source," Chainsaw said.

"Let's head him off," Lashley said.

Passing through the dining hall, they heard Mitzi Rhodes yelling. "Smoke, smoke! The building's on fire."

Back draft from the plugged chimney forced the smoke to seek its exit into the larger room.

The captain ordered, "Don't move! Don't move. Stay down."

Lashley located a double barrel 12 gauge shotgun from a gun rack, took a fist full of double-ought buck shots from a shelf and headed for the crew's loft.

"Guard the kitchen doors, Crisco," he instructed as he passed the cook. "Don't let anybody else in."

On the roof, above the loft where the guides slept, Lashley and Chainsaw heard movement. Steps communicated that the intruder had cleared the building's peak and was starting a cautious movement along the steep down side of the roof's slope. His destination was obviously the chimney that flued the cook stove. His final destination would be the chimney servicing the room where Heather Baldwin was confined. Without fire, there would be no cooking and limited heat in the Cottonwood. Cold food would produce touchy feelings where nerves were already ragged.

The construction of the crew's loft had been an afterthought. Originally, the log cabin had been built with a shallow-raised roof. The kitchen had been added to the cabin as a shed addition. As the Cottonwood expanded its clientele, attracting both summer dudes and winter hunting guests, additional space was required. The loft was constructed as a sleeping area for the employees specifically in late autumn and during the biting winters. Heat from the kitchen stove rose through the chimney as it passed throughout the loft. This made the room the coziest winter sleeping accommodations in the lodge. Cowboy carpentry had provided the labor for the addition. Serviceable, the room still fell short of complying with any standard building codes.

Lashley slipped two shells into the shotgun's double chambers, closed the weapon, and cocked it. He watched the rafters sag and bend under the weight of the stalker. Lashley waited until the resounding footsteps stopped just short of the chimney. He aimed, adjusted for the angle of the slope, and pulled both triggers. In the closed space, the noise was horrendous. On the firing range, he always wore ear protection. For a moment, he thought he was deaf. There would be some residual ear damage, but he could live with that. That is if he lived through this nightmare.

The double-ought shot tore a hole through the ceiling's half inch pine decking. The dry climate did not require many layers of decking material, and this roof had not deviated from that rule. The resulting hole was the size of a loaf of bread. For a brief moment, through the hole, Lashley could see where wooden splinters and pellets had entered the stalker's body through the seat of his pants, burrowing upward through his lower intestines with savage vengeance. Lashley watched the man pitch forward and disappear. He heard the body roll over the edge of the roof.

"You get him?" Poulen asked.

"Yeah," Lashley responded. "Let's go check his body and see what we can learn."

CHAPTER SIX

"Murderers! Murderers!" Joel Guarimo was yelling when grim-faced Howard Lashley and Chainsaw Poulen reentered the dining room.

Lashley stared at the raving man. Ignoring the outburst, he entered his room. Thick smoke still lingered. He discharged both barrels of the shotgun up the clogged chimney. Cleared of its obstruction, the flue would soon operate normally. But it would take awhile for the updraft to purify the air throughout the lodge.

"It's not right. You can't kill people," Guarimo continued pointing at Lashley when he re-entered the dinning room. "Thou shalt not kill. He lifted his eyes as if to call upon heaven to witness this abuse. "It says so in the Bible."

"Shut up, Joel," Beryl Carter responded, standing to emphasize the sincerity of his convictions.

"I'll not shut up," he replied in an injured tone, spinning to face another group. "Vengeance begets vengeance. Death is contagious. They kill one of ours. We murder one of their's. It's a disease. It spreads like the Hatfields and McCoys. It's not God's way. We must pray it through. Talk it out with Him.

"The demons of Hell abound. Look it up in the Lamb's Book of Life," Joel continued like an old fashioned tent revival preacher. "While on this earth, you've got to learn to row your own boat, because when you try to cross that Eternal River, you'll find there is no free ferry service. Only the sweet blood of Jesus can pay your passage."

"You're crazy, Joel," R.S. Farrow added. "We've been getting a lot of incoming literature in the form of bullets, and it's not been delivered by the Jehovah's Witnesses."

Pearl Gavin, attracted by the outburst, approached Guarimo. She placed her hand lovingly on his arm. Lashley characterized her as chunky, a heavy woman nearing obesity. Her sculptured hair, tailored by generous applications of spray, adorned her as a halo. It was stiff and gummy like cotton candy. Dangling earrings punctuated her angry movements.

"They wouldn't let me out of my room. Those men kept me in there with Heather. I've heard shots inside. What's been happening?"

Guarimo responded as though he were a cheerleader at a Super Bowl game. "Killers," he said, pointing at Chainsaw and Lashley. "Violators of the word of the Lord. They killed a man on the roof. Cold blooded murder!"

"Shut up, Joel," Carter promptly retaliated. "If you don't, I'm going to knock the shit out of you." The burly contractor moved forward to enforce the depth of his threat.

Pearl stepped between the men, shaking her stubble finger at Carter. "Now it's violence on the peaceful," she said. "Punish those who pray for peace. The vengeance of the Lord shall come down upon your head. You will be punished for your wickedness. What has been done is ungodly."

"Don't give me any of your holy roly bullshit," Carter exploded. "Sounds like you and Joel are kind of selective in your enforcement of the Ten Commandments. In my filtered memory, I seem to recall one about adultery. You two have been acting like it was rutting season in Tate's Hell ever since you've been on this hunting trip."

Pearl's body shook with such anger that the buttons on her blouse were stretched to their endurance. Her ample bosom rose with every breath.

"In the eyes of the Lord," Pearl asserted triumphantly, "Joel and I are one. Our prayers have reconciled us into unity. It's the sins of this group that have brought this wickedness down upon this lodge." Sweeping her hand to encompass the outside, she said, "Those are the Lord's enforcers. Pray. We must pray for the forgiveness of our sins. Those who will join me in prayer, follow me to my room."

"You sanctimonious bitch," Carter called after the departing Joel and Pearl. "Elliott Thornton's got a better solution than you have. I'm going to join his session with a drink in my hand."

Stunned by the outburst, no one moved for several minutes. Conversation resumed in hesitant whispers and remained at that tone for a while.

Lashley approached the two military officers seated with Patricia Stanford and Myrtle Wallace. Isolated by cultural differences, the four had selected a table nearest the kitchen. "Captain, I'd like you to join Chainsaw and me for a conference, please," he said.

Greer rose, "I'm the senior officer to Captain Mitchell. I'll attend all briefings of the current situation on behalf of our group."

"I'm looking for talent, not rank, Major," Lashley answered. "Fish are rank. If I want to smell rank, I'll go to a fish market."

It was an uncharacteristic catty remark and Lashley was well aware of its implications. The time had arrived to do a bit of testing.

Bowing up, like a toad after a bug, Greer's response was cut short by Patricia Stanford. She placed her hand on his arm and guided him to his seat.

Lashley nodded his thanks as he met her eyes. They were gray and cold - no nonsense eyes of authority. He had never before noticed, in detail, her appearance. Her accent was a mixture of tones acquired from southern Alabama with a touch of the

Midwest plains. She either disdained makeup, or stress was taking its toll, for she appeared older than his initial impression, mid-forties perhaps. She was lean, attractive, but tough in a feminine way. He did not seek a confrontation with Greer. His biting words had been uttered deliberately. He wanted information and he had just obtained it.

Stanford's slight wink was a returned acknowledgment of thanks, perhaps for placing the major in the proper perspective. He would have to make amends with Greer in the near future, if such a future existed.

"In five minutes, Captain," Lashley said, and after nodding politely to the foursome, departed.

At her post on the front porch, Grace Hancock, note pad in hand, was seated on the couch. Over the rim of her glasses, she observed Lashley approaching. Her suit cases and personal gear were haphazardly arranged on the opposite end of the couch. She was isolated in the porch corner, contentedly, remote from Rich's sexual demands.

"How's it going, Grace?" Lashley asked in a sympathetic tone as he knelt beside her.

"Good, thanks to you," she said bashfully, handing the man her notes for review.

"That's fine. Just what we need," he said as he glanced over the pages. "Don't leave your post unattended. Call Paige to relieve you. No one else. Your work is for me only. If anyone tries to inquire about your task, send them to me."

"Sure, Mr. Lashley. You can depend on me," she replied, winking her gratitude.

He turned to leave, then paused and returned, adding a departing thought. "Several of us are going to have a meeting over there by the billiard table. I don't think it will disturb you." He pointed for clarification.

A bullet thumped the wall causing Grace to return to her notes, recording the time, estimating the point of impact and orientation of fire.

Since the stove pipe attack ended, two shots had been fired. As Lashley studied Grace's work he learned the shots had alternated in origin. The first one was fired from the upstairs barn window. The other came from a place just to the right of the double barn doors. At the latter location, a break in the barn siding left a sizable gap. The cowboys stationed at the lodge's front door near the broken window were reporting to Grace, if she was uncertain about the origin of each shot and the point of impact on the lodge wall.

Fish Mackey, guarding the front door, beckoned Lashley. He knelt beside the wiry guide. "We're holding Wild Bill Hickock's hand, you know, two aces and a pair of eights."

It was not a question. It was more of a statement to which Lashley elected not to reply. He waited for the man to proceed.

Harshly, the cowboy whispered, "Something ain't right. It's like playing in a fixed faro game."

Lashley waited. He reasoned the man could not be pushed and would spell it out eventually.

"Out there, that's a bad party of ruffians, as my daddy would have called them. Lodge talk, I think," He continued. "But they's feeding us some Mexican oats if you know what I mean. It's less than the real thing."

Fish's eyes were cocked on Lashley as the men crouched by the door. Then the cowboy continued. "Neither of them fellows down there can shoot worth a damn. I've heard of not being able to hit the side of a barn with a slop jar, but I'll be damned if they's not that bad. Ain't been none of them shots that hit this building been within eighteen inches of the one before. Some have been so low they's hit the ground. Kind of figure them ruffians ain't had no experience with rifles. They must be mostly use to them rapid shooting weapons I've heard about. Or maybe hand guns. But they's never gonna win no sharp shooter medals the way they's handling that fire power."

The cowboy moved back to the peep hole. Lashley waited for him to continue.

"It's bad what they done to String. He didn't deserve that. I want the guy that done it in my sights. He'll see some real shooting."

"Thanks for the info, Fish," Lashley said as he rose to leave.

"One last thing, when you's ready to go bounty hunting, count me in. Before this is over, I want to see enough corpses down there to stock the Cottonwood's own Boot Hill. Make us famous like the O.K. Corral. You don't have to rub no saddle soap in my eyes. I know that this will be a tough fight, and some of us ain't gonna make it. But I'll go out firing."

"You're in," Lashley assured him as he moved back to the billiard table.

Fish Mackey was smart. Being pinned down as they were, the chances of getting out were minimal. Lashley had made the same observation about the poor shooting. But what was the rationalization? There must be some way to bring this madness to an end. He was operating in the dark. A walk in the darkness must halt before a last step over the precipice. If Lashley did not soon determine the solution, there would be a long fall into a gorge. How could they safely find the edge of the cliff? It would not be easy, but if it was to be done, Lashley needed help. Where could reliable help be found these days, especially if it meant dodging a few bullets?

Chainsaw straddled his chair backward, leaning his chin on the back brace. To his left, Frenchie's chair tilted precariously. Captain Tyrone Mitchell seated on a bar stool, towered like a disinterested observer. Lashley squatted against the billiard table, his hunting boots wrinkled like the forehead of an aging man.

"Cinch says they've got reinforcements coming." Frenchie reported. "Two vehicles at least. Possibly more. He saw sun reflecting on glass this side of the cattle's gap out near the asphalt road. He figures it was windshields. It's too far out to be definite as to the type of vehicle, even with glasses. He glimpsed the reflection until it disappeared behind Sleeping Camel Rock. Then he lost it."

Frenchie was referring to a doubled humped rock. When viewed from the eastern side, it resembled a camel hunched down with his long neck extended. A local land mark, the rock formation was two and one-half miles on the lodge side of the paved road. The formation served as a divider for the two trails leading to the Cottonwood.

The northern route was much longer. Any traffic along that trail road was obscured from observation by anyone at the lodge. The shorter trail, across the plains, leading directly inward to the lodge, was visible to occupants of the lodge for a majority of its distance. Any traffic coming directly to the Cottonwood along this southern route, except for an occasional dip in the road, was easily seen. Incoming traffic waved like a flag for the last ten miles. The reinforcements were using the obscure northern trail to transport reinforcements.

"When did he last see them?" Chainsaw asked in a worried tone, as he sipped from his mug.

"An hour plus thirty or forty minutes," Frenchie said.

"They can't get here until dusk dark. That north road is a long trip over rough country," Chainsaw informed them. "Where are we, Lashley?"

"My best guess is that we've got a reprieve for several hours," Lashley said. "It'll take them that long to get their reinforcements organized. Whatever they have in mind, it'll be tomorrow before they can activate a coordinated effort. In the meantime, they'll keep firing, rattling our nerves. That strategy is working. Some of the guests are about ready to cave in."

"Lashley, Cinch thinks we have another problem in the bunk house. That guy who climbed on the roof knocked the stove pipe off. Without a proper exhaust system, that fuel oil heater in the basement could put out some lethal gases. It might be dangerous sleeping in there tonight." Frenchie said.

"Let me check it out," Lashley ventured. "Keep everybody out of the bunk house. We'll meet back here, say, at about four fifteen. In the meantime, Frenchie, no, it better be Mitchell, talk to Leo Rich. See if you can determine what's bugging him. We need his help. Tell him we can't be fighting internally all the time. You," indicating to Frenchie, "circulate among the guests. I'll help for a few minutes. Give them the assurance we've been doing everything we can. We need their patience and cooperation."

The men departed to perform their assigned tasks. Lashley watched a few moments as Frenchie moved among the assorted groups, depositing ample encouragement while withholding the silver coins of detail.

Lashley observed Mitchell in a corner, engaged in an animated and heated conversation with Leo Rich. He felt Mitchell was a level-headed, cool customer. If Rick's hunting partners, Carter and Farrow, were not successful in controlling this hot tempered car dealer, he thought Mitchell was the next best candidate to reason him into cooperation, short of using force for submission. If force was required, Mitchell appeared willing to assist in its application. He had no love for Leo Rich.

A prayer session was in progress in the room opposite the pantry. Joel Guarimo and Pearl Gavin acted as the apparent leaders Lashley noted. Heather Baldwin, reclining in bed, stared through glassy and unfocused eyes.

The woman's condition remained baffling. Mitchell had reported his latest findings. He had checked her pulse and felt her forehead for evidence of fever. Both were normal. She should have been more coherent by now. More than twenty-four hours had lapsed since she had been assaulted. There had to be an explanation for her condition, but at the moment, he could not fathom one.

"You joining our group, Mr. Lashley?" Pearl asked pleasantly, holding a Bible outward for his inspection.

"No, I'm making the rounds," he responded, extending his hand negatively. "Telling everyone we're working on our dilemma. We need cooperation. The less conflict among our group, the easier it'll be for everybody."

The small room was overcrowded. Dark haired Mitzi Rhodes was flanked by Dunsey Martin, hiding behind her bandaged face. In a corner Lewis Fulcher stood. He seemed lost in admiration for Pearl's efforts.

Lashley considered Fulcher another unknown quality. A quiet person, Fulcher, the restaurant owner, seemed almost out of harmony with the rest of his boisterous hunting mates. Lewis Fulcher was the only hunter who had rejected the idea of a traveling mate. That did not appear especially peculiar, but he remained isolated from most of the group's contact.

From what Lashley knew the man was a success as a food restaurateur. Fulcher maintained a fleet of fishing boats plying the waters of the Gulf of Mexico. It was not an extensively large operation, but his fleet reached as far south and west as Belize in Central America. When Fulcher spoke, it was always with respect, but mostly humorless. Lashley wondered why Rich had reselected Fulcher for this his second hunting trip at the Cottonwood.

"Lashley, is there going to be any more killings?" Guarimo inquired in his best preaching tone. Then he shook his head sorrowfully as if for the departed souls of the recent deceased at the Cottonwood.

"We hope not. Right now, we're trying to analyze the problem. Find out what they want. Once we know that, we might find a solution."

"What are you saying?" Fulcher excitedly asked. "You're expecting some kind of demand?"

"Well, maybe something like that," he answered. "At some point there should be contact. Then we'll know how to respond."

"What if they want us to give up some person. Like what Beryl said. You know, if it's Leo's relatives gunning for him. Would we give him up?" Fulcher pressed.

"That's pretty drastic, Fulcher. Speculation is harmful. Let's wait and see," Lashley responded.

"What we need," Joel interjected with a clacking of his tongue, "is all of the heathens and sinners in this lodge down on their knees praying. Prayer is our one dependable weapon. It's also God's armor for men. Shielded by it, we will be saved. Jesus alone saves. The Lord will send us help when we need it bad enough."

Lashley wondered if Guarimo's Lord was the same one who had administered protection to General Custer at Little Big Horn. If He was, then the Lord was a poor Calvary officer. The Cottonwood Lodge needed help now. It was time for the Calvary to arrive with unfurled flags, shiny buckles, and a trumpet sounding charge. Somehow, Lashley felt that would not happen. What he expected was Crazy Horse and 5,000 more wild-eyed braves.

"I'll leave it to you and your committee here to construct our religious rampart. Behind it, we may be protected," Lashley said as he departed.

Jesus Freaks. They believed that praying was a cure all. If the Cottonwood was able to survive this ordeal, it would be through the definitive efforts of men like Chainsaw, Mitchell, and Frenchie. Use your God-given talents, Lashley believed. That was the answer.

Elliott Thornton and Katherine Pace were seated under the bar on the floor, confirming Lashley's expectations. An open cardboard case of beer was between them, six cans short. The outdoor stream cooler, exposed as it was, offered a substantial risk. Compromising their standards, the couple had resorted to drinking room-temperature suds they had located in the pantry. Indifferent to the amounts of consumption, Thornton demonstrated little evidence of intoxication. He spoke and functioned soberly.

Lashley wondered if the consumption affected the couple's sex life. Could he perform, or was

Katherine's sexual appetite satisfied by this elbow bending?

"How are you two surviving?" Lashley inquired, as he bent from his waist to bring himself closer to the couple.

"So long as the ferments of barley and hops last," Thornton responded, "we are content. Should there be a shortage upon the horizon, it will be Panic City. Judging by the ample supply I observed in the cupboard, there is no immediate short fall expected. We have withdrawn from the Boulevard of the Curious, allowing calmer and more sophisticated heads to wrestle with this evil facing us. And may they march in victory upon its pavement." He raised his beer can in salute.

Katherine Pace looked up with large, serious eyes camouflaged by heavy mascara, and laconically answered, "I endorse Elliott's observations. I'm also confident the glass splintered in his back is going to be okay."

"Good. Let Captain Mitchell know if you need anything. He's acting as a kind of unofficial liaison," Lashley said as he turned to leave.

"Lashley," Thornton said, "don't let my injury mislead you. Should my assistance be needed in ever so humble a manner, let not thou footsteps falter in thy haste to deliver to me such a message."

"I'll remember," he added with a grim look, as he moved on his rounds.

Beryl Carter, R.S. Farrow, and Thyus Harder were playing quarter stakes poker. Lashley's approach failed to detract the players.

"How's it going?" he inquired, standing with a view of Carter's hand which consisted of a pair of duces, a king, an eight, and a five.

"I'm down twenty bucks," Harder, the real estate agent, said. "Luck's treating me like batteries in a flashlight. Never works when you really need it."

"I'll raise you two, Thyus," R.S. said as he pitched change into the pot.

"I'll see you," Harder replied.

"I'm out," Beryl Carter said as he folded his cards. "What's the latest, Lashley?"

"We're evaluating several options. When we have something more definite, I'll be back to fill you in."

"We see Mitchell's been working on Leo. Hope he's got him settled down," R.S. said. "I don't want him to cross you. Man, you scare the pants off me. That was fast reaction, blowing that guy off the roof. I'm not saying I disagree with your decision, but I bet the balance of that dead man's companions down at the barn aren't exactly celebrating his demise. I'd say they're pretty well pissed off unless his life insurance policies were current, and only if they were named beneficiaries. Can't say as I blame them. Lashley, you may have brought the wrath of something down on us. It's not God though. It's most likely the devil himself who will shortly cast his dark shadow over this lodge."

He turned his attention back to the game. "I'll raise you two," R.S. challenged the card remaining shark.

Harder, ever the wise real estate broker studied his cards and folded. Farrow collected the pot. The cards were passed to Carter.

"What can you report?" the burly asphalt contractor, Carter, questioned, as he shuffled the deck.

"Not much," Lashley answered. He scratched his head as though he was trying to be helpful. "We're evaluating what we have. Maybe shortly something will break."

"It's like bidding time," the contractor added. "You study all the plans and specs and maybe visit the proposed construction site. You keep hoping you didn't miss anything important or that there are some ambiguities you misread. Then you put it all together in a lump figure. Everything's riding on one figure. It's your final and best offer. You submit your bid, thinking if you're low, you better not be too low or your hot mix will set up too fast and you'll bust your company. Lose your bonding capacity, and you'll have to go to work for a former competitor. That's the lowest humiliation for a contractor - working for a competitor."

He paused to deal the cards and continued. "So it's the same with you. Chainsaw, Mitchell, Frenchie and who ever you put on the committee. You'll evaluate more information. Put together a package. If the one shot deal works, you're heroes. But if it fails, it's the ultimate humiliation. A lot of people will die, and the survivors will be working for the contractor down at the barn. So whatever your final bid tallies, it better be based on the best input or this little company will fold before it's ever incorporated. There can be no error of judgment with stakes this high. It must be our final and best offer. I open with two," addressing his last comments to his partners.

"I understand," Lashley lamented with a quick response. He watched the contractor shift uneasily in his chair, as he studied his cards.

"If we didn't have these women here, I'd say let's charge out there, take our casualties, and hit them with our best shot. The men could take their chances, but with the women, that's a different batch of mix. If we weren't successful in the assault, then the women would be subjected to the same treatment Heather got, perhaps worse. The equipment you own limits the jobs you can bid. We do have substantial firepower. But is it enough? Another thing, we can't leave the home office unprotected. You'll want our help. There's got to be assurances that the women will be protected," Carter concluded with firmness.

"I think you'll agree that if you wait until every possibility is factored, nothing is ever done. But I understand the position," Lashley answered as he departed.

From across the room, Major Greer had watched Lashley making his rounds. Patricia Stanford and Myrtle Wallace sat beside him. Stanford leafed through a back issue of a hunting magazine. Myrtle was cleaning a pistol.

Greer bristled at the Lashley's approach. He spoke with hostility when the man arrived at the table. "Lashley, I don't expect to receive the last briefing. Hereafter, report here first."

Patricia Stanford said quietly. "I don't agree. He's better informed after he's made the entire circuit.

We're lucky Lashley's assumed command of this situation."

Greer's face twisted as though he resented the remarks and felt they were totally out of place. Lashley wondered if the major objected to a woman publicly disagreeing with him. It must have been humiliating to sign on to be an escort for a female hunter. Their roles should have been reversed. It must be crushing to his masculinity. He was a semi-veteran of the conflict with Afghanistan, only then to become the wet nurse to two female hunters.

To the extent of his knowledge, Lashley briefed the three, subjecting himself to the penetrating inquiries of Greer and Stanford on developing tactics, armament, and intelligence. Wallace remained silent during the exchange. Their questions exceeded his information and he said so. But Greer insisted, probing for details.

"That's enough, Greer," Patricia Stanford cut in.

The woman, hesitating a moment after her cutting remark stared curiously at Lashley, and then, just to start the conversation in a positive direction, said, "The situation is too fluid. If you have correctly calculated that the reinforcement needs time to get oriented, then we have until tomorrow to address our concerns. Let's look at something else. How do you analyze your leaders?"

"The Frenchman? Okay. He lacks leadership abilities except with his crew. He's good with them. As a resource, the cowboys seem partially reliable. They are facing this danger as though it were a continuation of the harsh life expected in this part of the west. At some time or another, they've all walked in darkness, killer snow storms, have had bad falls from horses. Surviving in this isolation is something they live with constantly. I have confidence in the lodge crew. All of them have some valuable assets, but in this dirty work, will they follow directions? Or more importantly, will the cowboys break and run under attack? They are untested and an uncertainty."

"What about Chainsaw? Why among the others here does he have your confidence?" she asked, turning their conversation into another yet deeper channel.

"He's resourceful. I consider him a good friend. Follows well. I think he is reliable. But we can't count on him alone extracting us from this Alamo."

"And you, Mr. Lashley, what are your qualifications?" she asked as an aside. Greer openly grunted his disapproval.

"Maybe none," Lashley answered. "What do you think they are?"

She smiled briefly. "I suspect you don't operate under the Rules of the Knights Templar. Don't ask me why, but I believe you're way ahead of us on this. You have accumulated substantially more information than you are imparting. You're searching for a pattern, a motive, or whatever. When you find it, you'll strike like a coiled snake. Vigorous callisthenic exercise has made you physically quick. But more than that, I think you are mentally quick. Killing that man on the roof had no more effect on you than if it had been a bug. The way I see it you selected that death as a method to communicate to our hostiles out there at the barn that this is a serious game.

She shifted slightly and continued. "The killing was also a method of gaining information. When you moved the body, I'm willing to bet you did a thorough searched of the deceased. It's just a hunch, but I'm gambling that there was some valuable data recovered. For what ever reason you're not ready to share. Lashley, you are playing close to the tarmac. However, you may be out to save your own shirt and then leave us to fend for ourselves. That is a strong possibility. I'm not ready to fully commit to you yet. Except, on limited issues, I will for the time being."

"Keep us informed of all details," Greer insisted.

"Okay," Lashley said. "I follow your message."

The clock over the bar registered 4:38 before Lashley returned to the front door. The sun was blocked behind the Hand. Evening shadows were advancing across to the barn. It was still a short time until dark, but in the canyon it darkened earlier. Mitchell and Chainsaw had assembled when Lashley arrived.

Chainsaw quibbled to Lashley, "I hadn't heard from you in so long, I thought my mail box had been stolen."

Lashley shrugged and smiled at the attempted humor. It was a good sign. Lose your humor, and all is lost.

When the head guide appeared his hands were full of black wire. "No wonder the ham radio wouldn't work. The cable connecting the antenna has been cut into a dozen pieces." He tossed examples on the floor among the men.

"Someone deliberately did it and hid the evidence. We found these pieces behind some cooking oil tins on the lower shelf. We only keep the radio for emergencies," Frenchie continued. "It came in handy the time that guest had a heart attack, but by the time the medic arrived, he was dead. Don't check it often enough. Sometimes we let several weeks pass. Could have been anybody in the past several months that did this. I find that hard to believe. To reconnect we'd have to go outside and attach to the end. But that might get us shot. Without the connection the radio is worthless."

At some time and place in his forgotten past, Lashley felt assured that he had faced similar hostility. Somewhere he had walked through this parallel, long, dark corridor of hostility. What lesson had he learned and now forgotten?

Lashley shrugged as though he expected the news. He looked at Mitchell. The officer paused, gathering his lines in preparation for his briefing. He began more for Frenchie's information than Lashley's. "After I finished with Rich I followed behind you. By my observations, overall the guests are under control. Joel and Pearl with their preaching are festering the group. They bear watching. Beryl Carter and his companions say they'll back us, but only if he is convinced it's damn near a foolproof plan. Want us to protect the women at all costs. Everyone is holding up better than I had expected, but their nerves are getting raw."

The captain hesitated. "Leo Rich is still a short fuse. He's extending his deadline through tomorrow morning. If this isn't finished, he'll make a leadership move. You can count on it. He's the Judas goat in this bunch, and he's got some sheep that will follow. Don't know how many, but there's enough for a power struggle. We need to avoid that at all costs."

Frenchie hung and shook his head as he arrived at a sad realization. "This is going be hard on the Cottonwood. I don't know how this publicity is going affect me with the balance of the hunters coming in and for years to come. I owe some debts and have purchased some new livestock. I even put some carpet down in the bunk house. Got a truck too. Man, if the guests stop coming here, it's going ruin this place. I will have to refund this group's money, and if we don't get this resolved in five days, I'll lose my second group of hunters coming in. It looks bad. Even if we solve the problem, I know it will have a long-term effect on me and probably the lodge too."

Lashley shifted in his crouched position, then rose to full height. "The bunk house is a lost cause. It must be abandoned. Absent a stove pipe that's vented above the peak of the roof, the bunk house will have back drafts that will force carbon monoxide into the rooms. It could be lethal. I cut off the furnace awhile back. There's no heat in there now."

"Can't we give the guests the option to stay, even though it's cold out there?" Frenchie asked. "Maybe we could move those portable kerosene heaters off the porch and into the hallway. That would reduce the chill."

"No," Lashley responded. "There's a more important reason. We can't protect ourselves if we're too spread out. Too much risk. The windows along the First Finger side of the mountain are too small for entry, but underneath, at ground level, there are several openings leading into the basement of the bunk house. Anyone getting into our underbelly would have us dead."

"Can't we secure it? Board it up?" Chainsaw asked.

"It will delay them, but it might not stop them entirely. It's imperative we set up a tighter defense."

"How do we play it?" Frenchie asked.

"Send a couple of your cowboys to the bunkhouse," Lashley responded. "Have them nail up every entrance to the basement. There's plenty of extra lumber stored down there. We'll get a few other men to pass some lumber to the porch. We'll board up all these exposed front windows. If anyone wants to shoot the glass out, we won't have any additional casualties from flying splinters. That limits our exposure and reduces their targets. Double brace each window. A thirty ought six magnum can penetrate even two layers of that one inch lumber at two hundred yards. If they shift their target back to the windows instead of the wall, we will have to increase the thickness. I want all of the lumber from the basement up here. Then we'll seal the trap door and board up the entrance of the bunk house from the lodge side."

"We're going to meet with some resistance. Be like tying off one leg of a calf," Mitchell interjected.

"Count on it, but let's move the most cooperative group first. Then the hard core is more likely to follow." Lashley said. "When we start sealing up the door, they'll vacate the premises."

"Okay," the Captain said. "How do we implement it?"

"First, start with your group, the military. Set them up here on this end of the porch. Between the billiard table and the wall of Guarimo's room. That will be their base. Use only necessary equipment. Don't bring it all. Pack in every weapon. Mattresses only, no beds. Next, move Elliott and his girl, Katherine. Set them up under the bar. Then have R.S. and Mitzi and one other couple set up over there in the dining hall. We'll tighten up on the tables. It'll be cramped, but we'll make it."

It was nearly midnight before Lashley joined Paige in bed. The moves had been completed, quarters shifted. As expected, Rich had initially been a problem. Mitchell, by masterful diplomacy, convinced Rich that the move had been an implementation of their earlier discussion. The committee had applied his original suggestion, dubbing it the "Rich Plan."

Rich took the bait, organizing the shift, and the rest fell into place. Guards were posted, and shifts were determined, as the lodge settled in for a stressful rest.

172

Paige shifted, tendering Lashley her warmed spot under the covers, a gesture of love. She snuggled closely, savoring the warmth of his body as he slipped his pistol under the pillow. His Remington leaned against the door, ready for any alarm. He extended his arm for her to rest her head on his shoulder.

"How do you feel, Howard?" she inquired tenderly but anxiously.

"Okay," he assured her belatedly.

It had been some day, beginning with his nightmare, that dreadful dream. Then he had remained constantly on the move since four a.m., facing interminable conflicts until past dark. Two deaths topped the day, the old guide and the stranger on the roof. Paige must wonder how he felt about killing the man. It had been a defensive act, not cold blooded as had been the death of String. Certainly she must know the shooting of a human being affected his emotions. But he noted she did not ask. Possibly she feared it would activate his dreaded dreams.

The picking and petty bitterness of the group provided a road block at every turn. That was

173

disheartening. Why were so many individuals uncooperative? There had been no shots since just after dark. The absence of shots was worse than the steady occurrence. With the pattern of shots, at least the next one could be anticipated and sparked the need for vigilance. The silence was like waiting for your first date to arrive. The anticipation was so great and anticipation often led to carelessness. Would the posted guards become careless tonight?

"Are we going to be all right, Howard?" Paige asked. "I mean, will we come out of this okay?" She turned to face him, molding her petite body closer against his lanky frame.

"Sure," he lied, brushing a few blond curls away as he kissed her forehead. "We'll make it."

She acknowledged his fabrication in the spirit of receiving a gift. She ran her hand affectionately across his cheek, feeling his whisker stubble. They lay for several moments in silence. The dry wood hissed as the flames bit the edges. A flicker of light cast by the burning wood dispersed dancing shadows around the room. Except for the reality of death, it could have been a romantic spot.

Anticipation of some romantic interludes was the reason she had consented to join Lashley on this trip in the first place. Now, the hunt had turned into a disaster. It had passed from love into the quicksand of death. There was no real way out. Hope existed only as a delusion.

"Who does Rich think those people are out there, pizza delivery men?" Lashley rhetorically asked in a soft voice. "They're human beings just like we are. In physical appearance, they are similar, but what's inside is the division. It's in their minds and hearts, their psychological make up. That's what distinguishes them from the balance of mankind. They aren't Boy Scouts."

"But you must have some idea?" Paige inquired.

"Not really. I'm certain it's a hastily recruited band of ill-trained mercenaries," he replied, muffling his comments. "That's all I know."

"You mean terrorists?" she asked, surprised.

"If this was Kabul or Dublin, I might be suspicious. Or even if we had some Jewish religious leader or diplomat in residence, it might lend some credence to a terrorist's theory. But the isolation of the Cottonwood doesn't appear to be a magnet for terrorists."

"Then, is it some type of frustrated freedom fighter looking for a cause?"

"Don't be misguided by the propaganda that these freedom fighters are frustrated, desperate people abused in their religious beliefs seeking revenge from alleged wrong. That's bullshit talk of some yapping street pimp. It's the smelly kind that lays on the ground, wet, slobbery, moldy, waiting for us to step in it and bust our ass. 'Freedom Fighter' is an oxymoron."

"But some of them do have strong political or religious convictions. Certain sects, because of various reasons, have suffered injustices," Paige reminded him of the unfortunate people.

"Again, that's propaganda. Every person has political or religious convictions, but that's not a license to kill. Circumcision for one faith, baptism by emersion for another. Those who are not true believers are ostracized to emulate those who differ. Injustices? When in the history of man have there not been injustices?

"One Neanderthal clan, by force, evicts another clan who has a warmer, dryer, and safer cave. Those disposed, in turn, overpower the weaker. The Romans overthrew a thousand separate clans and then were overthrown by the nomadic Galls. European immigrants overran the American Indians. Black tribes overpowered their neighbors, captured their enemies, and sold the surplus black captives to white slavers. Angry young blacks vent their spleens about southern slavery against modern whites. But they ignore that the basis of the injustice of slavery was instigated and nourished by Africans in the first case.

"So, young blacks indiscriminately shoot at and destroy white owned property, even that which belongs to those who might sympathize with their plight. And then they lose that support, and more racial strife follows. It's never ending until something breaks the circle. Then it receeds, left to smolder for years until it erupts all over again with even more violence."

"How will we know what or whom are we facing?" she asked.

"The question is who benefits from the bloodshed? Then we will have our answer."

Lashley continued with an angry tone, one that made Paige uncomfortable. "Now, if there are terrorists out there, they're cold blooded killers. If its terrorists, the only chance we have is to kill them before they kill us. There can be no compromise."

Even as he said it, he recognized the hopelessness of their situation. Barely hours ago, adversarial reinforcements arrived. As he rested, a plot was being developed to destroy the Cottonwood and its inhabitants. There was little he could do to prevent the destruction. He had no comprehension for the magnitude of the terror facing the lodge.

"Is it true what Joel said today?" Paige replied.

"What's that?" Lashley asked.

"That death is contagious. If they kill one of us and we kill one of them the process repeats itself. That it's a disease that spreads."

"Well, more or less. It works like that in an uncivilized society, or where law and order fail. When people put themselves above the law confusion follows. Look at Northern Ireland or Palestine. Terrorists abound. That kind of stuff breeds disaster. Death is contagious. It becomes a circle that never stops."

"What are we facing here?" she asked.

"I wish to God I knew."

This time he did not lie.

She kissed him, a wet, passionate implant. Slowly, she raised her flannel nightgown until the hem was above her breasts. Her nakedness pressed against him, its warmth stimulated his body. Awkwardly, he lowered his thermal underwear until his manhood could accept her femininity. Under the quilted covers, they made hurried, aggressive love. It was finished before she was ready. Lashley held her in a tight embrace. Finally, he pushed away, exhausted by the effort. Her satisfaction, though not sexual, he hoped, was bound in the knowledge that he would rest well this night. In the past, he had never dreamed that horrid nightmare after they made love. Falsely secure in that comfort, he joined Paige in sleep.

CHAPTER SEVEN

"I've got to talk with you," Lewis Fulcher hoarsely addressed the four men sitting at a small porch table placed off to the right of the front door. He spoke in a barely audible whisper. "It's me they're after. I'm the target," he sobbed openly.

It was seven minutes after ten o'clock, two minutes after the last shot had splintered the wall. The shot was the ninth since the sniper's morning ritual began in earnest. The firing had settled into an almost predictable pattern, some thirty minutes apart. The target was likewise predictable, concentrated under the broken window. Bullets constantly struck the logged wall in a random pattern. But the sniper was not consistent in his selection of the firing location. Sometimes the shots originated from the upper loft window of String's room. More often it shifted and came from the right side of the barn door frame.

Captain Tyrone Mitchell, finishing his report, looked up at the nervous, sweaty man. What was this bullshit, Lashley thought? Was it going to be another pile of misinformation. He was tired, racked by tension, uncertainty, and lack of sleep. Since daylight, he had been on the move and accomplished what? There was nothing positive that he could identify. The hopeless situation showed no improvement. Conditions were conceivably deteriorating. The movement of the clock, attached to the time bomb, swept hurriedly toward zero. He was uncertain whether the explosion would occur within the lodge or on the outside. But it would explode and soon, he feared.

As requested, all weapons within the lodge, not in use by the guards, had been centralized at the billiard table. Under Major Greer's supervision, Patricia Stanford and Myrtle Wallace compiled a weapon's inventory, evaluated the condition of each weapon as to its effectiveness, and assimilated each in its proper order. Appropriate ammunition had been separated by caliber for instant distribution. As the weapon's officer, Greer appeared to take his assignment seriously, expanding the inventory to include all hand guns possessed by the hunters and guides.

Safety regulations were instituted for weapons use within the lodge. Except for the weapons utilized by those on guard duty, all extra weapons were racked along the billiard table. Caliber classification was detailed to distinguish between magnum and soft point bullets. Each reserve weapon was loaded full clip or magazines, but all chambers stayed empty as a safety feature. Rifles with scopes were separated from those with open sights. Extra ammunition and clips had been collected from all hunters. Knives, field glasses, and other useful resources, though not necessarily collected, were recorded on an inventory. Greer located three hand operated radios with limited range. His list included all axes, hatchets, and specialty knives found in the building. Rounding out the list was two crossbows and four Bear Archery 40 pound test bows, with an ample supply of arrows for each type.

While conducting the detailed inventory, Greer matched individual hunters and guides with the weapon he determined best fit their familiarity and greatest skill. Frenchie Hebert, the head guide, and Cinch Wilkinson, the youngest cowboy, as the only individuals responding, appeared to have the greatest qualifications for archery. Lashley was satisfied the major had accomplished a successful match up of person to weapon. The lodge's armament was now in a defensive position.

Early in the morning the captain had checked on Heather Baldwin's condition. He reported she still remained in some type of coma. Her condition was mystifying. Medical attention was becoming a critical necessity for her. She was not improving. A continuing denial of a doctor might result in permanent damage. Help must be located immediately.

Dunsey Martin's and Elliott Thornton's injuries from the glass splinters seemed to stabilize. Neither of the injured appeared to be in any danger of infection. Thornton's mobility was mildly hampered, but his injury did not thwart his liquid consumption. Katherine Pace continued to match him can for can.

The captain had designated the pantry, off from the kitchen, as an infirmary. By default, olive-skinned, dark-eyed Mitzi Rhodes was placed in charge as the Cottonwood's emergency medical technician. She recruited some of the other women who were not engaged on Heather's nursing team as assistants. Together, the women had removed and relocated all the groceries and supplies, storing them throughout the dining and porch areas. It had been a monumental task.

Once cleared, the pantry was furnished with two folding cots, towels, and extra blankets. Personal first aid kits, secured from the hunting party and other items that might remotely pass as medical supplies, were collected. The effort offered only crude facilities, but it would have to suffice.

The stoop door, adjacent to the upward slope of the Trigger Finger, was considered the most vulnerable defense point. Across the yard downward to the barn, the front of the lodge was open, which afforded a broad defensive vision. The back door, by contrast, offered several cover points to launch an attack. To improve the rear passage, a team of hunters restacked the firewood around the stoop, creating an offset, side step entrance.

Beryl Carter and R.S. Farrow formed a carpenter's team. Under their direction, the front door was reinforced, and the side porch windows were double boarded. At all windows a small opening had been left for a firing position. Mattresses were relocated to make accommodations more comfortable within the main lodge.

As the majority of the guests set the stage for a defense, Lashley had observed obese Pearl Gavin and Leo Rich retreat into the women's restroom. He figured it was for a sexual quickie. Rich, by letting his moratorium pass, was apparently determined to maintain his conquest. Bible thumping Pearl exhibited no hesitation in violating the sexual moral code while insisting others give strict adherence to the Sixth Commandment of "Thou Shalt Not Kill." She adhered to a philosophy of 'Don't do as I do. Do as I say do.' At least the couple was occupied and not underfoot.

During the committee meetings, which had been scheduled every alternate hour, each member reported the ongoing defensive efforts to Lashley, who mostly remained silent. The real question was whether anyone believed that these efforts were of any consequence. While each individual responded willingly, it was questionable if anyone actually reasoned the defensive efforts would work. Should the enemies become well organized and sufficiently armed with heavy weapons or explosives, it would be easy to blow a corner off the porch. Then those inside would be unable to defend any frontal attack. Lashley was certain that most of the individuals trapped in the lodge, when facing a show down, would cow down and surrender. There was even a medical term used by head shrinks, the Stockholm Syndrome. During extended capture, an individual begins to sympathize with his captors. How long, Lashley wondered, until someone starts to feel sorry for those miserable souls in the barn?

There was always the fear of fire. The building could easily be burned. Lashley had not set up any escape route from the lodge. The occupants would be trapped. The absence of an alternate flight path bothered the group. That very issue had been raised earlier by Beryl Carter, the asphalt contractor.

"Let's load and head up the canyon," he had suggested to the "committee," as it was now called. "We'll build a stretcher for Heather and follow that back trail up and around the first knuckle of the mountain. We'll take turns with the stretcher. A couple of cowboys could follow behind to provide cover. I've talked it over with Joel and some others. They agree. Crippled Horne made the climb with Greer the other day. If he made it, it can't be too bad. Has lots of switch backs, so the trail is not that steep. The trees give cover till you get above the timber line."

"Once you reach the first knuckle, where then?" Lashley asked.

"To the closest ranch," Carter said.

"That route's been considered and rejected. You can tell Joel I said so," Lashley responded. "It's a two and a half mile trail up to the Knuckle. That's a rise in elevation of at least a thousand feet. With rifles and pack gear, we'd be loaded. Carrying Heather would slow us down. That's a steep climb. Some of the women, and I doubt Elliott, could make it."

"We've got to try," Carter insisted.

"We could only make that climb by going in daylight. Once we clear the tree line, if not sooner, we'd be spotted," Lashley checked. "All they have to do is send a team up behind and force us to rush to keep ahead. This group couldn't keep up that pace. Not with the women and the injured. Even if we did, the closest ranch is ten miles south, once we get off the Hand. That route is across some rough gulches, and it's a steep climb up that mesa to the ranch. Those walls are several hundred feet up. With pressure behind us once we leave the Hand, they'd use their vehicles and cut us off."

"How you figure that?" Carter asked.

Frenchie joined the discussion. "South of the Trigger Finger, there is a road where the sheep owner brings supplies to their herders in the summer. When we drop over the Knuckle, we'll be out in the open, visible again. They'd know which ridge we were using to come off the mountain. They'd ambush us there at the tip of that finger just when we got down to the road. Then we'd be too tired to fight."

"We could move at night," Carter said.

"Maybe," Lashley responded. "But you saw the weather yesterday. A front is moving in. It's going to be cold tonight. Could have snow on top. With the wind on the Knuckle, it will be below zero. It will be unusually dark too. Walking will be extremely difficult. How will the women do, especially Heather, being exposed to the elements?"

"Frenchie has a small cabin between the Middle and Ring Fingers. I've been there on previous hunts. We could hold up there," Carter interjected.

"And be pinned down with fewer resources than we have here? If we can't defend the lodge, what chances do we have of defending some remote cabin?" Lashley answered.

Demurely Carter accepted the defeat of his plan and returned to his carpentry work. It was obvious to Lashley the contractor was discouraged. He had evaluated their situation as desperate. Even a blind person could see it. Carter considered himself a fighter, and he would defend these innocent women. He had most likely never run from a fight, and he would not do so now. But how do you fight ghosts? The unknown enemy? Where was the sense of it all?

The committee had pressing decisions, and these constant personal interruptions were distracting the leadership from its primary function. Now Lewis Fulcher wanted an audience.

"What are you talking about?" Chainsaw asked, as he looked up to Fulcher.

"Those people out there, they want to kill me," he said.

"Why would anybody want to kill you?" Chainsaw inquired.

"Drugs. I've been involved in drugs," Fulcher responded in a halting whisper. "On my account, I've gotten two people killed, Heather raped, and now more will die if I don't go out and give myself up. Let them kill me, and they will disappear. Everyone here will then be freed."

"Mitchell, you and Frenchie make your rounds," Lashley directed. "Chainsaw and I will detail this. We'll meet again at twelve."

When the two men had departed, Lashley studied Fulcher in silence. The man was obviously nervous. His hands fidgeted. His feet shifted. By all appearance, he was being truthful.

Lashley nodded for him to take the chair recently vacated by Mitchell. This positioned his back to prevent eavesdroppers, inside the dining room from hearing his story. Nodding for the man to speak, Lashley leaned forward. Chainsaw joined suit.

"I've said enough," Fulcher said. "You don't need to know more. What you don't know can't hurt you. Besides, if I tell you and I'm tortured and talk, they'll be after you. They'll have to destroy any trail that leads back to them. If you know the story, they will come for you. It's better you don't know."

Chainsaw reached across, placing his hand on Fulcher's arm. "Trust me," he said. "We want to know. Please tell us."

A rush of sobbing engulfed the man like an incoming tide. His body rocked back and forth in sequence with his weeping. From all outward appearances, he was succumbing to the pressure of impending death. During the hours since the ordeal began, several of the women, especially the bandaged Dunsey Martin, despite her boyfriend Carter's comforting, had occasionally been grasped by uncontrollable crying fits. Fulcher appeared to be the first, but maybe not the last, man to be caught up in an outward burst of emotion.

Chainsaw secured a soda for the man. A few sips from the drink helped restore some of his equilibrium. Several additional minutes elapsed before he was in sufficient control to speak coherently.

"I'm ashamed. My family and all. The whole mess and my involvement. I can't believe it's happening."

His audience remained silent, letting Fulcher find his own denominator. No purpose would be accomplished in pressing him. He might break again. Eventually, the tale would unravel.

"When this started, when they abused Heather, I didn't want to believe that I was the cause. Damn it! Heather's such a sweet person. Did you know that every summer when she was in high school she worked as a waitress in my restaurant? She was good help. Reliable and mature for her age. Even now and then she comes in for a meal and tells me how my giving her that job helped her in life. Now look what I've done to her."

He paused for a sip, twirled the last residue in the can and gulped it down.

"When that man fell off the roof, I was on the floor near the door of the dining hall. I saw him through the kitchen window. Long, straight, black hair, darkened skin. I just saw a glimpse of him. Later, I saw him out the window on the ground. I recognized him as a Hispanic. One of those Colombians. It was then that I knew for sure it was me they were after."

"You recognized him?" Chainsaw asked, astounded by the disclosure.

"No, not him specifically. I just saw him for a brief glance. Maybe he is someone I've seen before.

194

But I did recognize the type. And that type is what's out to kill me."

Chainsaw allowed for a pause in the conversation, then said, "When we finish, I'll take you out for a look. Then we can know for sure. Now, tell us your involvement with killers."

It had started almost two years earlier. Fulcher's restaurant was successful and showing a substantial profit. The fishing boats, however, were creating a drain on his operation. Increased fuel prices caused by the unsettling political climate of the Middle East, obsolete equipment, and an unstable fish market hampered his productivity. Competition caused by over fishing, closed the historically favorable holes, forcing his boats to sail further into the Gulf of Mexico in search of more profitable catches. The economic answer was for Fulcher to acquire more modern vessels, efficient, less labor intense. Even with his restaurant and other hard earned assets, financing the fleet was a problem. The failing savings and loan associations resulted in tightened banking regulations. With the onslaught of the Comptroller of the

Currency's bureaucratic dabbling with the financial industry, the nation's economy worsened. Finding financing for fishing equipment became a difficult, if not impossible, task.

Every banking resource was closed to good businessmen like Fulcher, as tightly as an Apalachicola oyster. All efforts to pry them open were fruitless. Rejection became the norm. He examined the alternatives of shutting down his fishing operation, but he had too much money invested and too many notes due. The boats' crew and their families depended on him. So he kept the fleet in the waters, sinking financially deeper with each trip. There were no life lines for him.

It was essential to maintain a cash flow, so until he found an answer, he was desperate for relief. When the answer came, it emerged from a most unusual source. Good old Uncle Sam. In Miami, the government was selling modern fishing vessels, fully equipped, at bargain basement prices. These new vessels had been confiscated because of their involvement in transporting illegal drugs. The federal government impounded the vessels and then sold them to the highest bidder for cash. The successful bids were usually stricken off for one-third of their fair market value. Fulcher figured that if he could buy three of these confiscated boats for the usual price of one and dispose of his obsolete fleet at a sacrificial price, it would enhance him financially.

All he lacked was the cash for the bid. One of his boat captains, a short-time employee named Conroy, located a source for the money. The trail was charted by a fish-head friend of the captain from south Florida. X.C.X. Investment, Inc. of Miami advised Fulcher that the company specialized in financing fishing boats, especially those purchased from the government's impoundment program. Eighteen percent interest was discussed. Fulcher figured that since there were three boats involved, it calculated to about 6 percent per boat. Assured that the first payment was not due until ninety days after execution, the note was endorsed for X.C.X by Fulcher, his wife, and his only son, who was actively involved in the restaurant business with him.

It was not until later that Fulcher discovered he was hooked. X.C.X. dictated the choice of insurance coverage. The premiums, from pre-designated companies, proved to be triple in amount the coverage he could have secured from his own agent. Then late charges imposed by X.C.X were calculated for each twenty-four-hour delinquency. Payments were due on the tenth of each month. Even if the check was mailed seven days early, the drafts never arrived in Miami timely, or so Fulcher was informed. Ten percent delinquent penalties were added to every month's charges. Additionally, there were service charges for late accounting fees. The vessels proved to be swift, efficient, and sufficient for making profitable catches. But total fish sales were never adequate to service the loan. Fulcher was again in deep water in the middle of a hurricane.

During mid summer of the past year, a Hispanic appeared at the restaurant. When seated, he ordered Fulcher's famous seafood platter, accompanied by a bottle of local white wine. When he had finished his meal and lit his Cuban cigar, he invited, or rather ordered Fulcher to sit down. He told Fulcher the deal, and left without paying his meal tab. The bill was not the only item the man left. The Latino left the restaurateur stunned.

In August of that year, the first drug shipment was off loaded from local dinghies near the coast of Belize onto Fulcher's boat, commanded by Captain Conroy. Delivery was finalized at St. Andrews in Florida's secluded coastal waters. Six additional shipments followed without incident. X.C.X.'s note was paid current, with advance payments for six months. The crew received bonuses and promptly purchased new pickups with all the accessories. Fulcher attempted to counsel his captains about these luxurious purchases. Fish-heads, as the locals called the boat crews, with sudden wealth, new trucks, and fancily dressed wives or girlfriends, attracted undercover drug agents like tourists to a strip joint. However, the boss's warnings were to no avail, and the crews spent their drug money like drunken sailors. Strangers were coming to Fulcher's restaurant. For Fulcher, most did not look like tourists. He saw the look of a "drug agent" in every new customer.

He became paranoid, and his nerves were shot. He even sought medical attention. The doctor informed him that his symptoms were not that of an ulcer. He was under too much stress and was advised to slow down, enjoy life, and travel. His doctor told him to spend some of that money he was stashing away. But that advice could not be taken. He was committed to keeping his nets in the water. One snag and he knew the total catch would be lost.

The next drug trip was the first in a series of disasters. The crew became careless, failed to heed weather reports, and the ship was nearly swamped by heavy seas. One of the drug packages burst. How it happened, no one could explain. At the delivery point, the recipients were mildly angry, suspecting tampering but outwardly they professed understanding. Drug profits for that trip were radically reduced to accommodate for damaged merchandise and as a punishment for carelessness.

This past July, a Hispanic appeared again. He was not the same one as before. It might have been his brother or first cousin. But to Fulcher, they looked very similar due to their dark hair and skin.

The meal, the wine, and the invitation followed in due course. The exception to the previous conference was that Captain Conroy, who was in port, received a summons to join in the discussion at the corner table.

As Fulcher was relaying his story to Chainsaw and Lashley, he recalled the details of the conversation between Captain Conroy, the Hispanic, and himself as vivid as though it was yesterday.

"The last two shipments were each one bag short," the man said in his heavily Spanish accented English. "We were most unhappy."

Fulcher said he nearly wet his pants. "What the hell is he talking about, Conroy?" he had asked his captain.

"I don't know. One shipment we had a broken bag, but we settled on that. That's all I know," Conroy answered.

"We know how to deal with cheaters," the man said and left owing his board bill.

Fulcher pressed Conroy for details. If shortages had occurred in the drug shipments, the captain denied any knowledge, but promised to investigate. On the next trip, a deck hand overdosed and died. Frightened that the drug dealers could now piece together that the shorted shipments had been commandeered by the crew for their personal use, the crew became frightened. The survivors weighted the dead man down and buried him at sea. The Coast Guard received a radio report that claimed a tragedy. During a rainstorm, the report asserted, a crew member had accidentally fallen overboard and the boat, after an extensive search, was unable to locate the man. There was a cursory investigation by the Coast Guard. With no obvious evidence of foul play, the search was soon ended. Fulcher was beside himself. He then began to see a drug agent's reflection around every corner, not just in his restaurant.

Fulcher had called for a conference. A Latino came. Possibly, this one was an identical triplet of the first two. Fulcher was uncertain and really did not care.

"I'm closing the operation down," Fulcher said. "No more shipments. It's finished."

"We have ways of dealing with traitors." These were the only words from the man. He departed with an unpaid meal ticket.

A week later, one of Fulcher's crew members on shore leave was admitted to the local hospital. As he later explained it to the authorities, he had been sitting on his front porch reading his Bible when a man he had never seen before, and could not identify, walked up to him. For no apparent reason, the stranger shot him in the shin bone of both legs. Two days later, Captain Conroy disappeared. In early August, the boat captain was found floating in Basin Bayou, his throat slit.

Out of desperation, Fulcher joined this scheduled hunting party, absent female companionship, to allow things at home to cool off. The trip would allow him time to plan his next course of action. There was an additional reason for not bringing a female companion as he had first planned. He had first voted and supported the move to bring women. But now, his sexual performance abilities were about equal to his chance of survival. Zero.

"Take him out through the stoop door around back. See if he can identify the body," Lashley instructed Chainsaw as Fulcher finished his tale of woe.

As the two departed, Mitchell approached. "Our opposition is tightening the noose," he said. "Come, let me show you."

Lashley peered through a peep hole in the boarded window at the far right corner of the porch. What he saw disturbed him.

"Notice up on the tip end of the Thumb, on top there. They've built some type of cover behind bails of hay. Same thing on the tip of the Trigger Finger. Can't see it from here, but you can over by the front door. They've established observation points. From each point, they are offered a clear view of any activity we do on the outside. The motors we've been hearing are those of all-terrain vehicles. Must had brought them on a trailer. That's what they used to transport the hay up top," Mitchell said.

Chainsaw arrived to join the two men. "While I was out there with Fulcher looking at the Mex, I noticed something. There's somebody in the timbers out there about two hundred fifty yards out. I wouldn't have seen him if he hadn't moved. It looks like a sentry."

"What did Fulcher say about the deceased? Could he recognize him?" Lashley asked.

"No," Chainsaw responded. "But then I got the impression you didn't expect him to."

Lashley shrugged.

"So we're boxed in," Mitchell said. "They are positioned in a manner that suits them best."

"No. We've got them positioned exactly where we want them," Lashley corrected. "I think that's a direct quote from the Alamo. Colonel Travis, I believe. I think he said he had the Mexicans right where he wanted them."

CHAPTER EIGHT

Low telling clouds had slipped over the Knuckle of Hand Mountain, dropping down the draw and engulfing the guest lodge in a veil of mist. The barn, a mere 200 yards away, was barely visible, its features distorted. Beyond the structure, a gray curtain obscured the landscape. The existing daylight, now in short supply, was rapidly approaching night. It soon would be dark, truly dark.

Frenchie Hebert sat with his legs crossed, nervously picking at his teeth. His weathered face expressed his stress as vividly as words. His usual cheerful demeanor, which for years had charmed his guests, had vanished. He sat, absorbed by a personal fog as dense as the one engulfing the Cottonwood Lodge.

"We got to try, Lashley," Frenchie said. "We're losing our support. It's eroding away, washed out like our road."

"Tonight is wrong," Howard Lashley responded. "It won't work."

Captain Tyrone Mitchell had remained silent, while Hebert had explained the proposal. Mitchell had tactfully concurred with fragments of the operation. Frenchie's assessment of the overall morale at the lodge was accurate. Mitchell reported that his associates, dubbed now by the group as "The Military," were wavering in their support. A consensus prevailed that Lashley was confused. Either he was uncertain or he was devoid of the ability to perform any effective affirmative action to extricate them from this danger. It was murmured that he was possibly withholding vital information which the remainder of the party had a right to know. Neither aspect was encouraging.

Bible thumping Joel Guarimo had been openly soliciting recruits to support his philosophy. Lashley, Joel contended, must be replaced by someone with leadership abilities, not a possessor of killer instincts. An election should be held for the leadership position, a person whom the group would willfully follow. Joel boldly suggested that he might be their answer.

Bending to the pressure of a near mutiny by both guests and crew, Frenchie was demanding Lashley's consent to support a limited proposition. He suggested one of his crew members take a message, on foot, over the Knuckle, south to the Crosby Ranch on the mesa. Trapped as they were, the occupants of the Cottonwood had to reach the outside. The ranch on the mesa was the nearest contact. It was their only hope for relief. Some action must be taken, the head guide urged, to calm the storm brewing inside the walls of the lodge.

"Who goes?" Lashley inquired.

"I've volunteered," Chainsaw Poulen said.

"He's the best," Frenchie said. "He's lived in the mountains all his life. While Chainsaw's not as familiar with the Hand as my regular crew, he's a better outdoorsman. Cinch is my second choice, but he's young and not as mature. He's a good cowboy and marksman, but not on foot. I'm not so sure Chainsaw isn't the natural choice."

"It's the worst night for that," Lashley said. "The mountain is socked in. That front is moving through. It appears stationary for the time being. This overcast won't move out until early morning."

"I think I can make it, even with those conditions," Poulen reassured.

"Thinking is not good enough," Lashley said. "There'll be no stars tonight. There's nothing to judge a bearing. A compass might give direction, but it doesn't give a reference point on the ground. That mountain's not smooth as a baby's behind. It's rough. It's packed with crevices and draws. One missed step in the darkness, and you could fall a hundred feet. You wouldn't be found until next summer when the snows are gone. No, it's too risky."

"I'll compromise," Chainsaw offered. "I'll only go tonight as far as Frenchie's little retreat cabin on the west side of the Middle Finger. At first light, I'll start south. I'll break out at the butt of Middle Finger by eight o'clock at the very latest. Six or eight hours after that I'll be at Crosby's. Should have some help here by this time tomorrow."

"I can't endorse it," Lashley added. "By morning, the weather might be worse. Even if the weather improves, by the time you reach the open plains, you could be cut off. It is too big a risk. It's too much of a sacrifice in the event of failure."

"One man moving rapidly could make it," Chainsaw insisted.

"Negative," Lashley maintained. "I am opposed to that effort. Besides, we need you here."

Frenchie leaned forward and placed his hands on the table. "I'm over riding you on this, Lashley. If Chainsaw will volunteer, I'm sending him. If not him, then Cinch. Someone's going, or we'll have to whip Leo and Joel together, along with several others. And I'm not up to that."

Lashley shrugged in defeat, watching Frenchie move off to advise Rich and Guarimo the detail of the decision.

"How do you read it, Ranger?" Chainsaw addressed his remarks to the black officer.

"Travel light. Take high protein food. I've got an excellent night compass. Take a light hand gun.

Remember to drink plenty of water. You'll dehydrate quickly in high altitudes, even if you mountain men tend to forget that.

"First problem is to avoid the guard out back. Go up the Thumb diagonally. Avoid the lower trail. After you reach two hundred to two hundred fifty feet up the side of the slope, work due west along the incline. Up there somewhere, you should hit the trail. At that point you'll be behind the guard. Follow the trail from then on. After you clear the tree line, test the conditions. Move out several hundred yards and see if you are able to function safely. If not, return to the tree lines and hold up until morning. Then move on with the mission."

"What about any noise when I'm near the guard?" Chainsaw asked.

"If you're that high above him, he might not hear," Mitchell responded. "However sound is not muffled in fog. It's like sound over water. Occasionally, stop moving and shuffle around. It might sound enough like an elk or horse moving through. Irregular movements will confuse him. Only men move with a steady pace. Animals stop, listen, and graze."

"How about using a flashlight?"

"There is a disadvantage. If you use it, you'll be night blind for about twenty minutes. Sit down and don't move until your sight is restored. Using the light will be safer for movement above the timber line. With this fog, light can't be seen from any distance."

"Lashley," Chainsaw said, "I know you don't endorse this plan, but I think it has to be done. Wish me luck."

Lashley nodded.

"Frenchie, help me with my gear. I want to be gone by ten o'clock."

A while later, Mitchell and Lashley stood under the stoop as Chainsaw sidestepped around the escape door of stacked firewood. He turned right and disappeared into the fog. The men who remained were silent, each absorbed in their own thoughts.

Moments before Mitchell had been hurriedly briefed, in capsule, about Fulcher's drug confession. The captain expressed disgust at the possibility that

Fulcher was the target. The officer mentioned how he was struggling with the moral issue of allowing a volunteer to surrender to the opponent. He expressed his concerns to Lashley. If Fulcher was wrong and was not the target, they would have to live with that guilt.

"How do you feel about Chainsaw?" the captain asked as the fog closed in the back stoop.

"Not good. There's something just not right. It smells like Wednesday afternoon at the livestock sale. There's a pattern missing. I don't understand it, and I'm fearful," Lashley responded.

The men stood under the stoop for some minutes longer listening to the babbling of the stream.

The captain spoke first. "It's time for the enemy's second reinforcements to arrive. How do you see them making their deployment?"

"Well," Lashley responded, "no vehicles came close enough to the barn this afternoon for us to see them. There was no additional activity anywhere around that building. I figure they've set up headquarters somewhere else. They could possibly be up there at the new house by the landing strip. Or maybe they have camping facilities, and they're doing it at the bottom of the cliff. Whatever it is, I don't believe that they're using the barn for their housing quarters and meals. I suspect the barn is serving as their observation post only. It affords a high observation point within the lodge's compound."

"What about Fulcher? What additional information did he have to offer?" the captain pressed for a more in-depth briefing.

Lashley paused and thought before he responded. "He is firm in his resolution that he's the target. It's a plausible tale, but I don't think that Fulcher's our problem. It's something other than that."

"Could it be Leo Rich?" the officer asked. "Somebody, I think it was Carter, told me the details of his last family confrontation. It seems that Rich's wife is Italian or something. When he had his last fling and got caught, his wife brought in some mafia people who roughed him up real bad and also the girl. From what I understand, it was real bad the way she was treated."

"It's a possibility," Lashley said. "But somehow I don't think that's it."

"Why don't we let Fulcher go out and confront the people? What do you think that would buy us?" Mitchell asked.

"Nothing," Lashley responded. "Even if he were the target, how could we let him go and face a certain death sentence? Don't we owe some duty to protect the total group? I don't know. That just doesn't sit well with me."

"Yes, I believe there's a moral issue there," the captain said. "We can't let one of them go. Especially, if he is not the one they're looking for. That could really complicate our position."

"Yes, if Fulcher was wrong, we would lose another defender. We can't let that happen."

Lashley and Mitchell had relieved the hunting guide on guard duty to allow Chainsaw to start his mission. Their relief was not scheduled to return until one o'clock.

Abruptly, Lashley grasped the captain's arm and pulled him to a crouching stance. He leaned forward and whispered in his ear.

"What I am about to say is for your ears only, not your superior officer or Frenchie. Nobody, and I mean nobody, must know. Do you understand?"

"Yes sir, I understand what you say," the officer whispered back. He started to add an additional comment but was cut short.

"In the service, there's a saying, 'Need to know.' Are you familiar with that terminology?" Lashley paused for the officer's nodding acceptance. He detected the affirmation in the darkness.

He continued, "You are the only one that needs to know. If you fail in this assignment, I'll be dead. Then you and Frenchie will be all that are left to save these restless souls."

"What are you going to do?"

"Being socked in by the fog has an advantage. It's handy. It has handicapped our opposition. I'm going out on a reconnaissance mission. Gather a little information. Do some scouting. Who knows what we might find."

He reasoned Mitchell was astounded. The suggestion was a high risk operation, greater than Chainsaw's mission. It was a contradiction for him to suggest such an undertaking when he had resisted Chainsaw's back door effort.

"We can't afford to lose you. Have you examined other options?" Mitchell whispered.

"Yes," he responded. "This is maybe our last opportunity for a reconnaissance. Here are your instructions. Stay at this guard post. Only you. Don't let anyone relieve you until I return. If someone comes out here to chat or whatever, send them back immediately. Use any excuse, but get rid of them. If anyone inquires of me, say I went to the can, as far as you know. When I get back, I'll toss a pebble on the roof. That will be your clue that I'm coming in. Don't be alarmed. The password will be 'Davy Crocket.' I'll be gone no more than an hour, maybe less."

Lashley arose, stepped through the entrance and moved left, leaving a speechless captain. Outside, it was total darkness. He depended upon instincts as a compass. Moving cautiously, Lashley located the edge of the stream. Using its cascading sounds to muffle his steps he crouched as he moved. At 125 feet down stream, he moved upland. From his memory of the landscape, he judged his location. Within ten steps, he detected smooth ground under his feet, identifying the path. He had located the most direct route connecting the lodge with the barn. If he remembered correctly, this trail led down slope toward a crossing over the pond dam. He pivoted left.

Secreted in the foggy soup, he knew to his front, just off the path, was the old tack shed. It was no longer an active building but served as more of a shelter for discarded equipment, retaining its aesthetic looks as a western backdrop for the lodge. Kneeling, he crawled cautiously along the ground, hand extended outward, groping for the tack shed.

Lashley was gripped by the feeling of deja vu. Had he crawled this way before? In those lost years, reserved in a locked memory, had he practiced stealth before? His stealthy skills were apparent, an ingrained action that evidenced intensive training at some distant point. When and where had he been so intensively trained, and to what secret activities? And for what purpose? Who was Howard Lashley? It was a recurring thought that had possessed him for the past three years. The confusion started the day he awoke in Five Pines Sanitarium, located in the remote mountainous area of northern Georgia.

He suppressed the thoughts for now. Failure to give absolute attention to this mission could mean death, not only for himself but for all within the Cottonwood. He moved silently forward.

Then he found it. His out stretched hand groped the foundation of the log shed. He slid several feet and rested his back on the structure. On the far side of the shed, words, foreign in nature, were audible. A man was speaking half Spanish and half English no more than twenty feet away. Lashley understood this language as if he were a native. Language skills, was this another remnant from his former life?

Two men were conversing. One instructed his comrade on the details of his assignment. As Lashley listened, he realized he had missed the basics of their plan, but the bones were there. A time, a direction, and a place was mentioned. With a little imagination, he was able to fill the gaps.

Shortly, a living, breathing monster would be bearing down on the occupants of the lodge with spear in hand, seeking blood. Nothing would prevent the launch of the spear, but possibly he could blunt its point. If he were to succeed, desperate action must be taken. Time was of the essence.

Searching for any available resources, his groping produced a fist-sized rock and a short medal rod. He waited until the conversation resumed in full force. He then tossed both objects as far up the slope as his energies allowed. As he had expected, the rod and rock clanked upon impact. Yielding to the demands of gravity, the rock rolled downhill. The rod snagged and halted.

The metal had produced a different sound. It was more than the movement usually associated with a rock loosened and falling down an incline. It was metallic in tone. Intended to be construed as a manmade, the clatter resulted in a reward for Lashley. It sounded as if up slope someone had tripped on a loose rock, and a gun had struck something.

The conversation halted in mid-sentence, then recommenced in lower inaudible whispers. A few moments passed. Then a body movement followed. Something struck an object. In the gloom, it sounded like a slap. There were more whispers, inaudible. Then, Lashley heard the sound of a man's footsteps stumbling up slope. A search had been instituted just as Lashley had hoped. Someone was trying to ascertain the cause of the disturbance.

Cautiously, Lashley peered around the edge of the shed and stood. He stealthily moved along the down side wall. From the sheath strapped to his leg, he extracted a Bagwell knife. The custom-made weapon boasted an unusually narrow blade. Its length was no more than ten inches, sharpened at the tip as a Bowie knife. It was a deadly weapon. The knife was as much a part of Lashley's attire as his belt. Its purpose was death, and death was now its object.

"Shit," the man closest to the shed hissed. Then came a louder and longer "Shit" directed to the stumbling footsteps on the slope. The hissing muffled Lashley's movements. Locating his target by the sound, Lashley moved with deadly quickness. His final movements were concealed by the next "Shit."

Barely discernible in the darkness, Lashley identified his prey and attacked his target. He covered the man's mouth, jerking the head to the left, bringing the body to his chest. The knife moved upward to the point at the base of the skull. Twisting and sharply piercing, the blade severed the spinal column and drove deeply into the brain.

Death was swift, but not swift enough prevent the reflex action of the man's trigger finger. Six shots clattered from the off-safety automatic weapon before, in death, his hand went limp. The gun clattered to the ground. The impact discharged several additional rounds. There was a brief period of silence.

Lashley lowered the body and retracted his knife. Moving forward, he flattened his body against the steep slope of Trigger Finger.

Startled by the firing at the shed, the man up slope recovered from the shooting, yelled, "Aeeeee" and commenced indiscriminate, erratic firing. Exhausting his thirty shot clip, he stumbled blindly around the rough ground. Then he fell, tumbling like a rolling pin over bread dough.

Lashley, anticipating the fall, moved to intercept. He reached the bruised man, as he came to rest. His knife flashed, catching the downed man in the breast between the ribs. Severing back and forth, vital organs were cut. Death was quick.

Grabbing the jacket collar, Lashley drug the body to the shed. He broke the hasp, opened the door, and placed the body inside. He repeated the process with the other body. Closing the shed door, he was careful to make the hasp appear normal. Collecting both automatic weapons, he moved back to the creek, cautiously walking upstream.

For the past few minutes, a wind moving down the canyon stirred the fog, revealing patches of gray which outlined darker objects. This enabled him to locate the lodge. As he cautiously neared the chords of firewood stacked beside the stoop, he halted. Retrieving a small rock, he tossed it upward. The pebble brought a challenge.

"Davy?" someone asked.

"Crocket," Lashley responded.

"Lashley, is that you?" Mitchell asked.

"Yeah, and for gosh sakes, don't shoot."

"Come on in," the captain invited. As Lashley cleared the narrow opening between the firewood, the officer continued, "Son of a bitch was I startled. What the hell happened? I thought it was D-day all over. Are you okay?"

"Fine," Lashley answered as he slung the two automatics from his shoulder and handed them to Mitchell.

"Stash these somewhere away from prying eyes. Don't let anyone observe you. Stay here at guard duty for a few more minutes until I obtain you some relief."

"What happened?"

"I took two of them out, but we don't have much time to talk about it. Get ready. There's going be a lot of action in a short while," Lashley warned.

Silently, Lashley slipped into the kitchen. At the dining room door, he flashed three times with his flashlight, quickly turning it full into his face. It was a prearranged signal. Any person within the lodge building desiring to move in darkness repeated this process. After identifying their faces, the individual then shined the light in the direction of intended travel, whether toward the restroom or kitchen. The presence of numerous and readily available loaded handguns required the development of a safety system to deter some trigger happy, half asleep, tenderfoot from shooting a wanderer on his way to a bladder relief.

Lashley, following procedures, then pointed the light in the direction of Major Greer, who, in addition to his armory duties, had been designated as the inside control officer. As he wove his way through the guests bedded in the dining hall, muttered questions arose.

"Lashley, what happened?"

"What the fuck's going on? For God's sake, tell us."

At the door, as he entered the south porch, Lashley spoke in a modulated voice. "We think some of the

225

opposition's guards got spooked. Best we can figure they got confused in this fog. Shots weren't directed to the lodge, so it must be just a mistake."

"Were they trying to shoot one of us?" a female voice from the darkness asked.

"Not that we could tell," Lashley lied.

Further away, another question came. "It sounded close. Like it was just off the corner of the lodge."

Lashley continued the fabrication. "Sound carries differently in heavy fog. Besides, we're between two ridges, down in the mouth of a canyon. That also amplifies the sound."

"Scared the shit out of me," someone said. "I'm going to the john."

"Since everybody's awake now," Greer suggested, "let's all take a head break and then settle down. We can move without signals for the next fifteen minutes. Say at one-fifteen we'll reinstate the signal routine. Someone light a lamp. Those closest to the bunkhouse, get moving. I'll bell when curfew commences again."

"Greer, I need your help," Lashley murmured, as he knelt beside the major. The movement brought him level with Patricia Stanford and Myrtle Wallace sitting on the edge of their mattresses.

"You'll get my assistance when you cut the bullshit and start giving some straight answers," the major hissed with hostility. "It's time you lead the blind from darkness to light. Blind men aren't much assistance."

"To the extent I am at liberty to do so, I would gladly oblige. But time is a commodity in short supply. Something big is coming down, and it must have the highest priority," Lashley replied. His low voice caused the trio to strain to listen.

"Our discussion," he continued, "must be in the strictest confidence. No leaks. All the schedules I impose must be strictly adhered to. No deviations. Don't second guess what your instructions mean. None of that famous American ingenuity. It's got to be right by the book. Left, right, left flank, right. Absolute conformity. We've got less then an hour to be ready, and if we fail, there are going to be serious casualties in this lodge. You three are the keystones. Without you, our defense will collapse. Can I extract a promise of absolute confidentiality from you?"

"Yes, you can. It will be absolute," Patricia Stanford spoke for the group, joining her partner's affirming nods.

With unusual candor, Lashley described the time, places, and direction of the danger. It was a grim disclosure. Then he outlined the counter move. It was risky and simple, containing a limited chance of success. But it was the best he had.

"You made a reconnaissance," the major observed. "Those shots were at you."

"More or less," Lashley admitted.

"I suspected as much at the time. How reliable is your information?" Greer inquired.

"Very reliable, I would say. I went out there among them and got it."

"Gutsy," Patricia said.

Lashley shrugged.

"Who else is going to be involved?" Greer asked.

"Only four additional individuals will be included. Surprise is the nature of our defense. Some in our party may not be reliable under pressure, and I believe each of you to be capable of handling the stress of this assignment. Some others in this lodge could get buck fever and become a little trigger happy. Others might break into uncontrollable sobbing at inappropriate times. That will throw our timing off. That's something we can't risk."

"I agree," Stanford responded and continued. "What can we do to implement your plan?"

"During this curfew time, I need some equipment quietly transported to strategic places throughout the lodge. It's a good cover to move certain items with the least possibility of detection."

"What do you need and where?" Stanford asked.

"I need the twelve gauge Remington, the automatic, not the pump, plus a half box of double ought buck shot delivered to my room. Also, a dozen duck shots. If the plug is in the gun, take it out. We need it so it can take a full load."

"I've already thought of that. The plugs are out of all shotguns," Greer responded with pride for his resourcefulness.

"Break it down into two pieces. Miss Stanford, you can run the barrel down your pants leg. And you," he nodded to Myrtle Wallace, "the same with the stock. That should conceal the weapon when you transport it into my room. Leave the dismantled weapon and shells with Paige. Tell her to put them under the mattress. I'll be in shortly."

"What else?" Stanford asked.

"This is a little tricky. The cross bows and ten of the matching arrows. I need them delivered to the pantry. Cover them with a blanket or something. One of you will need to guard the archery equipment until Frenchie or that young cowboy, Cinch, comes. Only those two. Don't give the crossbows to anybody but them. If anyone else comes, tell them to get lost and quick. Be adamant. Don't let anyone else get a look. Frenchie and Cinch only. Understand?"

"Affirmative," Stanford answered.

Lashley was struck by the quickness of the woman's commands. She almost was a more dominating person than the major.

"The hand radio too. I need one delivered to Frenchie at the pantry, one to Paige, and one to Mitchell. Right now he's out under the stoop. I will send a guard out there to relieve him shortly. Brief the captain, and send him directly to me."

"O.K.," Stanford said. "Is that all the equipment you need distributed?"

"Yes,' Lashley said. "Those are the assignments. Frenchie and Cinch will be posted under the stoop as the rear point men for that entrance. You two women will be back up at the rear door."

"It's heavy duty stuff. Can we count on them? Frenchie and a kid cowboy?" Greer asked.

"Frenchie's tough," Lashley quickly responded. "Served in Nam. Saw a lot of action. He's solid and defending his home. Cinch is young. Never served in the military, but he's a skilled hunter. Killing's no novelty for him."

"But killing a man? Well, that's different," Greer said.

"He's the best we've got as a back up. But there's a second line that can't be weaker. You two women, if the guards on the porch fail, you'll need to do some killing. Can you stomach it?"

"Under the circumstances, with our backs to the wall, we'll have to," Stanford said.

"Take the double barrel shot guns with you. If there is a breach at the stoop, don't let anybody enter. Surely, if you can shoot a rifle as well as you have proven on this hunting trip, you can handle other weapons."

"We're both weapons qualified," Stanford answered for the women.

"A couple of other things before we break. Greer, make the rounds when you activate curfew. Congratulate everyone on being calm and holding it down during that last encounter. Reaffirm that if something similar happens again to stay put and keep down. Tell them to follow your instructions only. The guests must remain quiet, so they can receive orders.

And lastly, Mitchell will have a separate assignment, so leave him alone. Any questions?"

"Will it succeed? Can we do it?" Stanford asked.

"Every now and then, even a blind hog gets an acorn," Lashley said.

As he walked through the dining room, Fulcher approached Lashley. "I still know it's me they're after," the hash-jockey stated. "I'm ready to go. Get it over with."

"No, Fulcher, we can't give you up. We're not for sure that your calculations are correct. There could be many other alternatives that could be just as logical. Till we know for sure, we're not going to make any hasty decisions."

"But if I'm right and you're wrong, think how many lives it could save."

"We still have some alternatives. We may beat those outsiders at their own game."

Fulcher thought for a moment, then he added, "But in the meantime, a lot of people will be hurt, and hurt bad."

CHAPTER NINE

The wind whistled as it marched rapidly down the canyon, thumping an offbeat tattoo. Across the chimney top, it played a melody like the sound of a breath over a little brown jug. Back drafting, the dying embers in the fireplace emitted a puff of smoke into the room.

The plug was pulled, and the fog had leaked down into the valley below. It was rapidly replaced by chilled air and tiny flakes of dry snow, whirling in a mad-hatter's, helter-skelter direction. The moonless night darkened the landscape, resembling soot from a chimney. Outside, it was cold. The wind chill factor was near zero degrees.

Another log thrown into the embers would repel the unwelcome chill invading the cracks and crevices of the room. Such relief must wait. Any flame might reveal Howard Lashley lying prone on the shelf over the bed. It would also render him night blind, and that could be fatal. Alternatively, it would allow his opposition a view of the room's interior and its occupants. A cardinal rule: deny the enemy any advantage, no matter how small.

Lashley's face pressed the glass pane, his body extended along the shelf over his bed. He was alert and waiting. Moments before, he had noted the time. It was eight minutes past two. The attack was late. The opposition leadership, identity unknown, was experiencing the same personnel deficiencies Lashley faced, reliance on undisciplined, poorly trained combatants.

From the limited intelligence Lashley had obtained, somewhere out in the darkness, the opposition team was undoubtedly composed of experienced killers, assassins, and thugs. But their talent was restricted to street fighting. Here in the outdoors, in a foreign and hostile element, their cold-blooded nature was dulled.

"You want me to go out in that shit?" "You're crazy," they'd probably argue to their leader. "You ain't paying me enough." "There's an extra thousand in it," the bribes would be offered. Confused over the loss of contact with two team members on point at the tack shed, the leadership would have to improvise. Using threats and bribes, the attack would eventually move forward, thus accounting for the delay and off-timed assault.

Lashley's amateur team had one advantage. Lacking the killer instinct, they were desperate, being hemmed in as they were. For them, there was no retreat. The bully always engages in his toughest fight when he backs a coward into a corner. Would Lashley's backup support surrender when the first hostile shots were fired? It was one thing when shots were fired out side the lodge. That is impersonal. But when an individual was on the receiving end, it becomes crucial. Could his team stand direct fire? He would know soon enough.

Fifteen additional minutes passed before Lashley detected the first movement. A flashlight beam flickered, filtering through a gloved hand and darting about on the ground in its search. In a moment, it was extinguished. Someone needed directions and orientation.

This section of the lodge was U-shaped, with Lashley's room forming the base. To his left were the employees' restrooms, attached to an extended, sloped roof covering a root cellar. Oppositely, the guests' restrooms completed the right arm of the letter. Along the top of the extended arms was the service road leading to the rear of the lodge. The fuel oil tank, off to the right, composed the only structure within the "U." From the road, downward to the foundation of the log building, the slope was exceedingly steep.

Lashley's window, a single pane of glass, constituted the only opening on this portion of the lodge. Lashley recognized the window as the point of attack, but he could only guess at the method. If he were wrong, his defense would collapse in minutes.

"They're coming now," he whispered to Paige St. John as he slid backwards along the shelf, bending his legs. He positioned the shotgun for a hip shot. The first shot in the chamber was a number four duck shot. At such close range, he calculated that the duck shot pattern would dispense into a wider pattern than a buck shot. For additional firing power, the four remaining shells in the magazine were double ought. Stuffing cotton in his ears, he prepared for the onslaught.

Paige, covered with quilts, was crouched in the corner off to the left of the fireplace, using the small oak table for cover. Armed with a .38 Smith and Wessen, she represented the second line of defense should Lashley fail. Depending on a woman as a back up was risky. Even using a woman, with Paige's expertise, who had some weapon familiarity, was dangerous. Hours spent on the pistol range was one thing. Shooting a living, moving target was another task. But everything had to appear normal to the hunting party. If Lashley had assigned anyone else as a secondary guard in his own room, it would have raised inquiries from his fellow hunters. He could not afford that. There were enough nervous individuals in this affair, each with their own ideas for defense.

A signal from Lashley, three clicks on the radio, dispatched the message. The danger is here, the signal reported. Captain Mitchell was posted inside the kitchen door and armed with a twelve gauge, his line of fire covered both the stoop and bedroom door.

Receiving Lashley's message, the captain clicked once in acknowledgment of the signal.

At his station under the stoop, Frenchie Hebert delayed three seconds and clicked once in response. At that moment Lashley heard shots originating from the general direction of the tack shed muffled through his protective plugs. Bullets sprawled along the south porch breaking a boarded, glass window. The attack had begun.

Over the pandemonium, Lashley heard Major Greer shouting. "Stay down! Stay down! Don't move!" The first line of defense had shifted to the guards behind the firewood.

The firing from below the tack shed had been a cleverly staged diversion. Lashley knew the attack at the stoop door was a halfhearted effort, an off chance to penetrate the underbelly of the defending lodge. Lashley's room was the key. If the attackers gained control of this inside room, the defenders would have no alternative but to surrender the lodge.

Camouflaged by the exchange along the south porch, Lashley, through his cotton-plugged ears, detected muffled sounds below the window sill, announcing that a ladder was being positioned. Shades of gray cut across the glass window, contrasting with the darker background. A man's outline was identifiable. Lashley squeezed the trigger, the recoil bruising his thigh. The number four pellets shattered the glass and struck the man just to the left of his nose, tearing flesh and breaking bone and teeth. In the instance of the muzzle flash, Lashley briefly saw the face's hollowed features. The body, pitching backward, fell fifteen feet downward.

"Okay, Paige, okay," he said and slipped along the shelf toward the window. Before he reached it, there was a muffled explosion. An armed stun grenade, intended to immobilize the people inside the room, had fallen with the man to the ground. The plan of attack was designed to break the glass and toss the grenade into the room, temporarily disabling its occupants. Entering after the explosion, the attacker could easily take the disoriented occupants hostage, thus forcing the remainder of the lodge to surrender. But the snake had struck the flute player, biting the hand that fed it. The grenade had fallen among the assault team, inflicting a stunning effect.

At the window, Lashley paused, cautious of exposing his head to the firing. He was leery of traps. Cheek pressed against the window frame, he extended his arm and flicked on a flashlight, resting it on the window sill. The beam of the light faintly illuminated the area within the U. At the foot of the ladder, he saw a crumpled body. On either side of the ladder, men stumbled aimlessly, stunned by the grenade. Two double ought shells were discharged, and the men fell. Lashley had taken them out.

Higher up the slope just at the corner of the building, a figure struggled to escape. A load of buck shot caught him in the lower left leg. He screamed, fell against the wall, and then toppled around the corner out of sight. That was good. Let the wounded carry the message to Garcia. Tell your leader, Lashley thought to himself, that he might win, but it was going to cost him dearly.

Over the radio, he spoke softly, "All secure here." He then received a "Secure" from Frenchie and Mitchell.

"I'm going outside," Lashley said into the mouthpiece. "Mitchell, cover my back side. Keep everyone in place." And he climbed, with care, down the ladder.

Ten minutes later, he returned through the window. Frenchie waited at the door.

"Cinch and I were startled by the first shots. Off the stoop, we detected movement. A shadow appeared in the gap between the stacked firewood. I put an arrow in center of that bastard's chest. The man pitched forward. Behind him, his traveling companion stumbled and Cinch's arrow took this fellow in the windpipe, the shaft exiting through the man's spinal column. Snatching one automatic weapon, Cinch stepped around the firewood and discharged a burst of rounds in the direction of the tack shed. The firing and shouting downhill abruptly halted."

"You did well," Lashley said. "It's time we talked to our guests."

The men entered the dining hall. Frenchie lit a lantern, casting a shadowy glow over the room. All the guests began milling around like sheep in a pen, bleating and babbling.

"Tell us what the fuck's going on," Leo Rich demanded.

"We were attacked, and we beat them off," Lashley responded as a matter of fact.

"You knew it was going to happen, didn't you?" Rich demanded with anger. "You knew and didn't inform us."

Lashley shrugged in the affirmative.

"Son of a bitch, Lashley. I've had it with your arrogant ways. That was the last straw for you."

"Shut up, Leo," R.S. Farrow interjected. "It worked, didn't it? And we are okay, right?"

"Okay my ass," Rich retorted. "I've been scared shitless all night. Bullets and bombs going off like the Fourth of July. And Master Lashley treats us like feudal peasants. I'll not take it anymore. Out with it. What the fuck's going on?"

"It's me they're after," Lewis Fulcher answered, his head hanging to his chest.

"What are you talking about?" Beryl Carter asked.

"In my boat business, I got involved in some drug deals. The deals went sour. These guys out there are from Miami. They are Colombians. They are out to kill me. Murdered one of my boat captains a couple of weeks ago. Shot a crew member and now I'm on their hunting license."

"I don't believe it, Lewis. I've known you since school days. You're not that kind," Farrow said.

"Believe me. It's so. Lashley and I talked. I offered to give myself up. Let them take me and leave the rest of you to go. What's happened thus far to Heather and all of you is just too horrible. I can't live with it. If they don't get me, I'm going to kill myself."

"Lashley," Rich yelled, "it was your choice not to let him give himself up, wasn't it? Each of us should have had a say in that decision. You can't play 'Big Brother' of the Cottonwood. I'm going to toss you out of the rumble seat, you son of a bitch." He moved closer to narrow the distance.

Frenchie stepped between the men and pushed Rich backward. "It was a joint decision, Leo. Not Lashley's alone."

"Wait. Wait," Fulcher pleaded. "Tomorrow at first light, I'm going down there. That'll get it over with."

"Damn right you will," Leo Rich raged. "Dressed like a Christmas turkey with a white flag sticking out your ass. I'll deliver you myself."

"Leo, we can't give up one of our own. It's not right," Farrow pleaded.

"I got no sympathy for that son of a bitch," the car dealer emphatically stated. "He should have stayed out of the drug business. It's his own fault. Whatever he gets, he deserves as far as I'm concerned," Rich continued.

"Leo, have some compassion. We can't sacrifice one man's life to save ours," Farrow said, moving closer to the car dealer to emphasize his point.

"If it's my life or his, you can bet your sweet ass which one it's going to be. I'll dent his dash before I'll let a flake of paint get scraped on my model," Rich answered.

Thyus Harder decided it was time to deal his cards in with Rich. After Grace Hancock's failure to cooperate with Leo's sexual request, he could still make the timber deal fly. "I agree with Leo. Lewis, you've got to go."

"If it was just me, Lewis," Beryl Carter said, "I'd fight it out to the end. But there are women here. We got to protect them. I'll stand with Leo on this issue."

Sober for the first time since the trip commenced, Elliott Thornton interjected his opinion. "Lewis, Katherine and I don't see any alternative for you. If the bell is not here tolled, then it will toll upon your homeward journey. Sooner or later, you will hear death ring for your unfortunate mistake. It's best for the group, you know."

"It's decided. Lashley, you're out voted. Lewis' plugs are no longer a part of our engine. He goes down the hill with no breaks at first light," Rich announced in triumph.

"What if Fulcher goes, gets killed, and he's the wrong man?" Lashley asked. "What then? They're still here and won't leave."

"But I am who they are looking for," Fulcher said.

"No, Fulcher," Lashley responded. "In this case, you're wrong. That group is not looking for you. They're not from Miami or further south. These guys are from New Jersey."

"How do you know that?" Farrow asked.

Lashley tossed a paper on the table. Carter picked it up.

"A parking receipt," he said. "So what does that prove?"

"It's from a garage in New Jersey," Lashley added. "I just took it off a man outside my room."

"Oh God," Farrow stammered. "Oh God, they want me." He fell to the floor, missing a chair as he staggered to be seated. Mitzi Rhodes and Carter helped him up, seating him in a chair.

Here it comes again, Lashley thought. He should take some of this spare lumber, build a confessional, reverse his collar, and set up shop. He would be so busy offering twenty-four hour service that he would have to give up all other entertainment activities, like guard duty and serving on the defense committee.

"It's Angela, Leo. My affair with Angela," Farrow said hoarsely.

Lashley immediately took Farrow, Carter and Rich to his bed room. "Tell us the deal," he said and what he learned was more than he bargained for under the circumstances.

It was several years ago when it started. Farrow was married then, with two children. Farrow's insurance business was growing. He was specializing in commercial casualty coverage for paper and industrial forest plants and writing life policies for special friends. In some way, he became connected with a group interested in the location of a regional waste incinerator on the Gulf Coast. Farrow became the local front man. It was a highly controversial issue attached with substantial publicity. His wife could not take the pressure, divorced him, and moved to Atlanta with the children.

Farrow hung in there. He slugged it out through administrative hearings, countless court battles, and appeals. He received death threats, occurring as often as junk mail and local commercials. His insurance business collapsed when his office was fire bombed. Regular customers were afraid to do business with him. But when the final order was signed, awarding him a state incinerator permit, his luck changed. The big boys in the solid waste industry stepped in, paid him two million cash, allowing him to retain twenty-five percent of the business. As a bonus, he became the insurance broker for a chain of waste incinerators in seven southeastern states. His new, but specialized insurance business soared, exceeding all projections. Best of all, it required limited work. It was a self-feeding business with few claims.

Then Angela entered his life. Her father, based in Newark, New Jersey, was a Mafioso of a national garbage industry. He was a real guru of the waste disposal business. Angela had a Masters Degree in Business Administration from a prestigious, upstate New York college. She wanted a hands-on part of the operation. Not satisfied with being a frilly socialite bitch with a rich father, which more properly described her homosexual brother's ambitions, the balance of her father's heirs, Angela went to work in the family business.

Thirty-one and attractive, with clear dark skin, she waltzed into Farrow's life like a blast off at Cape Canaveral. He was in orbit. Assigned to the Gulf Coast to make the newly permitted incinerator operational, Angela stayed. The sand of St. Andrews filtered into her shoes, while Farrow filtered into her bedroom.

Angela's defiance was displeasing to her father. His long established plans detailed her to serve short apprenticeships in various family facilities to learn the details of operation. Knowing the way management cheats and experiencing pressures from the hard sale, was, to her father, true education. When her father retired or expired, whichever came first, she would be prepared for top leadership, succeeding his lead.

She was a woman endowed with hot-blooded traits, inherited from her old world linage. Her father had watched her numerous affairs from afar. Soon she would settle down, properly marry and have a few bambini, spaced properly so as not to interfere with her career in the home office. Meanwhile, the men in her life were a bother to him, but not a concern. After all, he had survived his own flings before marrying her mother. His was a late marriage at the age of forty. Now at seventy-five, he needed Angela closer to the New Jersey office.

Angela announced she was foregoing her next assignment and would remain in St. Andrews. This announcement was as disturbing to the old man as the discovery that his son was gay. Trusted employees made discrete inquiries about Angela. They returned with the name of Robert Stevenson Farrow. Angela ignored invitations, summons, and even direct orders from her father to return to Newark.

She purchased a penthouse in a luxurious condominium complex and decorated it like a modern American whore house, with mirrors, a Jacuzzi, and waterbeds. Farrow moved in. The first year was bliss. Thereafter, it ebbed like the tide - good, then bad; sweet, then sour; loving, then fighting. Angela was the most possessive woman he had ever known. She selected and purchased his clothes, down to his socks.

Each morning, she pre-selected his attire for that day, even to his casual wear for the weekends. She called him fourteen times a day, either on his cellular telephone or at the office. She furnished him with a beeper for instant contact. Even on the golf course, she paged him constantly. He became an extension of her alter ego, a subservient individual to the dominant personality.

During the months they had lived together, their one separation had occurred during last year's hunting trip to the Cottonwood. Four months earlier, Angela had announced that this year's trip was out. No longer could Farrow associate with the low life that frequented such expeditions. "Find another outlet," she told him.

So they split sixty days ago, through much yelling and broken glass. "Leave me," she threatened, "and I will turn my father's men on you. They'll track you to the ends of the earth." But he left her after continuous threats, tears, and curses.

In retaliation, all regional insurance policies on her family's business were canceled and placed with competitive agencies. Farrow had wisely invested his funds. He figured that with earned interest and his quarterly profits from the incinerator, he was financially sound. To hell with Angela and her family. He found Mitzi Rhodes, a younger, dark-haired, dark-eyed beauty, twenty-five years his junior. A hasty romance commenced.

During long years in the insurance business, Farrow had developed close contacts with the officers at Tyndall Air Force Base. He continued throughout the relationship with Angela to maintain that association. As a reserve Air Force officer assigned to training at nearby Duke Field, he had base privileges. He golfed and socialized on a regular basis with the base commander and other command officers.

It was through Farrow's acquaintances that the first inquiries were made concerning the possibility that Myrtle Wallace and Patricia Stanford might be invited along on this year's hunting expedition. Farrow, forever a braggot, was constantly describing the hunting opportunities at the isolated Cottonwood Guest Lodge. When Tyndall's general expressed an interest for two women under his command to join the expedition, Farrow convinced Leo Rich to extend an invitation for the women and their companions, Major Greer and Captain Mitchell, for the hunt. As the other hunters were bringing companions, it was appropriate that the women likewise invite company.

Out of spite to Angela or through habit, Farrow joined the hunting group with Mitzi in tow. Now Angela was making good on her threat. Her father's mob friends from New Jersey had found him. He, not Fulcher, must make the long death walk. It was he who had recently endorsed Fulcher's sacrifice for the good of the majority. He was trapped. How could he back out?

"Angela's come to kill me," Farrow said softly.

"My God," Rich said. "R.S., I can't send you out to the barn. We've been together too long."

"What do we do?" Carter asked, directing his question to Lashley.

"Get some rest," Lashley said. "Tomorrow will be a busy day."

As they left the room Fulcher asked, "Won't they come again tonight?"

"No, I don't think so," Lashley said. "Their casualties were too high. They'll make an effort to reorganize first. It'll take them till light. But we'll continue to keep our guards up."

"Casualties?" Joel sneeringly echoed from the kitchen door. "Casualties mean killings. So you've killed again, Mr. Lashley?"

Lashley shrugged again. How many killings had there been? Lashley calculated them to be String, the guide; the man on the roof; and the two he knifed at the shed. Add the three dead at the base of the ladder, now hidden under the fuel oil tank and the two beneath the stoop arrowed to death by Hebert and Cinch. These bodies were now hidden under the firewood. He counted a total of nine dead.

How many wounded? On their side: Heather, constant in her comatose state; Dunsey and Thornton, cut. Hostiles: the man he shot in the leg and possibly others on the receiving end of Cinch's shooting. Add a possible five to the casualty list.

"The disease is spreading," Joel reported. "Death is contagious. Soon it will devour all it infects. Vengeance is the Lord's judgment."

Lashley would later discover he had been mistaken. As he retreated for a few hours of sleep, little did he realize he was one short in the body count.

CHAPTER TEN

A pale, gray light announced the dawning. The overcast hung low like a Buddha belly, heavy, full of strength, slow in movement but dangerous. Wayward snow flurries danced in the wind.

Howard Lashley glanced through the peep hole, across the yard beyond the fish pond, to the barn. Nothing moved. It was a few minutes after seven o'clock. No morning calling card had been received.

He studied Grace Hancock's notes. The day before, a pattern had established. During odd hours, shots were fired a few minutes before the hour and the half hour from the barn's upper window. During the even hours, the pattern was reversed. A few minutes after the hour and on the half hour, shots were discharged from a gap off the barn's door frame. What did it mean? This pattern must have some rationality.

"Grace," he said. "You're doing good work."

"What do you make of all of this?" she asked, as she sat on the couch, her personal gear scattered in disarray around her.

"I'm really not sure yet, but any information, no matter how small, can be helpful at the right time."

"There've been no shots this morning," she noted. "Yesterday at this time, they had fired twice. I haven't seen any movement. Do you think they've gone? Left us?"

Lashley shrugged. "We can hope."

"Are any of us going to live through this? I'm worried. I've got a little girl who lives with my mother, but I'm close to her. Love her dearly and visit whenever I can. She needs me. I'm really scared."

The woman looked over her glasses across at him with mournful eyes.

"It's good to be scared, Grace. Keeps you sharp. Hang tough though, and we'll make it," Lashley reassured her.

"Oh, I want to thank you again for saving me from Leo's advances. I wasn't prepared to do what he was demanding. I'll always be grateful for what you did for me. If there's anything I can do to help you, all you have to do is ask. Anything. I mean it, anything."

"Thanks," he said, shrugging his shoulders in acknowledgment, as he moved toward the dining room.

Major Greer and Patricia Stanford were seated, picking at their breakfast. Lashley joined them. Myrtle Wallace, temporarily serving as the armory officer in the Major's absence, was stationed at the billiard table.

"Better eat well," Lashley advised. "I suspect today will be most taxing. You'll need your strength."

Patricia acknowledged the admonishment with a half smile. By appearance, she was holding up well under the stress. Her closely cut hair style demanded little care. The younger women of the hunting party, with their stylish hair designs, were showing more signs of fatigue. Absent the necessary styling products and equipment powered by electricity, their crowns had lost their once buoyant nature as the women adapted, as best as they could, to temporary styles. Patricia was a cool dame. She needed no adaptation.

"Lashley," Greer said, "I must compliment your tactics last evening. Brilliant. Timing, intelligence, and coordination were excellent. I owe you an apology for any previous misunderstanding."

Lashley shrugged in indifference.

"No, you are too modest," Patricia interjected. "I endorse Greer's observation."

"Others performed as requested. They deserve the credit, especially the major's control and dispersion of the weapons. Controlling the guests was essential."

"In the off chance you have not yet been informed, Myrtle Wallace and Pearl Gavin had a run in last night," Patricia advised, as she looked across at Lashley.

He responded, only by returning her stare.

"During the exchange of fire," the Major interjected, "Gavin attempted to leave her assigned area. Using force, Wallace restrained her. Gavin reported to me the circumstances with some trepidation. I gather she is most unhappy and intends to take her charge of excessive force to some higher authority. I suppose that includes you."

Lashley shrugged indifferently.

The major added, "I interrogated Wallace extensively. It was my conclusion her actions were justified. Gavin violated standing orders. She was clearly in the wrong. But I will leave it to your discretion to make the final decision."

"Lashley," Patricia said, bringing the subject to a more difficult stand. "We want you to know that we, the four in our group, support your leadership. We are committed to lending you backup support wherever you think is best."

Lashley nodded. With his coffee mug in hand, he rose to continue his morning rounds.

"Have you tried this venison Crisco fixed this morning?" Lewis Fulcher asked as Lashley passed. "It's superb."

Now that he was no longer volunteering to walk the proverbial plank to the barn to surrender to the adversaries, Fulcher had returned to his former chipper self.

"The cuisine wonders that cook can perform on that wood burning stove are incredible." The restaurateur continued, "There would be no limits to his talents if he worked in a modern equipped kitchen. He could convert trash fish into caviar."

Thyus Harder and Lewis Fulcher approached and requested permission to board up the shattered window in Lashley's room. Lashley quickly granted consent, and the men moved rapidly to fulfill their mission.

Beryl Carter devoured his food as if it was the last meal a few hours shy of the electric chair. R.S. Farrow drowned his sorrows in the bracing bite of cowboy coffee. The men watched indifferently as Lashley approached their table.

"Where are your companions?" Lashley asked.

"My Mitzi is changing Dunsey's bandages. There is some concern that a couple of spots might still contain some residue of glass. Real sore and tender in places," Farrow said, looking upward to the tall man.

"Mitzi, I understand," Lashley said, "is doing a good job. Thank her for me."

"I hear you did a good job last night. Laid them as flat as a parking lot," Carter said.

Lashley shrugged.

"R.S. and me, well," the contractor stuttered, "we support you if you have a showdown with Leo. It won't be easy on our friendship, but we've had competition before. I'll handle him if I have to smash him with my roller and pack him down with my sheep's foot."

Lashley nodded in acceptance. He wondered about the depth of support. Would it disappear as carelessly as it was tendered? Before he moved, Farrow asked, "If it's me they want, I'm ready."

"Stop that talk, R.S.," Carter said. "We ain't giving you up. Me and you, we've talked this out. We can beat that bunch of Ginny goons. Lashley's got it figured, haven't you?"

Lashley shrugged indecisively. Got what figured, Lashley wondered. There were real live, gun-toting killers out there taking a loose knit conglomerate of women and middle-aged men to task. For what motive? Drugs? Jealousies? Vengeance? Was it a dissatisfied purchaser of one of Rich's automobiles? Was either Elliott Thornton or Thyus Harder guilty of an infraction in a real estate transaction? Who else were likely suspects?

Carter's asphalt competitors did not seem likely candidates. All of his contracts would be bonded. All tradesmen would have a legitimate cause of action to obtain financial relief. From all elements considered, Lashley did not figure Carter as the object of the assault.

Conversely, Carter's woman companion, Dunsey Martin, likewise did not appear a choice victim. If it was a jealous boyfriend or ex-husband, the planning would require extensive resources and contacts to recruit a team of out-of-state killers. That appeared to be just a remote possibility. Dunsey's past connections did not seem to be sufficiently funded to undertake such a project.

And what of the youthful Mitzi Rhodes, the olive-skinned, dark-haired beauty? She spoke perfect English but she gave the impression she wasn't native born. Not long a resident of the Gulf Coast, currently employed by a travel agency, she had recently transferred from somewhere up north. She had caught

Farrow, twenty-five years her senior, on the down swing. Working her way into his void spot, she wrangled herself a hunting trip to the west. What was her background before moving to the Bay area? Was it possible that something in Mitzi's past would bridge the connection to this hostility? If such a bridge did exist, Lashley could not fathom its foundation. Possibly, the dark-eyed woman's history would bear some additional scrutiny.

There would not be any heavy losers on Joel Guarimo, the latecomer who was added to the hunt list because of the sudden illness of Tom Harley, Pearl Gavin's brother. A salesman for an electrical supply house, Joel lived over the line in Alabama and was a frequent visitor to St. Andrews. Carter claimed to know the salesman by reputation. Guarimo was accepted by Rich as he was tendered. The receipt of the note from Tom Harley implying he would be most grateful if Carter would add Guarimo to the hunting party was all that was necessary. A Bible thumper did not seem a likely target for a Hispanic hit squad. But today, men of the cloth, as visible as their profession had become through television, were less revered. Was it possible that Guarimo had conned some widow out of her life's savings? Had he been engaged in some failed promise to cure a dying convert? Had he transgressed from the edicts of his church and thus offended its elders? Stranger things had happened. In Miami, some religious guru had been convicted of hiring killers to eliminate wayward members of his congregation. Was Guarimo the target of such revenge? These thoughts were a possibility for Lashley's future exploration.

This assault operation was expensive. How many had been recruited? A minimum of twenty, Lashley figured. With airline tickets and rental cars alone, the cost would run in the tens of thousands of dollars. Killers do not work cheaply or on credit. Plus, calculate the food, weapons, and materials. Someone had shelled out a lot of money to accomplish this hit operation. And for what purpose? Why not a direct swift concerted attack? These lodge defenders would collapse under such pressure, place their tails between their legs and beg for mercy. But mercy would not follow, only death.

There was some rational explanation for the forbearance, but the reason escaped Lashley. A seed was waiting for the heat of germination. Like the cone of a jack pine which remained on a tree for up to twenty-five years until a high fire scorches it, opening the cone to release hundreds of winged seeds, Lashley was waiting for the fire to germinate his thought seeds. He hoped that the fire would not be too hot. If long delayed, it would soar into oblivion his fledgling ideas. Time was a commodity that was quickly being added to the endangered list.

Frenchie approached Lashley as he leaned against the door frame, casually sipping his coffee. Frenchie said, "My employees, Fish, Cinch, and Stumbough, are at their wit's end, what with carrying on the major's guard roster. My crew needs some rest"

Lashley nodded, acknowledging the cowboys' situation. "Carter and Farrow can do it for the next few hours. Send your crew upstairs till noon. That should suffice for now."

"That's good, Lashley," Frenchie responded, as he pivoted to leave.

"Make the arrangements for a shift change," Lashley called after him. "And I'll get Mitchell. I'll meet you over by the front door in a few minutes."

A huffy Pearl Gavin blocked Lashley's way. "That bitch," she stormed, "Myrtle Wallace, she struck me, knocked me down. I'm bruised all over. She hurt me bad."

Lashley, sipping his coffee, stared directly into her hostile eyes, and said nothing.

"What are you going to do about it? That bitch is crazy! I wasn't doing anything. She attacked me for no reason at all."

"When?" he asked.

"Last night when all that shooting was going on, I looked out the door to see what was happening. Just like that, she struck me. Knocked me down and slapped me."

"Why did you open the door?"

"There was shooting and noise. I didn't know what was going on. I needed to know."

"What had you been told?" Lashley inquired, knowing the answer.

"I don't care what I was told. Nobody, and I mean nobody has any right to tell me what to do. This is a free country. I'll do what I damn well please. What are you going to do about her?"

"Give her a medal and tell her the next time to shoot you between the eyes."

Pearl gasped, "You wouldn't dare."

"Try me," Lashley replied. "You think you can do a better job, then you assume command. Until then, you and everybody who has been given an order had better follow their instructions to the letter. If you don't, then accept the consequences."

"You weren't elected," she spit back.

"I took over. This isn't some governing board. It's absolute rule. If you don't like it, pack your bags and join those down at the barn!"

"You son of a bitch," she yelled, raising her hand to strike him.

Instinctively, he caught her wrist. "We're going to break out of here today. You have three choices. One, join the effort. Two, leave on your own. Or three, stay behind. Frankly, I don't care which one you select."

She pivoted and left huffing begrudgingly. "The Lord will judge you harshly"

Crisco tendered Lashley a coffee pot for a refill. Lashley gratefully accepted.

"That's a feisty mare," the cook said. "Someone needs to ride her till she's broke."

Lashley nodded his consent. It was time for his meeting, and he arrived just as the first shot of the morning was fired. Captain Tyrone Mitchell, reviewing a note pad, glanced up at Lashley.

"Where's Frenchie?"

"He'll be here shortly. He's trying to arrange for his men to get a few hours of sleep. This renewed firing won't help any."

"I was reviewing our armament," the young officer said. "I secretly stashed under the stairwell the two automatic weapons you recovered from your reconnaissance mission. This morning, Cinch obtained two similar weapons. They were found last night near the firewood immediately after the attack. These weapons were also stashed under the stairwell. The inventory reflects that in addition to those rounds in the weapons, we have twenty-five extra ammunition clips. That's a substantial amount of fire power."

Lashley nodded, preferring not to disclose two additional identical weapons he had recovered at the foot of the ladder. Now hidden under his bed, their existence, as well as the additional ammunition similarly stashed, would remain a secret for now. In this scenario you could never decide who you could trust.

Frenchie Hebert joined the two men as the captain continued, "As you instructed, disclosure of our control of these weapons has been reconstructed. Those with knowledge are the three of us and Cinch for the time being."

"Who's qualified to use them?" Lashley inquired.

"Somewhere down the line, I doubt Cinch has ever received training on similar weapons. I'll check. But he is a natural with firearms. Additionally, I received extensive weapon training. I'm not certain, but I suspect that Myrtle Wallace is qualified. I never asked, but she appears to be a marksman on numerous weapons.

"I'll assume that Wallace qualifies. Check it out first. You take one, and when Wilkinson is rested, issue him one. We'll disclose the existence of those two weapons only. The information that our fire power has substantially increased might be some comfort to those on our side. Let Greer do the issuing. Go through the channels when we are ready to disclose the weapons."

"What about you, Frenchie? Any report?" Lashley asked."

"Yea. Just before dawn, off by Sleeping Camel Rock, Stumbough thought he saw more vehicle lights inbound. There's still some fog down in the valley, but he's pretty sure he saw them."

"Additional reinforcement?" the captain asked.

Lashley shrugged, expressing uncertainty. "How do you evaluate our situation?" He directed the question to the officer.

"The morale is high this morning, reflecting unqualified support for the successful operation of last evening. Personnel are tired due to confinement and lack of sleep. By noon today, I expect we will experience bickering and disharmony as the pendulum swings."

"What is your analysis of our opposition?" Lashley asked the guide.

"I know more about a rodeo goat than I do about what's happening here at the Cottonwood," the guide responded. "This whole thing's as unbelievable as if we'd been chewing loco weeds. I'm riding side saddle and backwards."

"Mitchell?" Lashley asked.

"Some actions I understand, others baffle me. The methodical firing keeps us off balance. Guards on the ridges and to our rear keep us pinned down, minimizing our options.

"Their first probe to disable our chimneys was poorly and hastily implemented. Although, if it had succeeded, it would have been effective. The strategy to terminate our ability to cook and limit our heating capacity would have deteriorated morale rapidly.

"The second attack," the captain continued, "was well planned and executed. Its chance for success was high. Your reconnaissance thwarted the assault. Afforded us an opportunity to establish perimeters of defense. The simplicity of the defense minimized mistakes on our part, thus assuring success."

"What are your concerns?" Lashley asked.

"Their fire power," Mitchell responded. "It's superior to ours. Their personnel do not appear equal to trained operatives. But within the limits of their assigned mission, they are adequate."

"What do you see as their mission?" Lashley continued to seek the opinion of the captain.

"That's the most confusing evaluation. As a long range goal, I envision a total unified assault timed to work the various units uniformly. It could overpower our position. In point of casualties, it could be costly but not more than last night's effort."

Lashley nodded his approval. The captain was smart, and he continued to impress Lashley.

"Fire was an early alternative I considered but rejected," the officer proceeded. "Fire has limitations.

Remote as the Cottonwood might appear, the openness of this country would reflect a fire for fifty miles around. So fire seems a remote possibility, because it would bring in the curious. If fire was an option, that fog last night would have given the best cover. It would not have been visible at any great distance."

"Any other possibilities?" Lashley asked.

"Yes," the officer replied. "There is either some object or person in this lodge they're after. They don't want the object damaged, or it's someone they want captured alive."

"You have anything of additional sufficient interest at the Cottonwood that would motivate such violence? Something you didn't tell us before?" Lashley asked as he turned his attention to the owner of the lodge.

"Hell," Frenchie replied. "This whole thing don't make sense to me. I've been thinking it over since you first asked. I got one bull worth a couple of thousand. If they wanted him, they'd slip in on a couple of horses and drive him out to a hidden truck. That's how rustlers do it now-a-days. Of course, the Cottonwood is unique in one aspect. It's two sections of land, twelve hundred and eighty acres, surrounded by government-owned lands. Over the years, lots of ranchers that have government leasing rights have tried to buy."

"Other possibilities?" Lashley asked, stirring in his chair.

"Last spring, there were some prospectors through here. Maybe they found something. The old silver mine in the Thumb was played out in the twenties. During World War II, the government worked it for a while but nothing ever came of it. Besides, if anyone wanted the Cottonwood, they would bushwhack me on a trip to Alcova and buy the lodge from my estate. My younguns' left with their mamma more than twenty years ago. Not one of them ever visited the Cottonwood after their mamma took them and lit out. With me gone, you could buy the Cottonwood at auction on the courthouse steps."

"Prospectors find anything?" Mitchell asked.

"Not that I know of," Frenchie answered. "But them kinda fellas don't never say a word. They just ask permission to crack a few rocks and dig a couple holes, that kinda stuff. Then they disappear like flushed grouse."

"Any oil prospects?" the captain asked.

"Not as I know right here. Some wells to the north and east. But out there on the plains, down in the valley, there are dry holes as far as I ever heard. Course there's rumors that they were capped off, so they'd get cheaper leases from adjoining land owners. But the government owns that. So how does that help?"

"Anything else?" Lashley inquired.

"My grampy's gun collection. I've got it hidden behind a false wall."

"Who knows about it?" Lashley asked.

The owner pondered before he replied. "Years ago I used to take some pieces to gun shows. Never the whole wad. There's Sharps and early Colts and Navys in the collection. Those fellows that run that gun museum up in Cody, they have a complete list. I give them first buying rights should I ever decide to sell. When this attack gets out, it'll ruin the Cottonwood as a hunting lodge and dude ranch. To pay my notes, I'll be forced to sell my collection."

"Any idea of their value?" Mitchell asked.

"Ten years ago, I was offered one hundred fifty thousand. There's some real rare pieces in the lot. So even back then that was a low ball figure. Much more today. Maybe half a million. Even more to a hard core collector, one who specializes in rare pieces."

"What do you think?" Mitchell asked.

Lashley returned a noncommittal shrug.

"Then that doesn't eliminate a person as the target," the young officer interjected. "After my briefing on Fulcher's recitation, I'm still confused. But I figured he considered himself a prime suspect. Anything to substantiate his conclusion?"

Lashley responded with a negative head shake.

"You that certain?" the captain asked.

Lashley nodded this time affirmatively. He was certain. Accidentally, he had been at the far end of the restaurant when the Colombian, Fulcher, and the boat captain had their final meal. His booth afforded a clear view of the men. With lip reading, a skill acquired in his pre-Five-Pines life, he monitored sufficient details from their conversation. Intuitively, he realized Fulcher's peril but retrieved no details.

Fulcher was one of the first locals Lashley met after his hasty departure from the Five Pines and relocation to the Bay area. He liked the man, enjoyed his wit and companionship on the previous hunting trip. Fulcher had always given him advice and reliable information when requested. It always proved sound and effective. He never pried into Lashley's past. Fulcher accepted him at face value. Now it was pay back time.

The Hispanic had led Lashley east; through the Panhandle of Florida, along 1-10, south on 1-75, then forked left onto the Sunshine Parkway. The trail terminated in a seedy area of Miami. For several days, Lashley tracked and observed the man, his companions, and their headquarters located in a rundown, partly vacant, strip mall. After four days, he returned to St. Andrews and waited.

The same day the deck hand was shot and the boat captain's throat was slit, an attempt was made on

Fulcher's life, but the restaurateur was never aware of the assault. Closing the establishment at two o'clock a.m. on a Sunday morning, as he walked across the parking lot to his car, Fulcher failed to observe a man crouching in the azalea bushes. Nor did he see the swift moving knife that ended the would-be assailant's life.

Two days later, a series of fire bombings occurred in a strip mall in Miami. This triggered a drug war. Before it was under control, thirteen bodies lined Dade County's streets. The survivor's attention was directed to reconstructing their operation. St. Andrews was a long forgotten matter.

Fulcher, contrary to his fears, was no longer the bull's-eye for a soured drug deal. Unless the drug lords had recovered faster than Lashley had calculated, Fulcher was a free agent again. Lashley had listened to the man's account of his drug involvement to discover if some new element had developed.

"What about Farrow then and his 'fatal attraction' scenario?" the captain asked with skepticism ringing in his voice.

"That's one I'm not certain about," Lashley answered. "Territory disputes over garbage routes, they'll spill blood over that. Jealousy over a spoiled love affair? Sometimes, but not out in the open where it would involve other people. Mafiosos are too concerned about public relations. Don't take any chances that would bring adverse news coverage. If they wanted Farrow, they'd take him out in some quiet remote place and deposit his carcass in some incinerator they operate. He'd never be found. Remember Jimmy Hoffa? That's more their style. However, all the elements fit. New Jersey connections and all that. At this point, it can't be rejected."

"Whatever they're looking for, they're tenacious about it," the captain said.

"How's that?" Frenchie asked.

"If they were quitters," Mitchell answered, "they would have departed this morning. They took a beating last night. Suffered high casualties, considering the size of their force. How many can they have? Twenty or thirty tops? They've lost a third to a half of their personnel. Even with reinforcement, it's tough. Also consider the firepower we've gained. The odds have shifted somewhat. Unless they switch to explosives, with these automatic weapons now under our control, they face a tough fight to overrun this position. How are they set up for defense as you see it, Lashley?"

"As best as I can determine, the guards are only spotters," Lashley responded. "Those in the barn are the harassers. I figure that their sleeping quarters and food operation has been established in the new house at the north end of the little runway. That's the only place that's warm enough with cooking facilities and bunk space. There's a road along the butt of the cliff running toward that house. Below this butt is where I figure they are hiding their vehicles. They're shuffling the change of the guards between headquarters and the barn, staying below the rim, out of our sight. It keeps us from spotting any of their movement. Outside guards are replaced every three hours by those dirt bikes we hear. I would figure they miscalculated on a siege of this duration. So they are short on food and other supplies. Possibly the incoming vehicles of this morning will have additional supplies. But even that can't be adequate to sustain them much longer. So whatever they are planning, it's got to be done shortly. Time is now our ally at this point."

"What now?" Mitchell asked.

"I have a plan. It's still in the womb, not fertilized yet. It needs a few more lures to make it attractive. When it's impregnated, I'll let you know."

"In the meantime, we hope and pray Chainsaw gets through," the captain said.

Lashley did not respond. He observed Beryl Carter leave his guard post by the front door and approach the committee.

"There's a horse coming up from the gate by the fish pond," he whispered. "Someone's hanging across its back."

CHAPTER ELEVEN

Under the stoop, Howard Lashley and Frenchie Hebert watched through gaps in the firewood. The horse had stopped at the far side of the tack shed. Without a saddle, the horse's gear was limited to a halter. After a few moments, the animal dropped its head and nibbled on sparse sprigs of grass.

"What do you figure?" Frenchie asked, watching the horse's burden.

At this distance, a man appeared to be draped across the animal's back. All that was visible was a pair of legs and his backside. The rest of the body was on the horse's off side.

Lashley started to shrug, thought better of it, then said, "I'm certain that's Chainsaw tied to the horse's back."

"Oh, shit," Frenchie moaned in disgust. "Shit. Shit. Shit! How bad's he hurt?"

"Can't see from here. But he's not moving. Could be unconscious."

From inside, Major Greer's muffled voice was heard barking commands. "Back to your post! Away from the peep holes! Back to your assignments!"

A shot echoed up the canyon, reverberating between the Thumb and Trigger Finger. The bullet ricocheted, crossing rocks at the horse's muzzle. The horse shimmied sideways a few steps, angled forward, and then halted again. A second shot echoed, spooking the horse. It ambled to within a few steps of the stoop.

"They want us to collect the baggage," Frenchie said with a lack of enthusiasm and dread.

"I'll go," Lashley volunteered, as he moved forward.

"No," Frenchie restrained him, catching his arm with force. "The horse knows me. He might shy from you. Besides, if it's a trick to pick us off one by one, better me than you."

Clucking a familiar tune, the head guide stepped cautiously toward the squeamish animal, caught the halter, and stroked its muzzle. Cooing words of encouragement, he led the mare to the edge of the stoop, beside the firewood, where Lashley waited.

Lashley stepped out, and his knife slashed the rope that bound the limp body's hands to his feet. Together, the men lowered the figure. Lashley knew instantly that Chainsaw Poulen was dead.

Lashley handed Frenchie a short rope he had located. "Tie the horse."

Frenchie complied and knelt beside Lashley, who was examining the body. "He's dead, isn't he?" Frenchie asked. "Somebody blew out his lantern."

Lashley nodded. Chainsaw's face was a disarray of bruises, blood, and cuts. One eye was swollen shut. His features were almost unrecognizable. One arm was bent obliquely, broken by a brute force. Blood stains soiled his clothing. His torture had been excessive. When death finally came, it was probably received as a welcome friend.

A wave of rage swept over him. Lashley grieved for the loss. A hero's wreath would never crown this fallen comrade's head. But Chainsaw deserved one. His final hours of life had been sacrificed for friendship.

"It's my fault. I should have listened to you. Shouldn't have insisted Chainsaw go for help," the head guide expressed his heartfelt guilt.

"We'll have none of that guilt trip, Frenchie. Chainsaw wanted to go. Neither of us could have stopped him once he'd made up his mind. It's happened. We'll make the best of it," Lashley added. "Our job is to stay alive long enough to avenge his death."

"What will we do with him?" Frenchie asked. "Can't take him inside. That would upset the women. I'll be damned if I'll leave him in that graveyard of hoodlums we've started out back. Get a blanket, and we'll place him on the down side of this wood pile. We'll only be exposed to the gunman on the Trigger side for a few seconds. The guard is nearly three hundred yards out. Unless they have recruited better marksmen, we'll be safe enough."

The few minutes required for Chainsaw to be concealed under hastily stacked wood were charged with emotion. Guilt hung like a curtain. Though he had cautioned the guide to harbor no guilt, Lashley could not shake his responsibility in the decision. He had invited his friend Chainsaw to sign on as a guide for this hunt and had failed to veto the escape attempt.

Frenchie had failed to discourage Chainsaw's decision to walk out the back door to reach help. Both men shared the responsibility. A shift in decisions either way would have saved his life. Frenchie, he knew, would wrestle with his weakness in succumbing to Leo Rich's demand that a messenger must be dispatched. Regardless of Chainsaw's insistence, he should have listened to Lashley's superior reasoning.

"What now?" Frenchie asked when the disdainful task was completed.

"We must explain to the group," Lashley replied. "They have seen enough to suspect. We can't cover this one up."

"Will you do the explaining? I don't have the stomach for it," Frenchie asked with his accustomed caution.

Squatting in the kitchen door, Lashley addressed the gathering seated around the dining tables. Excluding the injured Heather Baldwin, Beryl Carter and R.S. Farrow at guard post, and the employees asleep in the loft, all of the occupants of the lodge were present. Crisco and Ray Horne, while attending their duties in the kitchen, listened attentively. In spite of near round the clock duties of administering to the lodge's needs, these two cooks, of all the staff, seemed the least stressed. Active duties kept their hands occupied, or perhaps the events were being blocked from their minds, much like Lashley's memory.

The group was uneasy. There was something amidst in the air. Coffee mugs clanked noisily. Chairs were pushed along the floor. The nerves of all were set on edge. It was like members of a class keeping their eyes on the clock, waiting for the conclusion of the lecture. Each time Lashley and Frenchie had brought them together, a disaster loomed like a duck landing along side a blind.

"Chainsaw was on that horse. They sent him back to us. He's dead." Lashley spoke matter-of-factly and paused. "He did the best he could do for us," he conceded at long last. He again paused and looked around the group, then added, "That he didn't succeed takes nothing away from his sacrifice."

An astonished hunter from the far side of the room said, "May he rest in peace."

From her post on the porch, Grace Hancock broke into sobs. Dunsey Martin and Mitzi Rhodes moved to comfort her.

"We killed one of them, and now they kill one of ours," Joel Guarimo preached. "The disease of death is spreading—it's contagious. Soon we will all be afflicted. Only the Lord serves. Turn to Jesus in our time of need. The voice of prayer is still louder than the noise of guns."

Surprisingly, Lewis Fulcher, uncharacteristically, spoke first. "Shut up Joel. One more sermon from you, and I'm going to jam that Bible down your throat. See if that won't muffle your babbling."

"Ask the Lord for guidance..."Guarimo urged.

"Cut it out," Thyus Harder interjected, directing his wrath likewise to Guarimo, cutting him in mid speech. "Let's hear Lashley out without violence between ourselves. Lashley's got more to tell us."

"How did he die?" Major Greer inquired.

"It's possible he fell from his horse in the dark, and they found his body," Lashley lied with this prompt reply. "There's no evidence that he was shot. But he was severely bruised. That's all we know."

Torture killed Chainsaw in a slow methodical way. Cigarette burns, severely bruised flesh, and broken teeth attested to the method and longevity of the torture. Revealing the details would not benefit this audience.

"Since we can't get out, we need to send them an ambassador. Talk it out. Reason with them," Leo Rich said, standing, then moving closer to the kneeling Lashley. "Everything has an operational manual. If you read it, you can repair most everything."

"How do you propose that?" Thyus Harder asked.

"Send someone out under a white flag of truce," Rich responded. "Talk to them. Come back and report on their demands. When we know what they want, it will be easier to compromise. Right now, we're moving around like bumper cars at the county fair. We don't know which way to turn. Ask what they want, and then we'll know what the deal is."

"It's too risky," Lashley said. He rose to meet the challenge from Rich.

Staring, he looked the car dealer eye to eye, or in more mechanical terms, headlight to headlight, as Rich would have specified the confrontation.

"Risky or not, we've got to get bumper to bumper with them. Race our motors, and talk it out," Leo defended. "It's like playing chicken with your auto. Start at the opposite end of a field. Race head on at full speed. First one to turn aside loses. We have to make those at the barn blink. Turn aside."

Lashley shook his head negatively. "It won't do. We don't need any more casualties. What you are suggesting is haste. Like the biblical reference to demon-possessed pigs running head on into the sea. We can't be like that."

"Then what the hell are we going to do? Sit on our bucket seats until the upholstery wears thread bare, the air leaks out of our tires, and we can't move? We've got to be affirmative, not a stalled contestant in a demolition derby." Rich was now speaking quite audibly.

"By noon, we will have a workable plan." Lashley compounded his lie. "It will take commitment from all parties. Until then, let's clean up our area and store our sleeping gear out of the way."

"I'm tired of you giving me orders," Rich yelled and accentuated his message with an appropriate obscene gesture, a rigid middle finger. He retreated to the bar and poured himself a straight bourbon, a direct frontal to Major Greer and his military authority. The officer had previously closed the lodge to all drinking. Drinking and driving do not mix. Neither do guns and alcohol. Even Elliott Thornton and Katherine Pace were complying with the 18th Amendment.

"What if they attack before noon? What then?" Harder asked.

"We'll repel them the best we can," Lashley responded. "Our fire power has increased. We now have two automatic weapons added to our arsenal." Again, he lied, but continued, "These weapons have been assigned to Captain Mitchell and Cinch

Wilkinson. Each is qualified with that specific weapon's use. These automatics will be used solely for defense and only if there is a determined out and out assault on the lodge."

"There's one thing I want to know, Lashley," Leo Rich spit out bitterly from the bar. "Who hired you as chief mechanic of this shop? Who handed you the golden wrench?"

Lashley stared him straight in the eyes. Even in the distance, Lashley was unflinching. "Nobody. It was lying on the floor, and I picked it up. Until somebody is ready to fight me for it, I'm going to keep it. Any more questions?"

His cold eyes swept the room seeking other challengers. Rich almost spoke, but changed his mind as Mitzi placed her arm around his waist. He mumbled under his breath as he broke the embrace and left the bar for the east porch.

"Let's all get back to our posts." Lashley said, and the assembly separated, each member returning to their assigned chores.

"Paige," Lashley called. "Relieve Miss Hancock, and ask her to join me, please."

Answering her summons, Grace Hancock found Lashley in a corner of the dining hall in conversation with Captain Tyrone Mitchell.

"Miss Hancock," Lashley said.

"Grace, please. I thought we had that understanding before," she interrupted.

"Okay, Grace. Mitchell and I have a job that will require your assistance. Before we engage your support, we need your assurance that what you observe will remain strictly confidential. You cannot discuss it with anyone, save us two. Not until you are released by either Mitchell or myself. That includes Paige, and I mean everyone. Do you understand?"

Shaking sorrowfully, she said, "Not really. I still don't understand any of this. But as far as talking, I won't. I understand that much. You have my word."

Lashley prodded, "You told me once that if I ever needed your assistance, I could count on you. We need you now, Grace. I know you won't let us down."

"I'm in for a penny, in for a pound," she said, adding humorously, "and I have a few extra of those." She placed her hands on her hips for emphasis.

Lashley smiled. "Okay. The captain and I are going in to give Heather a physical exam. I don't want anyone to say that in her physical condition we abused her. You are to be an impartial witness. Do you understand?" Lashley said, trying to be explicit.

"I think so, but isn't that going to make Pearl mad?" Grace asked. "After all, she's taken the burden of nursing Heather through this ordeal? Of course Paige and Mitzi have helped, but Pearl has taken the blunt of the work."

"She may be unhappy, but this has to be done for reasons I can't explain. So let's get on with the job," he responded.

Pearl Gavin answered their knock. Her eyebrows raised in confusion. "Lashley, what do you want?" she asked with an unaccustomed edge in her voice.

"For the next thirty minutes or so we will require the use of this room. I'd like you to take a break for a while," he responded.

"Heather can't be left to the likes of you. I won't have it. Go somewhere else to hatch your little conspiracies. Leave me with the Lord's work."

"It won't take long," Lashley insisted. "You could use a break."

"This is my room and my personal effects. I won't leave them or Heather with you."

Lashley shouldered passed her, dragging behind him a reluctant Grace Hancock inside the room. "Captain asked Miss Wallace to join us for a moment."

Momentarily, the black woman appeared at the front doorway accompanied by the captain. After Lashley instructed her, Myrtle Wallace beckoned Pearl with her finger. Resistance was short lived. Surrendering to a twisted arm, Pearl left.

Approaching the bed, Mitchell curiously checked the reclining Heather Baldwin. Her pulse was normal, and she had no fever. With a cold, wet cloth, he washed her face. She awoke, staring at him with glassy eyes. He whispered to her, "Heather, can you hear me? Nod if you can."

There was no reaction. Her eyes dropped closed. He slapped her cheeks firmly. "Wake up," he pled. "Hear me."

Her eyes fluttered open but remained out of focus. She stared. He moistened her throat with the cold cloth. She blinked. Her hand moved upward resisting the shock. He moved the cloth behind her neck. She blinked again and sputtered.

"What do you think?" Mitchell asked.

"I think she's drugged. Someone is slipping her periodic medication to keep her in a stupor." Lashley answered reflecting on those first few days when he had awakened at Five Pines. It had been a drowsy, listless feeling, accentuated by a limited ability to function. Reduced mobility prevailed until he had resisted further medication. His rapid recovery followed. He now saw a similar condition reflected in the infirm woman, a listless creature, spoon fed and carried to the bathroom four times daily.

"That's also my opinion," the captain said. "Let's check."

As discretely as circumstances allowed, they checked her wrists, arms, buttocks, legs, and feet. There were no puncture marks. Again, the process was repeated, unsuccessfully.

"Heather," the captain repeated. "Can you hear me?"

This time there was a slight nod. "Good," he acknowledged. "Grace here is going to help you over to the chair. I want you to sit there for a few minutes. We'll be quick."

Slumped forward for support, Heather sat in the high backed chair, staring through glassy eyes as the men's systematically searched the room. Methodically, the mattresses were flipped, corners explored, and drawers opened. A loose stone in the fireplace was removed and a cylinder checked, before returning it to its original position. Additional objects were found, examined, and replaced. As quickly as it had commenced, the search ended.

"Grace," Lashley said. "That's it. Let's get her dressed in some street clothes so she can be moved around. We are going to attempt to sober her up."

"What's going on?" Grace asked. She pushed her glasses up on her forehead, her eager eyes closely examining Lashley.

"For now, you don't need to know, Grace. Trust me, please. In the shortest of time, it will come out. Right now, it is sealed, okay?"

"Okay," she answered, helpless in her frustration.

"Get some help to take her to the restroom. Then sit her at the kitchen table. Get as much of Crisco's broth and any fluids down her as you can. She needs strength. Sober her up. She must flush those drugs out of her body."

Answering a call, Dunsey Martin broke away from Beryl Carter and entered to assist Grace.

As the men adjourned across the passage into the pantry, Captain Mitchell caught Lashley firmly by the arm and faced him. "It's show time, pal," the officer said. "The curtain just went up. I've looked at Act One, and I don't like this play. I need a program, so I can understand the plot and line up the actors. If it doesn't get any better, I might not be around after intermission."

Lashley gave a noncommittal shrug.

"That's bullshit," Mitchell gruffly responded. "I'm tired of it. You knew what we'd find before we searched that room. I've been the shrill for your con game long enough. Either you level with me, or I'm going to take my ball and start another team."

Shots and shouts interrupted their dialogue. Oh shit, Lashley thought. Had the assault begun? The defenders were unprepared. He retrieved his rifle and joined Frenchie who had already departed for the front porch.

At the front door, Carter moved aside for Lashley's observation through the peep hole. On the ground, thirty-five feet down from the corner of the house, a man lay with a white cloth crumpled over him like a fallen flag.

"It's Elliott," Carter said. "He came around that corner of the lodge waiving that pillow case. It was like a truce. A surrender or something. They shot him. He went down like a sack of cement."

Crouched to his right, Lashley heard Frenchie speak. "He's alive! He's moving."

"How did he get outside?" Lashley asked. "Who let him through the door?"

"It wasn't through here," Carter defended. "Must have been from out back. I understand Rich relieved Farrow at the stoop a few minutes ago."

"Greer," Lashley yelled. "Front and center. Frenchie, get Wilkinson down here now."

When the major arrived, he ordered, "Get everybody off the porch into the dining hall, except Carter. He stays on guard. Keep tight control. It's going to be rough for the next several minutes."

While the parties shifted, Lashley said, "Carter, you take the corner point at the far end of the porch. Just observe. Don't shoot no matter what happens. Is that clear?" Lashley received an affirmative nod and said, "Now move out."

Greer returned reporting the news that the porches were cleared. The guests were stationed in the dining hall, down on the floor.

"I need two thirty thirtys and two boxes of soft nosed ammo. Quick," Lashley instructed the major who rapidly departed to comply.

Stuffing his shirt in his pants, Cinch Wilkinson, barely awake, arrived panting and grunting. The young cowboy knelt down by Lashley. Mitchell approached from the doorway also crouching beside Lashley.

"I'm going out," Lashley said, "and bring him in."

You can't," Frenchie responded gruffly. "It's too dangerous. If they shot him, they'll get you. It's too risky."

"I understand the risk, but we can't leave him there. Bad for morale. I need some covering fire," Lashley said. "And only to the barn. The shooters in the barn must be penned down. Those guys out on the point of the Fingers are too remote. It'll be a lucky shot if they could zero a target from that distance. Especially if they are using automatic weapons. From what we have seen thus far, there aren't many marksmen out there."

Upon his return from the armory, Greer reached over the kneeling men, and handed Lashley two 30.30 Winchesters together with two boxes of soft nosed cartridges. Lashley, in turn, handed one to the young cowboy, Cinch, and tendered the second to the captain.

"That man out there on the ground needs assistance. I'm going after him. Can I count on you to stay on my team long enough to complete this task?" Lashley asked Mitchell. He looked the officer dead in the eyes.

"I'll stay that long," he responded indeterminately.

"Shit," Cinch said gruffly as he examined his rifle. "We'll need the thirty ought sixes with steel nosed cartridges. These Winchesters don't have the power you need. These soft noses won't cut through the barn's siding at this distance."

"Cinch, don't start your nagging. There's a purpose to this," Lashley said, moving forward to a peephole. "It's only cover fire," he continued. "Your target is that upper barn window. Keep them penned down. Shoot eighteen inches wide and the same distance off from the lower left-hand corner. Mitchell, you're to cover the barn door, same dimensions but peg your base shot right of the door hinges. All shots are to be wide. I only want cover, no casualties. Okay?

Now Frenchie, you cover my back side from the edge of the stoop. You two," indicating to Cinch and the captain, "don't shoot until Carter yells that I've cleared the down corner of the lodge. Space your shots at five second intervals. Do a walk down to your assigned base target with each shot. Give some spread. Don't let them suspect how well you can shoot."

Cinch smiled, "It looks like you're trying to steal the honey from the bee hive without pissing the bees off."

Lashley returned the smile, slapping the youth on the shoulder as he moved away. He halted long enough to instruct Carter on his assignment.

Back at the stoop, as Lashley prepared to step outside, Frenchie restrained him. "What the hell you doing? Those thirty thirties ain't gonna penetrate that barn siding."

"I know that. It's only a diversion. But it's what we need. Cover me now."

Lashley stepped between the firewood, moved quickly to the left, and jumped the creek, taking cover behind the beer cooler. Rolling sideways, he struck the lodge's south log wall. Elbowing along the foundation, he reached the corner, sprang up, and vaulted thirty feet. Exerting every ounce of reserved energy, he dove beside the wounded man, and in doing so reached his goal with a scant margin of safety. A bullet struck the ground six feet off to the right.

Elliott Thornton moaned. A left shoulder wound, Lashley noted. The injury was serious but not fatal. That was, if medical attention was not long delayed. He wiggled under the man, shifting the body for a fireman's haul. Behind him, shots spit from the lodge's porch. He rose to his knees, staggered to a crouch, and moved for the up side cover of the tack shed.

"Movement at the corner," he heard Carter yell.

Lashley hoped his action would activate the captain. Mitchell should revert back to his own personal combat routine. He would think to himself: breathe, hold it. Squeeze the trigger. Six inches for height, adjust. One thousand one, one thousand two, one thousand three, one thousand four, one thousand five. Shoot again. For the second shot, repeat the process. Eighteen by eighteen inch target. Just right off center, eighteen inches. Close in on the target. Squeeze. Repeat the process. One thousand one, one thousand two. His instincts were right as the captain's shots poured over his position.

As Lashley gathered his strength he pondered his options. Elliott had pulled this dumb trick just when the captain must have thought he had cornered Lashley. Mitchell figured he had Lashley in a bind. And he was just about right. The point was close where he would have to cough up all he suspected or he would lose Mitchell's support. It was a tough trade for him. The point had arrived where he would have to tell what the search of Pearl's room had meant. He was shocked at their discovery, the wealth of treachery. The discoveries were more than he expected to find. If he wanted Mitchell's continued support, it was time he coughed up the truth.

Lashley shouldered the man and stood. Staggering toward the shed, his balance deserted him. Missing a step as he crossed the stream, he landed in the chilly water. Quickly Frenchie was beside him, wallowing on his belly, in the water. Together, they drug Elliott to cover behind the shed.

"I told you to wait,' Lashley said between heavy breaths.

"You can't have all the glory. There's more than one winner in every rodeo," Frenchie responded. "Let's go the final steps. Ready."

Together they lifted Elliott and dashed for the lodge.

Elliott was placed on a cot in the pantry.

Dark-eyed Mitzi Rhodes bandaged Elliott's wound while his sweetheart, Katherine Pace, wrung her hands and moaned. The shot had entered the lower shoulder, exiting upward and shattering the shoulder bone during its exit. Elliott should survive, Lashley thought, but it would take some corrective work on the bone. Shock was of grave concern, the real killer following any trauma.

In the kitchen, Lashley stopped beside Grace, who was spooning soup to Heather. "How's she doing?" he asked, watching the process. The ill woman groaned openly. Grace, extremely perturbed, wrinkled her forehead. She leaned over, and with little success, tried to comfort and quiet the woman. The woman moaned again.

"Better, I think. She's responding some, but it's slow. I keep thinking she's going to be sick on me," Grace smiled blandly.

"Get more food down to her. And fluids. Walk her. Get one of the men to help. The more exercise, the better. We must work the drugs out of her system." He shivered in his wet clothing.

"She'll get it, but Pearl has been hassling me. What do I do?" Grace inquired.

"When she shows up the next time, call Myrtle Wallace. She'll keep Miss Gavin away."

After Lashley changed into dry clothes, it required considerable effort for him to separate Rich from the herd. It was like cutting out a calf for branding. Once a yearling watches a couple of his four-legged companions go under the hot iron, he reacts mighty shyly. Rich saw it coming and used one excuse after another to avoid the confrontation. Finally, Lashley had him cornered in the dining room. Sensing the situation, Rich moved around on his feet like a punch drunk prize fighter. Lashley stared him down.

"What's causing your plugs to skip?" Rich asked, trying to be indifferent but failing in his attempt.

"How did Thornton get outside?" Lashley impatiently asked the car dealer.

"I let him through," Rich grimaced under the staring eyes, "Elliott insisted. How was I to stop him? I couldn't shoot him." He was lying and knew Lashley was aware of the fabrication.

"Why didn't you call me before you let him out?" Lashley pressed.

"You were inside that room with Heather. I figured you were getting a cheap feel and you didn't want to be disturbed," he responded flippantly, running his fingers through his hair.

"Rich, I'd already warned you what could happen. That someone could get seriously hurt," Lashley stated, ignoring the gig.

"Yea, well maybe you said something like that. But I didn't put too much thinner in the paint when you were talking. You're against everything. You don't say anything helpful. Just negative things. The car's on fire, and you aren't even trying to use the extinguisher. Not even the one in easy reach."

"Who talked Thornton into that crazy idea?" Lashley asked, again ignoring Rich's comments.

"Well, most of us have talked about it, in general terms, I mean. But I think Joel convinced Elliott that he should be the specific one, if that's what you mean. He was to make contact with those guys in the barn. Kinda would make him out as a hero. Elliott needed that build up. He's lost confidence in himself the last few years. Been drinking too much."

"Who convinced you to let him out with his flag of truce?"

"Elliott did. He was real persuasive. Insistent, in fact."

"Anyone else involved?" Lashley inquired.

"Well, Pearl encouraged me some. Said it was like a good trade off. Sweet talked me. Said it was a good idea," the car dealer answered, hanging his head to avoid Lashley's stare.

"Rich, I know this is your hunt. You selected the members. In that regard, I'll respect your decisions. But outside of that, you're not in charge."

"Don't you race your motor at me like that," Rich growled in a demonstration of hostility. He raised his head to face Lashley. "Your muffler may be busted, but you've got no cause to talk to me like that."

"There's something going on here that's bigger and different than anything you ever handled. I'm not sure I can control it, but I know for damn sure you can't. We've always been compatible in our relationship. What's wrong with you?"

"Get off my windshield, Lashley," Rich demanded, disturbed by the direction of the conversation.

"You're a business man, Rich, and a damn good one. Let's get to the bottom line. Put the cash on the table. It's time to make a deal. Where are you coming from?"

Rich turned his head away, nervously rubbing his chin. Several moments passed before he spoke. "Lashley, the bottom line is I'm scared. Scared shitless." He turned, located an isolated chair, and exhaled loudly as he sat heavily.

"So are we all," Lashley responded. Following Rich, he selected a chair sitting oppositely. "I know I am. There's nothing wrong with that."

"It's more than that. It really affected me. I showed my ass when Heather got attacked. All that talk about paying her. She's a decent person and didn't deserve the abuse I gave her. I was concerned more about me than her. That was wrong. My conduct really bothered me," Rich confessed softly. He put his face in his hands. For a moment, he almost sobbed.

"These comments have paled into oblivion in light of the events that have occurred since," Lashley said graciously. He did not need for Rich to lose control.

"Even if the others have forgotten, I haven't. It was wrong. Very bad and heartless. The major's comments were correct. I hate that S-0-B, but he was right. I was worrying more about my wife vacuuming my floor mats than I was in transporting Heather to the medic. That was a loose fan belt. Right now, I'd give my bitch wife everything for Heather and us to get out of this with no more killing. I'm ready to go home. Repair the damage," Rich spoke in a low defeated tone.

"We'll make it, Rich. Don't give up. Things aren't as bad as you are making them," Lashley encouraged. Once more he felt like a professional liar. The situation was desperate, as Rich and several others suspected.

"No, it's worse. I tried to slip off with Pearl awhile ago. Couldn't get it up. Couldn't get a valve job. That bitch is a talker. Can't be trusted. By the time I get back to St. Andrews, she'll have it all over town. They'll say, 'Ole Leo lost both his sexual and business control.' These hunts really meant a lot to me. It's like having white walls on a fifty-seven Chevy, but now it's gone. I've lost it." Like a spanked child, Rich turned away, starting to rise.

"Wait, don't leave. Rich, I really need your help. There is a way out. You'll play an important role in a plan that is developing."

Leo Rich stopped, returned to his chair, and waited a few seconds before speaking. "Lashley, you're too much the gentleman. You and I know who killed that deer. Hell of a shot. But you never came forward even though it could be registered in 'Boone & Crocket.' Any hunter lives for that type of animal. You deferred to me. That's a true sportsman. Bragger that I am, if the car had swapped rear ends, you know I wouldn't have let you claim that trophy. No way. Don't drop bird shit on my new paint job. You don't need my help. Leave me a little dignity."

"Rich, you're wrong. I do need you desperately. It is for an extremely important role. We are close to a breakthrough. We need a little time. A team effort. You will play a major role. You might say, a post position."

The car dealer lifted his eyebrows and thoughtfully said, "I'll hear you out, Lashley. I at least owe you something for that deer."

"It's a tough assignment, Rich. Once you sign on, there's no backing out. You fail on your part, and we're all doomed. I must have your sworn commitment. No failure."

Rich pondered the offer. He looked Lashley square in the eyes. "Okay, you've got it. Strap me in tight. Complete commitment," he said. "What do I have to do?"

Lashley returned the stare unblinkingly. "Kill a man," he said, "in cold blood."

CHAPTER TWELVE

Ten thirty-two, his watch reported. It was barely midmorning. Outside, the overcast hung, rejecting the sun's command to vacate. The wind moved down the canyon and fanned out into the valley. Snow flurries, like fleeing sparrows, followed the suction of the rushing air, then fell, melting on impact.

The storm was buttressed against Hand Mountain. It bombarded the western slope with heavy snow, allowing through the leeward side filtered flimsy clouds, nearly devoid of moisture. The day was dark. Hurricane lamps lit the main room with a dim yellow aura that shadowboxed faces against the walls. A few hacking coughs and scraping chair legs broke the uncomfortable silence. Gloom, like a pale of stale cigar smoke, draped the gathered. Death had arrived in the early morning on horseback, bearing the corpse of George "Chainsaw" Poulen.

The white flag of surrender turned to blood red. Cherished and beloved in spite of all his short falls,

Elliott Thornton lay severely wounded. In the pantry, youthful Mitzi Rhodes with her petite fingers bathed Elliott's face with a warm cloth. Beside the cot, Katherine Pace held the fevered hand of the injured and cooed words of encouragement. The wound was severe. Professional medical attention was needed and quickly. Elliott had acted heroically, but foolishly. He had jeopardized all of them by this well intended act of folly.

Someone had to breach the defenses and get through for help. Or Elliott might die. Whatever long term operation Howard Lashley planned, Elliott's injury had upset the balance. Action must commence immediately. From across the dining hall, Lashley's soft voice floated dimly about the room. His words were occasionally indistinguishable to those on the far side. The guests, distant within the room moved forward to hear.

"There is a way out," Lashley addressed the group from his crouched position. "It's tough, but it will work if we all cooperate. Work together. Leo Rich has joined our command team, replacing Chainsaw. He is taking on a great responsibility in this effort."

"How are we going to fight our way out of here? Heather can hardly walk. Elliott's a serious case," Thyus Harder inquired. "You've already told us it was impossible, and that was before Elliott got shot."

"There's another way. Through the old mine shaft in the Thumb," Lashley interjected.

During World War II, the government had reinforced a part of the entrance for some secret training exercise. But the remaining shafts were dangerous. The head guide knew that it was no way out. Not through the mine, abandoned for almost fifty years. But when Lashley mentioned his plan, the guide agreed to give it support.

"What are we to do?" Beryl Carter asked.

"Teams will be formed, each having a separate assignment," Lashley responded. "Each group will be independently briefed. No team member will discuss their assignment with any person outside their own team. You are only to be concerned with your specific task. Concentrate on how well you and your team can perform. Nothing more. Give no concern to what, when, or where others may act. Nor should you devote any energy on the overall aspects of the plan. The plan will operate when your task is successfully completed. If you fail, the total plan fails."

He paused, shifted his weight to the other hip, and proceeded. "Are there any questions thus far?"

"I don't want any assignment," Joel Guarimo announced. "I'll not be a party to your depraved killings and murders. Count me out."

"To hell you will," Rich interrupted. He brandished a finger and yelled wrathfully. "If you fail on your job, I'll trip your lock, hot wire your engine, and you'll wish you'd volunteered for weekend floor duty."

Lashley added, "Guarimo, you have the one assignment that relates to no other team. No breach of procedures will occur if all others know your assignment. You are responsible for taking Thornton out. Prepare a stretcher and blanket. Mitzi will help you. Later, after other assignments have been completed, some of the men will, assist in the physical effort of transporting the stretcher."

"I'm not going to be stuck during an escape effort with some injured drunk. Let him take care of himself. His evil life shall be his own wrath," Guarimo responded loudly.

"Joel, you'd better get your stereo equipment repaired 'cause the sound isn't reaching you," Rich spouted back. "I'm fixing to polish your chrome with a guilt trip. You urged me to pressure Frenchie into sending Chainsaw out for help. Lashley was against it from the start. He had strong arguments. But you insisted. I saw the end result of Chainsaw's trip. He tried, and he's dead, just as Lashley warned. Then if that wasn't enough, I let you talk me into letting Elliott out on the raceway with the white flag. Well, he got run over thanks to you. So don't stall your GEO on my track, 'cause I'll flatten it like a crusher in a junk yard."

Sulking, Guarimo retreated to a seat at the far side of the room and sat down beside Pearl Gavin, who rose. "We may be outsiders in this group, not being from St. Andrews and all, but your treatment of us is unfounded. We came because my brother insisted that it would be fun. 'It's a great group,' he said. 'Nice people' What happened? I've been treated like a pregnant nun. That black bitch beat me," she pointed to Myrtle Wallace. "And nobody rallied to my support. After I spent days administrating to the needs of Heather, she's taken from my care, without even a thank you or anything. It's the wages of sin upon all of you."

"Shut up, Pearl," Rich yelled. "You were part of the dual system that talked me into the Chainsaw and Elliott fiasco. I thought I was getting something else. The whole time it was only a snow job for a blow job. You fasten your seat belt, and don't unlatch it until you're told to."

"This isn't helping anything," Carter interjected, attempting to add calmness to the heated discussion. "Let's hear Lashley out. Get to the base cost."

"What do we need to do to break out?" Lewis Fulcher asked from his corner chair.

"At two o'clock, we move. Three at the very latest," Lashley said. "Until then, we prepare. We must study our opposition. Each individual must get a personal tote bag. Put together extra socks, flashlights, things like that. The cook will issue everyone some candy bars, apples, crackers, enough to keep your energy up for twenty-four hours. I'll get with Major Greer to determine the weapons we'll take for best coverage. After you have packed your personal gear, I'll be around to make assignments and brief the various teams."

Lashley stood. He looked steadily around the room, stretching his muscles. He was tired, ready for twenty hours of dreamless sleep. Bickering amateurs. How reliable would they be when the tongue of truth flicked its spittle breath in their face? He was not certain he could count on Captain Mitchell. Frenchie, and the lodge's employees, for sure, would follow. The others were mere possibilities. In a few hours, he would know.

"Crisco will have sandwiches for us at one o'clock. Eat well as it may be your last food, except for snacks, for a long, long time," Lashley said. "Here are the assignments. Dunsey will help Grace spot from the front corner of the lodge starting immediately. Observe and report any activity. Take turns on assembling your personal gear."

Lashley paused and began, "Mitzi and Paige will assist Greer with the weapons. Mackey, Mitchell, Farrow and Frenchie will take the front door. Miss Stanford and Miss Wallace are joined with Fulcher and Harder. Their location will be designated later."

Lashley spit the instructions out like a drill instructor. "Carter and Rich, take the back at the kitchen window. Mitchell and Stumbough, take the stoop. Those who are working with Thornton will stay in that assignment. I'll be contacting the teams with their specific task shortly."

As the group separated, Lashley hailed Grace Hancock. "Take Heather back to my room, and keep her there. At about one o'clock, dress her in warm clothing, thermal underwear. Don't leave that room unless Paige relieves you. Send someone for Paige."

"Consider it done," Grace said and hurried away.

Cinch caught Lashley isolating him against a wall. "That part about the mine, that's bullshit ain't it?"

Lashley winked, "Yea, but keep it to yourself. We have to give them hope to trade for a wish. Brief the other guides to keep it under their brim. I have a plan, but it's not ready to be discussed yet."

Captain Tyrone Mitchell and Myrtle Wallace cornered Lashley as he headed for the kitchen "Myrtle must talk to you," the captain said.

"Not now. I'm busy," he said in a voice of warning.

"This is really important. She has confided in me. I think you need to hear her out," the officer insisted.

"Okay," Lashley answered reluctantly. "We'll use the crew's restroom, but make it quick."

When the trio had entered and closed the door, Lashley prompted, "Let's have it."

"I have substantial reasons to believe that you are the target of this assault. Those people out there want you," the woman started, obviously nervous in the cramped quarters.

Expressionless, Lashley returned her stare. Unwavering, she held her ground, staring back without a blink. She is cool and tough, he thought, a professional, of what classification, he was not certain. The woman was a person to be reckoned with if she became a foe. A strong ally if she joined your team. He needed her support as a key player. The plan will fall if she faulted. He shrugged indicating incomprehension.

"For my job, I have top secret clearance," she began. "It's important that I don't knowingly associate with any activities or persons who might jeopardize my clearance. Routinely, I use the military computer to run background checks on people with whom I have contacts. I'm authorized for that information. It assures my integrity. Two weeks ago, I ran a check on the members of this party, to the extent I was aware of its participants. I was surprised by the results. Even though I was not particularly alarmed at the time, I am now."

"So you were knowledgeable of Fulcher's problems?" Lashley asked, obviously upset by this delayed conversation. If the woman had information, it should have been forthcoming earlier.

"Only that the drug administration was investigating the death of one of his boat captains. Nothing was tied to Fulcher personally," she admitted. "But now, I understand that I should have pursued my research in more depth."

"And Farrow?" Lashley grunted, massaging his chin.

"He wasn't residing with a wife. Nothing unusual about that. Financially, he is well set. As an Air Force Reservist, he appeared clean. However, his business had reported a shortage of national business recently. But I failed to do a check down on his new girlfriend, Mitzi. I did not obtain her name until we got here. So I missed that completely."

"What about Rich?"

"His wife owned the auto dealership. At least it was titled in her name. Reports of domestic violence showed up. He'd been charged with striking her once, but the charges had been dropped. There was an investigation of her relatives harassing him. Someone trashed his car, but that was a year or so ago. I wasn't particularly concerned about that at the time. Appeared to be a typical domestic problem in a long term marriage."

"What about Harder or Carter?" the captain spoke for the first time.

"Harder has some serious financial problems. His real estate business might not make it. Nothing I saw other than that. Carter seems well off. His asphalt business is prosperous. He had a few assault charges when he was younger. You know, bar room brawls, but nothing else in the last few years. All of these individuals were substantial businessmen with the usual skeletons in the closet. Nothing suspicious. Basically, nothing out of the ordinary turned up."

Lashley pondered for a moment. "What about the women?"

"Well, I wasn't able to do a rundown, except on a couple of them. The men weren't exactly loose lipped about revealing their traveling companions. That kind of word gets around in a community no matter how tight you screw down the lid. Cross-checking the preflight schedules out of Dothan and Tallahassee, I caught some reservations arriving in Denver with connections to Casper at approximately our arrival time. Using that information and cross-checking, I was lucky to find a few of the women. That's how I located the names of Heather Baldwin, Dunsey Martin, and Grace Hancock. The women all checked out. Typical backgrounds. Divorced, etcetera. Nothing unusual. I missed Katherine Pace and Mitzi Rhodes completely.

She paused and then added, "As I later discovered, they flew out of Fort Walton Beach. But I've checked them out after arrival at the lodge. Asked a lot of personal questions. There doesn't appear to be any unusual problems associated with them. Katherine is a longtime resident of St. Andrews. A businesswoman in her own right, she owns a dress shop on the beach which attracts high class clients. Mitzi hasn't been there long. Just a couple of months. She came from somewhere up north. Now works in a travel agency part-time. Has independent wealth from her mother or something. She is young. About twenty, I'd say, but she claims to be older. Trying to impress the group, I suppose. She met Farrow about a month ago. He asked her along on a lark. She accepted, I think much to his surprise."

She continued hesitantly, "Paige St. John was a known participant as soon as you were identified as a hunter. Her background revealed her past connection with an unsavory character. But that relationship apparently was terminated about a year ago, and she wasn't personally involved. So I did not follow up on her as an individual."

Lashley let the comment slide for the moment. "What about Mitchell, Miss Stanford, and Greer?"

"I didn't need to check on them. Because," she stammered in protest, "Patricia, I work with her and know her clearance. As for Tyrone and Jerry Greer, I didn't see the need." She glanced sideways at the captain.

"Rather careless, wasn't it?" Lashley said.

"Not really. I casually knew Tyrone. With his background, it didn't appear worth the effort. With Greer's rank and such, it didn't seem necessary either."

"That doesn't account for Guarimo and Gavin, our malcontents."

"Gavin's brother had made this hunt before. He checked clean. Served some time as a reserve officer with top clearance. The late addition of his sister and her boyfriend didn't suggest any conflicts. Their roles as the substitutes weren't revealed to me until we arrived in Denver. There wasn't any way to follow up at that point. I did make a cursory investigation. Guarimo is connected to some off beat church in Atlanta. But that is the extent of my knowledge on him."

"When did you start your basic search?" Lashley inquired.

"Started it on Tuesday, two weeks before we left, if I recall correctly," Myrtle answered.

"We departed on a Saturday. Eighteen days or so lapsed after you certified the participants?" Lashley figured. "That's about right. By process of elimination, that leaves me. What did your search reveal under the name of Howard Lashley?"

"Nothing," she began nervously.

"Nothing?"

"Nothing," she added finally. "When the name was inserted and the proper code punched, nothing happened. Not a blip, nothing. So I inserted a higher clearance code. Again, nothing came up. That had never happened before. That is, to get no result on an individual. Usually, if there's no data on an individual, the screen will report the words 'NO INFORMATION AVAILABLE' or some similar comment. Then I inserted the highest level code I had been authorized to use. Trust me. It is high level. Nothing again."

"Did you figure that I was so squeaky clean that I might not be in the computer?" he offered.

"That was my conclusion," Myrtle said in response. "There are two point two billion people in the United States. All of them can't be in the data base. I figured that if there was nothing, then you were okay. That afternoon I checked around with some local people. You appeared to be a loaner, self-sufficient, but an okay guy."

"So?"

Myrtle glanced sideways and spoke as if to the wall, "I would have left it at that except for what happened later."

She turned to face him. He extended her an inquisitive look.

"The next morning, a dude shows up in my office flashing a government I.D. from some agency I'd never heard about. I found out later he'd landed at Tyndall in a Leer jet. That takes super clearance. Said his name was Tidewater. It had been called to his attention that I was making inquiries using some sensitive code number. This white-haired man wanted to know what I was doing. He scared the shit out of me. Figured I'd abused my code, and I was fixing to get the axe. Lose my job."

"What happened?" Lashley asked.

"I explained about the hunting trip and that my purpose was to verify the backgrounds of the participants. He asked a bunch of questions. Grilled me real hard about the circumstances. I told him the entire story, listed the participants who I knew at the time, scheduled departures, site location, etc.

Explained all I knew about the Cottonwood—its remote location, about the short and long roads to the lodge. I gave him the whole deal. Farrow had told me a lot of details and I had seen a lot of Farrow's pictures from previous hunts. He thanked me, cautioned me about using the data base for my personal use and left, leaving me as useless as a spent round."

"How does that tie into me?"

"It didn't for a while," Myrtle responded. "And I dismissed it. Until now. Back in my mind, there was something bothering me about the deal. Over the past seven years, I had accessed that data base in the same way, even using the high codes, maybe a hundred times. At no time did anyone question my right or use of the computer. Not until I inserted the name of Howard Lashley and drew a blank. That's the difference, Howard Lashley."

"How do you come to that conclusion?" he asked, fixing her with an accusing stare.

"That dude was a spook. A real cool spook. Like Ollie North, one that works outside the realm of an organization. With credentials straight out of the

White House. That dude asked about everyone on the trip I had accessed, but you. He wanted to know who was Miss St. John attached to? Carter, Harder, Rich, and their known companions. He quizzed me about every name I had researched. But he never said your name. Not the whole time. Your exclusion wasn't so obvious until now."

"So?"

"So man, you're hot. Hotter than a pistol after a tour on the range. Those spooks in Washington have their eyes on you. I don't know what you've done, and I don't care. By distributing our itinerary and details of the Cottonwood, I inadvertently set us all up. Somebody did a reconnaissance on this lodge. They were able to mobilize forces and pin us down. They must want you bad. Bad as in B-A-D, bad."

Lashley wondered. Was the exit from this labyrinth located in the Five Pines?

CHAPTER THIRTEEN

The room was gray, drab to a nauseous degree. It contained, as best as he could see, a hospital style bed and a night stand. He blinked in the dull light emitting from a fixture behind him. The windowless room disoriented him.

He was unable to distinguish if it was day or night. Attempting to move, he found his limbs heavy, listless, and barely responsive. Closing his eyes, he breathed deeply, and commenced a movement inventory. The fingers wiggled, though sluggishly. The toes under the covers responded. No injury was apparent.

Tilting his head slightly, he surveyed the rest of the room. Behind the door closest to the bed, he figured, was a bathroom or closet. Further down a short passage way, another door was barely visible. It must be the exit. To where, he wondered.

As he considered the alternatives, the farthest door opened, framing a young woman, plain, heavy, and dressed in white. She advanced to the bed and by habit, found the patient's wrist and checked his pulse.

"Well," she said clearly. "You are awake today. That is a surprise."

"Where am I?" he asked, his voice raspy and dry from thirst.

"Five Pines," she responded as she extended a thermometer to his mouth.

"What am I doing here?" he asked as he averted his mouth, to no avail. In a firm manner, she inserted the glass tube.

"Shush," she said, placing her finger to her lips. "Don't excite yourself. The doctor will be here shortly. He will explain."

Moments later, she extracted the cylinder, checked it, and made entries on the clipboard under her arm.

"What happened to me?" he asked, but she cut him off with a "Shush" and departed.

It was accounting time. The credits: he was mentally rational, his body parts were functional; he was warm and facing no immediate known danger. The debits: he had no idea who or where he was; he

337

had no name, no address; he had no family connections, nothing; and his prior life was zilch, a blank, a void. As a personal profit and loss statement, he was operating in the red. The bottom line was a loss. His throat was dry. He needed a drink, not of the chlorine variety. Rather, he needed bourbon on the rocks, three fingers deep and bottoms up.

Exerting extreme effort, he placed his feet on the floor and hazily stood. The hospital gown was his only garment. The night stand drawer revealed a box of facial tissues and a plastic cup, nothing else. The first door opened into a bathroom. He leaned against the wall for support. The room contained a toilet, hand bowl, and shower devoid of a curtain. He gulped a few swallows from the sink faucet. It was not what he needed, but it would have to do.

Moving toward the entrance, he was almost knocked down as the door swung opened. A man dressed in a pale green smock entered.

"Well, well," he said. "What do we have here? Miss Shock said you were awake. Let's get you back to bed."

"I don't want to."

"Doctor's orders," the man said, taking the patient by the arm and assisting him across the room toward the bed.

"Who are you?" the patient asked.

"I'm Dr. La Croix, a physician here at Five Pines."

"How did I get here?"

"About sixty days ago the police brought you in for treatment. Found you wandering in the streets."

"What is this place, a detox center?" the patient drowsily asked.

"Something like that," the physician said. "We prefer to call it a wellness center. We attend to the whole person."

"Who am I?"

"We had hoped you would supply that information to us."

From there, the conversation deteriorated. The only additional fact added to his limited reservoir of knowledge was that the Five Pines was located somewhere in Northern Georgia. The town, he was told, was of no significance.

Days added to days. Medication followed medication. Sluggish, lifeless, he marked time. Then, he revolted. First, he concealed the daily pills, faking their acceptance and fabricating his stupor. As his mind cleared, his strength returned. He felt normal, assuming that being stationary was a normal condition for him. Mentally, he charted the hospital routine. During the period perceived as night, he performed silent calisthenics, push ups, knee bends, and aerobic exercises. The clinic fed him adequately, as he was spoon fed his daily meals. Days primarily included sleep time, consistent with the aftermath of the drugs.

Two weeks passed on his self-imposed rehabilitation program. Mentally, he calculated it to be a month after his first conscious awakening. He had learned little else of a personal history. His age, he assessed in the early thirties.

He located scar tissue under his left arm. Its significance was beyond his reach. He was about six feet tall, in the range of one hundred sixty-five pounds by his estimate.

Faking a dopey conversation, his efforts to elicit further information from the nurse and orderlies were always rebutted. Nurse Shock shushed his inquiries, while Dr. La Croix skillfully dodged all questions as a man schooled in fencing. Persistence resulted in strengthened medication. Eventually, he ceased all inquiries, discovering that silence was the best rule.

He was a captive. The exterior door remained locked. It opened six times daily: three times for Nurse Shock to deliver meals and spoon feed him; twice for her temperature checks; and once for Dr. La Croix's visit. Occasionally, which he judged to be weekends, substitute mute male orderlies performed Nurse Shock's duties. The doctor's absence was noted.

He judged that sixty days had passed since he gained his first consciousness. The next day after the orderlies ended their duties he made his move. It was Monday, he figured, because that was the day Nurse Shock returned to execute her usual routine, following a two-day absence. Behind the door, he waited for her to enter for the final call of the day. Stepping around the nurse, he fled out the carpeted hall. Behind him, she called an alarm.

Closed doors lined the long corridor, ending at a partitioned nurses' station 100 feet away. Two male attendants cleared the partition and approached the patient with quick steps.

"Back to your room," the closest one said, reaching to grasp him. The patient went into a crouch, caught the man's extended arm and pivoted, throwing the man over his shoulder. Placing his foot under the arm, he twisted forcefully, jerking upward. The joint socket popped in a sickening sound. The orderly screamed as he lay at the nurses' station entrance.

The second attendant retreated·behind the partition, as the patient followed. The gap between the men closed. Holding a black aerosol cylinder, the attendant raised it toward the patient who ducked down and delivered a blow to the midsection. It drove the orderly forcefully to the wall. The mace dropped to the carpet followed by the gasping attendant. Instantly, the patient retrieved the canister, applying a full dose in the orderly's face, rendering the man incapacitated as he thrashed on the floor.

Behind the glass, a frantic matron nurse punched desperately at the telephone. Reaching over, the patient grabbed the chord and snatched it from the wall.

The patient stepped from the station, pulling the older nurse upright. He found Nurse Shock, kneeling in the corridor attending to the first orderly. She screamed when she saw the patient.

Behind locked doors along the hall, patients began banging and yelling.

"Ladies," he said decisively, "I don't want trouble. I want some clothes, and I'll be gone. Where are my things?"

"We don't have them. Please return to your room. Nothing more will be said of this violence," the older lady said.

He made a quick decision. The orderly on the floor appeared to be about his height, only heavier. Loosening the attendant's belt, he removed the trousers. Slipping them on over his pajamas, he found them baggy but a passable fit.

Next, he tried the shirt and finally the shoes. Hospital clothing. Too large, but they would have to do. Inside the pants pockets, he found a billfold containing a driver's license, credit cards, and $86.00.

Back at the nurses' station he took $43.00 from the maced orderly and a set of car keys.

He addressed the older nurse. "Make me out a receipt. I've got $86.00 from one and $43.00 from the other. Clean out your purse and Nurse Shock's. Put the amount down also. I'll send the money back in a few days."

He paused as the woman wrote, then asked, "Also, what kind of car does he drive?" He pointed to the orderly in the corridor.

"A dark blue Cavalier," she said, looking away as if afraid to meet his eyes.

"I'm borrowing it for a few hours," the patient said. "Put it on the receipt. Also, I want my medical files."

"They are not here," she replied.

He walked to the hall, heaved the screaming attendant to his feet, forcing him into the nurses' cubical. Twisting the injured arm brought additional cries of pain. Along the hall, the banging amplified.

"Quick, tell her to get my file," he said to the attendant, as he applied more pressure. "I don't have much time."

"Get it, Inez," screamed the attendant. "Get it."

Inez opened a drawer, extracted a folder, and placed it on the desk.

"What is the name of my file?" he asked and twisted the attendant's arm.

"Room 323. It's got no name I know of," the attendant yelled.

Reaching across the desk, he checked the file. The number did not correspond. Inez paled, staggered back to the drawer, removed another folder, and tendered number 323. He flipped it open. Lashley, HOWARD, it read. Now he had a name.

He twisted the arm again. "Where is your car parked?"

"It's behind this building near the big oak," he screamed.

Nurse Shock was pounding on his back with her little fists. Swerving, he administered a moderate dose of mace.

Up and down the hall, the pounding increased. The inmates of this loony farm wanted out. Call it a wellness center if you desire. But labeling a "cow" a "bull" does not alter its sex. The place was a prison with a different name.

"Open the door, Inez," he demanded, indicating a patient's room.

"I can't," she said. "It's against regulations."

Persuasion was required, but eventually he had the four employees locked in a patient's room. Using the nurse's pass key, he opened a door and instructed an occupant to release the remaining patients. Then he fled.

Dodging down the fire escape, he had a scare. Opening the ground floor door would trigger an alarm advertising his escape route. Calculating the alternatives he decided to use it for a diversion. He pushed with force. The door popped open. Instead of running outside, he broke right, pausing long enough to the strike the fire alarm. Charging toward the kitchen area he yelled, "Fire."

Startled kitchen employees stared in disbelief.

"Fire," he yelled again, and the staff broke, joining his flight toward the freight exit.

Locating the attendant's car proved a greater problem than he expected in the dimming evening light. Blue cars had varying shades. He lost valuable minutes in locating a vehicle that fit the keys.

Behind him, over the alarms, he could hear the hospital personnel getting a fix on the escape. The car cranked sluggishly. He backed in a screech of rubber. As he accelerated toward the hospital's exit, security guards began closing the gate. The car smashed through, crumpling the driver's fender. He gunned left along a winding paved road. Half a mile along, he quickly executed a U-turn, and proceeded cautiously in the direction of Five Pines.

As he passed the Five Pines, he observed security vehicles, turning left in pursuit of the escapee. He had a jump on the rent-a-cops, he thought. It would be a head start of only several minutes before they figure out his U-turn scam.

Two hours later, he located a MARTA station in the northeast section of Atlanta. Lashley joined the mass migrating into the belly of the city's transit's system.

For two days, he wondered the streets before locating employment as a dishwasher in a seedy restaurant. No name and no social security number were asked. None were given. Payment was made daily in cash at closing time. There were no withholdings. His hours were flexible, and his meals were part of the employment. Work as long as you are sober was the rule.

A fellow employee helped him locate a room that proved to be more despicable than the restaurant. Rent was payable daily, in advance. Conditions were deplorable, but they would have to suffice he knew until the heat was off. And they did so for seventy-nine long days.

He had become a fruit jar banker, accumulating a fair amount of change with his limited expenses, high hourly wages for long hours, and dependable service. Second hand clothes, purchased from Goodwill Industries, filled his moderate wardrobe. But circumstances made him move before he was ready.

The ambush occurred on a late Saturday night at the end of October. It happened in the back alley behind the restaurant as he left work. It was chilly. He hunched down in his wind breaker. The movement probably saved his life.

A swinging pipe glanced off his head with a stinging blow but with inadequate force to incapacitate him. He went down as if severely injured and rolled quickly toward his assailant. He took a swift kick in his money pouch. It was the move he had expected. Catching the assailant's foot, he twisted, and the man fell hard on the pavement, his head banging loudly against the asphalt.

Lashley rolled backward this time, catching a second kick in the lower back. It hurt, but it was not crippling. The second assailant was now located.

349

Spring jumping, he flinched left. His new opponent moved laterally with his motion. Reversing directions, Lashley dropped a kick in the man's knee cap. Gasping in pain, the man went down.

The first man, on his knees, was moving around the pavement, trying to locate the pipe weapon. Lashley gave him a size ten, steel toed shoe in the jaw. The bone snapped, and the man passed out, dropping on his stomach.

Lashley walked to the unconscious man and turned him over. In the dim alley light, he identified him as the Five Pines orderly who had involuntarily authorized Lashley's use of his vehicle. The other gasping prone figure proved to be the companion floor attendant on the night of Lashley's escape.

Lashley moved swiftly. He picked up the pipe weapon that now turned from foe to friend. Swinging it behind his back, he noted the high-pitched sound it made as it crashed, directed by Lashley's force of adrenalin, on the upper right arm of one assailant. With equal force the leg of the other was broken. He took their billfolds, hurried to his room and slipped out in the night.

As he reflected on the attack, the surprise for Lashley was that it was not the police who came hunting him. It had been the Five Pines, as an institution, who desired his return. Maybe they were mad, because he had not repaid the money he had taken during his escape.

One week later, Lashley crouched on a hill side in a heavy growth of bushes and watched a distant, weathered, brick building through field glasses. It was now an established pattern.

For the past four days, he had arrived early each morning, while the paper boys were still making their rounds. Secluding himself, he patiently watched the activities in the hamlet of Chatsworth, Georgia. The village was not large enough to warrant the classification of "town."

On the night of the alley attack, he had driven his battered, rusty, gas guzzling 1982 Chevy, with a dubious title, purchased for $300.00 cash, northward along Interstate 75. He located a rest area on the outskirts of Dalton. A chilly few hours of rest rewarded him with an empty belly and stiff muscles.

At a truck stop, he refreshed himself, ate, and prepared the rough outline of his plan.

For several days, he scouted the mountainous area until he was reasonably assured that Chatsworth would not lead to another ambush. Along a secluded road west of town, he located a fairly remote place to park his car, so it would be hidden from prying eyes.

Leaving his car, for the next four mornings he hiked into the hamlet. Under cover of the bushes, from daylight to dark, he kept surveillance on the law office of James Horne Chambless, II. It was a contact name that had appeared in the medical folder for room 323, taken from Five Pines. The name was the only clue to his past. Clipped in the file was a small sheet of paper which contained a simple notation: "In case of emergency, notify James Horne Chambless, II, Attorney at Law, Chatsworth, Georgia." The note concluded with a post office box number and a telephone number.

If the circumstances he now faced were not an emergency, Lashley would have to purchase a new dictionary. Cut off from all contacts, with no history, and with goons trailing him, he needed assistance. Should James Horne Chambless lend no rationalization to his dilemma, Lashley would have no place else to turn. But the name on the law office read "John Chambless." Lashley's trail was getting blurred.

His thoughts were broken when a now familiar car turned left off the main street. It drove into the darkened parking area, stopping under a massive oak tree. Its occupant stepped out. In the dim light of the car's interior light identification was made. The young, slim man Lashley had under surveillance had arrived for work.

For the past four days, the man's routine had developed a pattern. The lawyer arrived at his office at 7:00 a.m. His secretary put in an appearance about an hour later. At noon the lawyer walked two blocks to a greasy spoon café. Back to the office by one o'clock, the attorney usually departed about 5:30 p.m. Today was Friday. If Lashley was to act, it must be now.

As the lawyer walked toward the office door, Lashley moved on a silent intersecting course. The man reached the doorway two steps ahead of Lashley.

"Mr. Chambless?" Lashley inquired. Noting the startled reaction of the man attempting to insert the key in the door he added, "I'm sorry if I frightened you."

"My God," the attorney said as he spun to face his inquirer.

"I'm looking for Mr. James Horne Chambless. It's an important matter," Lashley insisted. "Do you know James Horne Chambless?"

Recovering, the man stared at his antagonist. "Yes, I'm his nephew. Uncle Horne is dead."

"Oh." It was Lashley's turn to be surprised. "When did he die?"

"About six weeks ago. He was murdered here. Right where we are standing. The police think it was robbery."

Dejected, Lashley sagged. A blind alley. His last contact had dissolved, dispensed with the shifting winds. His world began with his awakening in the

Five Pines. His last lead to his history was gone. There was nothing left here for him.

He turned and started dejectedly down the walk. From behind, he heard a halting inquiry.

"Are you by any chance Mr. Ashley? No, I think it was Lashley? Are you him?

"Why?" Lashley responded, halting his departure.

"I have a message for him."

I'm Lashley."

"I need identification."

Lashley was puzzled. What possible identification could he furnish?

"Your scar. May I see it?"

Lashley raised his shirt and exposed the scar.

The lawyer was apparently satisfied. "I was visited by some men after my uncle's funeral. They told me that if ever a Mr. Lashley contacted me to give him this phone note. Don't ask me who they were because I don't know and I am now certain I don't want to ever know." He opened his wallet and passed over a folded paper.

Lashley located the nearest phone booth and dialed a number.

When the party answered, he uttered the code he had been furnished. He was transferred to Ms. Smitz, who identified herself as an agent of the Midwater Trust Company. The lady informed him that she held in escrow $750,000 to be deposited in any account of his choice, and a substantial monthly allowance would follow.

Under instant questioning, the agent denied any knowledge of the creator of the trust. Her instructions were limited to distributing the assets to the beneficiary, Howard Lashley, once the proper code was furnished. That condition had been fulfilled. The remaining duty was to for him to name the account.

Lashley promptly established his permanent residence in St. Andrews, and the funds were deposited to the account he requested.

The selected town had been arbitrary. He wanted remoteness but with quick access to a large metropolitan area. Florida's Emerald Coast fit his standards.

Once established in St. Andrews, he watched, tracked, and back tracked. There appeared to be no sign of a tail or surveillance. He maintained an outward appearance of careless disregard for his safety. If you want to spring the trap, he reasoned, then set the bait. Nothing surfaced. Months passed. He continued to cross check, but allowed his life's pattern to stabilize.

Early on, he was obsessed with learning the secrets of his past life. Caution prevented any return to Five Pines. Selectively, he called anyone named Lashley in numerous cities. Did you know a Howard Lashley? He soon discovered it was a waste of time. Most considered them to be crank calls. No family ties were established. At the local library, he researched city directories, indexes, and old newspapers, all to no avail.

He turned to research. Medical dictionaries explained amnesia. Stress or trauma might have induced his lapse of memory. Eventually, the loss would return. But for Lashley, the passage of time lent no assistance. Eventually, he reached the conclusion that his memory had been altered by drugs at Five Pines. Whether or not that was correct, it sufficed as a palatable explanation. He could live with that.

So his resurrected life began. Gradually, he went outside of his self-imposed confines. He joined the world, although it was a limited association. Minimal contacts and social events, augmented with maximum physical fitness, absorbed his daily schedules. Howard Lashley began to exist as a normal person.

And now, here at the Cottonwood, his silent history was resurfacing. An incidental data check had brought him to someone's attention. It was difficult for him to believe he was the target. However, after his escape from Five Pines he had been attacked in the alley. Somebody had wanted him in Atlanta and it wasn't the police.

Myrtle Wallace's story had some validity. He could not question her concerns for there was a grain of reason in it. Possibly, at some point in his past life, he might have been a hot item. Somebody could have been hunting him for some wrong he had inflicted. But if he was the target, it would have been much easier to assault him on his own turf at St. Andrews. A high powered rifle could have easily taken him out while he jogged.

No governmental agency would stoop so low as to employ the low class street killers assigned to the Cottonwood. Whatever level of competency any agency placed on the closure of Howard Lashley, the paid assailants would be highly skilled professionals.

Wallace might be partially right, but Lashley was convinced he was not the primary target. It was someone else. But who? He now had some answers. But each answer produced more questions. Geometrically, not arithmetically, the trail forked every few feet forward and then branched again, until the maze became more complex. There was no exit.

There was no way to quickly reconcile his conflict. The answers would be clear when the battle was over. That is, if anybody survived.

CHAPTER FOURTEEN

It was pay day. All the action happens on pay day. The mills close down, and the workers head for town, the bars, and the fights. Fights are never restricted to the ring. Some of the most violent ones are fought on a saw dust floor or in a gravel parking lot. Once the pay checks are spent for who knows what, the long road home leads to the second and final round. These later fights involve the spouses. It may be about money, or the lack of it. It may be about lipstick found on a collar, a torn button, or neglect of the family. The list is endless. All over town, the scenario is the same, altered only by the actors involved and differing plots to fit the circumstance. Pay day is a tough day in a mill town.

It was pay day at the Cottonwood Guest Lodge. The fight was just shaping up. It was round two in which the opponent is within your own family.

"You got a saddle, Frenchie?" Howard Lashley asked, as he strolled toward the kitchen with the head guide in tow. "Paul Revere is about to make a belated ride. Or it might be more accurate to describe the rider as Benedict Arnold."

"There's a saddle up there in the loft under a bunk," Frenchie Hebert responded, amused by Lashley's comment. "Belonged to String. Don't think he'd mind you using it. You serious about this? A Benedict Arnold ride? Are you saying there's a traitor in the lodge?"

"Serious as mud in a rifle barrel," Lashley replied. He inhaled a short breath, one that signaled sleepless hours and weighted duties.

"Who's going to ride?" Frenchie half-reproachfully asked, fearful of the answer.

"We're fixing to select the lucky person," Lashley replied. "We're going to hold a lottery."

Frenchie dispatched the guide, Fish Mackey, to retrieve the saddle, directing him to cinch it to the horse tied at the stoop. This horse had brought in the body of Chainsaw Poulen. The mare would now be enlisted for another important ride.

Three men stood in Lashley's room, off the dining hall, as the operation was discussed. To provide more space, the bed stood tilted against the wall, the concealed automatic weapons placed behind the mattress. The boarded window darkened the surroundings. A smoky hurricane lamp, resting on the fireplace mantle, provided a dingy light. The mood was somber, apprehensive. It was 2:45p.m., and there was not much time left. A quick toss of the dice - craps, and you have lost your bank roll. Out on the street in your skivvies. Naked and exposed. Craps is the best odds for the house.

"The weapons are distributed," Major Greer reported to Lashley who stood with his back to the fireplace.

"The teams are ready and in place," Mitchell said. "Security appears good between the players. Everybody who has been briefed acknowledges their assignment."

"Let's get in motion," Lashley instructed.

The two officers pivoted and departed, leaving Lashley as the lonely man to mentally review his position. Another great lie. On equal footing with the joke that the check is in the mail is the corresponding observation that, when you are a leader, it is lonely at the top. Lonely was an oversimplification. A person could be lonely while standing in a crowded subway car. Loneliness was minute in comparison with isolation. A leader's isolation is self-destructive. Operating with abstract and unreliable information, furnished by traitorous squires and knights, the king is ultimately dethroned. Great battles have been lost when a drab detail was untimely delivered to generals.

Lashley felt engrossed in the most exaggerated form of isolation. He felt like a single astronaut in a space capsule whose only connection with NASA was a faulty radio. Every communication was static, with each repeated broadcast becoming more garbled than the preceding one. Until in final desperation, all connections would sever. Then there is complete isolation in a hostile environment. Rescue is leveled to basic personal skills. Doubts and uncertainties rise, as ghosts from the swamps of failure, the whole project birthed by the midwife of defeat. Would any individual or one of the Cottonwood's assigned teams perform, he wondered. If one failed, the craft would be in perpetual orbit, lost forever. Outer space wins, and Lashley was uncertain who was in charge of ground control.

Throughout the lodge, individuals struggled with the hand they had been dealt. They understood the cards that were dealt face up, but the difficulty was what to do with those cards facing down, the ones that cannot be seen.

Lashley moved to the door and cast a glance around the lodge. In the kitchen sprawling prone along a table, Leo Rich was well versed in his assignment. Rich had placed several quilts under him for comfort. His team member, Beryl Carter, knew little of the team's assignment. Through peg holes in the boarded window, the two men alternated, observing Rich's assigned target some 200 yards away.

For over an hour now, the two men had been observing activities of the sentry through field glasses. Up the canyon, snow flurries had ceased as the wind subsided. But it was still cold outside. It was the calm before the battle. Lashley wondered how well Rich would perform. Would he kill a person?

Lashley moved beside Rich squinting through a crack. Up the narrowing canyon, partially concealed by aspens, an outpost guard moved, shifting about for warmth. Inactivity had bred carelessness on his part. Along the steep slope, the trees, foliage, and scattered cottonwood stumps dictated a tough shot for Rich. Lashley had helped in the calculations, adjusting for the upward shot. With the 30.06, the target was attainable. Rich knew his abilities. He was a better-than-average shot. But the real question remained. Could he kill a man in cold blood? Two shots at best would be the limit. Then the target would be behind cover. There was marginal room for error. It was fifteen minutes until the count down would start.

Lashley patted Rich on the shoulder and moved to the stairs.

Upstairs, the loft was stuffy. Patricia Stanford stood on a bunk peering through a gap in the roof. A plank had been removed from the apex of the ceiling along the loft's north wall. He knew her target.

Through this opening, it was a clear view, revealing two men crouched behind hay bales piled high up near the tip of the Thumb.

She nodded as Lashley stepped on the bunk beside her. He saw two men smoking cigarettes. The slight wind blowing off the Thumb dispatched puffs into oblivion. The guard station was 325 yards out.

He watched as Stanford adjusted the open sights on her Ruger Model 77, chambered for the versatile 30.06 shell. It was her choice of weapon. Bolt action, for some sportsmen, was slower than a Remington semi-automatic. But practice had honed her skills. She mentioned she found it a strong, dependable rifle. He watched her fingers run over the clean, polished stock, her eyes admiring its walnut finish. In her hands, it would be fast, the second round microseconds behind a semi-automatic. But she would have to earn more accuracy on the second round. The second shot would be the most important. The woman had told him she had no qualms about killing these people. Lashley suspected Patricia Stanford had killed before.

Thyus Harder moved away from his peep hole, which had been similarly placed in the south wall loft as the one Patricia Stanford occupied. Lashley watched Myrtle Wallace relieve him. Harder stepped to the stair well to join Fulcher. The two men's assignment was to relay the code word from the ground floor to the loft's occupants.

Along the loft's south wall, Myrtle sighted her targets through a seven power scope. She tenderly caressed the .308 Winchester magnum as though it were a child's behind. Aided by the telescopic glass, the magnification brought the cross hairs first on one guard, then the other as she marked and measured her target. As Lashley had previously observed two men would be crouched 375 yards out on the Trigger Finger, with a 300 feet rise in elevation. The targets would provide a challenging shot. It was a difficult assignment, even without a strong cross wind. The shots required difficult mental calculations - six inches in height to allow for a trajectory drop for the long range shoot, two inches right for windage. A surprise or distraction would be her only opportunity for taking out both targets rapidly. All of her military training had probably been projected to killing. But this might be her first. Lashley gave her a thumb's up in encouragement hoping she considered herself mentally ready.

A double bunk bed had been moved crosswise in the loft. On the top bunk, Ray Horne, the assistant cook, lay prone, gazing through the hole Lashley had left when he shot the chimney stuffer off the roof. Three hundred fifty yards out, at eye level with the wind straight away, his target was higher up the canyon than the one assigned to Rich. The cook blew nervously on his hands. Killing a man was the same as a deer or elk to him Lashley knew. The rugged western mentality prevailed. Kill the son-of-a-bitch before he kills you. Shoot them on the wing. We will sort them out later and count our points.

"Good luck," Lashley said as he departed.

At the front door, Cinch Wilkinson sighted toward the barn's upper window. As Lashley approached he did not move. The cowboy was using a .405 Model, 1895 Winchester, the heavier caliber favored by Teddy

Roosevelt on his African safari. It was adequate for hippos and elephants. The weapon came from Frenchie's private collection. Frenchie loaded his own cartridges to fit his personal specifications.

When he returned from certain duties, Frenchie would join Cinch and cover the barn door. The head guide had selected a similar weapon, which was tilted against the wall beside the young cowboy. It was chambered with 330 grain bullets. This powerful, lever action rifle was selected to penetrate the barn's pine siding. Its cartridges would penetrate deeply into the interior of the building.

Flanking on the right and left of the guide, Fish Mackey and insurance agent, Robert Stevenson Farrow, sighted through 30.06s. Their assignment was strategic. Well-placed shots to a specific location against the side of the barn would give the false impression that the siding was adequate protection for those in the barn, causing those inside to commit. Once they had committed, their position would be exposed for Cinch and Frenchie's heavy weapons to zero in for the kill.

"Make them pay a heavy price," Lashley said as he continued his rounds.

At the stoop entrance, the guide, Fred Stumbough waited. Biding time, the cowboy curried the mare, careful not to expose his position. At ten minutes before the hour, he slipped the bridle on and saddled the horse. Sensing action, the mare sidestepped and strained on the halter.

"Bring him to my room," Lashley instructed the captain. "It's time to commence. See that Grace keeps Heather down. Crisco is responsible for keeping Pearl out here."

The young officer departed and returned moments later with Joel Guarimo.

"You want to see me?" the Bible thumper addressed Lashley, noting Frenchie deep to his left, standing in a darkened corner.

"Yes," Lashley replied. "We've selected you to ride the mare out. Spread the alarm. Go for help. Be a real hero like you encouraged Elliott to be."

Guarimo looked at the man in the room for a moment and then replied, "I'm no horseman. This has got to be a joke, and not a very funny one at that. They shot Elliott when he tried to talk. The white flag didn't give him any protection. I'm not going on any horse."

"We're serious, Guarimo," Lashley replied. "You are going. You're going to ride that mare down the hill. Once you clear the fish pond and break for the gate, you are on your own."

"You can't force me," Guarimo growled back. "It's dangerous. I could get shot. What happened to Elliott is warning enough. Those guys don't want to talk. That much is obvious."

Lashley was leaning against the wall, his right arm extended. "We're giving you a better chance than the one you gave String before you shot him," Lashley accused.

"What are you saying?" Frenchie spoke excitedly, breaking into the conversation. "Guarimo killed String?"

"Yes, that's what I'm saying," Lashley agreed with a firmness in his voice that could not be mistaken.

Captain Tyrone Mitchell stood silent and alert, waiting for the scene to unfold.

That's crazy," Guarimo sputtered. "You can't prove that."

"Don't bet on it," Lashley hissed. "You did it with a pistol. You shot String and the two dogs. We found the silencer under a loose stone in the hearth in Pearl's room. It was in the room you first occupied here at the lodge."

From the overhead shelf, Lashley extracted an object. Then he pointed the pistol, equipped with a silencer, at Guarimo. "Mitchell and I searched your belongings early this morning and found this pistol under your mattress. It's a twenty-five caliber. The same caliber as the spent casings we found near the dogs. The silencer we found under the loose stones in the hearth fits this weapon."

"What does that prove?" Guarimo said. "That porch room has had as many visitors as the Atlanta airport on a holiday weekend. That's no connection to me. How do I know you didn't plant it under my mattress? How do we know they're not your slugs? The captain here has been around my gear enough times."

"We had earlier found something else. When the bitch dog attacked you, your shirt was torn. There were green threads in the bitch's teeth when we found her. They match the shirt we found in your gear. Earlier today, I bumped your left arm. You winched. When that sleeve is rolled up we'll see those puncture marks. Those teeth prints are the proof we need. Roll up your sleeve for us," Lashley ordered.

When Guarimo hesitated, the guide stepped forward and snatched at the man's sleeve. The button severed. Frenchie raised the sleeve, disclosing bandages taped on the struggling man's arm. The guide tore away the adhesive and Guarimo's arm revealed the canine's puncture marks.

"You son of a bitch! I'll kill you," Frenchie hissed.

Lashley grabbed the guide's collar and separated him from the fray.

"I won't ride. I don't have to stay here and listen to any more of this bullshit. I'm leaving," Guarimo announced and moved toward the door. Captain Mitchell blocked the passage, as Frenchie moved closer.

"Hear me out, Guarimo," Lashley said, holding the pistol steady. "You have two alternatives. Move another step, and I'll kill you. Then I'll tie your carcass on that horse. Your second choice is to stand fast and let Mitchell tie and gag you. Then you go out on horseback alive. If you're lucky, your comrades out there will miss, and you might survive. But if you resist, death in this room is your only option. Which will it be?"

Frenchie gave a look of startled surprise. "His comrades are outside?" the head guide blustered. "Are you saying he's working with those wet backs down at the barn?"

"Yes, that's what I'm saying. Our hunting companion here, Joel Guarimo, has been a part of this conspiracy from the very beginning. He is our Benedict Arnold. He helped kill Chainsaw. Not directly, but he leaked the info."

"I'll kill him with my bare hands and eat his nuts like mountain oysters," Frenchie hissed in disgust. "Preaching the Bible to us like he was a saint when the whole time he was the devil himself. Those people are the worst kind. Hypocrites selling the word of God to hide their own sins. It stinks."

Frenchie, exhausted by his speech, moved forward toward the man. Mitchell intervened, "Wait, let him select his own option. It's more than he gave String or Chainsaw, but we're more disciplined than he is. Let him choose."

Guarimo unwillingly submitted to Mitchell's request. In the dim light, the captain examined Guarimo's left forearm and studied the puncture wounds. The bitch had been vicious in her final act before death.

"You killer," Frenchie said. "String was a harmless, kind person. If they don't get you out there, I'll hunt you down like a wild dog. I'll guarantee you death will be inflicted as heartless as an Apache's assault upon a lost Mormon."

Guarimo spit in Frenchie's face and took a stunning blow to his mouth in return. He went down in a semi-conscious state.

At the stoop, beside the firewood, Guarimo's hands were tied to the saddle horn. A rope tossed under the horse's belly bound his feet. Duct tape sealed his mouth. It was four minutes after three o'clock. The plan was behind schedule.

Lashley nodded to Mitchell. "Give the word," he said as he cocked the lever action, 30.30 Winchester.

The captain stepped inside. "Orange," he yelled.

From the stairwell, Fulcher forwarded the message to the loft. "Orange." he echoed.

Upon hearing the action command, Lashley flinched in anticipation. Grace, from her position near the dining hall door, relayed it to the team at the front porch. She was to comfort Heather. Something was happening, and it was important that Heather did not become upset.

He signaled Major Greer. It was time to place Pearl Gavin in custody. The officer waved in acknowledgement.

"Haw! Haw! Haw!" filtered in from the stoop. Stumbough jabbed the mare sharply in the rib and slapped its rump. The horse bolted down the trail. Lashley fired two rapid shots behind the horse.

"Seed," Lashley yelled, and the counter word echoed through the lodge. The words "orange seed" activated the plan.

Reacting to the gun shots and the horse's movements, the guards posted up the canyon and along the ridges altered their positions, attempting to ascertain the cause. In the canyon, peering around tree trunks, two men carelessly exposed their position simultaneously, as they strained to observe the occurrence around the lodge. Lashley watched the two men on the Thumb discharge a burst of automatic fire at the moving horse. The scattered shots fell short of the target, causing rocks to splinter along the slope.

"Fire," Lashley ordered as he aimed, firing again after the galloping horse. Guarimo slumped in the saddle.

"Fire," echoed the command through the lodge. The occupants responded. From the loft, porch and kitchen, rifles barked.

As quickly as it started, the firing halted. For several minutes, the lodge was quiet. Then Lashley ordered an audible "at ease." From within the building, individuals sighed relief and hesitantly moved toward the kitchen and restrooms.

"How many did we get?" Carter asked Lashley, as the hunting party gathered in the dining hall to receive a dose of Crisco's liquid caffeine.

Quickly and privately, Lashley conducted a casualty count.

Rich reported he took his target mid-chest. He had done it. Lashley's faith was well-founded. Higher up the canyon, Ray Horne's aim was cross-haired. He had marked his bull's-eye and squeezed. His target fell. Watching the man crash to the ground, Ray Horne said he felt no remorse. Patricia Stanford remarked she was surprised that both of her assigned targets stood when the horse bolted. She took out the one on the left first. She fast rammed the bolt action, and then scoped right and squeezed. Both men had pitched backward behind bales of hay.

In the south loft, Myrtle Wallace observed that her scoped targets stayed low behind their cover. It was as though they suspected some counter action before the group broke for the mine. The head of one was visible, shoulders up for the other. She opted for the head, cross-haired it, and squeezed the trigger. Not hesitating to verify her success, she had already swung to the second man, who was now ducking for cover. Her next shot was high, missing the disappearing act. The next three shots penetrated the hay bales. She reloaded and sent four additional, evenly spaced shots through the hay. Hay was no deterrent for a .308 magnum bullet. She wasn't certain whether or not the shots had found the hidden target.

Four rifles had barked from the lodge's front, concentrating on an equal number of muzzles firing from the barn. To the left of the upper window, Cinch had dropped a twelve-inch square pattern of .405's. The bullets splinted the siding under the onslaught. Reloading, he marched left to the right and drove six 300 gram bullets into the barn's loft.

Concentrating on the right corner of the same window, Fulcher dropped a full clip of 30.06's. He re-clipped, firing randomly into String's room. There would be some vengeance for the cowboy's death.

Zeroing in on the lower door frame, Frenchie's shot broke the upper hinge, and the barn door sagged slightly forward. Fish Mackey brought down a fleeting figure moving across the opening. Checker-boarding the siding, the two men's random firing chipped holes through the rough cut limber.

Major Greer advised Lashley he had difficulty in taking Pearl Gavin into custody. When the firing started, the major saw the woman move. Quick for her size, Pearl Gavin flashed a fist at his gun hand. Side stepping, he took her fist in his ribs. Closing, he brought the pistol butt down on her forehead. Blood spewed from a cut, as she fell limply to the floor. He had duct taped her hands and feet.

Rich Horne reported an affirmative single, as did Leo Rich. Patricia Stanford confirmed doubles. Myrtle Wallace, certain on one, expressed doubts on the second. From the front porch, Fish Mackey had the only confirmation. That confirmed a total of six for certain. The number of remaining casualties was pure speculation. His plan was a success. Silently, Lashley knew that any celebration was premature. Six points ahead at the end of the first quarter was inadequate to claim a win. There was plenty of time left on the clock for the opposition to go on the offensive.

"Where's Joel and Pearl?" Fulcher asked, noticing the absence of the hell fire and brimstone citizens usually present to condemn these reports. He spoke as if he had been expecting a chastisement for his participation in this deadly deed.

"Guarimo escaped on the horse," Lashley said. "And Pearl's in a room bound and gagged."

It was show and tell time for Lashley. The run down had been coming. It was time to lay the cards on the table and claim the pot. But he knew that he might not be in possession of the winning hand. There was one wild card outstanding for which he could not account. The joker was always a winner. He would have to bluff. Hopefully nobody would call. The limit had been reached, and he had nothing to add to the pot.

Several minutes passed before order returned, as the group reacted to the stunning news. Hissing, hoots, threats and demands had been hurdled, caught, recast, and rebound about the room. Carter, in his booming voice, brought it to focus.

"By God," the asphalt contractor demanded, "we are due an explanation. We have a right to know, Lashley. What the hell's going on?" Beside him Dunsey Martin nodded in agreement.

Lashley selected a chair, pivoted it, and sat down, resting his crossed arms on the upright. His back remained against the wall. Four lantern flames licked their dancing tongues upon the wicks. It cast moving shadows on his face.

"This will be very convoluted and might take some time. If we can, let's try to hold our questions until last," he said in a calm voice. The group nodded in acceptance.

"Back before we left St. Andrews, and we may never know how, the membership and itinerary of this hunting trip leaked. The information reached unsavory parties, who for their own purposes became interested. It appears that somebody within this lodge is a target. They have no intention of killing all of us. They are only interested in one individual."

"Like for ransom?" Dunsey asked, placing her hand over her mouth, remembering belatedly the agreement not to interrupt.

"Something like that, but possibly more complex," Lashley continued. "There is an outside chance I may be the object of assault. I haven't discounted it. It is possible that someone believes that I am in possession of information from my past that would help or harm some group. A remote hunting trip is an excellent opportunity to isolate me and extract the information. The trail would be cold by the time the dead are discovered. But that same logic could apply to any of us."

"Are you the key?" Thyus Harder asked.

"I said 'outside chance.' We'll leave it at that. Whatever their purpose is, it was of vital interest to them. They were willing to commit a lot of money, resources, and manpower. Once the Cottonwood was identified and the time of arrival was known, these perpetrators organized their tactics."

"First, they needed inside help. The easiest possibility was to compromise one of the hunters into giving them assistance. Find one in economic trouble and pressure him into cooperating. But if they failed to establish the desired support, most likely their contact would confide in his hunting buddies, and their plot would be exposed. The women were not likely candidates. Prior to departure, the men were close-mouthed about their traveling companions. Some, such as Mitzi Rhodes, we now know were last minute recruits."

"The alternative was to substitute a hunter. Late conflicts had developed before. Schedules change, even with the best made plans. Last year, there were two cancellations and substitutions within the final week. Thus, Pearl's brother, Tom Harley appeared as the most likely candidate. A veteran from previous hunts, he was only marginally connected to the nucleus of the hunting party, primarily Rich, Carter, Farrow, and Thornton. He resides in DeFuniak Springs, over a hundred miles from St. Andrews. Social interchange was limited. Personal habits and family connections restricted him."

"But Tom was in the Humana Hospital. I called to verify. I didn't directly speak to him, but I even sent flowers," Rich added. "I got a note signed by him, requesting that Pearl and her boyfriend be included. He didn't want to lose his deposit and still have to pay his pro-rata share of the trip for a no-show. We had done substitutes before."

"Granted, you received a note, but the question is who prepared the document?" Lashley said. "At the St. Andrews airport, when you explained that Harley was ill and Joel was the substitute, I also verified. What I found was that Harley was suffering from severe food poisoning. He had been admitted jointly with a woman, Mary Jane Bowers. I should have been more suspicious, because he had been in I.C.U. for three days. Now I ask myself, if he was that ill, how did he compose such a note addressed to you?"

Lashley left unexplained the balance of the reasons for his concerns. Check and double check your backside. Assume nothing. Be intense in your defense.

At some distant place in his past, his training must have been intense. Attention to details must have been impressed deeply upon his subconscious mind. Checking was as natural to him as driving a car.

Before departing Lashley had faked his credentials, claiming to be an insurance company employee verifying Tom Harley's coverage. He discovered several important details from the hospital. Harley had been on the critical list and was not expected to live. The police were investigating the circumstances surrounding his hospitalization, together with that of a white female companion. Poison was suspected. A cousin residing in Montgomery, Alabama was listed as Harley's next of kin. No sister had been mentioned.

"When we reached Denver, I called Humana Hospital again," Lashley continued. "Harley had died. It was a circumstance we couldn't control. Concerned that his death would dash cold water on the trip, I decided to withhold the information until our return."

Several gasps resounded, but no one interrupted.

"During the layovers in Denver and Casper, I attempted to contact Harley's next of kin but was unsuccessful. That wasn't unusual, though. The police had most likely notified the cousin, who would have been in transit to make arrangements for the funeral. The funeral home had not been in contact with the next of kin as of my last call placed just before departure for the Cottonwood. Severed communication, due to the remoteness of this hunting lodge, provided me with no opportunity to follow up on my leads," Lashley said. This failure had become a slip knot in his tight rope.

Lashley cast a glance toward Myrtle Wallace. He wondered how she missed a follow-up on Harley? Careless, maybe, but possibly he had a better feel of the players. He had known and hunted with them before. She had been careless not to back track. Any more similar mistakes, and she could expect an unwelcome assignment, like a transfer to Korea at some remote location.

"Then Pearl isn't Tom Harley's sister?" Wallace asked.

"That has now been confirmed," Lashley replied.

"Are you putting the blame of all of this on Joel and Pearl?" Carter pressed from the back of the room. He paced about aimlessly in frustration.

"No," Lashley answered. "They played bit parts but were strategically important." He took an object from the table. "With this radio which we found in Pearl's room, we now know that all the details of our planning within this lodge were leaked to our opposition at the barn. That included Chainsaw's attempt to walk out for help. We couldn't prove it until later, as I will explain."

He paused for some nonverbal feedback from the group. The group nervously twitched but remained silent. He continued, "The lid came off the operation when Heather Baldwin flushed the point men. Back in Casper, Joel had pumped information about the Cottonwood from hunters with previous experience. He posed it as innocent conversation. But it was extremely important for planning purposes. He learned about the layout of the land and the north road, as the alternative method of reaching the hunting lodge. He passed this information along to his contact.

By the first full day of our hunt, the first troops were here. The most likely operation called for the arrival of the main support the next day. While the hunting parties were out, they planned to sneak in and overpower those who remained behind at the lodge. As the incoming hunters returned, they could be easily captured. Succeeding in that endeavor, it would be easy to take their prey, destroy the survivors and leave."

Lashley deliberately omitted how Myrtle Wallace had inadvertently given details to the spook.

"You mean kill us, the ones they didn't want?" Grace Hancock interjected.

"That's what I mean. But by haphazardness, Heather stumbled into their nest. The members of the advanced party were street thugs, drug enforcers, or hired killers. All ill disciplined and rowdy. The ones we have taken and examined were either Colombians or Cuban Marielitos. They were tough, hardened criminals with no conscience but that which belches bullets."

"They abused Heather, left her to be found. It was a delaying tactic until reinforcements arrived. She was originally drugged to further delay our obtaining helpful information from her. Under Pearl's care, Heather was continually drugged orally. Neither Pearl nor Guarimo could take a chance that she had heard or seen something useful."

"Since she was moved to Grace's watchful eye, Heather has made steady improvements. In a few more hours, she will be close to normal. Not drug free, but she will be at least in an operational state."

"That's right," Dunsey Martin realized. "Heather's talking and everything now."

"Guarimo and Gavin," Lashley continued, "stayed at the lodge during the first hunt day. They used their time wisely, learning the characteristics of the main building, the barn, and the outbuildings. Joel located the ham radio in the pantry. Gavin was his distraction. It wasn't difficult to sever the cable. Rendering the radio inoperative, this eliminated the only emergency communication between the Cottonwood and the outside. Because the lodge is so remote, cell phones aren't operative."

"Can you prove this?" Carter asked.

"Some things we can, others are just conjecture based on hard evidence. My first major mistake was to explain our plans. I outlined to all the males of the group how we would obtain medical attention for Heather.

"At first, the attack on Heather appeared to be a random incident, even though the physical evidence was somewhat confusing. I was suspicious of Guarimo. But I couldn't initially draw a connection between the assault and his substitute for Harley. Our resolution to take Heather into Rawlins called for drastic measures, as the main force was not yet in place. So Guarimo disabled our vehicles. In the process, he killed String, who caught him in the act. That, we can prove."

"Fill us in on that," Major Greer requested in strong terms. "No shots were heard that night"

Lashley then explained how he had shifted Guarimo and his gear into the bunk house room to share with Fulcher. Under the guise of checking the security and defense of the bunk house, he had searched Guarimo's gear to no avail.

Unfortunately, it was the next day and after an extensive search that the silencer was discovered in Pearl's room. Lashley also explained that the torn shirt was discovered that matched the threads snagged in one of the dog's mouths.

"Guarimo was confronted with the evidence," Lashley further illustrated. "His arm revealed the teeth marks. He was finally placed on the horse for a diversion."

"What ties Pearl to this?" Carter asked.

"This radio," Lashley said. "Shortly after noon, Miss Wallace observed Pearl using it to convey our breakout plans for three o'clock. During her communication, we monitored her message by a similar radio I removed from one of the intruders who attacked the lodge last night. Intercepting that radio communication confirmed the depth of her involvement. She leaked vital information that disclosed our escape plans. If we had completed our plans to go through the mine as outlined, we would have walked into a trap."

"And where is Joel now?" Carter asked.

"He rode out of here tied to the saddle on the mare."

He wanted to add, WITH A BULLET IN HIS BACK. His final bullet had struck Joel's backbone just before the mare bolted down off the sloping trail, sidestepping to pass along the fish dam. Lashley had killed Guarimo.

CHAPTER FIFTEEN

The barrel of the Winchester flickered as the metal caught the flame from the burning wood. Fronting the hearth, Lashley sat, cleaning the weapon. He wiped the excess oil with a cloth, polishing the stock to a gleam. He levered and cocked the hammer back to the firing position. His thumb pressured the hammer. His finger squeezed the trigger. Silently, the hammer moved forward, returning to safety. Never dry fire a weapon, Lashley thought.

Sitting on the bed, Paige St. John watched him work. Weapons were almost an extension of his body. His ability to analyze a gun was uncanny. When handed an unfamiliar weapon, Lashley could instantly compute its features and craft it into tight knit bull's-eyes, yards down the range. Never a Maggie's Drawers for him. Lashley was a marksman par excellence.

Frenchie Hebert, when commenting to Lashley on the characteristics of this particular Winchester 30.30, observed, "It pulls left a half inch at two hundred yards. Zeros at a hundred and fifty."

"Any drop?" Lashley had inquired.

"Half to an inch at two hundred fifty yards," Frenchie answered. "Overall, it holds a tight pattern. I re-calibrated it about two weeks ago. Been in the rack ever since. No rough movement, so it should still hold a true sight."

Relying on the expertise of the head guide, Lashley had selected this specific weapon for the forthcoming task. Fully loaded, it held fifteen rounds. This provided adequate rounds for the handler. The lever action for the Winchester's ejection was extremely swift, its adequacy unquestioned. It contrasted with the more favored automatic weapons that were subject to frequent jamming and questionable accuracy at any distance. The Winchester had won the West. With its deadly and continuous fire against charging Indians, it turned the tide for the white man. It was still a powerful weapon in the crafty hand of a skilled gunman. If anyone was skilled with the Winchester, Lashley felt he fit the mold.

Several boxes of 30.30 ammunition were within a hand's reach. In the dim fire light, Lashley studied the labels, reviewing the power charge and bullet types. He loaded the magazine to full capacity, leaving the chamber empty. His safety training persevered to all aspects of fire arm use. Arm the weapon at the last possible moment before discharge. Forty-five additional loose, soft nose rounds were loaded in the right-hand pocket of his camouflaged hunting jacket. Twenty steel-nosed rounds filled the left pocket. He dropped two extra boxes of ammunition in his soft pack.

Paige loved him he was certain. She had loved him since early in their relationship, even with his strange silence, his unexplained absences, and his unusual lifestyle. These conditions appeared to enhance her affection.

At first, his disappearances had concerned Paige. A note attached to the refrigerator stating, WILL BE GONE FOR A TIME, constituted her only notice. Two or three days later, he would return with no explanation. Sometimes, he would return at day break, explaining nothing of his absence.

Occasionally she viewed his actions as taking their relationship for granted. Once or twice, she breached an inquiry about his absences, but he had shrugged off her question. The camel's back broke early one morning, as he returned with no explanation. She assailed him with tongue-lashing furry. She could no longer tolerate his careless treatment. Several minutes of her tirade passed before he interrupted.

"I'm sorry, but it must be this way. It is what I am," Lashley answered, and he explained to her for the first time of his rebirth in a hospital months earlier. He was an adult with no childhood, a life with no beginning. The explanation was brief, unadorned with details. He wanted no more discussion on the subject. From that day on, an acceptable routine of tolerance, unspoken agreement, and individual space merged them into an effective team. They became close and loving. On several occasions, usually following one of his harrowing dreams, he breached the subject of his past. Such conversations were limited in scope and rapidly terminated.

She continued her part-time work and supported his limited social obligations and major athletic jaunts. He, in turn, supported her commitments in his silent, effortless way. On those occasions when she mentioned a more permanent relationship, he demurred. He often asked himself what would happen should his memory return and his past be rediscovered. What if it included a wife and family? His alternatives could not be faced or discussed until that time. Until then, any ideas of a permanent commitment could gather dust on the back shelf. Still, she persevered in the relationship.

Paige's presence refocused his thoughts back to the present, to this dark room in the Cottonwood Lodge. Six months had elapsed since she had first broached the question of marriage. Now, he was leaving for a dangerous mission. Her question remained unanswered, a commitment unfilled.

"For a long time," she finally said to him, "I haven't questioned what you do or when or where you go. But, Howard, this is different. I'm worried."

He shrugged and began re-oiling a pistol he held. In the silence, only the burning wood spoke with a cracking sound. She waited and then continued, "Someone else can do it. It doesn't have to be you. Send Frenchie. He's the responsible party. He has a duty to protect his guests. Or Captain Mitchell. He's a professional soldier, paid to protect citizens."

Lashley shook his head negatively, discarding her arguments like water under windshield wipers.

"You have done your part," she persisted in a pleading voice. "More than any other person. Wait it out for a few more days. Other guests must be coming to the lodge when our hunt has ended. Those horrible people out there will leave before then. Besides, with their inside connections lost, now that Joel and Pearl are exposed, they're confused with all those losses. They must leave soon and let us be."

Lashley looked into the fireplace. He kicked the logs, arousing sparks and flames. His decision had been made. It was calculated, weighed and irreversible. He was going and soon.

"No," he said. "They will not leave. This party is composed of extreme fundamentalists. Certified fanatics. Tenacious as pit bulls. Vicious as panthers. Single issued as a spitball in a pea shooter. They may retreat temporarily, but abandon their target? Never! To end this, the heart must be cut from the body, the remains cremated, and the ashes scattered across the valley."

"Then death is contagious," she said bitterly.

Lashley accepted her sarcasm. It was an idea that offered him personal concern. He pondered his answer. "In a manner of speaking, maybe, as a concept, it is correct. When the Palestinians strike Israel, the Jews repay ten fold. It's counter attack after counter attack. One bomb explodes in the west bank. Then, ten bombs drop on some suspected P.L.O. guerrilla camp. Who dies? Mostly the civilians. It's the innocents who suffer. In that aspect, death is contagious. But only when the price becomes too costly does the cycle change."

He returned the pistol to its holster and continued. "For civilized people, it doesn't have to be that way. There are better methods of negotiating conflicts. But, as long as there are fanatics in this world, not bound by allegiance to law and order, then one death breeds another. Until then, that is, the bottom line becomes so expensive for the fanatics."

"Why is this different, Howard?" she asked.

"First, we must assume the ultimate target is limited to a specific person, piece of paper, or some type of information. Those guerrillas are not trained, professional soldiers. They're a rag-tailed, dangerous, hastily organized unit. That indicates that it's not an operation supported by a foreign government. That type of unit is bound to be better skilled. With that assumption narrows the possibilities of a clandestine organization like the I.R.A., Red Army, or something similar. Operating in small cells, they never joint venture any mission using a drug dealer's muscle. It would be too risky. If the deal went sour, people could be persuaded to talk. Identification could be made, and the cell would be penetrated to its core. The I.R.A., or a similar group, could never allow that to occur."

"Then what is left?" Paige asked.

"It's more of a personal thing," Lashley replied.

"Like R.S. Farrow's ex-girlfriend?" she asked.

"Possible. But I doubt it. This operation has been an expensive effort. I mean in capital outlay, materials, manpower, not to mention the casualties. That takes a serious commitment. I suppose it would have been easier to catch Farrow closer to his home turf, and take him out that way. My guess detects a deeper motive."

"Do you have a guess?"

"Not yet, but I'm getting close," he answered as he placed the pistol in the soft pack.

"But this, this volunteer mission you are so committed to, why this? Isn't it more death to heap on more deaths?" Paige asked.

"The weed must be destroyed, its roots obliterated. The seed must be demolished. You can't do that with a nation, a race, or a religion. There are too many hymns in the song book to erase all of them. But when it is a personal matter the odds can be narrowed. Wipe out the one who asserts some personal injustice and the torch burns out quickly. Then there is no one else to rekindle the flames."

"But if you kill him, doesn't he become the martyr?" she dubiously inquired.

"Sometimes. And that might be the case if those who surrounded us at this lodge were representatives of any government, sect, clan, or identifiable group. A tangible entity. When a government wrongfully kills, it's easy to rebel. A martyr might arise like a phoenix from the ashes. But here at the lodge, our best hope is we are facing a loose knit organization. It is intangible. There would be little or nothing for a cause to attach and hold. That is the best we can hope for."

"So you are going? And if necessary to kill again?" she nervously asked, dreading the known reply.

He nodded, and in the silent room turned to face her.

"But what about me?" she exclaimed. She spoke as if she needed to suppress the thought that she might be left to a lonely life. A life without Howard Lashley.

"I made financial arrangements for you months ago," he said.

"Damn, Howard, that didn't come out right," she said, drooping to the hearth and placing her arm around his legs. "I don't mean financially. I mean physically and emotionally. I love you. You have filled a void in my life. I don't need to lose that. Chainsaw was lost, murdered by those goons. I couldn't bear that to happen to you."

Lashley kissed her lightly on the forehead first, then passionately on her mouth. Charged with a depth of emotion, she responded, but he ended the embrace abruptly.

"When this is all behind us, Paige, are you ready to get married?" he suddenly asked. She was caught short by the question.

Astonished, she replied, "Yes, I think we've waited long enough."

CHAPTER SIXTEEN

On the trail, Howard Lashley paused at the low point on a switch back. Steps behind him, Captain Tyrone Mitchell's labored breaths broke the silence. The air was thin at this altitude, scrounging life's breath from lungs accustomed to a sea level existence.

The wind had died. The clouds, temporarily abated, revealed the jewels of the night brilliantly locked in the sky. Thinning timber signaled that the men were approaching the ridge line of the Thumb. The night's darkness had obscured the trail upward from the Cottonwood Lodge through the canyon, as they awkwardly climbed along its south slope. Usually, a forty minute effort in daylight travel, the men's hike had consumed twice the normal time. It was almost 2:00 a.m. Three more hours remained for preparation. The trip down the northern slope would be more difficult, as there was no defined trail. Silence was imperative. A rock slide of the smallest proportions would have the same effect as ringing the door bell - an announcement that guests were coming for a visit.

The steep north slope decent had been planned to go as far west as possible. The decent would be downward along the Thumb far from the tip. The distance was calculated to minimize discovery. The hike downward would be accomplished by a series of switch back movements, zig-zagging downward. The grade of decent was so intent that the men planned a staging of sitting and sliding downward on the rear of their pants. At the floor of the slope, they expected to enter into the bottom of a narrow draw, a half mile west of the Thumb's tip. This dry arroyo would provide cover, as they moved easterly.

Slipping his pack from his back, Lashley spoke softly, "Let's rest a minute."

Even in the darkness, clouds of vapor escaped his mouth as he spoke. In the stillness, it was cold. Close to zero degrees, he guessed. He removed his hat, running his fingers through his hair.

Mitchell gratefully accepted the offer.

The weight of Lashley's pack and weapon was becoming heavier with every step. A pound of weight seems to double with every mile hiked. Physically, he had considered himself in good shape, but this hike had taxed his energy reserves. Possibly, the short, erratic cat napping of the past several days was a contributing factor.

In silence, the men drank from their canteens and munched on candy bars, avoiding dehydration common in high altitudes. Carbohydrates mustered quick energy.

Lashley was disappointed. His final theory had burst, blown in his face like a balloon. He was back to square one. Either he had to accept a lie as fact, or he must be unwilling to embrace the truth, which he conceived to be disguised as a lie. It was all a grave masquerade party. Mardi Gras had arrived dressed in the fancy clothing of truth, while veracity had selected the garb of deceit. A wolf in wolf's clothing did not make good sense. But that was what he had left in his leaky bucket.

An elaborate drama had been written, actors employed, and the curtain rose with the Cottonwood Lodge as the setting. Somebody wanted someone or something. They were willing to kill and pay a high sacrifice. But what could have such importance in this remote Rocky Mountain resort?

Drugs were the most obvious answer Lashley guessed. Lately, drugs had been selected as the whipping boy for all the ailments of the American society. Certainly, drugs deserved its designation. Vast amounts of untraceable cash lead to deceit and corruption. Power corrupted, fostering bloodshed and street war, with the innocence more often a victim than a participant.

The first dead of the opposing force had clearly been a Cuban Marielito. The tattooed man Lashley had shot off the roof afforded an ample opportunity to examine a spectrum of his opposition. Drugs were the Hispanics' specialty, and Fulcher's connections to aborted drug deals had been a possibility. It was a tie through a weak thread. As the casualties mounted, and two died at the tack sack, Lashley's investigation revealed more dark-skinned, black—haired Hispanic bodies. Nothing more. There were no additional clues that would connect to any single national organization. Each body Lashley examined had no identification, bill folds or other data. Only one had a parking ticket in a coat pocket, and it was non-descript.

If they had been Arabic, then it would have defined some Muslim or Islamic fanatic connection. It would also eliminate drugs as the primary motivation. Islam, to date, had evidenced little propensity toward involvement in massive illegal drugs in the U.S. If the Arabs were involved, it would be small time compared to the heirs of the Marielitos and streetwise blacks. Their religion disdained liquor, also drugs. The Latinos' involvement was allowed as an alternative, possibly that this attack was a vendetta for some ex-girlfriend or relative seeking vengeance for a sexual wrong. That assumed, of course, that the couples around the lodge had enough connections with a Latino background. Lashley was reluctant to sign off Rich's Italian wife as an underlying factor. But such a connection seemed too remote.

Pearl Gavin had substantiated, to some extent, the hypothesis that these gangsters were well funded. Time was not an ally of the Cottonwood occupants. Lashley needed prompt and accurate information. Pearl resisted at first, but yielded when Lashley applied force. Under this pressure, she had revealed that Joel Guarimo, early in life, had been a fundamental Christian with a membership in some off-the-rack charismatic church. Dissolution with the religion's commitment of his fellow parishioners, he defected three years ago, joining an Atlanta mosque. Made up of distant followers of Malcolm X, the mosque was a modern, reform, Islamic movement. White members were rare but not totally excluded by this particular black religious order.

A member of the same mosque, Pearl made Joel's acquaintance there. Trained by a Muslim group as clandestine operatives in Central America, the couple had secretly undertaken assigned tasks against defectors of religious orders. Being white, they were unique in their cover. No one tied them to the Black Islamic movement. Their selection to be included in the Cottonwood hunting party had been arranged through contacts outside the Atlanta branch of their religious cult. Neither Joel nor Pearl was afforded any direct communication with their employers.

Their initial contact filtered through a convoluted route by way of a high priest named Haidar H. Twenty thousand dollars was jointly paid as up-front money, with a promise of an additional $15,000 each when the couple's job had been completed. Should a police investigation raise any connection between the couple and their employer, they had been promised safe passage to Libya and a secure position once relocated. Their assignment was to operate inside the lodge and report, by radio, all activities of the occupants.

They also sabotaged the lodge's radio and the vehicles. They were promised that they would not be necessarily included in any rough activities, but must be prepared to protect their presence inside. That was the extent of their job description.

Other operatives had poisoned Tom Harley and his girlfriend, Mary Jane Bowers, and set up the substitution request to Leo Rich. Pearl, delivering the fake note, had been briefed on Rich's sexual propensities. Behind a closed door and fast zipper, Rich had hastily approved the substitute hunters for the Cottonwood hunting trip.

The target of the proposed operation was never disclosed nor did the couple give it any concern. Secrecy had been essential in all previous assignments, and this operation was no exception. Questions often brought reprimands from their zealot leaders. Performance with zeal and fervency was the ultimate standard, resulting in homage recognition and capital rewards. They had accepted the assignment in ignorance. String's death had been accidental. From Guarimo's prospective, it was regrettable but excusable. The cowboy should not have interfered.

Information derived from a captured clandestine operative is at best questionable Lashley knew. In the event of capture, the operative is trained to delay as long as possible, furnishing any vital information. Ultimately, torture or drugs will break even the strongest resistance. Each operative is aware that ultimately he or she will break.

As the breaking point of each individual will vary, the operative has a preplanned cover story. Once captured, bare bones data, sufficient to be credible, is disclosed. Interlaced with minimum truth, the disclosure is clothed with deliberate misinformation, smoke screening the truthful portion actually revealed. The captor, understanding the process, must act accordingly to unravel what he has received. When the tale is eventually unwoven and re-stitched, valuable time has been forfeited, false leads traveled, and the operative has been able to function long past its exposure. The theme is to give sufficient and believable lies, and the truth becomes camouflaged.

Lashley had to assume that only a fraction of Pearl's information was believable. The balance was washed in the murky oil of deceit. The problem was to distinguish the gold from the pyrite. He had to peel the onion to its core without shedding a tear.

Logic grasped for a connection between an Atlanta Islamic religious sect, a band of Hispanics, the Cottonwood Guest Lodge, or its occupants. Conceived as blasphemy directed to Muhammad and his

413

teachings, a novel had been sufficient cause to activate an Islamic death squad searching for an English author. No readily identifiable blasphemers were in residence at the Cottonwood. There was no discernible tie back to the Arabs, except Major Greer's and Captain Mitchell's recent assignments to Pakistan.

Elliott Thornton's mother was Jewish Lashley had discovered. He had not practiced any religion since reaching adulthood, nor was he engaged in any Jewish political organization that might have alienated him with the P.L.O. Religion seemed to be a dead end. It was too distant a relation.

The Middle East had a dependency on oil. Those nations would not be elated should the Americans discover another vast oil field, tilting an imbalance in the petroleum trade. These ideas centered Lashley's attention back to the Cottonwood and its staff. For Lashley, local geological conditions did not polarize any conclusions on petroleum. Likewise, such a connection was remote and speculative.

Lashley and Frenchie Hebert had jointly reassessed the personal backgrounds of each guide. Nothing surfaced. There was no discernible lead to suspect any of these hired hands. Serving both as hunting guides and cowboys, the men were far removed from the influences of civilizations. Except for military service, none had traveled more than 100 miles from this valley along the upper North Platte River. Had Chainsaw Poulen or Hank Stringfield been the exception? If either of these two had been the target the intruders should have vanished after their deaths. No, Lashley was convinced there was something else. But what? He was at a loss.

Following Paige St. John's acceptance of his marriage proposal, he had again sought out Myrtle Wallace. He reflected on his second sequestering with Wallace and how he had extracted additional information from the research the woman had done, comparing her data with his separate investigation. Re-evaluating the available histories of the business men this trip revealed little more than that which had been previously discussed. The female companions were again cursorily rejected. Neither of these sources appeared useful for further attention.

"Except Paige St. John," Myrtle had said in her matter-of—fact tone.

"What about her?" Lashley asked, stunned.

Nervously, Myrtle delayed her answer.

Obviously she was concerned. Lashley knew people could become sensitive, even violent when the integrity of their lover was questioned. Wallace must figure he was not a person to cross. Treat the subject lightly, she must be thinking.

"Previously, I withheld info about Paige," Myrtle Wallace said with caution. "I didn't consider it pertinent at first. But I've had second thoughts."

She hesitated again then proceeded with caution.

"Her former associate, Leonard Matunes, was an arms dealer. He was real hot when he briefly moved his operation to St. Andrews. The feds were close on his trail. He knew it and apparently dropped out of international dealings. Then he became involved in a scam out of Miami with an off shore bank. He really became hot then. He's in hiding on a Belizean island now, last check I made."

Lashley's first meeting with Paige St. John had been at a Chamber of Commerce social. She was serving as a hostess. He was smitten with her charm and beauty. By design, Lashley made it his business to know her better. Investigating discretely, he discovered she had a tenuous relationship with an unsavory character, Leonard Matunes, who had recently moved in with her. Matunes divided his time between Paige's apartment and a unit in Miami.

Lashley purposely obtained invitations to functions that paralleled those received by Paige. After several social meetings, Lashley had established a speaking relationship with this charming woman. But Matunes' shadow prevented further allegiances.

Now, Myrtle's revelation stung Lashley. Matunes' dealings with a Miami-based company had been the catalyst Lashley had used to wean the crook from Paige. But his personal investigation had been superficial, careless, and single purposed. Discovering Matunes' unlawful activities with the Caribean financial institution had been sufficient for his use. A few innocent notes like THE TAP IS ON, THE

417

LOOKING GLASS SEES, and ALL IS KNOWN, were secretly delivered to the man's house or positioned on his windshield. These notices were all that was required. The guilt-laden rabbit fled the security of the briar patch.

Matunes' abrupt departure stranded Paige emotionally and financially. Lashley filled the void. But he had not dug deeper after Matunes' background or connections. It was a gross mistake.

"How bad were the arms deals?" Lashley asked.

"Real bad," she responded. "The cover up on that one originates from the Clinton White House down. Matunes was involved in an arms deal to exchange hostages in the Middle East. The deal fell through and an American, a military officer advisor assigned to the U.N. peace-keeping force, was killed. Murdered. Matunes reportedly kept the money and also hid the arms. Both sides were gunning for him."

"Where did Paige fit in?" Lashley asked.

Myrtle shifted uncomfortably. "I'm not too sure. There had been a personal relationship between the couple several years before. When Paige separated from him, she returned to St. Andrews where her mother lived. Occasionally, after their separation, Paige would meet Matunes for weekends or holidays. Those meetings may have coincided with the aborted arms deal. Briefly they lived together in St. Andrews. However, he departed hastily. There were suggestions that Paige was personally involved in the arms deal. But who knows? When I first noted the connection, I rejected it. But now I'm not so sure. I should have explored the connection in more depth."

"That connection is too remote," Lashley defensively answered. His poker face leaked a glimpse of shock.

"Not necessarily. There are several possibilities. One, that Paige has information that could lead to the location of the money or the arms. More particularly, the arms. That inventory included some of the most sophisticated weaponry the U.S. has ever authorized to be sold to any Middle Eastern government. The arm's destination was never disclosed, but it appeared to have been headed for Jordan."

"Israel was some kind of disturbed," she continued. "They figured that this manifest would upset the balance of power in the region. The arms disappeared. Reportedly they are stashed in Central America. Matunes can sell them at any time. When they appear on the market, the purchaser will be in a strong position. Emerging countries from Russia's providences also look like possible buyers."

She paused. Her face bore a look of uneasiness as she walked a tight rope.

"Alternatively," she continued, "Paige may have been involved, and someone has finally figured it out. So, it's accounting time. They want those arms bad enough to capture her, extract the info, by whatever necessary means, and kill the survivors at the Cottonwood. To the world, Desert Storm proved the superiority of America's sophisticated war weapons. This weaponry has now become the most desirable war commodity for third world countries. It was reaffirmed in Afghanistan. That's a sufficient motive. The ball's back in your court, Lashley."

Her voice had been hesitant. But just from hearing her own words, she finished with more confidence. Lashley returned her nod as he departed.

His deep concentration of that earlier conversation with Myrtle muffled the sound of Mitchell's question. He shivered in the cold, his back braced against a rock.

"How's our timing?" Mitchell repeated in a low whisper, fearful that the echo might carry beyond acceptable distances. They had discussed the possibility of finding a guard posted somewhere in the draw along the base of the slope.

Lashley checked his watch. 3:18 a.m. There was plenty of time left. A few seconds passed before Lashley answered.

"Okay on the time. But let's move on. If there's any surplus time, let's spend it in the arroyo down below."

The trip down the north slope of the Thumb went smoother than expected. Within an hour, the two men crouched in the sandy bottom of the dry gulch. Protected from the wind by the rocked wall, the temperature appeared almost warm. Secure from the bellow's movement, the gulch felt twenty degrees warmer at the bottom.

Lashley's attention had been equally divided between the difficulty of the silent decent and his thoughts of Paige St. John.

Mitchell was operating as the point man, picking the route downward. Descending was more straining, taxing different muscles. Back packs and slung weapons adversely tilted their center of gravity. This slow progress had tested their physical strengths, but it afforded Lashley an opportunity to access the alternatives.

Paige identified as the target? The suggestion did not make sense.

"Still determined to go?" Paige had said hastily when Lashley cornered her in the bedroom, following his last conversation with Myrtle Wallace.

"My objections mean nothing?" she said, then smiled. "Freshly engaged, and we're having an argument already. Isn't that a bad omen?"

Lashley spoke, looking somber. "Paige, it's important. I need to talk to you about Leonard Matunes."

It was the first time he had ever spoken the name "Matunes" in her presence. Paige's face flushed in the pale light of the lantern on the mantle. Gasping, she raised her hand to her throat. During their entire acquaintance, Lashley had never raised a query about her past companions. It was a breach of etiquette between them. She must have despised his remark.

"That's cruel, Lashley," she spoke in anger. "I've never asked about your personal relations before we met. I never expected you to inquire into mine."

She sobbed, as she added, "It's personal and private. I'll not discuss it with you."

She turned her back to him and smothered her face in her hands. He stepped toward her, placing his arm over her shoulder and drawing her body into his chest.

"I didn't phrase that well," he said, as he stroked her hair. "I want nothing personal. No details or anything like that. I need to know what connections Matunes might have had. What his involvements

423

were. Could there be any reason that someone was out to get at Matunes indirectly by going through you?"

He felt her body shiver. Her knees weakened. Only his strength prevented her collapse.

"Oh, my God," she whispered. "Oh, my God."

He moved her to the bed, seating her between two sofa pillows. She placed her arm along the head board. Her head sank into the bend of her arm, and she sobbed openly. Lashley had located some water and lifted the glass to her lips. He waited patiently.

"About a week and a half before we left, there was a man," she spoke calmly while deliberately telling her story.

She was alone for lunch in a local restaurant when a distinguished, well-dressed, light-haired gentleman called her by name and asked if he could join her for a business discussion. A crowded restaurant appeared to be a safe surrounding, so she consented. He displayed some identification and introduced himself. His name had something to do with water, like flood, or a similar reference. She had forgotten, but maybe if it was important, she would remember. The identification attached him to a branch of the U.S. Government, with which she was not familiar.

Idle conversation about the weather and the beauty of the white sands of the Gulf of Mexico at St. Andrews ensued. Then the man delivered the bombshell, the purpose for his trip.

"He was investigating Leonard Matunes, and this guy, Flood or whatever his name, wanted to know if I could assist the government," Paige told Lashley.

She further explained to Lashley that she responded to the man by stating she had previously talked to the F.B.I. She had made a full disclosure. She knew nothing of Matunes' involvement in off shore banking activities. He never discussed it with her, not the slightest hint of what he was doing. She remembered her shattered feelings, when she came home one night to find all his personal items, clothing, and gear gone. He had disappeared just like water down a sink, only faster. Since that date, she had heard nothing from Matunes.

She suggested to Mr. Flood to review her F.B.I. report. It was all there. She had spent hours with the federal agents who, in turn, had recorded her interrogation. Surely, government agencies would share their reports with another agency.

Mr. Flood, however, was not concerned about the financial affair. His interest was directed toward an earlier period, specifically, trips to the Caribbean and to Panama. Paige recalled the details of the trips where she had swam, sunned, and partied. Other than that, she was not much assistance to Flood.

Yes, Matunes had met some associates on each trip. He always abandoned her when he supposedly attended daily business meetings. Matunes never disclosed to her the nature or purpose of those meetings.

Occasionally, in hotel lobbies, she would see Matunes conversing with different individuals. The men would leave together and sometimes she had, from a distance, observed them returning in the same car. She had never been introduced to any of Matunes' contacts on these trips. Certain individuals, she had observed, had met with him on more than one occasion. Two had been in attendance at all locations.

Some, she had observed only once. In total, Matunes had been in company with more than a dozen.

Mr. Flood had pressed Paige for details, but she was unable to amplify more than she had already supplied. Was it possible that she could identify, by photograph, any of the participants? It was possible, but not likely. It had been more than two years. It was closer to three, in fact, when the first trips were taken. Would she try?

She suggested it would be best to allow her time to think that out before committing. Her relationship with Matunes was over, tearfully buried. Resurrection of a skeleton's bones might generate more pain than she was willing to experience. She explained that she would shortly be leaving on a hunting expedition. When she returned, if Flood was still interested, she would then discuss it. But she made no promises. Flood had accepted her explanation and withdrew from the restaurant.

She had more or less forgotten the encounter, with her excitement of preparing for her first trip to the true wild west. There was one additional point that she was not clear about. Somewhere in the back of her mind, she was certain that later that same day, she saw Flood passing her in a car with some person she knew. But to save her life, she could not remember who that other person had been.

"Howard," she had said, concluding her dissertation. "It can't be me those people are after, can it? I'd never forgive myself if I was the cause of String's and Chainsaw's death. I couldn't live with that. Am I the one they're after?"

Lashley departed, offering the woman no answer. Now squatting in the arroyo, Lashley determined it was forty-five minutes before the operation would start. Even in the dark, a cautious quarter mile walk down this deep draw would be a twenty-five minute hike. The mouth of the draw would exit just north of the Cottonwood's "new house," which was Hebert's in-law's abandoned dwelling. By allowing ten minutes for reconnaissance and preparation for the operation, they still had a few minutes remaining.

And still he had no answer for Paige. Her connection with Matunes was the most solid lead. Had

Matunes double crossed some companions in the Caribbean? If so, this combination of Colombian drug lords made sense. Paige had moved to the number one spot as the target.

"You ready, Mitchell?" he softly asked, crouching with his back against the rock wall.

"Ready," the captain replied.

"Need another check down?"

Apprehension cracked in Mitchell's voice as he answered, "I'm briefed adequately. The waiting is always the hardest part."

"We'll delay a couple more minutes," Lashley said, adjusting his rifle sling to a more comfortable position.

"How are you and Miss Wallace making it?"

Coming from left field, the question surprised the officer, Lashley guessed.

"Pretty good," he responded.

"How's the trip been for your sex life?" Lashley pried.

"Not much since this fiasco started, but before that it was super. Thought I was going to lose my strength."

The Mardi Gras dancer had been unmasked, and it was a lie. His backup, Captain Tyrone Mitchell, who was to cover his tail, had just lied to him. Lashley was going into a dangerous operation with an unmitigated liar.

CHAPTER SEVENTEEN

Lashley gave Captain Tyrone Mitchell's sleeve a tug. The officer stopped. Varying shades of darkness signaled that the men had arrived at the mouth of the draw. The house was no more than 200 feet off to their right. Through the ground floor window, a pale yellow light from a lantern fell like death's beacon. Lashley tugged again. Mitchell went down to a crouch. Lashley joined him.

"Stay here. I'll be back shortly," Lashley whispered in his ear.

Removing his pack and his rifle, Lashley stacked his gear neatly against a rock. Arming himself with the pistol, he spoke softly, "I'll whistle low when I return. Don't shoot me."

He silently crept away. Had he not crossed the officer's line of sight, thus blocking the window's light, Mitchell would not have been able to detect his direction of movement.

Lashley moved with the silence of a night hunting panther. Shit, he thought silently. I'm in a helpless, perilous situation. A sitting duck on an open pond surrounded by who knows how many camouflaged blinds. Each structure occupied by multiple armed hunters, desperate to cut a feather. That is what I am, a feathered duck with a wet, cold ass. Either way I move, I'm dead. Stay still among the decoys and maybe I'll pass off as a dummy duck.

Minutes passed as he moved closer to the structure. How many, he was uncertain. Fear had disrupted his mental timing device and tossed it over the side of a cliff. If he failed, could Mitchell run the operation alone, and finish it. The officer knew the mechanics, the what and how. But the why of the totality of this affair eluded him.

To the extent Lashley knew the "why," he had been tight-lipped about it. Mitchell had probably reached the conclusion that Lashley knew more than he was revealing. The revelations to the group about Joel Guarimo and Pearl Gavin's double cross did not complete the total picture. Many gaps were missing.

The underlying objective was bypassed. Lashley had tried to convey the impression he was a cool cat when in fact he was little better than a cold sitting duck? What did he really know, and how much was guess work?

Lashley's prying questions to Mitchell back up the draw had a purpose. To inquire about the officer's sex life with Myrtle had an underlying purpose. What business was that of Lashley? None, except during his last meeting with Myrtle Wallace, Lashley demanded some answers.

"Cut the bullshit, lady," he had said. "It's time I learn about your group."

Wallace had been reluctant at first until finally she disclosed basic facts.

Truthfully, as Wallace explained the details to Lashley, it might more appropriately describe their relationship as the absence of a sex life. Possibly it would have been unmanly for the captain to admit abstinence. No red-blooded man wants to confess that he had been conned into a trip with an ostensible girlfriend for a platonic romance. All that ballyhoo about being black on Saturday night was a reputation not easily defaulted.

Captain Mitchell was just completed his divorce when he met Myrtle at the Officer's Club at Tyndall Air Force Base. They had casually dated a few times. Myrtle reported he acted most surprised when she invited him to be her partner on the hunting trip.

However, whatever his expectations, they dissolved when they arrived in Denver. In the Mile High City, the captain received a briefing. Myrtle advised that he would be sharing a room with Major Greer, a man he found to be boring and barely tolerable. It was a secret to be held inviolable. Outwardly, Myrtle explained that the couple would fake turtle dove affection, withdrawing to separate quarters at the appropriate intervals. Major Greer and Patricia Stanford would likewise play the same doubles game.

The captain protested and threatened to leave for home. These protests were quickly smothered when Myrtle reminded him that his military orders had temporarily assigned him to Major Greer's command.

If he wanted to discuss it further, then he was to take it up with his temporary commanding officer. Otherwise, he was to follow orders just as she would likewise obey those orders assigned to her.

With their differences explained, the couple had developed a routine. In the presence of the members of the hunting party, Myrtle was the affectionate, tender, dutiful sweetheart. Privately, they were strangers. The mood swinging frustrated Mitchell she susptected. He was unable to distinguish play acting from affection. During the couple's earlier dates prior to this trip, he had suggested a maturing relationship. Myrtle, he hinted, could well be the next Mrs. Tyrone Mitchell. Since arriving at the Cottonwood, he had evolved, in all aspects, into a eunuch, serving a lady in waiting.

Then, Heather had been raped and String killed. Lashley noted an abrupt transformation in Myrtle and Mitchell. Both had been as dramatic as the evolution of a cocoon to a butterfly. Especially did he note a change in the woman.

No longer was Myrtle a fluttering sweetheart. He watched as Myrtle became a callused, withdrawn professional. Cool, calculated, and determined, she had functioned under pressure more efficiently than some of the men. There was no doubt she had been well trained, but she likewise possessed an inner quality that distinguished humans, dividing the sheep from the goats. She was a wolf. She had taken out her targets without qualms or hesitation. At least one, and possibly two. bodies attested to her skills of marksmanship, done with no expressed remorse. Then she had stood toe to toe with Lashley, her chin to his chest, and unloaded a barrage.

He retained his doubts about the captain.

His reconnaissance completed, Lashley crept back. He gave a low whistle, followed by three mouthed clicks. The muffled sounds floated through the darkness. He was relieved when Mitchell clicked back. Lashley slid beside the captain, crouching low.

"One guard was in the front doorway. I took him out," Lashley whispered. He hunched closely and continued. "Lamp's on in the lower floor. There appears to be six men on the ground level. Four are playing cards. It's possible that two on the cots are injured, but we won't count on it. We'll assume they've transported out or otherwise accounted for their wounded. At this level, all have to be considered as active hostiles."

He paused to confirm Mitchell's acknowledgment. Then he proceeded. "No idea on the upstairs occupants, but we will assume it is at least equal to the lower floor. It's six minutes after five. Frenchie and Cinch should have their ambush in place by now. Let's go."

Lashley untied the pack's flaps and removed a container of kerosene. Mitchell followed suit. Both slung their weapons over their shoulders and stuck the pistols in their belts.

"You flood the back doorway and north side with kerosene. Heavy on the door, but don't let any leak inside. Fumes might tip them off. I'll cover the east side. Don't light the kerosene until I break for the edge of the plateau. Then, get back here to the mouth of this draw. Use that rock over there as cover. From there, you can cover the door and the rear window." Pointing, Lashley indicated the cover. "Good luck," he said.

Lashley crept to the far south corner of the building, unscrewed the container's cap and sprinkled the liquid along the wall. A single window on the lower floor faced west. Over the years, while vacant, the house had become a nesting place for pack rats. Mustered into use as a barracks, the building's most recent occupants had cleaned the interior, dumping the nesting material outside under this window.

Lashley soaked the rat's debris thoroughly. It would serve as the basic kindling for the fire. When Lashley reached the northern corner, Mitchell was waiting.

The officer nodded affirmatively. It was time for the operation to begin. It was all or nothing. In the next few minutes, the success or failure of the defense of the Cottonwood would rest on the actions of these two. There was absolutely no margin for error allowed.

Lashley broke into a trot. His designated protection was fifty yards away. Covering this distance was the most dangerous exposure in the operation. If he were spotted darting for cover, he could expect a bullet in the back. Mitchell was likewise vulnerable, especially if anyone stepped outside to relieve himself or to change the guard. It would be worse yet, if there was a roving guard patrolling this area. Lashley was banking on dull senses caused by inactivity. Once the fire was illuminated, both Lashley and Mitchell would be clearly exposed, scraping for coverage.

A flicker of light broke the darkness. Mitchell had dropped his match. Flames gripped the dried siding of the building, erupting in intensity. In moments, the flames would alert the occupants. Lashley had the advantage of foreknowledge. He held the upper hand.

Diving for the rim of the plateau, he dropped down, located a stand and rose with his left arm extended along the Winchester. His elbow rested on the ground. It was a textbook classic supported firing stance. He waited, and his wait was short.

439

The two-story house was possibly twenty feet by thirty feet with the two exterior doors. The building's east side harbored two windows, one upper and one lower, centered in the structure to catch the rising sun. The south wall marked single windows, upper and lower. The fire was creeping up the rear of the building and shooting over the roof. The pack rat's collection was performing well. The landscape radiated in a red glow.

Inside the house, shouts joined the noise of the burning wood. Even at a distance, Lashley could distinguish the cursing. The awakened occupants organized a fire drill along the lines of mob confusion.

Lashley heard Mitchell fire. Evidently, someone attempting a rear exit had braved the flames devouring the door. Upstairs, silhouettes framed the window. Lashley squeezed the trigger, taking the back figure. Re-sighting, he drew down on the one remaining and squeezed. Two were down on the upper level. At the south wall, a man attempted to crawl from the upper window. Lashley dropped the man. A body plummeting through the glass of the lower center window struck the ground and sat up. Lashley aimed and took the man out where he landed. Another figure appeared at the same opening, flames covering his clothes. One shot was sufficient.

An automatic weapon barked. Showers of rock spewed fragmented rocks over Lashley. He ducked below the rim of the ledge. The weapon spoke again. This time, bullets sprinkled the rock ledge Lashley had just abandoned. The sniper had zeroed in on its target a moment too late. Lashley quickly side stepped two lengths, cautiously rising so his eyes cleared the cover.

The dry wood of the building fueled the fury of the fire. Flames cleared the peak of the roof by ten feet. The intensity of the inferno was evident to Lashley fifty yards out. The landscape was illuminated by the power of thousands of candle watts. It was both a curse and a blessing.

The sniper in the upper story could observe Lashley's movements. But, conversely, the man could not dally long, or he would be burned alive. The advantage shifted back to Lashley. He removed his hat and tossed it several feet left along the cliff line.

Instantly, the automatic responded, targeting the hat. Lashley's Winchester coughed twice, and a weapon fell out the upper window. Lashley's rifle was empty.

From behind the house, Lashley heard the reports of Mitchell's rifle in defense of the rear escape route. Lashley's aim, after reloading swiftly, was drawn back to the upper center. Another bullet was fired. A shadow fell in response.

During the brief pause, Lashley automatically slipped a single round in the chamber and inserted several cartridges into the magazine. The upper window darkened. Smart, Lashley thought, as he watched a mattress sail through the window followed by a man who flopped on the bed cover to cushion his fall. Lashley shot him on the first bounce. The building was now consumed with flames. If any survivors remained, they would soon be devoured by the inferno.

Five hundred yards down the abbreviated runway, a glass windshield and chrome reflected against the flames. Reinforcements were coming. Lashley dropped below the rim's edge, moved 100 feet south, and assumed another classic firing position. The Jeep Cherokee accelerated across the terrain, bouncing like a bucking horse at a rodeo.

At seventy-five yards out, Lashley fired. The front tire on the driver's side blew. He leveled the Winchester and dropped a round through the passenger side windshield. The vehicle traveled another 100 feet then careened to its side, belly angled toward the rim. Two rapid discharges pierced the fuel tank. Gasoline poured on the ground. He extracted a soft nosed cartridge from the chamber. Locating a steel nosed bullet in his left pocket, he inserted it into the chamber.

The steel bullet struck the vehicle's frame, activating a shower of sparks. The gasoline exploded, engulfing the Jeep in a curtain of blaze. On the top side, a door opened. A head appeared. Moments later, it flew backward in response to a round that pierced its forehead, leaving organic debris scattered on the ground. The tailgate opened, and a man rolled out. Lashley caught him on the third roll. Inside the vehicle, death screams competed with the cracking of popping safety windows, bursting tires, and expanding metal.

A momentary pause in activity at the house caused him to glance southerly toward the barn. Even at this distance, the fire was sufficiently intense in scale to illuminate the far end of this plateau. Lashley was able to observe a couple of hostiles entering separate vehicles expecting to escape the surprise attack.

The leading vehicle spun wildly in the rutted road, halting crosswise in the trail. Closely following, the second car turned sharply to avoid broad siding the disabled vehicle. Reacting too slowly, the rear car swerved to the right, striking the stalled auto a glancing blow, driving it out into the sage brush. Leaving the road, both vehicles trailed erratic courses through sage brush and broken rocks until the debris became too thick to proceed. As each vehicle halted, its occupants burst from the doors discharging automatic fire to the south corner of the barn. Frenchie Hebert and Cinch Wilkinson would be their targets. The guides were ambushing from a point Lashley had stationed them.

Lashley watched for a brief moment to observe several escapees retreating into the shadows.

Below the rim and to his left Lashley detected gun fire. Frenchie and Cinch were actively pursuing the escapees with accurate firing.

Lashley rested with one comfort. Every rancher in the valley within fifty miles would have seen this fire. Five o'clock a.m. had been selected as the ideal time for the attack. At that hour, adjoining ranchers would be attending to early morning chores and livestock. Traffic on the highway would have been altered. Soon, help would arrive. Frenchie had agreed to sacrifice his in-law's homestead as the signal for assistance.

The most difficult and dangerous task lay ahead, mopping up the stragglers. Lashley knew that the surviving fanatics at the barn would not surrender. Those hostiles would only go down in a hail of fire.

CHAPTER EIGHTEEN

Far to the east the rim of the sun broke over the mountain chain. Light struggled with darkness and slowly won. From his concealed location, Howard Lashley looked down on the barn eighty yards away. The structure's rustic red paint reflected the morning sun.

Lashley plotted his attack on the building. Flushing the remaining pocket of resistance in the barn was the next order of business. He was certain no one had survived the fire in the "new house." Doubt remained concerning the whereabouts of those who survived Frenchie's ambush on the escaping vehicles. Most likely, the survivors were scattered across the plains. Any additional straggler among the hostiles would be those trapped inside the barn.

He reflected on his enemy's strategy. The barn was a large structure with numerous hiding places. He attempted to recall the building's footprint.

The barn, a typical rustically constructed, western building, was 175 feet long and sixty feet wide. Behind the west side double doors, off center, Frenchie always parked his pickup, tractor, and farm wagon. The ground floor was sectioned into numerous horse stalls, reserving the south section of the ground floor and loft for hay storage.

Along the back, a fence served as a corral for the wet cows that satisfied the Cottonwood's requirements for milk, butter, and cheese. The fence had been constructed to enclose almost an acre. During harsh weather an open rear section of the barn wall allowed the cows, calves, or any stalled horses to retreat from the pen into the sheltered interior.

Frenchie Hebert climbed up the ledge and joined Lashley. Together, they watched the landscape as it was revealed by the rising sun. Lashley munched on a candy bar.

The men lay crouched where they could see through the partially opened rear pen gate to a portion of the cow lot. Within their sight, nothing moved inside.

"Whose kill is that?" Lashley asked, pointing to a body lying on the barn's upper deck doorway leading to String's loft room. At the top edge of the stairway, two arms dangled into open space.

"I figure he belongs to that black woman, Myrtle Wallace," the guide replied. "She was assigned to cover the stairs. She's stationed at the lower ledge of the bunk house. When that fire was blazing, there was enough light down here to see people moving. I figure that's when she picked that one off. That girl is one damn fine shot."

"How did you and Cinch make out?" Lashley inquired between bites.

"Two vehicles tried to break out," Hebert said, "a few minutes after the fire started. I guess you might have seen it. We jumped them both, but several of the passengers are out on foot somewhere there on the plains. When the barn's secure, I suggest we catch some horses and track them down. From the weapons we found abandoned in the cars, I'd say they have limited fire power. But I wouldn't count on it. Meantime, Cinch is still covering the southeast corner of the barn. Fish is at the corral, covering higher ground on the southwest. Myrtle still has the north side well covered."

Lashley carefully scoped the building, spending a long time watching the window framed in the upstairs door. "Is there any other way from that top room down into the barn?"

"Yes," Frenchie responded. "Through the trap door from the underside. It can be reached by ladder. In extreme bad weather, when a real northerner passes through, String could climb down and care for the cows and several of the horses we keep in the stalls throughout the winter. A storm might keep us holed up for a couple of days at a time. It is difficult in that kind of weather to make it from the lodge to the barn. So String would care for the livestock until the weather broke"

"Who's holding the radios?" Lashley inquired, as he washed down the candy with a swig from his canteen.

"Cinch, Fish, and that woman, Myrtle, have the little hand held jobbers we had at the lodge. You and the black captain have the big ones we took from these wild Indians. Cinch recovered another one of the bigger jobs in one of those vehicles we ambushed this morning. So, through Cinch, we can talk to all our outposts."

Lashley rummaged through his pockets, locating his radio. "Mitchell," he said. "Come on down to the lower end of the runway. Join us there."

"Roger," the radio replied in the captain's voice. Lashley had assigned the officer a post position on the south corner of the barn. The response was without enthusiasm. Mitchell would have to belly crawl across an open area, keeping his butt low when passing the barn. Lashley hoped the depression was of sufficient depth, so he would not be seen from the barn's loft.

The radio spoke, catching the men off guard. The voice was heavily accented, but the static made the dialect difficult to discern. "I'm inside the barn yard, hurt bad. I need help."

The men remained silent, contemplating this developing situation. Lashley again scoped the barn seeking the slightest movement. At the window, he detected motion, but it was gone in a flash.

In reflection, he was not certain that what he had glimpsed had been more than his desire for confirmation that the loft was occupied. He was tired, exhausted to the limits of human endurance. In three days, he had very few hours of sleep, stolen mostly in cat naps. Adrenalin pumping in excess quantities kept him motivated. When that supply was exhausted, he would collapse like a wet blanket. Was there a sufficient amount of energy remaining to supply his strength for another hour? That was all the time he needed to finish the job of clearing out the loft.

"Sounds like a trap to me," Frenchie said, visibly shaken by the unknown radio voice's plea for assistance.

The instrument was heard again. "Hurt real bad. I need help soon."

"Identify yourself," Lashley said, pressing the transmission button.

"A friend," the radio responded. "Name is of no consequence. I was sent to oil the waters. They

451

rejected my offer of peace and shot me. Now I oppose them."

"What is the situation in the barn?" Lashley asked.

"There are five, possibly six still active. I am on ground level outside the barn away from the equipment parked at the other end. I am inside a fenced area. Some of them are downstairs. I'm not sure how many."

The transmission was interrupted by the sharp report of a shot. Lashley heard it simultaneously on the radio and as it echoed against the slope of the prodding Thumb.

"They've got me pinned down. But they don't want to take the chance to rush me," the wounded voice said.

Captain Mitchell slipped in beside the two men, clearly exhausted from his efforts. He peeked over to view the landscape stretched out below. It was reminiscent of a western ranch scene from a jigsaw puzzle. The sun sparkled on the fish pond. Fish nipped water bugs, tracing ever enlarging circles on the surface. It was restful and serene, defying the death call waiting to peel.

"I've been listening to the transmission. What do you think?" the captain asked.

"I think it's a ploy of some kind," Frenchie responded. "Like the hen grouse faking a broken wing to lead the coyote away from her brood."

"Could be," the captain added. "But then it could be legitimate."

"That confirms part of the info," Lashley said, speaking under the field glasses. "Movement at the windows confirms at least two hostiles on the upper deck. I'm going to operate under the assumption that the entire building is under hostile control."

"Frenchie," he asked, as he continued his scoping. "Who, besides yourself, is good with a rope?"

"Fish is the best," the head guide answered, as he selected the chief wag of the hunting guides for the rope detail.

"Here's the operation," Lashley explained, detailing each assignment. "It will be a combined effort. Let's get in position within thirty minutes. Move out."

The young cowboy, Cinch Wilkinson, covering the southwest barn corner, received Lashley's short message. In turn, he alerted Myrtle Wallace to expect Captain Mitchell at her post.

"Don't shoot him," Cinch warned on both radios' frequencies. "He's coming up the drainage ditch on the far side of the road from you. Then he'll cross over through that culvert. Follow his instructions."

"Roger," the woman reported.

From his vantage point, Lashley watched Mitchell start his crawl up the ditch. Simultaneously, Frenchie drifted toward the cow pen, staying below the line of sight. In minutes he saw Frenchie joined Cinch. Although his radio remained silent, Lashley knew Cinch was communicating on the smaller lodge radio set, which was on a band frequency not accessible to the larger set. Unless by accident another type of radio was in the barn, the hostiles would not be able to intercept all of the transmission. He watched as Fish Mackey cautiously approached the exposed side of the corral, removed an object, and retreated from vision. A minute later, Fish appeared at Cinch's post where he handed something to Frenchie. The plan was in operation.

Lashley visually assured himself that Cinch was moving to cover his newly assigned position. He lowered himself, creeping to a boulder adjacent to the road leading westward to the lodge. Frenchie, with lasso in hand, joined him.

"Can Fish do his part?" Lashley asked, as he stripped off his jacket, discarding his field glasses and Winchester. He checked his pistol, extracting the clip to determine its load. He accepted the 12 gauge Remington that Frenchie tendered.

"Count on it," Frenchie responded, as he similarly discarded his surplus equipment. In tight quarters, it was best to travel light. "He'll come in from behind the walk-in cooler. I'll go up along side those parked vehicles. The handles on the barn door are like a half goal post where you can drop down a bar to secure the doors. It may take several tries, but I think we can lasso those handles."

"Your danger point will be if you're seen from the upper window. If you stay low, you shouldn't be exposed. If either of you fails, the other must jerk a single door panel open. Mitchell will be placed in front of that opening. You and Fish should cover the flanks of the door. When Cinch is up in the cooler at the trap door, I'll go in through the back gate into the cow pen. I won't move until I hear Mitchell firing. Move out."

Crawling to the back fence line, Lashley studied the interior of the cow pen. Through gaps in the diagonal fencing, he saw no movement. He kept low. To the east, the sun was on his back, casting his shadow along the fence. It troubled him. Seen by those inside, his low moving shadow would reflect between the gaps in the boards. With the sun's position, there was no alternative. His shadow, portraying his location, made him a visible target.

As he cautiously moved along the fence, he paused. Inside the closure, something moved. Whatever it was, it was parallel to the fence about fifteen feet ahead. Lashley crouched just short of a gate, hanging partially open. He peered between two boards. Cloth was visible. Moving backward the length of a couple of boards, he again peered between a gap. He observed a pair of cheap new boots, the type usually purchased at a discount store. He eased silently along the fence, taking the time to gaze between each section.

Two panels up, he noticed blood on the pants leg. From his limited view and judging from the amount of blood on the cloth, the wound was severe. Further along, he heard labored breathing, gasping, and choking moans. The sounds were truly authentic. Separated from him by an inch of board fence, someone was laying on the ground in the cow pen. The man was suffering with pain.

At head level, Lashley could see patches of dark hair, thinning on top. He judged the man to be more than six feet in height, slim in bone structure, and in his mid forties at least.

"Careful. Don't make any sudden moves," Lashley hissed softly through the fence to the prone figure.

The effect of his warning telegraphed a startling jerk in the prone body.

"Were you the one speaking over the radio a few minutes ago?" Lashley continued, positioning himself at a full panel down from the head. Should the man attempt a pivot to shoot at Lashley, he could see any shoulder movement long before it could materialize into danger.

"Yes," the man acknowledged in an accented, Middle East tone. "I'm hurt. I need help. I'm not one of them blokes."

"What's the situation?" Lashley queried.

"Those inside can't get a clear shot at me. But then, if I stay here long enough, I might bleed to death. Blokes can't rush me, because they don't need to risk me shooting them. For now, they are bloody well content in defending the rush they are expecting from your side."

"Let me see if I can get you out," Lashley responded, and added in caution. "But don't make any sudden moves."

"Not as severely as I'm hurt. It's a bit of a pain," the man admitted through clinched teeth. "Blokes inside are crazy. They won't help me. You are all I have left."

Lashley slipped his finger between two boards and pulled outwardly. Weathered by years of exposure, the nails were loosened. The board moved forward a few inches, its nails giving along the lower cross bracing. Attempts to widen the pathway more than a few inches were fruitless.

"I'll need a pry bar of some type. Be back in a jiffy," Lashley said. "Momentarily, there will be some fireworks. Keep still and down. You won't be hurt."

No sooner had the warning been issued than the action commenced. Fish or Frenchie or both had uncoiled their lariats Lashley hoped. Practice, based upon years of experience, allowed one loop to skillfully dropped over the barn door's hatch. The coil tightened as the guides jerked backward on the ropes. The door must have opened because Mitchell was shooting toward the barn.

Mitchell, from the lodge side of the bunk house, discharged into the lower deck of the barn a full clip of thirty rounds from his automatic weapon. Bullets struck Frenchie's truck and farm equipment parked inside, ricocheting throughout the interior. The plan had been for Lashley to use the diversion to enter the cow pen gate and come up on the downside of the barn. But Lashley had elected to deviate from his plan. He was intent on getting the wounded man into the opening. Moving inside as originally planned, would have placed him in a cross fire, for he would have to enter the pen with his back to this wounded man. The pre-described plan needed some innovation during execution. Lashley now proceeded with his alternative.

"Cinch," Lashley beckoned on the radio, "I'm still outside. Pass it around. Ask Frenchie to come back to my last position. Tell Mitchell to drop another full clip inside."

"Roger," Cinch acknowledged over the radio.

Lashley crawled backward to retrieve his shotgun and immediately returned to the fence gap. He observed the injured man had not altered his position, right shoulder down, left injured leg off the ground. Hebert joined him at the fence.

"What's happening?" the head guide asked, panting from his excursion.

"The man on the radio we heard some time back, he's here." Lashley pointed to a place along the fence. "I've confirmed he's been injured. We need to get him out. Help me loosen a couple of these slats."

Using the shot gun as a prying bar, the two men widened the space. One board broke at midpoint. Two other boards completely separated from the cross braces. The open gap was approximately thirty inches wide. It was the best they could accomplish from a prone position. The leverage was inadequate.

"This is going to hurt," Lashley warned. "Bite down on your hat brim," he continued as he retrieved a hat lying on the ground. "We don't need those inside the barn to discover that we're getting you out."

As Mitchell discharged a second clip, Frenchie and Lashley drug the injured man outside the fence into the open. They moved him down slope to cover. With each jar of his body, the man moaned in pain. Lashley removed his own coat and covered the man. Shock, the medical phenomenon, would be the killer. They searched him and extracted a 9mm pistol from his jacket pocket. Through glazed eyes, the man stared at his two protectors. He wavered, trying to focus.

Lashley spoke into the radio. "He's out of the pen. Hold all positions for a couple of minutes."

Hearing Lashley speak, the injured man turned his head toward him. "Otter," he said, grimacing with pain. "The River Otter. You're alive. We were told you were dead. That you had died in the fire that killed your wife and two sons. When was it, three or four years ago?"

Lashley was stunned. Was this man addressing him?

CHAPTER NINETEEN

"Lashley, we can't leave him here," Frenchie Hebert spoke, as he kneeled beside the wounded man. The head guide removed his jacket, rolled it up, and placed it under the man's head. The kind effort was not helpful, but it would do for now.

"The ground's too cold. If we let him stay here too long, he'll suffer from hypothermia. That's as fatal as shock for his condition," Frenchie added.

"It's too difficult to get from here to the lodge. Carrying this burden, we'd be too easy a target. They'd pick us off like grouse roosting on a bush limb," Lashley responded, continuing to stare at the man.

Lashley did not recognize the injured man. Nothing jogged his memory. He had always hoped something would occur similar to this. Suddenly he would meet someone from his past. A contact, some person who could unlock his mind and make the present join hands with bygone days. It would be like antiquity merging the gap toward modern history.

It was possible, he had desired that his infrequent travels would bring him to a long forgotten but familiar location that would open the early volumes of his life. He had read books, studied maps, and briefed himself on current events. Nothing clicked. The lapse continued. His life extended by each day, but the starting point always brought him back to that drug filled day when he awoke in the Five Pines hospital. Prior to that day his early life was irretrievably locked in the file cabinet of his mind. There was no precedent life.

And now it had happened on this cold windy day in central Wyoming at the edge of a cow lot. And it was nothing. The contact, who claimed to have known Lashley in the past, brought a blank. This was not what he had expected. Not what he had ever anticipated. Was this to be another dead end? Would he ever know his ancestry?

The injured man seemed so sincere. It was difficult to assume he could have been mistaken. Was it a case of mistaken identity? Lashley could be mistaken for a similar featured person. After all, the man was severely wounded, suffering from pain and shock. Or was it a set up? A baited trap? Were these hostiles leading him down another false trail? That had to be the explanation. To be called "Otter" did not make sense.

The man moaned behind closed eyes, his face distorted in glimpses of pain. His breathing labored. Lashley extracted his knife, split the bloody pants, and examined the left leg.

The bullet wound in the upper thigh was small. Bruised flesh around the circumference of the point of entry was turning blue. He rolled the man to his side examining the back side of the leg. Through the split cloth, he found the exit wound of the bullet. Fortunately, the shot has passed through the upper thigh. A meager examination failed to reveal that the bone had been broken, but it was difficult to pass judgment based on such a superficial examination. The wound had produced an excessive amount of bleeding. However, the projectile appeared to have missed the artery. The bleeding could be stopped.

"How about let's move him to that jeep down there," Frenchie pointed to a vehicle 200 yards down from the cow lot, parked on the road leading to civilization.

In the distance, the men could observe its shattered windows, a result of the ambush that Frenchie and Cinch had sprung earlier in the morning. One escaping fugitive's body lay on the ground off the passenger's side. Another crouched figure lay slumped behind the steering wheel.

"We can use the back. It'll get him out of the wind and off the ground."

"I don't think that's good," Lashley responded. "It will still be exposed to fire from those upstairs. They would note our activity and pick us off. It will have to be another vehicle."

From the ground, the man moaned again, "The blue one over there."

He pointed across the road toward the cliff base to a parked Bronco at about a 300 feet distance. "I rented it. Keys in my right-hand pocket."

"It will suffice," Lashley said. "But it will be a risk. A hundred fifty feet over open terrain, crossing from this fence to the start of the outcropping won't be easy. Taking you on my back will be painful, very jarring. There is no way to be gentle."

"We don't have much choice," Frenchie interjected.

"I will make it, Otter," the man said. "Do it. We can't fold up here."

Lashley addressed Frenchie, "We need a diversion. Help me get him on my back. When he's set, radio Mitchell and Wallace. State that we need full clips thrown into the upper barn. At the first burst, we will break across the road. You bring our weapons. Stay just down step of me. If I fall, it will be in that direction. You can break the fall."

Frenchie hefted the man upon the stooping Lashley. The injured man was no light weight, 185 pounds by Lashley's best estimation.

Mitchell and Wallace acknowledged their instructions. As their first shots showered the loft, Lashley stepped forward in a jerking and halting kind of motion. At mid exposure, Lashley stumbled, went down to one knee, recovered with Frenchie's assistance, starting forward again. A bullet flicked the shoulder of his shirt, stinging as it creased his flesh. But he did not hesitate.

Up the hill, he heard the chatter of rifle firing. He suspected Myrtle Wallace was concentrating her firing on the door window of the loft. That portal gave the enemy the only view of the running men. If Myrtle could keep them pinned down a few more seconds, Lashley was confident his burden could be delivered safely.

He landed twenty-five feet short of cover. His breath and energies folded simultaneously. Lashley went down in a heap. To his right, Frenchie grabbed the wounded man's jacket collar, and dragged him the few remaining feet, causing him to cry out in pain.

Several bullets struck within inches of Lashley as he lay gasping on the ground. It was a sufficient motivator. He rolled sideways, regained his balance, and dashed for cover, collapsing against the truck's tires. Frenchie, breathing in huffs, reclined beside him. Pale from shock, the rescued man lay on the ground at their feet.

Several minutes passed. Neither of the men were able to respond to Mitchell's urgent calls on the radio. The captain, from his cover at the bunk house, had seen Lashley drop. But being obscured from the balance of the rescue efforts, over the radio, he expressed concern that Lashley was shot.

His voice was near panic as he bellowed, "Frenchie, check in." He delayed for a moment and repeated, "Frenchie, Lashley, check in damn it! What's happened?"

Finally, Lashley breathed a labored, "Okay, here." A long pause allowed Lashley to struggle for his next breath. "Give me a minute. Over."

Five minutes passed before either Lashley or Frenchie were able to minimally function. The injured man lay face down on the ground, obviously unconscious. The pain attendant to the moving had been severe. He had finally passed out.

At last, Lashley, accumulating the strength to straighten up, reached over, extracting the vehicle's key from the man's pocket. He unlocked the door. Checking the interior, he found a 9mm pistol concealed under the front seat. Among clothing in the rear, he located a small first aid kit. The contents, though limited, were sufficient for emergency purposes. Removing the rear seat with Frenchie's assistance, they placed the man lengthwise inside. Spare clothing and personal gear were shaped into a makeshift bed.

Crawling into the vehicle, Lashley poured antiseptic on the man's wound and bandaged it, being careful to apply sufficient pressure to stop the bleeding. In a cooler, he located a Coke. Lifting the tab, he let the man sip from the can. The fluids appeared to revive him. Excess liquid dribbled down his chin. With some prodding, he swallowed several Tylenol.

"Feeling better?" Lashley inquired.

The man nodded affirmatively between sips. Lashley studied the man. Medium-sized lips supported a thin mustache, giving a sinister effect to his tan complexion. A twisted nose attested to a tough background of loose fists. Otherwise, his features were average.

"Ready to talk?" Lashley added positioning the drink can for another sip.

After sampling a mouthful of the beverage, the man signaled, with a wave of his hand, an end to the consumption. Using his elbow, he turned to Lashley and said in a raspy voice, "I'm ready."

"Why don't you start with your identity?" Lashley requested.

"You jest, of course. I am Ganyor," he responded, confused by Lashley's demand. "Suleiman Ganyor. The Turk. Surely, you recognize me, ole bloke. We worked about off and on for ten years. Went a full round, you might say."

"That's bullshit," Lashley answered in denial, frustrated by the direction of this conversation. "You

471

have confused me with some other individual. I don't know you."

"It's been three or four years at the outside since our last job together was a bit of a riot in Central America. Unless you have a twin, I cannot be confused."

He spoke in clear, concise English, spoken by a person who most likely learned the language in a school taught by residents of the British Isles. His accent was Middle Eastern, indicating that English was not his primary language.

"You could not have forgotten your former chum in such a short period of time. Remember Lebanon? Now that was a rough and ready number. We went in together to rescue that Red Cross official. It was all so hush-hush. Succeeded though didn't we. Said we would right from the start. Rescued the chap with hardly a scratch. But I could not say the same for the kidnappers. They received the big bang, like the IRA in 'ole London town. You might say you blew their minds."

"Tell me some more about it. Give me the details," Lashley urged, desperately searching for some sanity in this conversation.

Ganyor looked at him reproachfully. "If you like. But I must say I am a bit confused. You don't recollect the bomb you placed under the auto seat of the head participant. Triggered so that it exploded when he exited the auto. The device was only strong enough to break his spine. Incapacitated him for life. It was a masterful stroke. Don't kill them. Thus, they become martyrs, so on and so forth. Let them live as invalids. After a time, their memory fades and quickly."

Frenchie, from the tailgate, listened in silence to the conversation. He ventured to interject a remark, "What's he talking about, Lashley?"

"Lashley? Who is Lashley?" Ganyor inquired, lifting his head so as to better observe the man seated at the tailgate of the Bronco.

"You're talking to him. My name's Lashley," he said.

473

"So Otter has taken another name. Gone under water so to speak. Does all this have to do with the loss of your family?" the man said. He indicated a request for another sip.

When he finished drinking, he continued, "We heard about the fire and your loss. The lid was tight on that container. Eventually, some of the details of your tragedy leaked. Couple of the blokes in the business were told you had perished also. We asked questions. But the lid got tighter. Squashed everything down. None of our business, if you like. Don't inquire, was the official command. When you failed to be assigned on further joint assignments with your old players, we all assumed it was true. No rumors ever surfaced that you were still alive and working in some other capacity. So we finally accepted it was fact. Followed protocol. We pursued our assignments, mournful of your demise."

He paused, sipped, and then continued, "I might say in the outset that working with Crest, our control officer, was a bit of a hard biscuit. But we were a small, tight knit team. Losing a chum like you was hard on those surviving. It is similar to losing a family member. Your absence hit us all hard. Silver headed Crest assured us that it was a tragic accident. Though we had never met your wife or children. To do so would have been against the rules. Their loss was deeply felt. To find you alive is staggering."

Passing a hand over his forehead, the man paused for a breath, as he surveyed his dubious benefactor. Then he pointed a scornful finger.

"At the onset," he declared, "I should have guessed the Otter would have survived. Crest gave you the code name, River Otter. With him, everything had to be nicknamed as something connected with water or the sea. He cabled me - 'Dolphin.' He conferred your title with honor. You were so quick. He would say in that boisterous voice that a person could have a dead aim at a river otter. By the time you squeezed the trigger, the animal would be a hundred feet up stream. Bragged that Jason Tyson was so fast in his movements and thought he would never be killed on any mission. Crest said, if you were ever killed, it

475

would be by some accident. And for all we understood, that's exactly what happened."

"Jason Tyson?" Lashley mused. "How does all of this relate to me? I have no memory of any of this. You have mistaken me." Lashley was dubious of a trap. Exhaustion gripped his body like a vise. He was unable to think clearly.

Ganyor was indignant. "To work as tightly with a chap for so many years and not recognize that individual is impossible. For days, we were glued together, on missions. We were tight, you know what I mean? Inseparable. Sweated and stunk the same. You brought me out of Honduras. Saved my life, you did. Severely injured in the effort, you were. Do you still have that scar under your left arm? That should be sufficient evidence that I know my ole chum."

Lashley was silent. This concept was beyond his capacity to understand. Possibly, Ganyor was correct, and he was Jason Tyson. Conversely, it was just as likely that the whole tale was a fabrication. It was some ploy to divert his attention. A guise to allow time for those in the barn to organize and possibly slip out.

It occurred to him that the back side of the cow lot was no longer guarded. The cowboys were spread thin at holding down guard duty. Cinch Wilkinson was holding point along the front, using the top side trap door of the cooler as his cover. From the corral, Fish Mackey guarded the south barn wall. Ray Horne and Fred Stumbough, from their post at the back side of the lodge, assured a defense against a rear attack. Lashley assumed that any of those hostiles who had escaped from the ambush might climb the Trigger Finger to attack on the lodge's unprotected rear flank.

The captain remained to cover the barn door. Myrtle clung to her assignment of observing the upper exit from the barn.

Throughout the lodge building, the remaining hunters, under the command of Major Greer, were supposed to be distributed at the doors and loft sites and prepared for any counter-assault.

Lashley reasoned that long periods of inactivity would cause the guards to become careless. Or even worse, they might become trigger happy and suffer from a severe case of buck fever. The original plan had to be finished quickly. Whatever the consequences for him personally, this conversation must end. There will be time enough later to reminisce about Ganyor's knowledge of Jason Tyson. It was time to return to the primary objective to force the hold outs in the barn to surrender.

Lashley knew he could not leave the barn's rear flank exposed much longer. The final remnants of fighters in the barn could easily exit the cow lot and drift east several hundred yards, taking cover in the shallow draw. From there, if they used a cover of thick bush, it would not be difficult to reach the water hole. Disbursing from that watering hole would be easy.

Considering all the hostiles, who had earlier escaped Frenchie's ambush and were already scattered across the vast valley, the possibilities of catching the entire assault team would become more remote. The wider the covey scatters, the more difficult it is to flush out the singles. Surely, some flushed birds would escape the muzzle flash. Some feathers would not be ruffled. Lashley could not afford a single survivor. The goal was, at all costs, to forever quash this infestation before it is germinated in the test tube. It must be terminated now. With one tiny cell survivor, the disease breaks out somewhere else. Total eradication was necessary and imperative.

Lashley shifted to face Frenchie. "Cover the backside of the cow lot. Give me ten more minutes with our patient. Alert Mitchell to hold his troops fast for a little while longer. For safety, work down to the shallow draw, cross the road beyond that first disabled vehicle. They can't see you from the barn if you cross that far down. When I finish here in a few minutes, I'll join you on the same route. Then we'll return to our original plan. Pass it along to Mitchell to hold positions."

As he spoke, he heard an exchange of shots. It was a good sign. Mitchell was keeping some action going. Idle hands produce careless mistakes.

When Frenchie departed, Lashley directed his attention toward Ganyor. After an interval, he said, "For purposes of argument, I'll accept our past companionship. But for now, I'm more interested in the present. What are you doing here?"

"There can be no secrets between old chums. I changed jobs. Quit the Crest crowd. I am employed by my own government at the present. I have been so engaged for the last two years. No more of that freelance work. I was never certain who was giving the orders and whether I was in conflict with my own government. After you departed the scene, Crest changed. The white-haired bastard became moody and so forth and so on. Though the free lance pay was excellent, suspicions arose concerning my assignments. The Russians had long past fallen apart. Their boundaries became fluid. But Crest still viewed the Ruskie as the enemy."

He breathed deeply and continued. "So I became dissatisfied. Signed on with the Turkish embassy. Still had my good state side connections. So it was natural to be assigned to Washington. More recently, I have been directing my efforts to Middle East problems. Of course, all of this is confidential. Except for our past association, I would never talk so freely.

Your presence here confirms my suspicions that the Americans were aware of this mission. You were sent to protect from the inside?"

"What are you doing here at the Cottonwood Lodge?" Lashley asked insistently, letting the Turk's comment pass unanswered and unchallenged.

"I'll directly address that inquiry," Ganyor answered promptly. "For several weeks now, there have been rumors concerning a developing mission in the U.S. It was a follow up to the planes crashing into the Twin Towers. Supposedly, it was spearheaded by some fanatic Muslims but not the al-Qaeda. Our embassy was unable to get a handle on it, but the feedback information was strong. The sources would not be ignored. Something heavy was occurring. It was different from a simple drug related endeavor. The basis was political in nature. Automatic weapons were being purchased. Recruiting was taking place. Money was changing hands. But nothing checked."

He shifted positions. "Finally, we Turks got a break. One of those Colombian street lords got caught delivering a drug shipment on board a Turkish ship docked in New York. We Turks do not subscribe to the concept of due process as dearly as Americans. Excessive police force doesn't have the same meaning along the Caspian Sea. Based on my expertise in Southern and Central American issues, I was requested to investigate these persistent rumors. A major portion of my expertise in that section of the world I owe to you. You were my teammate. We worked well together. I remember one time . . ."

Lashley interrupted, "I don't have time for a history lesson, Ganyor. Get to the train on track. I'm concerned about this place and time. There are bodies scattered all over these plains. Still, there is a resistance pocketed in the barn that has got to be flushed out. No more memories. I want the bottom line."

"Okay. I'll accept that. On board the ship, my government had, as you Americans say, jurisdiction. I brought in some help, persons skilled in persuasion. Some pressure was applied to that Colombian. He eventually talked. He was a terrible bloke. We were not interested in anything but the drugs. Inquiring about his contacts aboard the ship and in Turkey was the limit of our knowledge. As we applied pressure to his body, he wanted to make a deal. He offered to trade information for his life. We listened, took the information, and also his life. He was a real pig."

"How did that information lead to the Cottonwood?" Lashley impatiently pressed for a detailed explanation.

"This bloke explained, with limited details, efforts to recruit a team of Colombian street punks. There was a need for personnel to accomplish a mission somewhere in the U.S. Shooters were needed. Every drug gang has a premier shooter or hit man. Efforts were under way to collect some of the best gang hit men. Top dollars were being offered. Guns would be furnished. Iraqi connections were mentioned. He was not exactly informative on the details.

"With effort, we were able to extract several names within his drug organization. This afforded an opportunity to follow up with leads. Secure that we had milked the totality of his knowledge, he remains now at rest in the hole of the ship awaiting entombment in the Atlantic."

Lashley was becoming impatient. Where was all of this leading? Would there be an end to this man's recitation? Where in the dialogue resided any useful information for him? What connection existed between a drug dealer captured on a Turkish ship in the New York harbor and a remote hunting lodge in central Wyoming. Iraqis here at the Cottonwood? Two thousand miles from New York? He was more confused. He felt he had been screwed. But by whom? It was time to turn on the lights and find out.

"I followed up on the squealer's disclosures. Brought in some of my resources. I avoided Crest and any of the old team. I reasoned for some time before I terminated my association that there was a deep mole in Crest's organization. This was especially true after Jason Tyson's absence. Through extreme detective efforts, we were able to establish a rough outline of the mission. But the effort took a couple of days."

Ganyor grimaced in pain. Lashley checked the bandages. The bleeding was abating. He located two additional Tylenol and held the soft drink for the man to swallow the pills.

Ganyor continued, "What we uncovered was an operation germinated in several eastern American universities. A bloody new organization patterned along the lines of the original Arab Student Union. Secretly, it was copied after the original Iraqi Ba'th political party that undermined the British after World War II. It is a clandestine organization which recruits Iraqis attending various American universities. Its members are restricted to youths from the ruling class of that bastard Saddam Hussein. We Turks despise him more than do the Israelis. He is a maniac and a bit of a pip. A mental dwarf. A degenerate."

"Cut the political recitation. Get to the bottom line," Lashley insisted, his patience near exhaustion."

"You Americans," Ganyor smiled, "have no patience. Everything must be reduced to the lowest common denominator."

He paused, catching Lashley's aggravated eyes, then continued, "This Union had millions of dollars of family oil money in secret accounts available for their use.   Their oath is founded on that abstract Iraqi concept, SHU'UBIYYA. More properly, it is an Arab concept which is accepted only by the extreme fundamental elements of Islam. It is steeped in hate. A hate so bloody burning and consuming it defies translation. As a concept, it vigorously defends basic Islamic history while rejecting all foreign influences within Arabia."

Again, Lashley faced confusion. Where was this leading? What did some student ethnic hate fraternity have in common with the Cottonwood or any of its occupants? Buried hatreds had, throughout history, invoked wars and rebellions. It served as a common front. But here, it did not make sense.

"It is ironic that the very students who selected America as the site for their education would harbor such hatred of their host country. But such is the illogical rational of youth."

"Cut the lectures, Ganyor," Lashley spoke harshly. "Where is this leading?"

"To this place, but the route was camouflaged, many detours. It convolutedly revolves around Desert

Storm and America's involvement in Afghanistan. Do you recall the deep concrete bunker that the American's smart bomb penetrated? I never could understand how anything of such a destructive force could be labeled 'smart.' But leave it to the Yankees to place a monocle on everything in sight.

"Recall that bunker? CNN covered it in detail. Saddam got a lot of mileage out of that bomb. Placed a guilt trip on Uncle Sam's populace on that one. Claimed all those innocent women and children were killed. Bloke even asserted that it was a refuge for the homeless and orphans.

"That was a lie. Its occupants might have been innocent and young, but the truth was that Saddam was using all of his bunkers to protect the families of the elite. Families of his cabinet officials. The remainder of the population took its own risk out in the open."

Determined to give his limited audience a full accounting, Ganyor continued, "Like the atom bomb that fell on Hiroshima, Japan, ending World War II, this smart bomb brought an abrupt end to Desert Storm. It happened when Saddam's regime realized that their families were at risk. The defensive bunker constructed at a cost of millions of dollars was no more secure than the straw house of the Three Little Pigs. They had to capitulate. His surrender followed a short time later."

"That's interesting and educational," Lashley sarcastically added. "But so what?'

"Ever the impatient man, the Otter," Ganyor interjected. "I calculated that by now, with your quick mind, you would have seen the connection. Maybe Crest was wrong about you. You aren't the Otter."

Lashley responded angrily, "You have had the advantage of observation from a remote distance. I've been in the bastion of this fray. Get on with it."

"Enter the newly revived Arab Student Union, the young messengers of Islam. Their Union was a deliberate introduction to a passion cause. An indictment for revenge. But what would be the focus? They adopted the code name, ZOROASTRIANS or FIREWORSHIPERS. The Union commenced, planning an operation for vengeance against

Americans. Some of these students' families had been killed in those Iraqi bunkers."

The man shifted for a more comfortable position and heaved a deep sigh before continuing, "We were able to confirm that the Union provided assistance for those involved in the crash at the World Trade Center in New York City. They taught the al-Qaeda how to get American passports. The Union masterminded and underwrote several additional terrorist attacks, most of which failed or were aborted. Frustrated with these failures, they contrived one massive operation. A kidnapping was planned. It consumed much commitment, time, and money. But once it was operational, the trail ended here in this remote place."

"Who is the target?" Lashley probed. This was the bottom line. With this name, the whole scenario would fall into place. At last, he would understand.

"There is one reason I confide these secrets with my chum, the Otter," Ganyor continued. "These fanatics must be stopped. At last, I have failed in that objective and lie here wounded, once again to be saved by the Otter. You must complete the objective.

Destroy the Union. Abort this horrid, bloody deed they are planning."

"Tell me the name. Who are they after?" Lashley pleaded in a shallow tone.

"That's peculiar, Otter," Ganyor replied. I never discovered the target."

CHAPTER TWENTY

"What do you think, Lashley?' Frenchie Hebert said. "It looks bad to me."

The two men lay on the ground, peering through the opening in the fence. The interior of the lot was cross-fenced into sections. The cross-fencing lacked paint. The bare wood revealed the aging of the boards reflected by years of exposure to the elements. Gates dividing these interior stalls were either missing or hanging open, loosely attached by rusty hinges. The ground disclosed a mixture of discarded hay and piles of aged manure.

Lashley judged the fenced area to be roughly an acre. The rear of the barn had been designed to accommodate this fenced lot. Half of the building's east wall was open. The opening marked the barn's sole entrance from the rear.

Two hundred feet separated the outer back side of the fence and the main structure. But the distance offered no direct route to reach the barn. It would be necessary to weave around the interior fenced sections. Dodging to reach the protection of the barn's wall would require a lengthy time of exposure. Was it worth the risk? Was there a better method of gaining entrance? Did any safer way of reaching the underbelly of the barn's defenders exist?

Lashley had considered and reconsidered the alternatives. One option was to do nothing, simply maintain the guard posts as he now had his sparse resources assigned. But how long could he manage that? His personnel were spread too thin. Each was exhausted beyond human endurance. Should just one guard break for a personal relief, that post would be unguarded, exposed, and vulnerable for a break out.

The defenders held the high ground. From the barn, they could observe the lodge's guards in their scattered positions. Should any opportunity afford itself, the wedge would start. They would attempt to escape. Once these fanatics reached open ground, as heavily armed as they appeared to be, the chances increased that some of the fleeing fugitives might succeed. They would possibly join with the estimated five or six stragglers who, at early morning, survived Frenchie's ambush and were now scattered throughout the valley.

Additionally, the likelihood that inbound reinforcements were in route still must be considered. The Cottonwood was a long way from being secure.

Also, Lashley had calculated the risk factors involved in a simultaneous assault, each guard post moving forward in a coordinated effort. A rush on the barn constituted a weak alternative.

How many casualties would that effort produce? Captain Tyrone Mitchell, a professional soldier, had volunteered for such risks when he trained as a ranger. Possibly, Myrtle Wallace had similarly enlisted to whatever extent her governmental contract required. She might be committed to sacrificing her life to protect the civilians of her own country.

Frenchie's employees' obligations required performing roles as dude cowboys in the summer and hunting guides in the fall. Those were the outside limits of the employees' obligations. Nothing more. String, one of their own, had been murdered, and revenge against his killer was strong motivation. How deep would that feeling go? That emotion might drive them to shoot men like they would a bolting deer. But to request the cowboys to rush a well defended building and possibly lose their own lives was a substantially different request. Lashley was confident that their hatred would not extend to such foolishness.

Frenchie and Lashley had argued. The conflict had been partially reconciled. With Frenchie acting as backup, Lashley had finally elected to lead the advance through the cow lot maze. Lashley selected a 12 gauge Remington loaded with buck shots. He pocketed a .45 caliber army pistol. Theoretically, the .45 pistol contained sufficient power to knock down a hostile, even if it struck an insignificant part of the body.

"How many you figure?" Frenchie asked again.

Patiently, Lashley responded. "Five. Six at the most. Depends on whether Mitchell took that one down when the barn doors were yanked open. Mitchell's pretty sure that he hit one. But he's not sure it was a kill. If that man is in there wounded, we have to count him as an active. Until there's a confirmed body count, each must be considered a danger."

"How much faith do you place on that Turk, Ganyor? He looked like a bronc gone wild to me. Can't trust that kind if you want my opinion. He'd pitch you in the first bunch of cactus you pass, laugh while you struggle to get up, and piss on you while you try."

"I'm not a hundred percent convinced either. But it is the best information we have. There were sufficient facts in his story that have been previously confirmed. He knew about the leaks inside the lodge. Parts of his story had a ring of truth to it. I'm assuming that he was correct on the configuration of the leadership of this fiasco. I see no reason to doubt him on that. It was evident that they shot him. That wound wasn't self-inflicted. It was too severe. It would be too risky to shoot oneself that severely. So he has no reason to fabricate their strength. I'd say we can rely on that."

"But you let him leave," Frenchie stated with determination. "I still don't understand that."

Earlier, the head guide had been aggravated when he had seen the blue vehicle make a hurried U-turn and commence a dusty retreat northerly, distancing itself from the Cottonwood. He had raised his rifle to wing a tire but had been waived off by Lashley's warning. "Let him go," Lashley had said.

The last information imparted to Lashley by the Turk disclosed details about those held up in the barn. Of the original ten members of the ad hoc committee of the Arab Student Union, planners of the attack on the Cottonwood, six to his knowledge, remained alive in the barn. That was the final count preceding the disagreement with Ganyor. Three Zoroastrians had been killed earlier when the occupants of the lodge had counter-attacked. Bullets penetrated into the room's interior, killing the three students in rapid succession. One leader's whereabouts remained unaccounted. Ganyor had not been informed as to his identity. At least, the final survivors had not disclosed his whereabouts. All of the nails were not driven home. The coffin box was not yet ready to close.

"Your Bible, The Old Testament, I believe," Ganyor had said, "teaches vengeance is God's way. Arabs instruct their young that vengeance must be done by the family. A family member must inflict bleeding from the head of the offending party. To die for your family is noble. Only those with a fanatic Islamic mentality can comprehend such a commitment. Few understand the hatred of the Zoroastrians. The survivors will not be captured alive. If escape is possible, they will seek that route to regroup and fight another day. But capture is not an alternative. For fools, death or escape are the only alternatives."

"Describe them to me," Lashley pressed the Turk.

"Typical college students. Some very young. One or two are maybe twenty-three or twenty-four. Something like that. It's the younger members who you must be the most concerned about. They are the most fanatic. They are the most uncompromising. They will kill within their own members if they detect a sign of weakness."

"And their capabilities? What of them?"

497

Ganyor clinched his fists, more in anger than in pain. The bandages and medication appeared to be giving him some relief, Lashley noticed, as the man appeared stronger and more rational.

"One of the Colombians was serving as the man in charge of field operations. But he deserted sometime this morning. His lieutenant was killed earlier. This leaves one of the youngest students in charge. He is unyielding. Still has faith in the success of the operation. Armed with modified Mac tens and assorted other weapons. Must be ten automatics in that structure. Several boxes of ammo. They don't appear to be experts with weapons, but then, with automatic fire and close range, they don't have to be experts. A direct assault wouldn't be advisable."

"Are they expecting reinforcements?" Lashley inquired, shifting in the vehicle to a more comfortable position. The injury to his arm disturbed him. The bullet had creased the muscle, but the injury was more of a discomfort than of any serious nature.

"Can't say for certain," Ganyor replied. "They never imparted any of their high level strategy to me. My assignment here was very limited."

Lashley raised his eyebrow, surprised by the revelation. "What is your assignment?"

"Once I had obtained sufficient information to confirm a terrorist activity within the bounds of the U.S., my embassy sent me to confer with the Brits first. We have more confidence in their intelligence agency. Less leaks than there are in the American C.I.A. In the States, whenever someone retires, they write an expose of the agency. Destroys the world's confidence in American security. The Iranian arms deal would have never been exposed by the English press. National Securities Act and all that prevent such disclosures. The Brits' press is too absorbed in exposing monarchy transgression then reporting foreign affairs."

"Cut the crap, Ganyor," Lashley responded. "Get to the purpose."

"The Brits would not touch the issue," the Turk continued. "But they did agree to forward around a confirmation request to the Iraqis through the Swiss. Nobody has established diplomatic relations with Iraq since the Desert Storm affair."

"Contacts within Iraq denied knowledge of the plan. Insisted that if such an operation existed, it would be an independent action, disassociated from the Iraqi government. Little reliance can be placed on Saddam Hussein's underlings. But the Swiss reported their source was well placed and had been reliable in the past. So we Turks elected to bypass my usual American contacts. Too risky. We conferred with the Saudis, Jordanians, and several Middle East countries. It was decided that so soon after the Afghanistan invasion, the Arab countries could ill afford another confrontation with the Americans. It was jointly decided that the operation must be defused."

He paused, shifted on his temporary bedding, and then continued, "Consider how an Arab kidnapping on U.S. soil would affect public opinion. Follow that with a sham trial to vindicate fanatic Islamic principals. The recent war in Afghanistan cemented the Arab countries into a fragile union with the States. They are vis-a-vis closer than they have been in years as they fight terrorists. Israel is no longer a favored nation recipient of American arms.

"In the broad scope, Islam is now receiving a lion's share. But consider how its delicate balance could easily tip if these Arab student militants were successful. It would be a catastrophe for the majority of the Arab countries.

"The average American understands little of the subtle differences between Egypt and Turkey, for instance. They perceive them as Islamic dominated, religiously similar. If this fantastic kidnapping plan succeeded, Israel would again emerge as the favored nation. All would be to the detriment and disadvantage, not only to individual countries, but to the Middle East as a whole."

Ganyor paused for more cola, elbowing his body upward to view his surroundings. When he continued, his voice was stronger. "Of supreme importance are the peace talks between the Israelites and their neighbors. Any disharmony, no matter how insignificant, could destroy the progress of the negotiation. To emerge as the spokesperson for the Islamic fanatic ethnic cause, Saddam Hussein needed to destroy the peace effort. It is essential to Hussein that the Israeli issues never be resolved. So my embassy concluded that if Hussein was not directly connected with the Zoroastrians, he was covertly connected. It was essential to my government's position that this plan would not be successful. Thus, I was dispatched to diffuse the Student Union. Restore sanity to the insane in one single motion, like the flying carpets of Persian legend. Magic, but there was no magic for Suleiman Ganyor. I failed."

"What did you try?" Lashley asked.

"I tailed in yesterday on the backside of a team of their reinforcements. It was an easy task. For the past several days the Colombians on the ground here had been sending coded radio messages to New Jersey soliciting more recruits. We intercepted those messages and I was able to follow some Marielito enlistees to Casper. Rented this auto and drove behind them. They were especially careless. Assumed I was bit and pieces of the operation.

"After my arrival, it required substantial persuasion to gain an audience with the student leaders. At first, they were determined to terminate me. They calculated I was a foreign plant. Later, I was given a reprieve when I impressed them with my broad knowledge of the Koran. At least for a while, for a brief time, I was allowed into their inter-circle. Once admitted, I attempted to persuade them on the futility of their mission. I argued for a staged withdrawal taking their fallen companions, leaving behind the dead Colombians and Marielitos. The authorities would assume it was a bad drug deal. Drugs and Colombians. They are brothers. The hand and glove, as the Americans say."

Lashley was becoming impatient with the magnification of the details. Ganyor was boring him, preventing him from getting on with the business of ending this affair. But within the disclosures, the Turk's revelations were grains of salt sprinkled liberally on a frosted cake. To savor the cake, the salt must be bypassed.

"I was finally successful in temporarily separating the Colombian in charge, so to speak, from the Union alliance. The chap briefed me on the field aspects since they had implemented the operation. As for the troops that had early on broken rank and assaulted the woman, each had been severely disciplined and returned east.

"He expressed surprise that his night attack on the lodge building failed. Since arrival, the chap had inside communications directly from the lodge, detailing every plan and counter-plan of his opponents. Chances for success were weighed in his favor. He wanted the assignment to be resolved quickly, with prompt payment followed by a swift departure from this cruel land.

"The attack's failure was a personal devastation. He concluded that he had been betrayed. Double-crossed. Casualties were severe. The Union was in a tirade. Threatened to kill him. The chap was really confused, because his planning and execution were flawless. The inside informants let him down. Gave no forewarning about the lodge's defense. Something went wrong with his scheme that he could not understand."

"He can blame me for that," Lashley inserted. "I penetrated his outpost. Once I knew his plan, the defense was easy. After he lost contact with his outpost, he should have aborted. That was his mistake. Other than that," Lashley said, "I agree it was a well-designed plan. It was luck that I discovered its implementation."

"Luck? No, it wasn't luck. The Otter designed his own destiny. That's not luck," the Turk responded.

"What else happened?" Lashley asked.

"Earlier, the Marielitos had captured one of your people trying to relay a message to the outside. His death was an accident. Too much pressure applied. The Colombian wasn't happy about that. Nor was it his idea to send the body in on horse back. The students made that decision. Figure that should there be any survivors in the lodge, he would be hunted down like a wild animal. He wanted me to convey a message to the proper authorities, should anybody survive, that the cowboy's death occurred through the

505

hands of the lunatic Zoroastrians. He didn't want that posted to his account."

"And you? How did you get shot?" Lashley asked.

Ganyor paused for a moment. He smiled, "I do not particularly want to discuss it, but I suppose you will insist?

"You figured right," Lashley answered affirmatively.

"The old Otter. Once his sharp teeth engage, it's useless to try to pry them loose. He'll hold until one or the other is dead."

"Come on," Lashley pressed. "Out with it."

"When the counter-attack started this morning, it caught everyone by surprise, most especially the head Colombian. The chap was planning an assault later in the day. His men were resting up, regrouping. He was conferring with the Student Union on the details of how he would implement the attack when your assault commenced. The shooting, closely followed by the fire, caused him to lose control. Some of his men drove down to check on the situation. That lorry met a similar fate. Went up in flames."

"The rest of his team broke for the remaining autos. The chap tried to stop them. Failing that, he joined in the mass hysteria of retreat and went head first into the ambush you had set up. That left me isolated with the Union. It was really scary. I felt more threatened than on our mission to Honduras. I resolved I would not survive."

"They turned on you?" Lashley queried, knowing the response before the question had left his lips.

"Did they ever. Like a mongoose on a cobra. Calculated that I had somehow betrayed them. Accussed me of sending a message to the inside. I fled down the ladder under a hail of bullets, as the Americans say. One caught me, but I managed to seek refuge out there in that stinking cow lot. It is a most distasteful place to observe your life's blood oozing from your body.

"I lay on the ground longer then an hour when you ultimately located me. I was unable to locate a safe, unexposed exit. I feared that I would die there. I was successful in keeping the lunatics at arms' length by returning an occasional shot. But my ammo was fast being exhausted. Shortly, I would have been at their mercy."

Satisfied that he had received Ganyor's maximum information, given the time allotted, Lashley was ready for his move to return to battle. No music or waving flags. No tattoo of drums. Just a messy, bloody battlefield strewn with bodies. In the thick of the battle, there are no heroes, only ordinary Joe's doing their individual small parts. If each performs, the battle's tide shifts to victory. One lost nail, and the battle is unsalvageable. With all of Lashley's nails loosely set, it was time to go.

Ganyor caught Lashley's arm before he moved. "Otter, I need one last favor," he plead.

"What?" Lashley responded apprehensively.

"Let me depart instantly," the Turk said.

"Leave? Why?"

"I'm no longer a participant in this party. I have lost my role. The balance has shifted. Soon there will be local authorities on their way. I cannot further assist in the cause. I cannot believe that the burning building went unnoticed. Somewhere out on these plains, someone is moving forward with a curiosity kindled by the fire. A Turk assigned to his government's embassy can ill afford to be caught at this scene. No matter the outcome, it can be bad water for a Muslim Turk. Besides, if I go out the way I came in, I could be a rear guard should reinforcements approach. Crest always preached caution to protect your rear."

"Can you drive that far in your condition?" Lashley asked.

"Possibly. It will be tough. If I bleed to death elsewhere, there will be fewer explanations required. I am willing to take the risk," the Turk added with a determined look.

And so, with care, Lashley moved the injured man into the driver's position behind the steering wheel. Returning his pistol and moving food and drinks to a more handy accessible position, he prepared for the Turk's departure.

He then cautioned, "Don't leave until I'm across the road. That cowboy over there trusts no member of the Islamic faith. If Frenchie thinks you are escaping, he will shoot you as easy as he would a coyote."

Armed with Ganyor's limited intelligence on the composition of the Zoroastrians, Lashley now peered into the cow lot, calculating the risk and evaluating Frenchie's support and the strength of his enemies.

"I'm going in," he advised. "Cover me."

CHAPTER TWENTY-ONE

Lashley rose to his knees and spoke softly into the radio, "Now, Mitchell."

Upward toward the lodge, the captain's automatic rifle barked its death message. Further to the right, Myrtle Wallace's Winchester echoed in affirmation.

Twisting, Lashley drove through the fence opening and landed in soft manure. Rolling forward, he halted with his back against an obstruction. Nothing. He assumed his entrance had not been detected. But that was an unsafe bet. The enemy awaited his next move. At that point, he would be most vulnerable. Go ahead and get it over with, he thought. The water's cold when you first dive in. After the initial shock, the body gets accustomed to it. Then it isn't so bad. You can handle it. The first bullet through the flesh is the hardest. Afterwards, you adapt. Unless, of course, the first is a death message.

Like a gymnast swiftly performing, Lashley stood and hand-vaulted over the intrusive fence. The top rail

511

broke under his weight. The break saved his life. Bullets passed over him as he tumbled ungracefully to the ground. Behind him, he recognized Frenchie's challenging gun fire. Then, silence reigned again.

Because the protection and cover, afforded by the flimsy interior fencing, was discomforting to Lashley, he searched for more adequate protection. Moving to his left, he sprinted across the lot, diving behind the broken gate hanging loosely on its rusty hinges. Bullets chipped the boards behind him. The dash left him breathless. Frenchie again fired, protecting his flank.

Squirming on his belly, Lashley positioned himself for a better view into the barn's dark interior. The darkness inside the building contrasted with the rising sun behind him. The illumination of the cow lot was a definite disadvantage. His enemy could observe him, but he could not see his enemy.

Along the far fence just to his left, he observed a small boxed trough about three feet off the ground. Easing upward, careful not to overly expose his position, he ran his hand into the box. Inside, he located the small remnants of a salt lick. About two pounds remained from a larger block. The cows pinned in the lot had been working on this salt lick for some period. Despite its small size, it would suffice.

Holding the lick as a baseball, Lashley hurled it over the gate. It struck the barn's lower overhang and fell noisily back into the lot. Lashley was ready. When the anticipated muzzle flashes illuminated inside the darkened barn's interior, his twelve gauge, in rapid succession, answered three times. His efforts were rewarded. Inside, he heard a moan, followed by harsh thrashing against a stall retainer. Then silence.

Immediately, Lashley sprang again. His body struck the barn wall with force. Nothing moved inside. He sprinted around this section of the barn and entered the interior with a rolling, twisting movement. The maneuver carried him into an open horse stall. He rose to a kneeling position, which prepared him for defense.

Lashley slid three new rounds in the magazine. Fully loaded, the gun waited for its master's next move.

To the best of Lashley's calculations, the survivors had posted this final guard on the ground floor to protect their flank. He assumed that the guard had been taken out by his last shots. Four stalls down, he could partially observe an automatic weapon protruding into the walkway among a setting of scattered hay. He slipped a stall closer, waited, then moved forward one more stall length.

As his eyes adjusted to the dark interior, he became better oriented. Further along the corridor, closer to the north end of the barn, Frenchie's truck and farm equipment were barely visible in the shadows. Even with the open front barn doors, located on the off side from the rising sun, that area remained shadowy.

His memory of the layout of the barn was somewhat cloudy. Though he had been inside twice, he had never studied the details of its layout. This was a flaw in his preparation. He was a poorly trained Boy Scout. Remotely, he recalled a lesson taught to always be prepared. Expect the worst. The unexpected will always happen. Study your surroundings. Know your mission site. But the Cottonwood was never a mission for him. Why prepare for a happenstance so remote? The odds of happenstance were beyond the realm of possibility.

Crouching low in this smelly stall, Lashley cursed his carelessness. Frenchie had briefed him in general terms on the barn's footprint. But second hand information, while useful, does not replace a personal study. It is like cramming for a final exam with a schoolmate's class notes. What makes sense to him may not necessarily compute with you. Here in the barn, knowing the generalities was helpful, but the details that would save or forfeit Lashley's life were not specific. Measurement of feet and inches could spell the difference in success or death.

Knowing the exact location of the trap door to the loft was vital. Lashley wondered what range of vision a person upstairs would have to peer down into the stalls? When would his movements fall into their line of sight? He backtracked two stalls, motioning for Frenchie to join him.

"What's the situation?" Frenchie inquired, as he crawled into the stall.

"One man's down. Up forward about four stalls. I don't know if he's really out or just hurt bad. Take a look. You can see his weapon out in the corridor," Lashley whispered.

Cautiously, Frenchie peered around the corner post. "I think I detect slight movement in the hand, but it is too distant to be sure,"

"We'll operate under the assumption that he's still a danger. Have you notified Mitchell that we're inside? Can't have him shooting at us."

"Yea, he knows," Frenchie answered in low breath, crouched in the stall, his back resting against the wall.

For Lashley the whole thing was becoming an irritating habit. Seeking protective cover, crouching, sprinting. Would his life ever return to normal?

"The captain is on hold. Said everybody outside is aware," Frenchie continued.

"Let's see if we can smoke them out," Lashley said. "Identify for me the exact location to the trap door. The right side?"

"See that closed stall, the one with the solid door where the walls go all the way up? That's the tack room. The ladder to the loft is just this side of that room about four feet. 'Cause of the rafters, you can't see the trap. But it's right there."

Lashley found some comfort in the location. The upper floor rafter operated as an obstruction for those upstairs. It limited their line of sight. Without these huge, wooden, joist beams, a person upstairs could observe the ground by backing away from the opening and moving back and forth. These rafters restricted that opportunity. Only limited observation within the stalls was possible from the loft.

Lashley could now better judge his critical movement areas, the spots where he would be most visible through the trap door. Mentally, he calculated the restricted areas that hereafter he would avoid. He needed a diversion now. But did he have any left?

Using his hands, Lashley motioned Frenchie to jointly move forward. Together they halted two stalls back from the ladder, he studied the arm in the corridor. No movement. Still he could not risk it. The assumption remained that the man was a potential danger. He waved Frenchie to move to the far rear corner, motioning him to use the top rail for a gun rest.

Lowering his body among the strewn hay covering the earth floor, he sought additional cover behind a stout support post. It was a barkless log, unsawed and twenty-eight inches in diameter, running from the ground to the apex of the roof.

Constructing the barn, the original homespun contractors had used natural materials when possible. No pressure treated dressed lumber adorned the Cottonwood. The upright was a substantial barrier.

"Hey," he yelled. "You upstairs, let's talk this out."

Lashley had calculated that this challenge would produce one of two results. One would be an acceptance, which he figured was less likely than the other, a hostile rejection. His evaluation proved to be accurate, though he wished it was not.

Like a belly gunner on a World War II bomber, bullets, directed at the location of Lashley's challenge, spewed from the trap door. Wood chips disseminated around the post. The aim was high but erratic. Along the ground, chips splintered from the post and stall walls. But the rejection had one affirmative result.

Off to Lashley's left, Frenchie had a glimpse of arms holding the gun and the top of a head. His quick reflections and marksmanship skills paid off. Any man who can bring down a flushed jack rabbit with a single rifle shot could target this gunman with as much ease as spreading butter on a hot, sourdough biscuit.

The first shell from Frenchie's shotgun caught the down-turned head, opening the skull. Pellets of buck shot delivered instant death. The body's arms reacted first, dropping the weapon, which clattered noisily on the earth floor. Suspended momentarily, the body then slid over the lip of the trap door landing in the corridor with a resounding thud.

Lashley moved cautiously along the stalls. He reached the closest body, kicking away the weapon lying in the corridor from its outstretched arm. No movement. Kneeling down, he felt along the neck for a pulse. Nothing. There was no need to check the body that had just performed the swan dive from the loft. Frenchie was too accurate. It was two down since they had entered the barn. How many left?

Suleiman Ganyor estimated there were five or six. The Turk was uncertain as to the number of survivors within the loft. Lashley's role had now changed from being an attacked victim to the aggressor. It was possible there were two or three remaining upstairs. He must know for certain. But at this juncture, there was no additional data on enemy strength he could obtain. He had exhausted his resources.

Ganyor had mentioned the Islam leadership was composed of a team of ten. The Turk had been certain of that. Where was the mysterious last player? Ganyor had confirmed nine hostiles alive in the loft hours earlier. No mention was made of a dead leader. Was the missing member hidden here on the ground floor? There were abundant hiding places among the stalls, stored equipment, stacked hay, and feed sacks. It would have been a simple matter to restack hay bales or feed sacks, design a tunnel, retreat inside, and close the mouth. A perfect place to institute an ambush.

The unsuspected searcher would be on top of the hiding place before the trap was sprung.

It was risky business to forego searching the crevasses of the building. Such an effort would be time consuming and dangerous. It was better to bring in additional people to protect the backside of the searcher. That effort would have to be shelved for now. A balance of risk had to be measured. It was best to smoke the possums out of the loft.

Lashley motioned for the head guide to join him. In a soft voice, he outlined his plan. "Cover me from down here. Stay out of sight away from the trap door. I'm going around to the outside stairs. I'll do my approach from there. Advise Mitchell and Wallace. I'm using that route. Cinch should hold still in the cooler. Have Fish come around through the cow lot and join you here. Just before I go in the door, I'll yell. You and Fish discharge a few rounds up the trap door. Ten minutes. Have everyone in place."

Lashley stood on the lower step. He hugged the barn wall with his back. He counted twelve squeaky steps before reaching the platform. At the top step, a body lay with its left arm dangling over the banister. The loft door was flushed with the wall. After he reached the seventh or eighth step, he would be in the line of sight from the door's shattered window. The weight of his steps, while climbing upward, would announce his advance. No welcome mat would be rolled out for him. At least no friendly one. It was time to move. Almost ten minutes had passed. He had to move.

From the ground, he selected several rocks. Holding the shotgun in his left hand, its butt resting on his thigh, he hurled a rock upward. The stone landed on the platform at the threshold of the door. As the rock crashed along the wooden structure, Lashley quickly advanced four steps. Nothing.

He knew Wallace, with her marksman's eye, was covering the window and door. She had moved from her earlier position and was now prone in a small depression directly opposite the door. Lashley was concerned that this new position would expose her. From his elevated stance on the stairs, Lashley could clearly observe the woman. With the added height as seen from the loft, Wallace would be even more exposed. Her defense rested in her quick reflexes. Her opponents would have to reveal their location before they could sight their weapon on her. She had only one area to cover. They had to first locate her, then sight, before firing. Those few seconds were her last defense.

Lashley tossed another rock in an arching motion. It struck the door frame mid-height. No reaction. He moved three more steps and tossed another stone, which sailed through the shattered door window. They were biding time, he thought, waiting until he was irretrievably committed and past the point of no return. It was time for commitment. Tossing his last rock against the door and shifting the shotgun to his right, he fired his first buck shot. The full load hit the door frame at the upper hinge. The second round, targeted at the same location, severed the top hinge.

He reloaded. Five rounds for full defense, he thought. One in the chamber and four in the magazine.

Three full loads of buck shots finally broke the lower hinge. The door sagged but was held in place by the door handle. Reload. He acted automatically. From his standing position close to the wall, the door's latch was obscured from his vision. He started to move to the outside rail for a clearer shot. A reflection detoured him. From the upside of the window, a bolt of automatic fire rained down, chipping the stair rail and steps below him and to his right. Just as his vision was obstructed, the occupants of the loft had no clear vision of him.

Myrtle Wallace quickly sized up Lashley's situation. She reclipped, firing three quick 30.06 rounds into the lock. The lock broke and the door fell inside the loft. As on key, she fired five additional rounds into the darkened room.

Lashley moved to the wall as Wallace reloaded, discharging his shotgun four times inside. Falling back to the rail, he reloaded. Lashley heard Frenchie and Fish firing upward into the loft through the trap door. Discharging his shotgun in the direction of the loft again, Lashley paused to reload.

Stooping low, Lashley advanced the three final steps and yelled to Frenchie. Reaching forward, he pointed the gun around the door frame and unloaded the full load. He scattered the charges through out the room.

Frenchie, advancing up the ladder, reached over the lip. The head guide, in rapid succession, unloaded five shots into the loft. Gun powder hung in the air as smoke from a clogged chimney. The furry of the discharges rebounded within the closed room in a deafening thunder.

There were two dead spaces in the room from Lashley's viewpoint. Both walls, adjacent to the door, were beyond his range. It was risky now. More so than before. Using minimal cover, any survivor had a built-in ambush plan. The first person through the open doorway or crawling inside from the ladder would be exposed.

He stuck the muzzle inside and discharged three rounds parallel to the forward wall. One round each struck at heights of twelve, twenty-four, and thirty-six inches. Reloading, he checked his ammunition. Eight buck shots and five duck shots were left. It would have to do.

Lying flatly on the platform and using the barrel of the gun, he rolled a rock off the platform to within his reach. He retrieved it and waited a moment, then shouted to the head guide, "Hold off, Frenchie. I'm going in."

Quickly, he rolled the stone across the floor like a bowling ball. Automatic fire came from the closest corner down from the doorway. Frenchie rose from the ladder and shot three times into the corner. Lashley sprung through the door, firing toward the same spot. A weapon clattered to the floor. Silence followed, but the ringing in Lashley's ears continued. It reverberated like a church bell on Easter morning.

On guard, Frenchie and Lashley surveyed the room. The scene was reminiscent of the Alamo. Bodies lay haphazardly among the meager furnishings of the room. The pot belly stove lay on its side, its smoldering ashes miraculously still contained within its black belly.

"Notify the others that this room is secure. They should not stand down on their guard. We don't have a full head count yet. Cinch and Stumbough should move inside the barn to assist Fish on a search of the ground floor. Wallace and Mitchell should move behind the barn to guard our back along the road and water hole. We have several loose canons out there. They're on foot, but they could be extremely dangerous."

He wiped his face with his sleeve and continued, "Maintain strict security on the rear of the lodge. Some hostiles might still attempt to circle around, climb over Trigger, and catch us napping."

Along the far wall, there was a slight movement. The motion was followed by a low moan.

"One has survived," Lashley said, as he moved around a bed, exposing a body face down. A hand reached outward toward a gun. Lashley kicked the weapon aside, turning the body over with a swift motion.

The youthful face, distorted by pain, revealed a boy of no more than eighteen or nineteen years of age. His dark complexion disclosed handsome features. But his piercing eyes accentuated his face. As black as his hair, the eyes gleamed in obsessed hatred. No defeat emitted from their depth. A single purpose of revenge reflected in his stare. The youth crossed his arm over his chest, looking up at Lashley with hostile eyes.

Lashley instructed the head guide, "Get on with your assignments. I'll attend to this one myself."

Frenchie hesitated for a moment and reluctantly obeyed.

When he was alone with the youth, Lashley found a pillow and blanket and placed them appropriately to furnish some comfort to the boy. During the process, the hateful stare never faltered. His Samaritan's mission of mercy completed, Lashley tendered the boy a cup of water. It was refused with a sneering grimace. Acceptance would have been an unforgiving sign of weakness. To accept gifts from an infidel defiled the true believer.

He spoke to his benefactor in accented English. "Will I live?"

"Possibly, if we get you medical attention soon enough. We have a qualified person down at the lodge who will be here shortly," Lashley lied.

His observation led him to the conclusion that there was little chance of survival, but he did not want the youth to know the extent of his injuries. There was still information he needed. If he could find a trade out, a basic need the boy desired, then he might still produce results.

"I cannot survive. I must die," the boy said automatically and matter-of-factly. "Will you kill me?"

The fanatical Islamic ethnic code Lashley wondered would allow no error for failure.

"You help me, and I might assist. No help from you, and I'll do everything I can to see you survive as an invalid in a U.S. prison. You'll spend the rest of your life behind bars.

"What do you need to know," he asked through pinched lips.

"The identity of the tenth team member," Lashley answered.

"By the sweat on the beard of Allah, I'll never tell. Live or die on that," the boy responded.

"I'll accept your loyalty. Forget that request. But this," Lashley pressed, "is my final question. Answer this and I'll assist you in your final solution. Shortly, I can arrange for you to find your seventy-two virgins in the hereafter life. At least I understand that is your anticipated reward when you die in battle for your faith."

"What are your conditions?"

"Tell me your contacts, how you came to be at the Cottonwood. Who was your target? Give me the name or at least a description of the target at the Cottonwood Lodge," Lashley inquired.

"How will I know you will perform your end of the bargain?" the youth asked.

Lashley gave a quick glance around the room. Visually, he located what he desired. He walked across the room, retrieving a .38 short-nosed revolver. Checking its cylinder, he extracted several rounds, leaving one bullet. Returning to the injured boy, he handed the pistol to the prone youth.

"There's one round in the cylinder. But it's off center from the barrel. You'll have to pull the trigger several times before it fires. That's my insurance you don't try to shoot me in the back as I walk out the room. I've performed my half of the bargain. Where is your consideration to seal the deal?"

Through pinched lips, the boy revealed a few details, a name. It confirmed Lashley's existing hunch. The target had been identified, and the conspiracy partially unveiled.

CHAPTER TWENTY-TWO

"I know we are all tired. Taxed to the limits of our endurance. But I need your support for a while longer." Howard Lashley addressed the clustered group standing along the south side of the barn. The sun warmed the group, as the shelter blocked the morning wind.

The cowboys had finished their search of the barn. Satisfied that no one was hiding on the ground floor, the group abandoned the inspection. It had been determined that searching the hay loft would be too risky and time consuming. As an easy solution, the two entrances to the hay loft were sealed shut, nailed tightly enough even to contain Houdini. If a pocket of resistance *was* hidden there, it had been neutralized.

Frenchie Hebert and his guide crew, now composed of Fish Mackey, Cinch Wilkinson, and Fred Stumbough, stood off to the left separated from the rest of the group, their backs to the cow pen fence. In the center, Major Greer, Captain Mitchell, Patricia

Stanford, and Myrtle Wallace faced Lashley, who stood with his back against the barn. Squinting into the sun, Leo Rich and Beryl Carter rounded out those attending. The group welcomed the nourishment of coffee and biscuits that Crisco had distributed.

"What happened up there?" Frenchie asked referring to the barn loft. "I heard a gun shot after I left."

"The last survivor elected to join Allah," Lashley answered without emotion. "For religious reasons, he didn't choose to live when his companion in arms had died. Either way, he would have died. His wounds were too severe. We could not have secured adequate medical attention in sufficient time for him to live. He would have suffered excruciating pain until his death. It was his selection to terminate early. Such is the way of extremist followers of Islam."

"Damn shame," Frenchie added. "He was such a young colt. Didn't appear to have been old enough to be halter broke."

"What now?" Major Greer spoke, bringing those gathered back to the purpose of the conference.

Lashley made eye contact with each individual as he spoke, "We need outside contact, and we must capture those who escaped Frenchie's ambush. As long as they are loose, we aren't safe. I have some assignments for each of you. Can I depend on your individual support for a couple of more hours?"

Lashley watched as each person reluctantly accepted his request. The guests at the lodge had alternately guarded and slept during the night. There had been no rest for anyone since the fight began at five o'clock that morning. The cowboys had taken the blunt of the night guard duty. Thus, they, as well as Captain Mitchell and Lashley, had foregone all sleep during the past thirty hours.

How much longer could he tax their strength? Tired bodies made careless mistakes. Mistakes in warfare meant death. And the Cottonwood was a battlefield. Soon, drawn by pure fatigue, the friendly became the enemy, fighting among themselves. At first, there would be slight bickering, then quarreling about mundane tasks followed by hostilities. The conclusion of this affair must come quickly, or they would become their own worst enemy.

Lashley continued, "Carter and Rich will arrange a guard system for the lodge. Set up a post in the rear among the trees about two hundred yards up the canyon. Don't move about. Be especially quiet. Rotate the guard every hour or so. Get everyone inside not on guard duty to take a nap. They will need their energy later."

He paused to sip coffee from his tin mug. "Set the other guards up by the old tack shed. Use the same rotation. Don't worry about the barn. If they come back, they will try to over run the lodge. Stanford and Wallace should take the first shift to the rear up the canyon."

He turned to Frenchie. "What's shaping up from the outside?"

The owner replied, "There are at least three vehicles coming in on the south road. Locals I'd say. They are using the most direct route, so they have apparently been to the Cottonwood before."

"We don't need any visitors in this battlefield. If what has happened leaks to the outside, there could be international consequences. It must be avoided. I have now joined Leo's plea for silence, but for different reasons. No public notice. We are going to have to close the gate."

"What the hell's going on here?" Rich inquired. "We've got a right to know."

"Yes, you have," Lashley answered. "But now isn't the time for a detailed explanation. And even if I could tell, there is so much political intrigue that national security might prevent it. It might be better for your long range safety not to be informed. This whole affair boils down to a union of Arab youths joining with Colombian drug lords in a terrorist attack to detract from the Israeli-Arab peace talks. To the extent that we were innocent, randomly selected victims, is irrelevant. Let that briefing suffice."

Lashley was telling a white lie again. But it was the best cover for the time being. Rich was not whipped, nor was he a former shell of his boisterous, vulgar self. He was a new individual. A team player accepting this role, who stayed with the game plan. He was earning a lot of respect from his team mates. When the chips were counted, he would be ahead.

Lashley dispatched Carter and Rich to the lodge to coordinate the efforts of the people remaining within the main building.

"What is the balance of our assignments?" Major Greer inquired.

"That depends on who in your group can make the best contacts with the government. We need a silent government clean up unit. One that can put a cap on this mess. Bury the dead with no funeral. No fan fair. Repair the damage swiftly," Lashley requested.

"Count me out," Captain Mitchell answered. "I have no such inside connections."

"Let me confer a minute with Wallace. I'll get back to you shortly," Greer responded and quickly moved out of ear shots with Wallace and Stanford in tow.

"Frenchie, let's get back to your crew. What are our resources for the horses? How hard will it be to corral a few heads?" Lashley asked.

"We're lucky on that. Before daylight, Cinch caught the mare we dispatched Guarimo on. That body had been removed, but the reins had dropped. So the horse didn't range far. She's now been fed and watered. With Stumbough in the saddle, we can have what horses you need in ten minutes," Hebert answered.

"We'll need a string," Lashley said. "We must round up all of those fugitives that escaped down into the valley."

The top guide turned to the cowboy, "Stum, take that mare. Bring in eight or ten. Fish will help you saddle them. Move like a calf under a hot iron."

Stumbough was in the saddle instantly, while Fish moved to open the corral gate for the reception of the gathered horses.

"We sure could use the dogs now," Lashley said. "I expect our prey has gone to cover in that thick bush out among the lower draws."

"We'll use the pack mule instead," Hebert responded. "Old timers always used a mule as their alarm. It is said a longeared hoss can detect a stranger approaching camp a mile before a dog can. They swear by the mules. We'll catch one for our use. Make a tracking dog out of it."

Major Greer and Myrtle Wallace rejoined the informal conference. Stanford remained a few steps behind.

Greer said, "It appears I have the best credentials. I think, if I can get to a base line telephone, I might be able to get the appropriate assistance you requested."

Lashley looked the officer straight in the eye. "We don't need any 'I think' stuff. We need 'for damn certain,' it can be done. Top clearance, top secret. Delta force or something even more secure."

"Let me rephrase my last statement," the major answered. "I understand your requirements. It can be accomplished. I can and will perform. I just don't know how long it will take to activate such a unit. Or more appropriately, what time will lapse before it can reach this location. The unit exists. They are subject to activation on short notice. Travel time to reach this lodge will be the only unknown factor."

"Good," Lashley responded as he tossed a set of keys to the officer. "I took this set from one of the operatives upstairs. If you can match the key, I think it will fit one of those vehicles parked behind the cliff. We can assume it is operative. Your job is to drive to the wash out on the incoming road. There, you should intercept some of the locals driving into the lodge. Tell them a bull story, that some hunters accidentally started that fire. But that all is well now. You tell them you need a ride to Alcova. The closest phone is there. If you're asked questions, explain that someone was supposed to be coming in at noon today and was to meet you at the bar there. Say that Frenchie has had an unusually wild group this time and hasn't had time to fix the road. Shortly, he will attend to it. Take Ray Horne, the assistant cook. Post him at the wash out to turn back all the rest of the locals inbound."

"Okay. We can handle that," the officer answered.

"One last thing. There are five or eight hostiles out running loose in that valley. If they were to set an ambush, an ideal place would be at the wash out on the road. Caution Horne to be especially careful."

"Take your rifle," Lashley continued, before the officer left to locate the vehicle fitting his key set.

During this conversation, Stumbough drove in nine horses and one mule. Cinch roped the mule and tied it to the post. The three cowboys set about, cutting the best mounts and closing them in the corral.

"What is my assignment?" the captain asked. "Will I be mounted?"

"Not this time," Lashley responded. "You are to be in charge of the interior. With Pearl Gavin under arrest, you might say there needs to be some tough leadership inside."

Off to the side, Lashley yelled to Frenchie, "We'll only need five mounts saddled. You four and me." He pointed to the cowboys. "Each man should be armed with a shotgun and a rifle of his choice. The longer the range, the better."

The captain remained standing, riveted in his stance. Lashley knew the officer could not be ignored any longer. This morning during the assault on the new house, his ass had been on the line. He had paid his dues. His membership was current. Lashley could no longer treat him like an outcast field hand. The captain expected to be informed.

"I'm demanding to know the basis of this calamity. What's going on?" the officer demanded.

"You've earned that right," Lashley responded in a quiet tone. "But at this juncture, I am only partially informed. If this man hunt is successful, and I can capture a certain Colombian alive, then we may both know. Should I be unsuccessful, our ignorance may follow us like our shadow for the balance of our lives. Wish me luck."

"I do, Lashley' Mitchell said. "Forget my hostilities. You have been fair with me. It has been a pleasure serving under your ad hoc command. More superior officers should have your talent. I thank you for your confidence in me."

"No thanks required. You have done your duty. Your next assignment is a different one. Now that Pearl understands that there will be no rescue for her, she may be very hostile. She is a dangerous woman. Don't let your guard down. Take charge of the interior of the lodge."

"Consider it done," he answered and tendered his hand in friendship.

Lashley accepted it. The men shook firmly, neither willing to openly acknowledge the dangers ahead.

CHAPTER TWENTY-THREE

"There's something hunched down in that bush," Frenchie said softly. "That mule is shying away."

"It's nearly too thick for the horses. Let's flush this one out on foot," Lashley answered, as he swung out of the saddle, simultaneously extracting his Winchester from the saddle scabbard.

Concealed in the thicket was the third fugitive the trackers had cornered since the trailing began. The tracks were difficult to read, but foot prints indicated seven people had escaped from Cinch and Frenchie's ambush early that morning.

It was now after ten o'clock. Five hours had passed since the fighting started. As recorded in the old outhouses, the job was never done until the paper work was completed. Capturing the escapees was like the drying-in of a house. After the roof was on, there were still jobs and details to attend to, but it was dry work, even when it rained. But flushing out hostiles was bloody, detail work. It involved the installation of a blood bath.

Tracks leading from the stalled vehicles close to the barn had not immediately been readable. Over rough country, the survivors had first fled toward the watering hole, and turned easterly, following the stream bed until it flattened out. There, cutting across a sand flat, the signs were more discernible. Fleeing, the men had formed together as a unit, moving slowly away from the lodge. Wearing inadequate footwear for this rough terrain made their traveling erratic.

As soon as the trackers picked up the sand trail, it was evident that one man was limping badly. Ultimately, they knew he would be abandoned by the party.

The trackers soon overtook this solo hiding in a rocky crevasse within a narrow draw. Requests for his surrender were answered by hostile fire. Lashley did not have time to wait for the cornered man to exhaust his ammunition. Cinch was sent on flank. It was an easy 300 yard shot, and one more man was counted in the deceased column.

The second man was cornered, fifteen minutes later, as an almost duplicate concealment of the first. The selection of a poor defensive position allowed Frenchie to skirt around and pick him off.

Now the trackers were facing the most difficult concealment of the hostiles. Discovering one holed in thick bushes was risky business. Fish and Cinch had been stationed along the far sides of the bramble, should the fugitive, once flushed, attempt an exit in either of those directions. To prevent an escape out the back, Stumbough covered the rear down through the open draw. A fleeing man would be visible to at least one of the flanking cowboys.

Lashley offered one last option. He yelled, "Come out with your hands showing. Nothing will happen. You will be protected. All of the Arabs are dead. There are none left but you."

He was surprised by the acceptance. Within the bramble, he detected the motion of leaves and branches. Cautiously, a man appeared, bent over as he fought the entanglement. Stumbling into the clear, he spread his hands awkwardly outward, palms up. His thick, black, greasy hair hung upon his forehead. His torn coat verified that his testy flight across open country had not been easy. Trousers ripped at the knees hung loosely. With several buttons missing, his shirt was opened at the throat.

Lashley judged him to be in his mid-thirties. The back of his hands revealed crude tattoos, a sign of the Marielitos, successor of the scum of Castro's prisons.

"Don't shoot," he pled in heavily Spanish accented English. "No weapons."

"Turn around," Lashley instructed.

When the man complied, Lashley cautiously approached him from the rear and hastily searched him. With his curiosity satisfied, Lashley backed away. "Where are the rest?"

"Two are in there. They will come out when I assure them no harm will come. Should I give them such assurance?"

The announcement surprised Lashley. He had expected another delay tactic to allow others to escape.

"That's two unaccounted for. Where are they?" Lashley asked, watching the man carefully from a distance.

"We left two far behind," the man responded.

"We found them. They didn't surrender and went out the hard way. Seven tracks started down this draw. Two, we found a ways back. Three here, you say? Where are the rest?" Lashley pressed.

"We had differences. Could not agree. They are also in there," the man said sweeping his hand carefully behind him. "But," he said, "they will not be coming out. They are dead."

"Tell your lying companions that they can come out. You have my word. But they must bring two bodies with them. No bodies, no safety."

"Si," the man answered, and he gave instructions in Spanish, loudly enough to be heard over the thicket. Answering, a voice inside expressed some reservation. At the thicket's edge, the captive yelled a response, which was followed by more conversation.

Feigning ignorance, Lashley followed the conversation with interest. He had been the recipient of a lie, cleverly concealed as the truth. There were not two bodies in the bush, only one. Three live men were still concealed. The fourth survivor faced the barrel end of his Winchester. Only one body was in the thicket. The men had a dilemma. They had not anticipated that their pursuers would demand an accounting for each individual who had escaped. The plan had allowed for three to surrender, leaving one behind to make a get away to carry the details of the defeat at the Cottonwood. The inability to produce two bodies was creating a problem for those still inside the thicket.

"They said they can only drag one here," the man said.

"Then that's tough," Lashley replied raising his gun and firing, throwing gravel against the man's leg. "The deal is two bodies. Nothing less," he repeated.

The man flinched and yelled, cussing in Spanish to his companions for a total surrender. From the bushes, the terms were accepted. The fight had departed these weary, trapped men. Hours on the run with no food, poor clothing, and fragile footwear for such a harsh terrain had altered their will to resist. The white flag of truce became their banner.

"There will come out to bring one body," the frightened man said. Three men emerged, two dragging a body. Lashley focused on one. He had been the last man to emerge from the bush. Even in defeat, his dark eyes reflected a humor. His trick to fool the "gringos," had failed. But the trick was clever even in its failure.

"Well, general," Lashley said. "It's time we have a talk. Join me over there, please." He pointed to a distant rock.

Seated, the Latino looked upward at Lashley who was standing, his boot resting on a rock and his leg bent. The captor measured his captive, a lean man.

Who was this man who now surrendered? Given his due he had fought well. True, his men were not trained soldiers in a military sense. But they were hardened men. Some had probably fought against their government's troop in the jungles. Others had been survivors of capture and prison escapes. Final education had been earned in big city streets. Now they lay dead, scattered along this barren land.

The man must realize by now it was a mistake for him to have agreed to this assignment to assist a bunch of crazy Arabs. The Holy Virgin might forgive him for associating with those who reject the Blood of the Cross. Helping a band who swore by the beard of some prophet would be intolerable. He would have to attend a confession real soon. Purge his soul of this contamination.

"Cigarette?" he asked Lashley.

"All nonsmokers," Lashley shrugged an apology.

"Then maybe some whiskey?" He pronounced the word as do the Mexicans, long on the "whis" and strong on the "key."

"I could use, how you say, a warmer. It is cold. By misfortune, I left behind the warm clothing."

"Sorry, I can't accommodate you. We left in a sort of hurry this morning ourselves. Other than water and bread, we are limited."

The Latino, waiting for Lashley's move, shrugged his shoulders in a noncommittal, indifferent way and gazed across the landscape.

Lashley, in kind, remained silent. It was a contest of nerves. The captive broke first.

"What will you do with us?" the man asked.

"That depends on you and how cooperative you want to be," Lashley answered, now diverting his gaze to the activities of the cowboys.

Fish and Cinch were taking a snooze, while Frenchie stood guard. The three captives under his care were seated on the ground, huddled together under a rain slick provided by one of the cowboys. Stumbough attended to the horses. Although the sun was high in its midmorning rise, the day was cold. The breeze, drifting down the draw, lowered the chill factor substantially.

"But you promised. It was a pledge," the man protested, his voice uncertain.

"I also lie," Lashley answered, turning to stare directly into his opponent's eyes. The stare was returned unwavering. "I intend to kill you if you don't buy your way out."

"I'm not a rich man," the Latino said.

Lashley detected bravery in the man. Either that or he was a good poker player. Lashley figured he was bluffing at this point, repressing the fear that was building up inside.

"That's not what I mean, and you know it."

The man shrugged again. "Forgive me, Senor. But in English, I am not so good."

"You also lie. I figure you have had an adequate education in the U.S. and have a better command of the language than those local cowboys over there. So don't pull that Juan Valdez routine on me. I don't have time for it, general."

Since the days of Santa Anna's assumption of power in Mexico, every Hispanic who led even the smallest band of gorillas assumed the rank of general. Lashley was playing with the man's vanity.

"It is an undeserved title," the man demurred.

"For my purposes, it will do. Any name you furnished would be a fake. 'General' is as much of a fake as we can get."

"But to be a general with no army is nothing. All of my soldiers have been discarded upon the field of battle. If we need a name, Juan Valdez is adequate. He was a man of humble origin like myself."

Lashley noticed the man was no longer speaking in an accent, but rather with a clear pronunciation of a city thug. The language barrier had been a cover, as Lashley had suspected from the start.

"Okay. Juan, it will be. Let's get down to the nitty gritty. You have some information, and I want it. Simple as that."

"But first," Juan protested. "We must talk terms, get assurances. Nothing is free."

In a swift movement, Lashley unsheathed his Bagwell knife and pointed it at Juan's crotch.

"I don't know how they do it in Colombia, but here in these mountains when a sheep herder castrates a ram, he eats the testicles raw. They call them mountain oysters. Maybe in the high ridges of the

Andes it's called 'eating coffee beans.' But whatever the terms, I'm fixin' to castrate you and feed you the results."

"You wouldn't do that. Even a man like you is bound by a code. Your government would never allow such activity," Juan responded, but now there was deep uncertainty in his features. His poker face failed him at this most crucial time.

"Don't count on it, Juan. Don't let it be your most critical mistake yet. It was a colossal mistake to join with a bunch of foreign, fanatic lunatics. You entered this assignment with ill-trained troops, unfamiliar with the terrain or their enemy. The bully tactics of street warfare do not work in these isolated mountains. Most fatal of all, you failed to obtain basic information on your opponent. Even football teams scout their opposition. If you had done the most basic study, you would not have underestimated the talent in the Cottonwood."

"What talent?" Juan asked sarcastically. "Average, soft, American businessmen, who mostly drink and are hindered by their camp-following women. Military officers who were not organized. And a bunch of western clowns. That was defined as the occupants of the lodge. My sources were described as reliable. Besides, I had insiders working."

"But you didn't make an independent investigation yourself," Lashley said.

"And if I had, what would I have found?"

"An undisciplined group all right. None of them had ever killed a man in cold blood before. American ingenuity works. That bunch of cowboys are crack shots. So are some of the guests at the lodge. Your data was faulty."

"And I overlooked you, I suppose. The leader of the unit. The government's assigned body guard of the person the Arabs sought."

"No. That's where you're wrong on two counts. It was an accident that I was on this hunt. I knew nothing of the purpose for the attack. Totally ignorant. Nor was I the leader. I was a defender, but not a leader. Your other basic conclusion is wrong too. I'm not tied to any governmental agency, bureau, or department whatsoever. I'm completely independent.

And for that reason, I have no code that binds me. Castrating you is no more to me than a burp after a big meal. It's going to give me pleasure."

Lashley moved forward, mincing with his knife. The man's fear that previously evidenced itself and disappeared during the monologue, reappeared. No amount of concealment worked. Juan Valdez was scared.

"Hey, man," he plead. "There's no call for that. What's the deal?"

"Deportation for you and those thugs. Within hours, you can bask in the sun of your homeland. You waive all hearing. If you ever come back to the states, I'll personally hunt you down and complete my threat. I have adequate connections on the outside. I'll know of your return and will find you. Cross me and you get to eat well."

"I'll need some traveling money. The Arabs had more than a half million in cash hidden in that hay barn. It was our final payment for the job. That should do for starters."

"Ten thousand, if we locate it before you leave. Nothing more. End of deal. The owner of this lodge keeps the balance for his damages," Lashley added with firmness.

"No way man," Juan began his rejection.

The knife caught his left pants leg six inches down from his crotch, splinting the material upward toward the zipper. The gash in his leg opened, allowing a rush of blood to run down his split trousers.

"Okay. Okay," he yelled. "It's a deal. Stop!"

Juan grabbed for his vitals only to have his hand slapped away. The knife pricked the flesh on his right leg. He squirmed under the pressure.

"I need confirmation about your contacts that set up this operation and the name of the tenth member of the Student Union. The last of the Arabs," Lashley pressed.

"Those are things I don't know, "he answered and gasped as his pants again split under the knife's sharp blade.

Reluctantly, Juan revealed his story. Lashley was satisfied he had the truth. Juan rolled over moaning, clutching his family jewels.

"Lashley," Frenchie called from down the draw. "Hustle over here quickly."

When he arrived, Lashley knew it was bad news. Frenchie's face was a distortion of conflicts.

"It just came in on this radio. Captain Mitchell called to tell you Paige has been hurt real bad. He needs you in a hurry back to the lodge."

The jaded horse covered the four miles with Pony Express timing. Lashley arrived in time to witness Paige St. John die in his arms.

CHAPTER TWENTY-FOUR

Fatigue seized his body. It assumed control of every muscle, nerve, organ, and cell in total surrender. Howard Lashley collapsed beside the lifeless body of Paige St. John. For days he had operated on minimum rest, extending his endurance to its outer limits. Stress capitulated to uncertainty. Uncertainty merged with deceit. Operating on a self-induced high served by a super charge of adrenalin, he had labored under a false hope that he might safely extricate these civilians from this horrible nightmare. But that hope proved false, as he had feared.

There was no room in his mental capacity for anything. No prayer arose for the soul of the departed. Light no candle in memory of a loved one lost. Sing not the song of ashes to dust. All of these emotions had been exterminated. They were nonexistent in a body racked with fatigue.

But in their place, another type of candle was lit. It flickered briefly, almost relinquished its life, and flamed again. And then it grew as if it begged for more flammable material. Once firmly ignited, it grew in astonishing strides. The intensity of his growing anger fed the flame to an uncompromising roar.

This was the flame of revenge, a primate motivation of man. As a client of mankind itself, revenge converts rational thinkers into savages. It alters the civilized man into a beast. Its power transcends love, compassion, hope, and faith combined. Unrestrained, it consumes all other emotions.

As he knelt by the corpse, crushed by his personal defeat, within his guts the flame kindled. He could not cry, for his tears might quench the fire. Add fuel, not moisture, he reasoned. Don't cry, he thought, whatever you do, don't cry. And he did not.

"What should we do?" he heard someone whisper.

"Let him come to grips with his grief," another one responded in a shushed tone.

Lashley turned loose and fell into a dreamless sleep, kneeling on the floor, his arm draped across the corpse of the woman.

He felt a hand on his shoulder shaking. He was aware that time had passed.

"Lashley," a voice said. "Wake up."

He opened his eyes and stared into the friendly, brown face of Captain Tyrone Mitchell.

"Come on, pal," the officer said. "We need your help." He reached under his arm to assist him in rising.

Lashley blinked again, looked at the body on the couch, and finally yielded to the offered assistance.

"How long have I been out?" he asked.

"A little less than an hour," Mitchell responded.

From Lashley's left, Myrtle Wallace handed him a cup of coffee. He accepted it with appreciation, walked to a table, and sat down. Wallace appeared with a plate of biscuits and gravy. Again, nodding, he expressed his gratitude and began eating from habit more than desire.

"How are you feeling?" the captain asked.

"Groggy," he replied between bites. "But I'll make it. What happened to Paige?"

"I can't tell you exactly. Guard duty's spread everybody kind of thin. I requested those in the lodge to catch a few winks in order to be prepared to relieve the others later. Paige selected Grace's couch to rest. Grace returned later and found Paige as you found her. She was stabbed. I called you to come in, because it was obvious she wasn't going to make it. There was nothing we could do for her except to make her comfortable."

"I understand," Lashley responded. A degree of emotion, despite his stoic conditioning, crept into his voice.

"She asked for you. It was a mumble mostly. I tried to understand her, but it wasn't clear. I had the impression she was attempting to identify her assailant for me. Try as hard as I could, I wasn't successful. She did say something about warning you of a danger. Water or something like that. She tied two people together. Finally knew who was with Flood. To be careful. That much I understood. It was my responsibility, and I failed you." The captain's head bowed in defeat.

563

Lashley hesitated between bites and answered, "No, you didn't fail. This assault came from a most unexpected direction. Neither of us could have anticipated it."

"My failure extends beyond Paige," the captain said. "You warned me to be careful with Pearl Gavin. Somehow, she got loose. Either she found a knife to cut her bindings, or someone assisted her. However it occurred, she got loose. I figure she stabbed Paige. Crisco struck her with a meat cleaver when she attacked him in the kitchen. She hurt him, but I think he'll be okay. It appears to be an emotional thing with him more than the injury. Killing a female has disturbed him deeply."

"Shades from the past, I suppose," Lashley added.

Myrtle Wallace, noticeably silent during the conversation, finally spoke, "The dilemma doesn't end there. There's also Grace Hancock. She's secluded herself in the cowboy's loft. She is afraid. She envisions that she was the target, because Paige was sleeping in her place. She thinks that the killer mistook Paige for her. Grace is armed and won't let anyone come upstairs. She figures that the killer in the lodge is after her."

Lashley was silent for a moment as he attended to the last few crumbs on the plate. When he spoke, his voice was calm, devoid of emotion. "I'll speak to Grace. You two stay here. Keep everyone off the stairs." He rose and departed the room.

Halfway up the stairs, he halted, calling in a modulated voice, "Grace, it's me, Lashley. Can you hear me?"

A few moments passed, and he heard no reply. He repeated his first request. Far into the darkened room, he detected a noise. Then, a soft voice spoke, "Don't come up here. Go away. Leave me alone."

"Grace," Lashley responded. "You once told me that if I ever needed you, I could count on you. You've helped before. I need you again. Please help me."

"I'm scared," the woman answered. "I thought I was frightened before, but now I really am."

"I understand that, and I can appreciate how you feel. I have been scared myself. The whole morning, I have been fighting with fear."

"But someone tried to kill me, and they got Paige by mistake. I don't know if I can live with that," she said, her voice filled with emotion.

"You're wrong, and I need to talk to you about it. I'm coming up. Give me a chance."

He flipped on a flashlight, turning it upward so as to illuminate his face. Cautiously, he climbed the steps, entering the room slowly. Moving along the bunks, he walked toward the woman standing against the far wall. Her pistol pointed at his midsection as he advanced. Her hands wobbled, and Lashley feared the weapon would discharge by accident. Stopping, he positioned himself within inches of the gun. Hesitantly, with his right hand, he took the weapon from her. She fell against him, sobbing hysterically. Stroking her hair, Lashley spoke soothing words.

"It's all right, Grace. Cry. It will help. Cry for both of us. I have no tears."

"It's my fault for letting Paige use my space. It will be hard for me to live with that."

"No Grace, that's not right."

"But someone is trying to kill me," she said between sobs. "Why me? What have I done?"

"You were not the mark. Paige was killed, because she knew something that she could have passed on to me. The killer knew Paige was resting on your couch. No one is after you. It's me they are after."

"You mean this whole affair has been because someone wanted to kill you."

"Not exactly," Lashley answered, tightening his grip on the woman as though the idea was painful. "The attack on Paige was a diversion. Bait to distract me, to afford time for the killer to escape. As we stand here, the killer is making an escape with a two-hour head start."

"What are you going to do?" she asked as she pulled away from his embrace.

"Come downstairs, and help me get organized for the hunt."

* * * * *

The wind off the Knuckle bore down on the rider. Loose snow flurries darted, scurrying before the wind. Dark clouds forecasted an impending storm. Soon, the heavy snow would obscure his tracking, and the killer would have the advantage. Establishing an ambush a few feet off the trail, hidden by snow flurries presented an easy opportunity. Waiting until the unsuspecting rider closed the gap, a well-placed shot would terminate the pursuit. After the ambush, the hunted would escape undetected down the mountain with the pressure relived.

The snow would conceal movement on the mountain to those at the base who might attempt to flank the escape. The inability to observe the direction of flight left too many trails to cover. The possibility of heavy snow was a call for haste.

Lashley turned his horse broadside to the wind and spurred its flanks to impress the importance of speed. The animal responded reluctantly. Behind, the spare horse resisted momentarily, then moved forward as the tie rope jerked its head. The rider sensed the happenstance of the animals desiring the necessity of turning their tails to the biting winds of the approaching storm. The barn corral was east, not west, as the rider insisted.

To the greenhorn, a mountain wraps its features in mystery. A smooth trail through a high, sage grass flat abruptly ended at a broken slate rock formation. Crevasses and draws severed the surface, causing the game trail to twist and wind in disjointed directions. Rock slides, activated by cascading water from melting snow, frequently obliterated well-established hunting routes. No road map could chart the high elevations of the west. There are no freeways. Travel becomes a series of trials and errors where carelessness is a prescription for death.

Lashley had been in the saddle for almost an hour, pressing his horse to the extreme. The fugitive had possibly a four-hour lead. Attempting to shorten the lead, Lashley had taken a dangerous risk by pressing the animals to unaccustomed steep climbs off the regular trails. Demanding speed, Lashley had taxed his mount to a point of abuse. They had covered seven twisting miles he judged. He recognized the jaded condition of the horse, as he observed its nostrils flare and exhale clouded breaths in the freezing air.

Lashley, anticipating the fatigue that a demanding ride would produce, had brought a spare mount, fully saddled. The time had arrived to switch horses, but he wanted to cap the approaching ridge line before halting for the transfer. The crest would afford a broad vision down the western slope, even with the scattered snow flakes. From this observation point, he expected to catch sight of the fleeing killer, his first since the chase had begun. The one fact squarely in his favor was that the killer was on foot climbing in rough country.

His pursuit was calculated on his limited intelligence work. Thyus Harder, guarding the back side of the lodge and stressed by many sleepless hours of fear and anxiety, had carelessly napped at his post. Lashley had found him in a deep sleep against an aspen tree. Patricia Stanford and Myrtle Wallace, alternating guard duty to the lodge's front, alerted Lashley that each person passing their post had been accounted. Escape for the killer was most likely up the canyon along the trail leading to the Knuckle.

It was reasonable to assume the killer had no intentions of heading south along the route Chainsaw had taken in his ill-fated trek meeting death. The killer would reason that Lashley would dispatch a team along the same sheep herder's road that the Hispanics utilized to ambush Chainsaw. South was out. As a precaution, Lashley earlier dispatched Mitchell and two cowboys along the south road to prevent an escape out to the ranch on the mesa.

A better route suggested a run to the north, hugging the east side of the Arm and avoiding the blunt of the storm. The heaviest snow and wind would batter the western side of any finger ridge. Keeping to the east expressed a more reasonable approach. The Diamondhead Ranch some fifteen miles north was the most logical destination, given all the alternatives. Stealing a truck parked in a barn would present little challenge. In these remote, isolated regions, car theft was seldom a concern. The owners' keys were invariably, by habit, left in the ignition.

Just beyond the outer limits of the Arm, across the boundary fence, a rutted road led directly to the Diamondhead headquarters. If the killer reached that road before dark, Lashley's expectations for a capture would be diminished. The killer, upon reaching the ranch road, might make a clean escape. Lashley, pressing hard in pursuit, measured against a dwindling time of vision, knew he must prevent the killer's decent from the Arm.

But the slope proved to be a false ridge, a common mistake for those not fully knowledgeable of the territory. Like a mirage in the desert, the eye plays tricks on humans in the mountains. Judging from below, a hiker sets his sights on a tree or other marker up the trail, swearing that when he reached that predetermined point, he will have reached the summit of a ridge. Disappointment prevails when the object is reached, and the hiker discovers that the actual crest is still higher, it being previously obscured by the structure of the sloping contours.

Lashley had misjudged his point of reference. It was a false ridge. The true crest was some 300 yards up slope. Delaying his decision to change mounts, he spurred the animal again. The horse advanced 100 yards before it staggered in mid stride and halted. Lashley heard the shots as the horse's front feet folded. The animal collapsed and rolled on its left side. Numbed by fatigue and cold, Lashley's reactions were delayed. The report of the rifle, muffled by the winds, reached him moments after the bullet penetrated the mare's chest. Simultaneously with the animal's collapse, he swung to dismount, but his motion failed to timely clear the saddle. The animal's dead body trapped his left foot. Pain, like a charge of electricity, cascaded through his nervous system as his head, in reaction, swung back and hit the cold ground.

He was uncertain as to how long he had been unconscious, but he guessed it had only been seconds. The pain was now a steady throb, as raw nerve ends nibbled at his brain cells. He struggled to free his trapped leg. The dead weight of the horse lay upon his foot like a vice. The struggle was useless. He reclined full length in frustration.

James. E. Moore

A bullet chipped a rock inches from his head. His movement had notified the killer that Lashley was still alive. Twisting his body against the fallen animal, he presented a protected silhouette, as he reached across, located his rifle and withdrew it from the saddle scabbard.

Studying the ridge line, Lashley selected his best guess as to the killer's concealment. He followed a boulder that was 250 yards away and off to the right of the trail. Watching carefully, he detected a slight movement. Firing across the dead horse's neck, he placed two shots, inches apart, at the boulder. Nothing moved. He fired three more shots into the lowest crevice of the rock. Reloading, he prepared for a final play at this deadly game. If the cards fell wrong, he was busted. The stakes were high.

Slipping off his jacket and hat, he felt the stinging blunt of the wind breaking over the lip of the ridge. He shivered involuntarily. Unzipping the hood of the jacket, he stuffed his hat inside the extended head cover, giving it the appearance of a form, as he crouched behind the horse. Quickly, he tossed the jacket out upon the ground, duplicating his reclining position where he had drawn fire only minutes before.

The jacket had hardly flattened before two bullets, in rapid succession, clipped the material. The muzzle flashes revealed a shift to the far side of the boulder. Lashley's rifle spoke an instant later. Four additional bullets followed in a tight pattern. The Winchester .30-30 bucked against his shoulder. His awkward firing position had prevented the required tight grip of his rifle to the shoulder as in a proper firing position. His body would later suffer the bruises from this breach of firing etiquette. Such concerns would only matter if he survived. At the moment, he was not prepared to give odds on his chances of success.

The storm broke its restraints. Snow flurries became a shower of whiteness. In minutes, he was curtained in a white out. Visibility was reduced to a few feet. The altered conditions were both a blessing and a curse. The killer's sight was encumbered. There would be no further distant sniper shots directed at him. But more hazardous conditions existed. The killer would now have to come to him. He was trapped, pinned down by 1100 pounds of dead weight on his foot.

By now, the killer must have figured why Lashley had not moved away from the downed horse. He was caught like a bear in a steel-hinged trap. He could struggle helplessly about until the trapper came closer with the gun. Or alternatively, he could escape as the bear might have chosen, by amputating his pinned foot. The second alternative was not much of a decision. With such a severe injury, the cold would rapidly take its toll. He would die of exposure.

Lashley felt the sharp prong applied by the horn of a dilemma. He appeared trapped in a perpetual crisis decision making process, all of them potentially fatal. Chained in a mode of stress management to the ultimate extreme, his long range planning cycle covered the events of the next five minutes. Short range planning embraced the next sixty seconds. As he lay on the ground, survival for the forthcoming minute became his highest priority. How long would it be before the killer circled through the snow storm zeroing in for the execution? To avoid death, he must extricate his trapped foot from a half ton of dead horse. And he needed to perform the magic act as fast as instant grits.

He examined his retaining snare. The foot had cleared the stirrup of the saddle and was jammed below the flank skirt of the seat. As he pressed his body against the cantle, the saddle moved slightly but insignificantly enough to accomplish any useful purpose. It was obvious that with his own strength, he would not be able to dislodge the foot. Wedging the rifle butt under the lower end of the pommel did not afford sufficient leverage for movement. His boot, fastened tightly, was within the standards of hiking footwear. However, it offered no chance of slipping off his foot. Rejecting these options, he directed his attention to other possibilities.

The surrounding ground under the saddle appeared to be firm and mostly rock. He probed carefully with his knife edge, searching for yielding, salient features. None were apparent. Quickly, he reached the conclusion that the solution lay in the need of heavy earth moving equipment to dent this terrain. A week should be sufficient time to transport a Caterpillar tractor of sufficient size, equipped with a blade, from Casper to this remote spot. That was not much of a choice. Digging was discarded as an escape route.

At the end of its hackamore lead strap, the spare horse stared indifferently through the snow scene. The sorrel was a cow pony of mixed origin. Any horse that survived the harsh Wyoming winters was tough. And this sorrel fit that description. Tough and wiry, with a protruding under jaw, Frenchie had called the stallion 'Stargazer' for its habit of holding its head too high and its nose out, like a cheap, aristocratic circus horse. This rogue horse automatically became Lashley's final hope.

He caught the lead rope. Tugging, he brought the sorrel in closer. Snub tying the rope to the saddle horn, Lashley moved the horse within a few feet of him. After untying the lariat from the far side of the saddle, with several tries, Lashley watched the lasso finally fall and tighten over the sorrel's saddle horn.

Lashley short tied the lariat rope snugly under the pommel of the downed animal. Reaching over the dead horse, he raised the right stirrup fender, exposing a cord girth cinch. With speed, he severed each individual cord until the final restraint was cut. The saddle was free from the underbill of the carcass. The saddle was trapped by the weight upon the mount side. Lashley untied the spare horse's lead strap. His life now depended on the stout leather of two heavy duty stock saddles and the strength of this bandy legged sorrel.

Lashley was betting the animal had been exposed to some calf roping. A cow pony was expected to perform sliding stops and quick turns. But more importantly, this breed of horse was trained to recoil from the sudden impact of several hundred pounds of bolting calf on the hoof. On cue, the cow pony jerks the slack out of the rope. Lashley hoped this horse was traditionally calf-schooled, to timely step backward, bracing its fore hoof to keep the rope tight. Strength in both the saddle and the horse was an absolute requirement.

Reaching for his jacket, Lashley tossed it at the sorrel who reacted by retreating to the length of the lariat. The rope pulled tighten, its slack now gone. But the effort was not adequate. Dropping his arm over the taut rope, Lashley put his full weight against the twisted hemp. The sorrel, interpreting the weight on the rope as a struggling calf, back stepped. The saddle moved a few inches. Lashley applied his weight again, and the sorrel responded, stepping backward with more force. The saddle moved, and the boot cleared its trap.

Retrieving his rifle, Lashley rolled over the dead animal, crouching against the flank and taking precaution to place his jacket in a position next to the saddle. Lashley waited. He reasoned the killer needed the spare horse to expedite escape. It was a waiting game.

The sorrel signaled the alarm of the approaching enemy. The slight movement of its ears was all Lashley needed. He crouched lower in a defensive position.

The snow flurries obscured the terrain. Visibility was reduced to 100 feet. The sorrel turned its head and pointed its ears up slope. The killer's approach was charted to arrive on the back side of the supposedly trapped rider.

Lashley slid the Winchester over the ribs of the downed animal, silently cocked the hammer in the firing position, and waited. The wait was short. The killer moved with silent skill. When first visible, the outline revealed no more than patches of gray against the flurries. But the sorrel could see the figure, and it snorted a brief alert. Lashley strained for a better target. If his shot was released prematurely, the killer would forever disappear into the snow patterns. Lashley forced himself, with measured breathing, to be patient. His effort was rewarded.

The flurries parted, as the curtain for Act I of a drama. And the killer stepped into center stage, firing a rifle at the discarded coat. Lashley's Winchester barked a single round. The killer stopped in mid step, moaned loudly, and pivoted for a new target. Confused by the distracted movement of the sorrel, the killer's rifle wavered and turned toward the horse.

Lashley leveled his weapon, jamming a cartridge into the chamber with measured skill. The trigger squeezed, discharging a high velocity bullet into the chest cavity of the standing enemy target. The impact of the bullet projectile drove the body backward. It hit the ground in a spread eagle position.

Lashley waited. No movement was noted. He could not take a chance. Using the lariat rope, he guided the sorrel around the hind quarter of the dead horse. Untying the rope from the saddle horn, he hobbled beside the horse toward the prone body, using its mass as a shield. When he was close enough, reaching between the horse's legs, he kicked the rifle away.

Still no movement was detected. He was convinced that the solar flex shot had been fatal. But he could not take any chances. A hidden handgun would present the most danger. He walked the horse counter clockwise around the figure. As before, there was no movement. A bulky, parka's hood had fallen over the face, and Lashley was unable to detect any feasible sign of breathing. In a swift movement, he dropped down, placed the barrel of the Winchester against the prone body's ribs, and jerked the hood back.

Patches of dark hair pressed against olive cheeks, contrasting with the dark trickle of blood from the corner of the taut mouth. He stared into the dark, glassy eyes. A sibling's duplicate of those dark eyes he had observed on the dying youth in String's loft. The tenth and final member of the ad hoc Arab Student Union lay dead at his feet. The last of the Zoroastrians had been eliminated.

Mitzi Rhodes, even in death, stared back in defiance. Then Lashley understood. Paige had been killed because, belatedly, she recollected a chance meeting she had fleetingly observed. Unwittingly, Paige had glimpsed Mitzi as a passenger in the wrong automobile driven by a man who called himself Flood.

CHAPTER TWENTY-FIVE

Howard Lashley sat on a flat rock along the lower edge of the dam. To his back, the midday sun warmed him. The excess water, cascading through the rocks, overflowed across the retaining wall of the dam. The noise absorbed his dulled thoughts. Like the free floating twigs in the water, his mind bobbed and twisted recklessly, avoiding any commitments or entanglements.

More than forty hours had passed since he had returned to the Cottonwood Guest Lodge, bearing on the rump of the sorrel the lifeless body of Mitzi Rhodes. During the succeeding hours, the lodge had been a beehive of activity. Lashley had been only a peripheral part of the operation. For that, he was grateful.

While Lashley pursued the final member of the Arab Student Union, an early contingent of an elite military unit had arrived at the lodge.

As he sat on the damn, Lashley observed the unit at work and reflected on the past two days' activities.

Neither the commanding officer nor any member of the force wore any identity of rank or unit. Even the branch of the service to which they were assigned was not discernible. Each wore the standard, camouflage, military uniform favored by the U.S. Army, but that was deceiving. The Marines, Air Force, and Seabee also wore similar attire. The unit's helicopters used to reach this remote location were devoid of identification marking. Skilled, physically tough, and well disciplined, the unit functioned with the precision of a drill squad.

Immediately, efforts to repair the damage to the lodge were applied with enthusiasm. Remnants of the burned building were leveled and, without delay, hastily buried. Disabled vehicles were repaired, and a majority of the hunters packed their gear in preparation for an early departure.

Boarding was removed from the porch windows. The lumber was nailed in place over sides of the lodge and barn where evidence of bullet holes showed.

Hardware and siding was shuttled in by helicopters to repair additional damage. Rustic, red paint covered the new siding as a cosmetic approach to the corrections. The stove pipe on the bunk house was installed, and the bunk rooms were again ready for occupancy. Window measurements were made, and shortly, glass replacements would be flown in by choppers.

The swift action of the elite unit was restoring the Cottonwood Guest Lodge to its original configuration. The next hunting party was expected to arrive late tomorrow afternoon, and with the progress being made, those incoming guests would have no physical evidence to reveal the horror of the past several days.

The unit's officer had debriefed the guests and guides, separately, as well as in a group session. The hunting party was cautioned about the willful disclosure of the previous days' events and the consequence that such disclosure could bring. It was explained that the attack on the Cottonwood was activated by a group of deranged Islamic fundamentalists. Motivated by an attempt to scuttle the ongoing peace talks between the Israeli and

Arabian countries in the Middle East, these students intended to create an event of sufficient magnitude to distract from the peace negotiations. It was also explained that the U.S government had no authority to prevent a citizen from expressing any details of the events of the assault. But should the disclosure be made, the government could not provide round-the-clock protection for the surviving hunter should other Arabs desire to avenge the death of the ten students.

One alternative explained was for any volunteer to join the Federal Witness Protection Program. There, the participants were assigned into hiding by making complete life changes and assuming totally new identities. The down side was a total severance with all family connections. If a breach of that security requirement was ever made, the participant would be expelled from the protection program, subjecting them again to the danger of assassination.

During the siege, camaraderie had evolved among the survivors. They had become bound by a thin web of sacrifice and friendship. Weighing the alternatives, each guest, except Lashley, took a voluntary oath, of sorts, to remain silent for ten years about the events at the Cottonwood.

Of the original nineteen members of the party, four had died: Paige St. John, Pearl Gavin, Joel Guarimo, and Mitzi Rhodes. Paige's death would be officially reported as a hunting accident, her body transported to St. Andrews for entombment. No report would be made on the remaining three. Discrete remarks would be released to the Atlanta Islamic mosque to which Joel and Pearl claimed membership.

As the officer had briefed the group, a suggestion would be disclosed to the mosque leadership that two of their members had been engaged in illegal activities which might require an I.R.S. audit. The purpose of the inquiry would be to assess the church's right to maintain its tax-free status. Threatening such an audit would discourage any investigation by the mosque leadership into the whereabouts of their missing members.

Out on the plains, the elite unit had dug a mass grave site wherein were placed the ten members of the Arab Student Union and the Colombians burned in the fires or shot while escaping. The unmarked spot was quickly returned to as near as possible to a natural condition. No notice would be offered directly on these deaths. It had been planned, through diplomatic channels, for vague leaks to be released hinting that the Iraqis had escaped the country, possibly into Mexico or Central America just ahead of an American investigation into their activities. The students' families could always assume that the youths were the victims of some bandits, their bodies forever lost in the jungles of the tropics.

Chainsaw's body was returned to Rawlins with the explanation that his death was attributed to a fall from his horse. Lashley, from his personal assets, planned to assign a trust fund for the maintenance of Poulen's widow and children. By Lashley's selection, Chainsaw had joined the hunting party, and Lashley accepted responsibility of his fallen friend.

The night before, Lashley had attended a simple graveside service for Hank Stringfield. Up canyon behind the lodge, the guides had dug a shallow grave for the cowboy. A crudely constructed pine casket had served as the final bedding for their deceased saddle buddy.

Before the dirt and rocks filled the hole, Frenchie Hebert, in his capacity as the trail boss, spoke a few words and prayed. Limited family connections made notification of his death a simple matter. Frenchie wrote a simple letter to a distant niece explaining that her uncle had died in his sleep and had been quickly buried, cowboy style. Even with the advent of civilization, on the open plains, death is met with an openness not exhibited within the confines of a city. Burial must be quick so that life might continue.

It was considered that because of the distance between the residences of the various deceased, it would be difficult for an outsider to make a connection and join the deaths into a larger conspiracy. It was a calculated risk, Lashley reasoned, but one which offered few alternatives. The less complex scheme for the cover up equaled a greater assurance of success.

A thorough search of the barn by Frenchie and Lashley had finally uncovered the cash hidden by the

Zoroastrians. The aggregate amount exceeded the estimate of Juan Valdez, the Colombian.

Reluctant at first, Frenchie finally acquiesced to accept the money. He offered it for Paige and Chainsaw's families, but Lashley persuaded him to retain it for his damages and as a bonus for his crew. Lashley suggested, and with a strong basis, that the Cottonwood had permanently lost the revenues from the annual Leo Rich party. Doubtless, none of the group, Frenchie's most reliable and profitable hunting party, would ever return. The lodge owner would have to rebuild his clientele before he returned to his current cash flow status. Besides, considering the effect of Pearl's death on Crisco, the lodge might well lose its cook. Crisco should be compensated for his traumatic experience should he elect new employment.

The three Columbians hurriedly signed deportation papers, and Juan Valdez accepted the $10,000 cash Lashley handed him. The Colombians were flown to a nearby air base. There, Captain Mitchell explained to Lashley, the three would be transported by military aircraft to an undisclosed airport in Colombia and then released with an admonishment to remain perpetually beyond the jurisdiction of the U.S.

And so the reconstruction of life, as opposed to the buildings, had begun. Two hours before, six men and four women of the hunting party departed by helicopter. Leo Rich volunteered to accompany Heather Baldwin to a special, discrete government hospital for evaluation and tests. To receive medical attention for his wound, Elliott Thornton was being transported to the same facility. Katherine Pace, ever yielding to his support, elected to attend Thornton while he recovered. Beryl Carter, R.S. Farrow, Lewis Fulcher, and Thyus Harder scheduled flights from Casper to St. Andrews via Dallas. Dunsey Martin and Grace Hancock ticketed to Atlanta and then home. Scarred by their experience, each departed a different person.

A separate helicopter embarked with the body of Paige St. John. Lashley had stood beside the aircraft as the body was loaded. It appeared obscene to him to view the remains of such a tender, caring person confined in such a vulgar container as a plastic, body bag. Outwardly, he showed strength. Inwardly, he was devastated. The loss of this dear friend offended his sense of justice and fair play. Where was the reason of it all? Finally, he succumbed to tears. His body shook with uncharacteristic emotion.

Frenchie, standing to Lashley's left, extended a hand to touch his arm, a welcome tender of friendship. Lashley nodded at the friendly gesture.

Now, as he sat on the rock absorbed in mindless wondering, his eyes swept the surroundings. The elite unit was attentive to each detail of restoration. The cowboys assisted in assigned carpentry.

Inside the lodge, Crisco had insisted on cooking for the unit. He expressed extreme rebuke at the suggestion that the military would offer emergency rations. A compromise was negotiated. Crisco would feed all of the military who stayed over night. Those, temporarily on site, would eat the rations furnished by the unit. Lashley had hopes that Crisco's duties would soften any guilt the cook might harbor associated with his part in the death of Pearl Gavin.

It required some supposition on Lashley's part to reconstruct the final events of the waning hours of the assault. Prior to her escape, it appeared that Mitzi Rhodes had cut the binds of Pearl Gavin. Pearl's actions were intended to create a diversion for Mitzi to stab Paige and to depart the lodge undetected. The cook had been an additional, unwilling victim of the Zoroastrians.

But the termination of the Zoroastrians' final members, the death of Mitzi Rhodes, did not eliminate Lashley's interest in the totality of the Islamic fanatics' purpose. The "who" was known. The "how" was obvious. But the "why" still lay behind the dark cloud of obscurity. Lashley needed a resolution. To suspect is never adequate. Confirmation was the final jewel in the crown. But only an expert could determine if the last jewel set was counterfeit, dazzling to the mind's perception but worthless in value. He suspected that soon he was to be handed a fogged jeweler's loupe with permission to scope among the jewels for the certified gems.

The process was an insight into the secret world of intrigue. He had enough of that crap in the past few days to last a lifetime. Additional deceit from the government was unpardonable, considering the sacrifices he had made. Among all the dead bodies, Paige, String, and Chainsaw were the innocents, drawn into conflicts beyond their comprehension. Poulen had assumed the risk by volunteering, but Paige, in purity, was blameless. The loss of life of the faultless and untainted extracted the greatest grief. He had lost both Paige and Chainsaw, the two closest companions he had known in his short years of conscious existence. Those losses could not be easily replaced. And he would be damned if he were going to sell them for a few shekels of lies.

He watched the figure approaching, weaving along the broken ground. The probe had begun.

Lashley recognized that the military considered him as the most uncertain element of the hunting party. The elite unit's officer had purposely excluded him from an individual debriefing. Likewise, he had not received an invitation to the group session, although he had attended. He had neither been requested to join in the oath of silence, nor was he offered the Witness Protection Plan. Throughout the planning and reconstruction stage, he had been treated with respect and courtesy, although distantly offered. But now, the time had come. There must be a resolution of Howard Lashley's future role in the prospective plan of this affair. No man could be left upon the deck, a loose cannon in a stormy sea, to reek havoc with every gust of the wind. No, Lashley must be lashed to the bulkheads, secured in troubled waters. The military must extract its pound of flesh. The· government would not leave any exposed flank.

Captain Tyrone Mitchell's huge figure cast a shadow on Lashley's sanctuary of seclusion. "May I join you?" he asked.

Lashley did not respond but gestured in a sweeping, friendly, hand motion to the officer.

Mitchell selected a rock for a stool. Finding it uncomfortable, he moved latteraly until he located an adequate place. Lashley, in silence, watched the activity.

Silent moments passed before Lashley spoke. "So, you have been detailed to bell the cat."

"Come on, Lashley. Don't be difficult toward me," the officer replied.

"I had expected a party of higher rank," Lashley responded in a harsh tone.

"It was discussed, and I was selected, considering our close affiliation during the recent hostility. It was decided that I was the preferred person, on site, to approach you."

"Proceed," Lashley said, shrugging his shoulders indifferently.

"You aren't going to make my mission easy, are you?" He paused for a response. Receiving none, he proceeded, "My superiors want to know what you intend to do. What is your analysis of your future commitments toward the suppression of this affair? They are satisfied that the women and the businessmen associated with this hunting trip will remain silent. The crew here at the lodge isn't likely to talk to the press or any congressman. But you, Lashley, they aren't certain about you."

"Why?" he asked.

"Maybe I don't understand all of the implications of the whole fiasco. I'll admit that you were way ahead of me on the strategy of our hostiles. Possibly you know, even now, more than I do. Being in the military, I'm accustomed to operating on partial information. We are ordered to perform without details of the background. Obeying orders is our earliest indoctrination. So I have learned at the end of a mission to attend the debriefing, ask no questions, and move onto the next assignment. But you aren't cut out of that bolt of cloth. You operate within an independent framework, outside the measured realm of conformity. So you've got my superiors concerned."

"Concerned? How?" Lashley queried.

"I'm not sure I know. So maybe I'll speculate. But I suppose they fear that you will blow the whistle on this affair. Something like that. Maybe that will bring bad publicity to the President and military intelligence. Such a thing as this should never have happened. Terrorist attacks should be anticipated. The intelligence was faulty in this instance. The military might get its budget cut or something. How should I know?" the captain finished in frustration.

"What do they want?" Lashley asked.

"A commitment of silence. A pledge or understanding as to your future role. They recognize that with the loss of Miss St. John, you paid dearly. More than any other of the friendly participants. Also, you must receive deserved credit. Without your leadership, the students' plans might have succeeded. You are owed a lot for that."

"What do they propose?" Lashley was zeroing in on the substance of the military thinking.

"Some type of employment? A commission with Military Intelligence. You could accept or reject any assignment offered. In practicality, you could stay home, draw your salary, and never work for the military. It's a twenty-year contract, with retirement and benefits at a Lieutenant Colonel's salary."

"That's it? That's the pay back?" Lashley said.

"No, there's more," Mitchell hurriedly interjected. "You'll be awarded the civilian equivalent of the Medal of Honor. It will be presented by the Secretary of Defense in a private ceremony. The award will remain secret for twenty-five years. But you will be afforded all of the privileges that pertain to the award. Extra pay and such."

"I have a price, but what you offer isn't even close," Lashley answered.

"I expected some negotiations. You're too sharp to accept the first round. Give me your terms, and I will convey them to my superiors."

"It will be expensive. I'm not sure it's worthwhile to waste your time mediating between two sides."

The captain smiled. "I expected you would be expensive. But what the hell. The government's got plenty of money. That's no problem. And don't be concerned about my time. I'm paid a straight salary. Give me your offer to convey. It may take some time, but I promise I'll get you an answer."

"Nothing personal, but you can't be the next messenger. It will have to be someone that can commit. The one who can sign the check, so to speak," Lashley added.

"Tell me your terms, and I will get someone to deliver your request."

"They won't like it."

"Give it to me anyway."

Lashley paused a long time before he answered. "All I want is the truth. Nothing more. Nothing less. Those are my terms."

CHAPTER TWENTY-SIX

The fire in the hearth, supplemented by a wick lamp, furnished dim lighting for the room. Leaning forward in the chair, Howard Lashley extended his hands, savoring the warmth of the tiny flames. His back hunched with fatigue. Since returning from the mountain, Lashley had retired on several occasions to seek the relief of sleep, but the efforts had proved wasted. Stress, confusion, and uncertainty had taken its toll. Sleep was yielded in short dream-filled snatches. And thus, he remained unrested and tired.

Outside, it was dark. It would snow tonight on Hand Mountain, he expected, a heavy snow as a forecast of an impending hard winter. Soon the Cottonwood Guest Lodge would be blanketed under feet of white crust, cocooned away until spring. The big timberline bucks, retreating from the higher altitude, would shortly be seeking winter feeding plots in the lower valley. The hunting season, brief in duration, would close in the next several days, leaving the lodge in isolation, except for the skeleton crew who elected to remain for the winter months.

Lashley, sipping bourbon, waited in silence. He glanced around the confines of the room. The sole window, broken during the assault, had been recently replaced. The balance of the interior had been restored to its normal configuration as it had been when, only days before, he and Paige St. John arrived, with an exchange of laughter, brought their baggage into this cubby hole, and deposited it on the bed. In this room, the couple had shared disagreements, love, a marriage proposal, and their final departing words. For Lashley, Paige's presence penetrated the walls like sweet perfume, identifiable but not visible.

These final moments, surrounded by lodge pole pine walls, would be his last connection with his deceased lover. Reconciled mentally, his departure from this love nest would constitute his final farewell to his beloved, Paige St. John. The instant he departed through the room's rough-hewed door, the healing process would start. Paige, filed in a dusty mental volume, would be sealed away, retrievable from the secret vault when the hurt was at last endurable.

Lashley recognized a responsibility to reconstruct a new existence once more as he had done previously, after escaping from the Five Pines Sanatorium, some three years earlier.

His personal gear - hunting clothes, boots, and camouflage had been packed away - except for bare necessities needed for tomorrow morning's toiletry. Rifles, prepared for shipping, stored in the carrying case, now rested against the door frame. At early light, Lashley planned to depart from the Casper, Wyoming airport. His final flight destination was as uncertain as the reconstruction of his life. With the loss of Paige, his anchor stabilizing his life's boat was gone. Aimlessly, following the ebb and flow of circumstances, he was adrift.

But Lashley's mission at the Cottonwood Guest Lodge was not yet complete. And so, in this darkened room, he waited, not with anger but rather reinforced with a stoic commitment to purpose. The offer had been tendered, through Captain Tyrone Mitchell, to the appropriate official possessing the authority to accept or reject Lashley's offer. The conditions for a counter-offer had long since passed. His terms, as explained to Captain Mitchell, must be met in their entirety. Lashley, considering the simplicity of his settlement terms, would compromise for nothing less.

The consideration to consummate the bargain, as demanded, was insignificant compared to the total picture. Deaths, injuries, and property damage had been excessive. The price extracted from Lashley's part had been substantial. Paige St. John and George Poulen had been only a part of his contribution. Circumstances, necessitated by deceit and subterfuge, had caused him to kill, in hand to hand combat, several humans. He had shot, with malice, a double hand full. No rational person is so callus as to be unaffected by such action. Death is heavy baggage to carry, no matter what the circumstances. Paige had been his major contribution. Was his demand from the government unrealistic?

If the ante was raised to extreme heights, the card game would be over. Everybody would fold. The

605

players, short of their losses, would depart for home or what other retreat they savor. And so what is left, being alone with maybe a few bucks ahead. But the real motive, the desire to win, is lost. With the ante excessively raised, the game ends. Nobody desires the finality of the play. The curiosity lies in the hold cards. A total bluff against the balance of the players was never the intent. The ultimate desire was not to know if a single hand was won, but to continue the challenge of future wins. Abrupt departure is never a win. It is a total rejection.

So Lashley pondered, as he had all afternoon. Had he made the stakes too high? Would the government fold and leave Lashley disappointed? Unknowing? His bid had been the "truth." He had raised when his show cards revealed little. In actuality, Lashley knew the truth. He had finally figured the total scheme. The "why" of the fiasco had ultimately come together. Lashley possessed the answer. What he wanted was confirmation, from those in possession of the information, that his conclusions were correct. It was so simple, so uncomplicated.

Would the government deal with the truth? What was the "truth?" Could the term be defined? To Lashley, the resolution was uncompromising. Truth was the opposite of lying. No more lying. In any multi-complex act, such as that which had so tragically unfolded at the Cottonwood, there were many actors. Thus, no single individual was involved in events from beginning to end. No one person knew the total picture. That vision had to be constructed, piece by piece, as one builds a house. Lashley, by contacts with many players, knew the deal. Minor finishing work was required to give Lashley a final product.

The "how," covering the students' planning and implementation, Lashley had confirmed from the Turk, Suleiman Ganyor, and the captured Columbian, Juan Valdez. The "who," those who had perpetrated the assault had been confirmed. The Zoroastrians' involvement, including their cash commitments and recruitment of the Hispanics was not in dispute, as was the "who" behind the assault. But the unanswered question was why did the shoot out at the Cottonwood occur in the first place. Knowing how the operation

607

developed structurally, and how it was carried out by the students, was informative. However, the "why" behind the "how" must not remain behind the veiled curtains, perpetually obscured. Until the "why" was resolved. Lashley would be forever wandering the uncharted ghostly trails of the curious. He must have confirmation of the "why," explained to his satisfaction, or heads would roll on the table of public inquiry. Nothing, short of death, would stand in his way.

At the conclusion of this early afternoon conversation with Captain Mitchell, Lashley had distantly observed the continuing activities of the elite military unit in its efforts to create the "before" condition of the Cottonwood. The unit's efforts, more than just the rehabilitation of the damaged buildings, caught his attention. Rather, his focus was directed to individuals scurrying to and from the helicopters, parked on the landing strip atop the plateau, north from the barn. One craft had landed midday and had apparently been pressed into duty as the command post.

Unobtrusively, Lashley had been mentally tracking those persons hastening to the chopper. Captain Mitchell, Major Greer, Myrtle Wallace and Patricia Stanford, previously dubbed "the military," had been frequent and lengthy visitors. On summons, Frenchie Hebert had made one trip, lasting thirty minutes. The officer from the elite unit and one additional man, whom Lashley figured was an executive officer, were the primary persons in attendance.

Occasionally, Lashley observed a glimpse of a stocky man appearing at the door of the chopper. Over the man's shoulder, additional civilians in the chopper would peer out toward Lashley. No one requested Lashley's attendance, nor did he volunteer to confer. But he observed and watched and waited.

Lashley understood the dilemma he had placed upon the military. Telling the truth was a tough assignment. Misinformation, double-talk, and bureaucracy were service specialties. But revealing the truth in unconditional, unvarnished, and precise terms was a task so foreign to the same military thinking and capabilities that the truth was avoided at all costs. The old adage applied: the military had rather lie, when telling the truth would suit their purpose better. The scurrying of individuals about the chopper, Lashley realized, related to the construction of a cover story, one savored with a tinge of truth. But unveiling to Lashley the truth in unconditional, unbending terms was going to be difficult.

The primary problem facing the military's decision was the uncertainty of how many facts Lashley had obtained about the underlying cause for the students to center their activities upon the Cottonwood in the first instance. Uncertainty as to the depth of Lashley's knowledge, obtained either from the Colombian or the leader of the Zoroastrians, left the military in a quandary. If Lashley had acquired sufficient and detailed information from these inside sources, any revelations made by the military must parallel that knowledge in all material aspects. The slightest deviation in any military briefing, conflicting with Lashley's knowledge, would cause the entire story to be suspect. Playing close to the vest was difficult for the boys in camouflage uniforms, under these circumstances.

In late afternoon, as the shadows moved easterly across the valley, Lashley positioned himself on the barn's stairs and sat. Two days earlier he had climbed these same steps, in the peril of his life, blasting with a 12 gauge shotgun. Reflecting on the contrast between the two events associated with reaching the same step, Lashley wondered about the necessity of his assault and the resulting deaths of the students that had followed in the loft. Had these deaths been necessary? Did other alternatives exist, short of the loss of so many lives? Lashley realized he might never know the answer to those questions. And in retrospect, he did not care. What he had done, here at the Cottonwood, was done. It could not be undone. Lashley had made the decisions instantly, with the best information available under combat conditions. Leave it to the historians, who never faced hostile fire, to criticize his actions from the safety of their ivy towers. Lashley could and would live with his decisions.

At a 100-yard distance, joined by two civilian types, the portly man stepped from the helicopter. He wore a trench coat and a dress hat as protection against the chilling wind. A gusty updraft, catching the brim, blew his hat from his head, exposing a salt and pepper crown. Stretching, he loosened his muscles from the long confinement in the chopper. With deliberation, he stared across the space toward Lashley seated on the barn stairs. The contours of the terrain placed both men at equal elevations.

Even at this distance, Lashley was able to observe, from the deep wrinkled face, a man in his early sixties. The two men locked eyes. Lashley, unwavering, returned the stare. He wondered if this government official had now become his enemy. Had the hostilities shifted from the Zoroastrians to officials of Lashley's own government? After a time, the well-dressed man broke contact with Lashley, retrieved his hat, and reentered the helicopter.

Hours passed with no contact. Now in the darkened room, Lashley, extending his hands, relished the warmth of the glowing embers. He hesitated, considered that it may be some time before anything happened, and decided to place additional logs upon the fire. Selecting three split pieces from the adjacent wood box, he tossed the timbers carelessly upon the coals. Using a bent tire rod as a poker, he stroked the embers to life. Quickly, the new fuel caught fire, crackling under the encouraged flames.

From the mantle, the flickering lamp cast an erratic light through the room. He stood, adjusted the wick, and the light stabilized, accenting his surroundings. Earlier, he had rejected the option to retain this room as his final base of operation until his departure. Pain associated with these surroundings was intense. Coming to grips with his grief associated with the loss of Paige was a necessity. Thus, with deliberation and intent, Lashley had remained in the final sanctuary he and his lover had shared together. And he waited.

CHAPTER TWENTY-SEVEN

An hour passed. Additional logs were added to the fireplace. Tired of continuously adjusting the lantern's wick, Lashley let the lamp go out. The room was darkened. He sensed, more than heard, a presence at the open door.

"Come in, Colonel," Lashley said without turning around. "I have been expecting you."

"Expecting me? I'm surprised," the officer responded.

Lashley shrugged indifferently. "Yes. Ultimately, I suspected that you would come. Sit down."

He offered a chair facing the fireplace and waited for compliance before continuing, "How about a drink? My resources are limited, but I have some Jack Daniels, Black, if that interests you."

"A light one, please, if you don't mind, thank you."

Reaching for a spare glass on the small table next to him, Lashley poured the bourbon, a finger deep.

"All I have for a mix is water," Lashley apologized. "There are sodas in the kitchen. I could get you one."

"Water is fine," the colonel answered.

Lashley mixed the drink and handed it to the officer.

"So you're the officer designated to be the negotiator." Lashley spoke flatly, with no hostility in his voice.

"Yes," the answer came back in a similar tone. "I suppose so. At least to a limited extent."

Even in the dim fire light, Lashley was aware of starched, creased, camouflage pants, joining combat boots in a military tuck. He kept his gaze on the fire.

"Are you prepared to meet my terms?" Lashley inquired.

"The terms of your offer are extremely vague and unrealistic, don't you think, Mr. Lashley?" the colonel interjected.

"In the last week," Lashley answered, "more than forty people died here at the Cottonwood. Mostly Hispanics and ten very young students. A woman was raped, and three innocent bystanders died. Several persons have been wounded. Those events were harsh and very realistic. No, the terms of my offer are fair and just. Also I might add, the conditions are uncompromising."

"Should you be furnished with the information you desire, what do you expect to do with the data?" the officer asked.

"Nothing," Lashley replied.

"Then what difference does it make to you whether you obtain the information. Idle curiosity does not appear to be your motivation. Your request demonstrates a more subtle purpose. Possibly you possess a hidden agenda. If so, the government has concerns about complying with an idle request. Military secrets are not easily bantered among those who seek answers for mere curiosity purposes."

"My motivation should be of little concern to anyone. I earned my request," Lashley responded harshly. "I paid a heavy price and have discharged the right to the terms of my offer. I expect no trifle quibbling. Either accept or reject the offer."

"You are rather decisive," the officer said.

Lashley shrugged nonchalantly and said nothing. The room was awkwardly quiet. Finally the officer broke the silence.

"Let's progress and determine the extent and limits of what we can accomplish. If I am able to adequately respond with your guidelines, then your mission has been accomplished. Should I fail, we can address that issue at the appropriate juncture. How would you suggest we proceed?"

"By not beating around the bush," Lashley advanced. "A good offense is never poor tactics. I could establish the broad perimeters. At the conclusion of Desert Storm, many Iraqis wanted revenge. Not only had Iraq been humiliated in its holy cause but had also lost face before the world of public opinion. Even their fellow Muslins had rejected them. Saudis, Jordanians, Egyptians, together with other Islamic countries, had all joined with the American infidels to defeat Iraq. It was a mortification for those who believed so strongly in a holy principle. Iraq became the butt of crass street jokes of the most vulgar kind. How is this for background?"

"Reasonably accurate," the colonel responded.

"Into this conflict the GBU-twenty-eight bomb, the so-called "smart" bomb of Desert Storm, enters this picture. For years, the Iraqis had been preparing for war. At exorbitant costs, Saddam Hussein had constructed extensive military communication and control bunkers. These concrete and steel structures were beyond the destruction capabilities of the U.S. Military as they existed at the commencement of Desert Storm. The then-existing GBU - twenty-seven, a two thousand pound bomb, guided by laser beams to the target, was the best hardware in the U.S. Military inventory. Bomb drops with the GBU - twenty-seven upon Iraqi bunkers proved unsuccessful. Sufficient penetration into the depths of the bunkers was not sufficient. As a fall back, the military realized the necessity to convert existing weapons to produce more effective results. Using fast track construction and design, modifications were quickly laid out on the drawing board."

Lashley continued, "What was required was a bomb capable of being delivered from the air, at a high altitude, with high-impact velocity and the correct angle at contact. The task was assigned to Eglin Air Force Base's Armament Laboratory. Cutting the red tape and normal delays usually related to the Federal Acquisition Regulations, the brain trust at Eglin, in our own backyard in the panhandle of Florida, configured the modifications. Using short circuit construction, the revisions were completed in a couple of weeks. Early on, it was decided not to use the B-52 bomber for delivery but rather to opt for a fast jet fighter. With these predetermined factors in mind, what the Armament Laboratory produced was a forty-seven hundred pound bomb, with an attached laser guidance kit. It was a modification of the older BLU - one-o-nine bomb, lengthened and adapted with a laser guidance system. Hurriedly tested, the modified bomb was quickly transported to the Persian Gulf. Its delivery on the major Iraqi bunker was a devastation to Hussein."

"You've done your homework," the colonel interjected.

"Not really. All of these events I have just described in detail were thoroughly and adequately published by the news media," Lashley replied.

"That is correct, but few people have the understanding you have just displayed. Thus, there is nothing required for the government to confirm. You have those facts, which you recited, as substantially correct."

"But that is not the issue," Lashley added hurriedly. "What remains critical is why did an assault occur at the Cottonwood Lodge in this remote area of Wyoming? The GBU -twenty-eight or the 'smart' bomb, as it is usually called by the press, ended the conflict in Kuwait, post haste. Saddam Hussein had little alternative but to end the war. No longer could his bunkers be considered a safe haven. Overnight, these bunkers were converted to coffins for the living dead. Iraqi military realized that, one by one, the U.S. would zero in on each bunker and eventually Hussein himself would have been a casualty. Being trapped in a sealed bunker awaiting a horrible death was no rejoicing thought for the leader of this third rate military force. Earlier, Hussein had evidence of a frightening bunker death. Family members of the elite had sought shelter and were trapped in a bunker where a smaller bomb penetrated to some depth. American television furnished the viewers with a front row seat exposing the aftermath of that bombing run."

"I have no disagreement with your dialogue thus far, but I am uncertain where you are leading," the colonel interjected.

"I suspect you do follow my direction, because we are now approaching the most critical issue. Many Iranians were killed in the short-lived action of Desert Storm. It is usually the fanatical survivors of a war who become residual trouble for the victors. And as in other conflicts, Desert Storm was no different. It was the relatives of the ad hoc Arab Student Union, operating under the code name of Zoroastrians, who died in those bunkers. Younger sisters, brothers, and cousins, ever how distant, perished. The elite had been caught in the crossfire and died. Blown to pieces.

621

Such an occurrence should have never happened to members of the ruling class. The ruling class is never intended to be a victim of war. But it did occur in a massive way in Iraq. The war ended, and the survivors sought revenge."

Lashley paused, mixed a mild bourbon, and then recommenced his assessment. "The students, charged with hatred beyond a normal person's conception, plotted for the revenge of their dead relatives. The war in Afghanistan escalated their hatred. Each retaliatory attack planned by the students, assisted by al-Qaeda, was designed to reach a high classification to produce maximum press coverage."

"So some students, not necessarily these, assisted bin Laden in plotting and planning the first World Trade Center bombing. The students funded that vigilante assault through a convoluted method. The bombs reached a level of mass press exposure, more than anticipated. The coverage lasted on the front pages for weeks. Likewise, the assault on C.I.A. employees in Washington, D.C., was a maximum news coverage event. Those kids had access to vast sums of money. Oil money easily funneled to cash.

"But the Student Union became frustrated. They wanted more assaults. The early arrest and exposure of the participants in the World Trade Center and C.I.A. assault quickly moved the stories to inside page coverage. What the students had always needed was a news story with a long life span. The coverage of the kidnapping of Americans in Beirut, especially that of reporter, Terry Anderson, spaced a five year period. Convinced that a kidnapping of a selective target, coupled with a staged trial, would fit the outline of their purposes, they activated a plan that had been sitting on the shelf."

Pausing again as though the effort was tiring, Lashley regrouped. He then commenced talking, "So the students plotted to reactivate focus on a particular person most singularly associated with Afghanistan.

"Arrangements were contemplated to capture an appropriate military officer, transport him out of the *U.S.* Then a People's Court would be constituted and impended. An indictment, as drawn, would specify how the accused was guilty of the crime of deliberate assassination of innocent women and children. A sort of modified genocide allegation, modeled after the Nuremburg trials.

"Possible it was more analogous to the Nazi, Adolph Eichman's trial. Israel kidnapped him from Argentina thirty years after Germany's surrender. That trial was covered by the American press for months"

"Our government would not have been privy as to the activities of these Arab students to which you allude. Thus, I would be unable to comment on that subject," the colonel added.

"We will pass that issue for now," Lashley said. "The original subject for the students, early on, was possibly, General Franks. However, as the overall commander of the assault on Afghanistan, the government recognized he was subject to terrorist attention and offered the general discrete protection. The students' emphasis shifted then to the person who delivered the smart bomb. The pilot of an airplane who dropped a load in Afghanistan where they could claim innocent women and children were murdered.

"Like the scholars they professed to be, the students undertook a massive research project. Pouring through magazines and newspaper articles, a pattern developed. The trail was obscure, but they persisted in pursuit of a thread. The students shifted their research to government documents. The average American citizen has never understood the wealth of vital military secrets that are available to terrorists through the Freedom of Information Act.

"Simultaneously with the other militant activities, this intense research took the students more than a year to confirm the identity of a pilot who dropped a 'smart' bomb in Afghanistan. Additional months were required to study the target, plan an operation and then move operations into position.

"Pearl Gavin and Joel Guarimo were recruited through the Atlanta based mosque. Mitzi Rhodes, a primary member of the Student Union, moved to St. Andrews to be closer to the identified pilot stationed at Tyndall Air Force Base. But the student needed a break to isolate the pilot. And they found the break by a most peculiar method, through Myrtle Wallace."

"You are accusing Myrtle Wallace of disloyalty," the colonel challenged. "That's preposterous."

"No, you misunderstood. Not Miss Wallace individually. But inadvertently, she raised the flag that disclosed the itinerary of the pilot."

"How so?" the colonel asked.

"When Miss Wallace inserted the names of the hunting party into the computer, the name of Howard Lashley, for whatever reason, alerted some governmental agency. An official from that agency flew to Tyndall, where Wallace was stationed. There, this official confronted Wallace. She, not being aware of the totality of the circumstances, explained the roster of the hunting party and details of the plans to this super spook.

"There are employees within the U.S. government bureaus that are just as desirous as fanatical Muslims to witness the collapse of the ongoing peace talks between the Israelis and the Arabs. Certain of our own government officials' jobs depend on the continuation of global conflicts. When hostilities cease, in a hot spot, those officials, assigned to monitor the conflicts, may find their jobs are no longer needed."

Lashley continued, "You have to be naive to believe that our various agencies were not knowledgeable of the activities of the Arab Student Union. Our government's spooks had pre-warning about the plot for the airplane to crash into the Trade Center, even if the F.B.I. wasn't informed. When a single group spends vast sums of money, especially cash, it attracts attention. Even the Turks had previous forewarning of the impending student activities."

"What you are asserting is beyond any personal knowledge I possess," the colonel interjected. "Also, if you expect me to agree with these wild assertions, you are wasting your time. I will not enter into any debate on the merits of any political issue."

"It's possible some of this is beyond your knowledge and even political in nature," Lashley conceded. "But in the final analysis, you are privy to the salient fact of that matter. It is now apparent that certain well-placed U.S. employees had been, for sometime, conferring with the Student Union, encouraging them with inside information."

"You can't prove any of this," the colonel challenged.

"Don't bank on it" Lashley said, no longer bluffing. "I conferred with some insiders in this affair. You weren't present at the student leader's capture in the loft. Neither was anyone else present at my confirmation with the Colombian. So don't challenge me on my fact."

"What does that have to do with me? What do you expect of me?" the colonel asked, backing away from the challenge.

"Let's move along, and your contributions will become apparent. When Mitzi Rhodes moved to the Gulf Coast, with help, she attached herself to R.S. Farrow, the insurance salesman. This decision was predicated upon his connections at Tyndall. · As an active Air Force Reserve Officer and Desert Storm veteran, Farrow had constant social contact with base personnel.

"Mitzi Rhodes needed an excuse to gain admission to the inside of the base to better scope the target. It was a mere accident that the target and Farrow were teamed on this hunting trip. But it happened. If events had fallen differently, there were additional students working at Tyndall who would have developed different scenarios to implement the overall plan. Mitzi's accidental pairing with Farrow was a stroke of luck for the students. But from day one, Mitzi was being fed inside information and given invaluable assistance about the target. With these connections, the students' plan was almost guaranteed."

"Except that Howard Lashley's interference destroyed the plot," the colonel added.

"Not exactly. I will not accept credit, because I had substantial help. I suspect that if I had failed to fill the void, someone else would have stepped forward. I am reasonably certain I know how the command would have been handled. However, if, early on, some logistical assistance had been offered to me, the results might have been altered."

The colonel delayed answering for a moment. The response was in a cautious tone. "What assistance were you denied?"

"The truth. It would have avoided following false trails," Lashley stated. "And more importantly, it could have established a line of trust, a base of security in team members. That credible revelation, at the start, might have altered the outcome in a more timely fashion. I don't mean to place the blame of Paige's death on any individual for the failure to disclose. But the outcome might have been different for separate players."

"How could you have been trusted with such vital military secrets? Wasn't it just as logical to those in the know that you had connections with those assaulting the lodge? It was peculiar that your name didn't appear in the computer request. After all, you assumed command without any authority. You planned no retreats or probing counter-assaults. Playing a wait-and-see game gained you no confidence from the occupants of the lodge," the colonel said.

Lashley stroked the fire and added two pieces of wood onto the dying coals. "Possibly, part of your observation is correct. But well into the operation, circumstances were different. Even then, I continued to receive a substantial dose of fabrication."

"Had you known the identity of the target, in retrospect, would you have done anything differently?" the colonel asked.

"Yes. I would have exerted less energy on unimportant details. Truth would have established the reliability of support. By midpoint in the operation, I had earned the right to be informed."

"I'll grant you that," the colonel responded. "But it didn't happen, so where does that lead?"

"To my bargain. I want confirmation, Colonel Patricia Stanford, that you were the primary target of the Zoroastrians. As the pilot of the jet, you delivered the newly-designed 'smart' bomb, forty-eight hundred pounds of explosives to some target in Afghanistan. The students sought revenge against you."

Patricia Stanford, in the fatigue uniform of a U.S. Air Force Colonel, leaned forward toward the fire. She extended her hands to accept its warmth.

"Certainly, you are aware of published military regulations. Female pilots are not authorized to fly combat missions over hostile territories during war conditions," she said.

"Yes, I'm familiar with that stated regulation. And that is what threw me off the trail for a while. Ultimately, I reasoned it out. Every rule has its exception. The delivery of the GBU - twenty-eight to the bunker at Al Taji Air Base on the outskirts of Baghdad, Iraq, was not designated as a combat mission. Neither were those delivered to Tora Bora. America isn't at war with Afghanistan. I concluded those latest flights were classified as test flights. Test flights are your specialty, is that not correct, Colonel Stanford?"

"Yes, you are correct that I am a test pilot," she answered softly.

"And you delivered a 'smart' bomb in Afghanistan?" Lashley asked.

She hesitated a long time and then answered firmly, "Yes."

"A few days following the delivery of the 'smart' bomb, Desert Storm came to an immediate halt. It took longer in Afghanistan."

The woman nodded affirmatively, acknowledging the correctness of the statement.

"Captain Mitchell, I assume, was ignorant of your position and your potential prospect as the target."

"Yes, only Major Greer and Myrtle Wallace were privy to the possibility of my involvement. As you have most likely assumed, Myrtle Wallace has been assigned as a body guard to protect me against such contingencies. For some time, we have suspected that I might be the object of a terrorist attack. We never anticipated that it would occur here, in such a remote area."

"Before Paige died, she suggested to Captain Mitchell the final evidence in this bizarre tragedy."

"I'm not familiar with that," Stanford admitted.

"I didn't expect you to be. But what she mumbled was extremely critical. As she lay mortally wounded,

633

she mentioned something about a man she knew as Flood and a contact with a woman seen with that man. Because of those associations, Paige St. John lost her life.

"Before leaving home, Paige had inadvertently seen Mitzi Rhodes in the presence of a man. It made no significant impression on her at the time. In fact, she forgot about it. It was only at the end of this fiasco that the connection cost her life."

"I don't understand what you are saying. Are you asking me to confirm something about this recitation?" Stanford asked.

"Not really, except to tie this scenario together for me. The man down at the helicopter, the civilian, what is his name?" Lashley asked.

"He calls himself Shoreline. That's all I know," Patricia Stanford answered.

Howard Lashley's worst fears materialized. It had been a light-haired man called Flood, or a similar name related to water, who had contacted Paige St. John about unrelated details. Paige had accidentally observed Flood and Mitzi Rhodes driving together. A white haired man named Tidewater had confronted Myrtle Wallace. Crest, a silver haired man, control officer for the Turk and Jason Tyson, also called the River Otter. Suleiman Ganyor, the Turk, had described their control officer as having a penance for names related to water. Crest is the cap of a wave. Each of these gray-headed individuals was the same individual.

Patricia Stanford, the pilot of the super fast jet fighter, deliverer of tons of explosives, was not the ultimate target of the assault on the Cottonwood. True, the students wanted to kidnap Stanford. But Shoreline, a/k/a Crest, Tidewater and Flood, desired this terrorist assault to be the subterfuge for the true purpose of the events occurring at the Cottonwood Lodge.

Howard Lashley, the alias for Jason Tyson, had been the primary bull's-eye from start to finish. The use of the Arabs had been a clever cover to camouflage the genuine purpose of the assault. Shoreline wanted Lashley dead.

And knowing that fact, Howard Lashley sealed his fate. He had just signed his own death warrant unless he killed Shoreline first.

Death is indeed contagious, Lashley reasoned.

ABOUT THE AUTHOR

Moving from the stage of yarn spinning and storytelling, James E. Moore brings his talents to the adventure novel. Moore has published numerous historical articles and has authored two books on the history of the Florida Panhandle. He also co-authored a humorous book of Southern short stories. A graduate of Florida State University and the University of Florida, Moore is the owner of a Holiday Inn Express.